My Noble Fight

THE ROYALS
BOOK THREE

C. R. RILEY

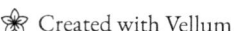 Created with Vellum

Hermosa Islas

This book is dedicated to all those who are brave enough to start fresh. It's not easy to take a leap of faith. Putting past choice behind us can be difficult and often held against us. Therefore, when a person decides it's time to make a better life for themselves, I find that worthy and commend them for it.

Note from the Author

My Noble Fight mentions the acts of physical, mental/emotional, and sexual assault which I understand be subjects some readers wish to avoid.

This romance novel is a work of fiction. It is about the healing of a woman determined to have a better life for herself and her daughter. I do not go into great details, but do discuss those matters so you as a reader can understand the heroine's strength. Then hopefully you will be able to celebrate her as a survivor, warrior, and a champion to her daughter. Reader Discretion is advised.

If you have found yourself in a similar situation as Violet, I am genuinely sorry for all you have endured. I hope that through my telling of Violet's story you can find some healing and that I was respectful in my telling of it. If you are in need of some assistance or want someone to speak with please reach out to the National Domestic Violence Hotline: https://www.thehotline.org/

CHAPTER 1
Lorenzo

The Royals

I've never been more infuriated with someone before in my life. If you were to ask why I am so bothered on why this individual has such a hold on me, I don't even know if I could provide you with an honest answer.

I'd have dealt with her sooner. However, extreme circumstances took a great deal of my time these last couple of days, so I've had to put it off until those matters were settled. Now I intend on confronting this woman for the unacceptable offense I feel she is guilty of. There is no excuse for what she did, hence the reason I am determined to get to the bottom of it once and for all.

If I hadn't been derailed during the party when Winifred's estranged sister showed up a bloody and confused mess, I'd have handled it that night. As one might imagine, that situation became a priority. It required our undivided attention. In fact, we've been dealing with that mess for most of the week. I've been running interference with the press. Feeding them just enough information to satisfy while my other brothers managed everything else.

Now that it has settled down, I am finally free to confront the most frustrating woman in the kingdom. Clearly, this woman holds little respect for the King's family, along with the office where she works.

Although my brothers strongly disagree with my opinion. They have it in their delusional minds that it's me she has an issue with.

And perhaps that is what bothers me the most. I cannot for the life of me understand why she has a problem with me. I've never done anything to make this woman, not like me. Never once was I rude or treated her disrespectfully. I never dared to belittle her alone or around others. If anything, I'd like to believe I had done just the opposite.

I pride myself on treating everyone respectfully, no matter what their social status might be. Striving to make all feel extremely comfortable around me. It happens to be one of my many talents, especially when it comes to the ladies. Women always like me. I have had no problems interacting with them, until her.

It began on the first day I walked into my brother, the King's office, and was introduced to his new secretary, Miss Violet Blanc. I got the impression almost instantly she didn't much care for me. Not understanding why, I've done my very best to change her mind. Took a little extra time when I stopped by, making a point to speak with her. Endeavored to get to know her while letting her also get to know me. Except she always ignored me, tried to dismiss me, often suggested I not waste my time. Claiming that me trying to impress her was never going to work and then proving her words true by her body language.

I thought she only needed to get to know me better. Therefore, I kept making a point to not allow her actions to bother me. Doing my very best to always smile genuinely at her, even though she only scowled at me.

Even tried to bribe her with treats I'd witnessed her enjoying from time to time. Only to watch her dispose of them in the trashcan next to her desk, as if she didn't trust me. It was as if she believed I would lace them with something. Something I would never even consider. I found it disturbing she'd consider that a possibility. My father died because his wife slipped drugs into his nightcap. Thus, I have no tolerance for that sort of conduct.

Then the day came when I made a very demanding request of her. It was two days before my brother threw his wife—who also happened to be my best friend—a surprise party. I was tired of all the animosity between us I felt was undeserved, so I challenged her. Invited her to attend the party as my date. Not surprisingly, she declined immediately. Then attempted to blow the entire event off by claiming she had other plans that evening, which couldn't be changed.

I'll admit I might have overstepped my role. Gave Violet an ultimatum she'd not be able to refuse. Explained how when a member of the royal family extends such an invitation to a private event—one that was a celebration—one did not blow it off, first and foremost. I went so far as to suggest should she forego the festivities; she might want to start searching for a new job. Dared to point out that it would be in her best interest to show her support. Let those she worked for witness firsthand how she was more than appreciative of an invitation to such an event.

I myself could hardly believe what I was suggesting. All because I knew no one in my family would hold it against her if she declined. That wasn't how our family treated its employees or friends. Thankfully, Miss Blanc hadn't figured that fact out yet.

With a very angry disposition, she agreed to attend the celebration. Declining however to be my date. Wild horses, she'd mentioned, couldn't drag her there should that be a requirement.

I felt guilty about lying to her after I'd had time to cool off. Started to realize my behavior was uncalled for. It was then that I offered a sincere apology. That is the very reason I returned to the palace later that afternoon.

Upon my return, I overheard Esteban's secretary discussing a subject that struck me as quite inappropriate. It took no time at all to grasp it was Violet she was gossiping about. Daring to belittle her choice of clothing and style. All of which had me giving it my all to figure out what was wrong with her choices exactly. I took significant effort to recall several of the outfits I'd witnessed her in. I suppose they were simpler than what the other women in the office wore. They certainly were not so dire to draw this kind of attention.

The other woman seemed to disagree. Pointed out to whoever she was chatting with how rotating the same three ensembles, mixing them slightly, was not acceptable for a person who worked in the palace. Even less so, it seemed, when said person reported directly to the king himself. Violet had lowered standards, being allowed to dress in budget department store clothing, making the rest of the staff appear like fashion amateurs.

Needless to say, I thought the woman was crazy. Possibly jealous because Violet had acquired the position as the king's secretary instead of her. There were reasons that woman hadn't been assigned such a promotion. Her loyalty to feeding the gossip pool was high on the list. Antonio needed someone he could trust to keep tight lips. Not having to worry if this person had issues offending even the most powerful and arrogant men. Something Violet had proven several times she had no problem doing, me included.

It became apparent that Violet had overheard the other woman once I entered the king's main office. She'd been standing a few feet away, checking out her reflection in the window before she caught sight of me. I might have even witnessed a tear or two building. Though I cannot be sure once her ice princess persona slipped into place the instant she realized I was standing behind her.

I can recall that conversation as if it happened only yesterday.

"What brings you back twice in one day, Your Highness?" Violet asked me as she took her seat behind her desk and then pretended to work. *"His Majesty is not here. I believe he has left for the day, even. You should go."*

I ignored her while I took a step closer. All while I gave her outfit a respectable once-over. She was wearing a black pencil skirt, silk pink blouse, a pearl necklace with matching earrings, finished off with black stockings and pumps. A black suit jacket was hanging off the hook behind her. I could easily distinguish the outfit was not of exceptional quality, but it was in excellent condition. More than acceptable for this office.

I then took a second peek at her necklace, easily recognizing it was not real. Not that it mattered one way or the other; it was classy enough and worked just fine.

"Is there a reason you are still here?" Her annoyed voice questioned while I stood there and blatantly checked her out. It was clear when our eyes met that she was self-conscious about my openness. Possibly wondering if I felt the same as the other woman across the hall. Believing her outfit was not good enough for this office.

"Sorry," I shook my head as I did my best to refocus. *"I've come with a peace offering. Earlier I might have..."*

"No," she interrupted, not giving me a chance to explain. "Take it with you when you leave."

Not interested in accepting her request, I stepped even closer. I then set down the wrapped box and crossed my arms. "Since I all but forced you to agree in attending Princess Winifred's birthday bash, I thought I could at least make certain you were properly clothed for the occasion."

Her eyes darted up. For a moment I believed I saw a flash of vulnerability behind them. It didn't last long, because Violet wasn't one to display those emotions easily. Nevertheless, she was drawing the wrong conclusion about my being there.

Her next words clarified that for me. "I believe I am capable of dressing myself."

"Clearly," I motioned to her ensemble. "You seem very capable, in fact. But one can never have too many cocktail dresses in her wardrobe, correct? I presumed a new dress would be nice. My sister, Gabriela, seems to always light up when I splurge on her. I assumed you don't like wasting your hard-earned money on frivolous things, therefore I decided I'd indulge you. See if I could make up for my earlier rudeness."

Violet started to say something. I'm certain it would have been epic and put me in my place very quickly, but she surprisingly stopped herself.

"Just open it before you dismiss my over-the-top gesture. It's not every day I go shopping with the intent to make amends. So, before coming unhinged on me, at least take a peek. That way you can criticize my taste along with the gesture."

A slight twitch at the side of her lips made me think she might actually smile. Making me nudge the box closer, hoping to at least tempt her curiosity.

"I cannot accept this." Violet stared at the box with uncertainty, "It wouldn't be right."

"One might suggest that it would be less right for you to deny a gift from your prince. Although I get the impression that you, Miss Blanc, don't give two cents what others might think. You are your own woman and do as you dare choose. To hell with what others think. However, it would be a shame to not at least appreciate what you are refusing before denying it. Don't you agree?"

"Why?" she tapped the box skeptical. "Do you always buy gifts for your women?"

"My women? I don't have women, Miss Blanc. So no, I don't buy them gifts or offer many apologies." I shoved the box toward her, "You would be the first."

"Why don't I believe you?"

"Seems a pattern you have crafted where I am concerned. I suppose there lies an answer somewhere in your mind, although I don't know what or why that is, only you do." I'd like to though; know why she disliked me so.

"You remind me of someone."

It's the first time I'd been given a hint as to why she held some animosity against me; it certainly gave me something to ponder on.

"What a shame. He must be a real putz since you seem to sincerely dislike this person so much. My apologies." Should I ever meet that man, there is no doubt that we'd exchange a few words.

Violet blinked several times as if thinking that over. "You really are something else, you know. Apologizing for someone that you have no control over and could not even change."

I had so many points I wanted to make about that statement. I decided it best to leave it for now, though. "Open the box and stop stalling."

"Gaw, you are extremely bossy." She vented as she took the box, then began untying the ribbon that was holding it shut.

I watched closely as she opened the package and separated the tissue paper. It became evident to me that this woman didn't receive nearly enough gifts.

"This is too much," her weak voice stated. "I can't..."

"Debaixo de bom saio está o homem mau." (Judge not according to the appearance.)

I am a firm believer of that statement. Judging a person is never a good idea. First impressions can at times be deceiving if we have preconceived notions. It is obvious Violet did since she claimed I reminded her of someone else.

"Peace offering, Miss Blanc."

She pulled the dress from the box and then let it hang from her fingers. The black dress was nothing special, really. Every woman, I *believe, owned one more than one, probably. It was nice enough she'd be able to wear it to any formal event, yet casual enough to wear it when going out with her girlfriends. The style didn't imply I'd gotten it for her to suggest something I was not suggesting. The dress was elegant and modest and would look so very lovely on her. Although if I'm honest, I imagined it could also be extremely sexy while remaining classy. I guess I would only know that if she actually accepted it and then wore it later.*

"No more gifts please," she folded it and set the box aside. "Promise me this."

I hated to lie to her because I knew it was one I could not keep. Therefore, I moved on and ignored her request. "I'm glad you have come to your senses. So about me picking you up and escorting you..."

I'm not sure how I'd gotten Violet to allow me to pick her up for the party, but somehow, I had. Although she'd refused to let me come to her flat and retrieve her there. She insisted I meet her at a friend's instead. Something about needing to go there anyway, because she had swapped her previous plans. This friend was now doing her one huge favor by letting her get ready there.

The evening of the party, I'd thought we'd moved past it all. We'd been having a nice time. Spoken to each other like civil adults and not once had she gotten cheeky with me. We were two hours in when she received a text that caught her attention. Everything from that point forward shifted. I sensed her pulling back and slipping her mask on. And when I questioned her about it, she asked me to mind my own business and kindly stay clear of hers.

I'd excused myself to go speak with someone I needed to talk to, only gone fifteen minutes at most. When I returned, all her belongings were nowhere to be found, and she too was missing. I did my best to dismiss it. Excused her absence by assuming she was using the lavatory. Thirty minutes later, I knew she had disappeared without so much as a goodbye or explanation.

It had rubbed me completely the wrong way. I tried my hardest to not let it, but nothing I did seemed to work. Perhaps it was that I had come to realize she had returned to her stony ice princess persona, directly after someone had interrupted our evening. My assumption was that it had to do with the person I reminded her of. And because I was there instead of him, I was to bear the expense of her emotions.

So here I am, just outside her building. I am in my vehicle staring at it, trying to decide how to proceed. This place isn't exactly what I had expected. I was certain she could afford something nicer with the salary she received, or so I hoped. Although, I hadn't actually looked into her financials. I assume because she is the king's secretary, she makes an adequate salary.

My driver stops me with his words as I am reaching for the door handle, "Sir, I must insist..."

"Hush," I pause only long enough to give him a direct order. "You may join me, but you will keep your opinions to yourself."

Rico sighs, a sure sign he expected that answer. Thankfully, he doesn't argue with me. "Certainly, Your Highness."

I climb out and wait for him to follow. "Enough with the attitude. Shall we?"

"After you, sir." He motions for me to move first while he does a surveillance of the area.

"Do you suppose it is unlocked?" I ask as I reach for the security door and yank it open with no problem. "Do me a favor. Have Javier do a full background check and financial assessment on Miss Violet Blanc. This is unacceptable for any woman, in my opinion. Surely Antonio pays her better than what it costs her to live here. If not, then I shall be having a harsh word with my brother the second I am finished here."

A rat scurries out in front of us, making a quick exit from the building. "Even the rats agree that the conditions are not up to standards," I state as I begin to make my way toward the elevator bay. As soon as the door opens, we are bombarded with the stench of urine and stale cigarette smoke. "Perhaps the stairs will be healthier?"

"Doubtful sir, but at least we won't be trapped in a public urinal should this deathtrap get stuck." Rico looks and sounds almost as disgusted as I am. "Are you certain you have the correct address?"

I push open the stairwell door and realize he was correct when the odor inside washes over us. "I hope for her sake this is not the correct address, that it was somehow mistyped into the system. Be ready to fight a feral cat should I find her here and decide to vacate with her over my shoulder. It could get ugly."

Rico chuckles behind me, but it's not because I believe he thinks this is funny. "Might be easier to knock her out before transport."

We don't talk the remainder of our climb to her third-floor flat. When we reach her floor, we exit the stairwell into a hallway that isn't any better. By the time we arrive at her door, I am beyond furious. There are no words, no explanation she can come up with that will be good enough to explain this away.

Before I can knock, the door swings open. I come face-to-face with a man I know all too well. He's slightly taller than me, but with the same dark hair and brown eyes. We often have been mistaken as brothers during our younger years when it was difficult to tell any of us apart.

His smug expression explains way more than I wish. "Hello, cousin."

"What are you doing here, Ruben?" I try to remain calm.

Reaching down, he zips his trousers, even though I'm not convinced they were actually undone. "You know the usual. Visiting my whore and baby factory."

"Don't call her that." I long to punch him for disrespecting Violet in such away. My hands form a solid fist but remain hanging by my sides.

"Sorry. I believe your type refers to them as mistresses and surrogates, but I'm rather confident this one is the former rather than the latter." He takes a step back and invites us inside as if it is his right to do so. "I didn't realize she was extending her services to others, although I suppose that is understandable. Once I've successfully secured a second heir, I'll be done with her for good this time. Lady Amber is not interested in more than two, and as you know, I give my wife what she wants when I can."

"You son of a..." I start to lunge for him, except Rico holds me back.

"Careful cousin. Do not forget who you are dealing with. You are no one to me, to the people really. Third born only makes you a nuisance, one no one would miss all that much." Ruben lifts his head slightly and squints his eyes as if studying me. "Do not push me."

"You need to leave," I warn him. "Don't come back."

Ruben laughs in that sadistic way he has perfected. "I'll keep returning to see her until I decide not to, Your Highness. Please do not disturb her, unless you want me to return sooner than I first intended. Tell her to come by the house in a few days. Since she was a *good girl* and didn't give me nearly as much trouble this time as last, she's earned her reward. Charlotte will be happy to see her."

I close my eyes as my mind recalls the young daughter who seemed to appear out of thin air. She had to be over a year by now if memory serves me correctly. A dark-haired, beautiful little angel who looked like Ruben but nothing like his wife, Lady Amber. Rumor suggested his wife was barren after an accident. He had promised to not let that stop him from giving her a child, though. I dare not think how Violet fits into that promise. I refuse to believe this was a choice she would have made freely.

We watch him gather the rest of his belongings as he keeps a close eye on Rico and me. He only takes his eyes off us for a second when he does a quick perusal of the flat and agitates his head. "She'll probably be sore, so you should be extremely gentle with her cousin. And please, double wrap, to ensure our swimmers don't intermingle. That could become a tricky situation should we achieve a positive result. Do you not agree?"

He opens the door to her flat and then leaves me with more to think on. "Don't worry Lorenzo, she isn't spilling any palace secrets. Not even after given my special serum. I don't honestly know what she finds so repulsive about me. I've never been anything but good to her. Took care of her when she was all alone and needed some extra cash. Funny how they so quickly forget, isn't it?"

I stare at the door for what seems like hours once it closes. Wishing I'd gotten my hands on him before he left. It isn't until Rico speaks, do I take my eyes off it and try to put the pieces of the puzzle together.

Why was my cousin really here? What did he want with someone like Miss Violet Blanc? How did Violet get involved with a man like Ruben?

All questions only she could answer should she choose to do so.

"Sir," Rico holds up an empty syringe he discovered on one of the side tables. "We should probably check on Miss Blanc."

I glance at the only other door in the flat that happens to be closed. "Call Gayle and Laney. Have them meet us at my place in an hour. Make sure they call Dr. Wilson. Give her a rundown of the situation we will need her assistance on."

"And what is that exactly, may I ask?" Rico runs his hand over his head, displaying his frustration.

"Just tell her... tell her... tell her we suspect a rape, but cannot confirm it yet. Possibly one where drugs were involved and who knows what else. Express that we expect full disclosure on the matter.

"While you do that, I'm going in there to establish what the damage is." I point to the closed door. "Be ready Rico, this could get ugly way faster than I expected."

I place my hand on the doorknob and turn it.

The first thing I notice when I step inside is the dress I bought her. It has been shredded as if someone took scissors to it and went to town on it to prove some point. I'll obviously replace it for her.

As the light overtakes the darkness in here, it is then that I spot Violet on the bed. She is awake and staring at me with a drug-induced gaze. Her naked form attempts to coil up and retreat. But because of the drugs that are affecting her, she barely moves.

"Please, no. No more. I've done as you've requested. You promised if I was good, you'd let me see Charlotte." Violet does her best to cover her naked body, except there is nothing to cover it with. The very reason I can identify the bruises, bite marks, and old scars. They stand out, along with the new ones she will likely soon acquire.

"I'm going to be sick." I hear her announce, right before she clutches her stomach and then retches its contents all over the bed.

I don't bother with decency at that moment, I simply react. Scoop her up in my arms so I can carry her off to the bathroom where I deposit her in the tub.

"Sir," I hear Rico behind me. "Don't wash her."

"I have to clean her up," I argue, blocking him from seeing her clearly.

"Sir. I understand where you are coming from, I do. But if you wash her..."

He doesn't need to explain more. I understand what he is advising.

Not that it will matter, because I also know my cousin, along with the connections he holds. It is why he wasn't worried about us finding him here. He does as he pleases and no one touches him. No one messes with a Del Markov or his family. Most fear them for good reason, I suppose, since they run the other empire that thrives in Hermosa Islas.

Every country has to deal with organized crime in one form or another. Ours is no different. The exception, I guess, being that my father's youngest sister Marjorie ended up married to the second most powerful family we have in our great kingdom. A family my father hated more than he hated all those opposed to his reign. That hatred had put a wedge between the Reyes family and the Del Markov family, had them fighting to destroy the other without considering the financial cost.

"You look like him," I hear Violet express as she stares at me blankly. "I hate him. I'm afraid I'll never get out from under his thumb. No matter how hard I try or what I give him. Even when I don't want to give it to him. Please leave. Just... please leave me be. Maybe this time I'll die before it wears off and I'm forced to face the reality of my situation again."

Violet's body convulses almost instantly. I climb in the tub with her so I can protect her the best I am able to. Afraid she will do more damage than has already been done if I don't secure her safely against my body while I protect her head.

It kills me to know this is all I can do right now for her. If I could, I'd suffer all this for her, take away her pain, give her something else to focus on.

Her words break me in a way that I've never been broken before this woman entered my life and somehow changed it. I hold her against me, doing my best to be there for her. Even though I'm sure it is not what she wants. However, knowing it is what she needs. What she is going to get from here on out.

"I've called for an ambulance. They should be here in five minutes." Rico announces as he drapes a blanket over Violet's shaking body. Protecting her too, because that is what my team does.

CHAPTER 2
Lorenzo

The Royals

I 've been camped out in this white sterile room for three days now. Not once have I left it since they wheeled Violet inside. I've remained by her side after a nearly fatal reaction to whatever drugs my cousin injected into her system.

She's suffered so many seizures the doctors are concerned about the effects it could have on her long-term. Watching her brain diligently for any signs that suggest complications she'll have should she ever wake. It isn't clear yet if and when that might occur.

Right now, the doctors are hopeful, but Violet is not out of the woods just yet. They can only understand so much while she sleeps and her body does its best to heal. The seizures have stopped finally. Even the minor ones that could only be detected by monitoring her brain waves. Now everyone is playing the waiting game. Only Violet can determine when this game will end.

I've had three days to sit here and reflected over the last eleven months I've known this woman. Recounted it all over in detail. Bringing each and every interaction I have shared with Violet to mind.

The first day Antonio introduced us, I remember catching her retreat slightly. Taking a step backward and trying to play it off. When I extended my hand to shake hers, it took every ounce of strength she had inside of her to allow me to touch her. I recall how her hand trembled when I captured her fingers with my hands, while I expressed it was a pleasure to make her acquaintance. She couldn't yank her hand free of mine fast enough. Her hasty retreat behind her fortress of a desk where she could place a solid barrier between us seemed odd. I didn't miss how she kept a close watch on me from that point forward. Rarely saying more than necessary when addressing me.

That was how those first several months transpired between us. I'd come to the palace to discuss Reyes Capital with my brother, and Violet had regularly done her best to avoid me as much as possible. She pretended to be busy or made some excuse to leave shortly after I arrived. Never participating when I attempted to make small talk, always acted annoyed by me. At first, I assumed maybe she did that to everyone, so it never truly bothered me much.

Until the day I walked in and heard her laughing with Alejandro and Dane, my brother's personal secretary and one of his fiancée's guards. I only caught a portion of the conversation, but enough to realize Dane had basically asked her out on a date. Violet gratefully had declined. Told him she was flattered he considered her in his league, but that at the moment wasn't dating. Her life was way too complicated for her to add a dating life into the pot. She barely had time for herself as it was, didn't feel as if it were fair to disappoint another person. Especially someone she was supposed to be trying to impress, and hopefully later convince she was a catch. Dane had chuckled, as had Alejandro. He expressed that when she found her life slowing down, where she discovered she had time on her hands, to give him a call or throw him a bone even, so he could call her.

I proceeded into the office thinking I'd find her in a good mood and flip matters around for us. Except as soon as Violet laid eyes on me, I visibly watched her demeanor transform to the icy, unemotional princess she always was around me. The one who noticeably thought very little of me. It was also clear that the other two gentlemen had caught on as well, because they did that tennis match spectator move with their heads.

Instead of drawing more attention to it, I, for the first time, ignored her the best I could. Announced myself and asked if His Majesty was

14

ready to see me. Wondering out loud if I had time to visit the heir Prince before he graced me with his presence. Yeah, I was bitter, and it showed.

I'd wracked my brain after that day to determine if we'd possibly met before and I'd somehow offended her. Paid way more attention to how she treated every other male she came in contact with. Only to get more frustrated when she was civil, even to the worst of them. No matter what I did or said, Violet was unmoved. Each gesture only seemed to irritate her more than the last. Unbeknownst to her, it only fueled that fire inside of me that was determined to make her see me differently.

It also was how this woman snuck into the one place no other one had been able to get inside before. Her constant denial of me made me that much more attracted to her for some odd and unhealthy reason. Suddenly I wasn't interested in entertaining other women whose only objectives were to manipulate me. Not that I'd allowed myself to be manipulated, or bothered really, to grant them more than a single date. If you could even call them dates.

Was it a date if you only went out with a woman once? Not allowing any real physical contact with them? Did your best to be there in the present with each woman, yet found you were often bored with it all? Wishing you were anywhere else but there?

I cannot tell you the last time I went on an actual date with someone where I got caught up in it all. My guess is never, honestly. Not even when I was a teenager, did I find myself infatuated with all the very eager ladies who threw themselves at me. I can probably count on one hand the number of females I've kissed on the actual lips, and I'd done that a few times under protest.

As a man, I'd been extremely careful. Although I'm sure most will argue that at twenty-three, I haven't been a man all that long. Except I'd argue that at eighteen, shortly after I left for university, it took me all of three seconds to figure out what kind of man I had to be to protect myself. There were way too many female prospects willing to do whatever they had to do to trap a prince like myself, so they could keep him. I'd vowed at that point to not allow myself the pleasure of getting caught up in it all. Not until I was certain I'd uncovered the one who would forever be mine. Kept my hands to myself, for the most part.

Touching only when dancing or maneuvering them in the direction I wanted them to move. Determined to kiss nothing more than the back of a hand or a cheek when it seemed appropriate to do so. Making sure to not lead any to believe I was interested in pursuing them. If needed, I had no problem letting my words be straightforward and to the point. Which, as you might imagine, often gave me the reputation of being the prince who played the field. When in reality, I wasn't playing at all. All I was doing was what I always referred to as sleight of hand. So that those who might be paying close attention to my dating life were left to assume I had one. In reality, I did not.

Nor did I want one. Until recently, that is, when the very irritating Miss Violet Blanc started messing with my mind. I do trust that was in no way her intention. She was unaware of what she was doing by treating me the way she did. If she had a clue to the fact that I'd become infatuated with her because of her actions, I'm confident she'd have done her best to figure out another way to steer me clear of her. Although now that I've had time to deliberate about it, I'm not sure it would have mattered.

Something drew me to her. At first, I'd written it off as being all because she wanted nothing to do with me. That, however, made me want to encourage her to change her mind where I was concerned.

I stand from my spot in the chair I've spent hours in and amble over to her bed. As I stare at her, I am reminded of the fairytales my sister Isabel is often engrossed in. She and I have watched them so many times that I could give you a play-by-play. It is also a great possibility that I'd win some trivia games about them.

Two of those countless stories come to mind while I watch Violet lie perfectly still. Her body is fighting to stay alive, denying her earlier request when all hell broke loose. She looks as if she is only sleeping when in reality it is way worse. It has me truly frightened that we've wasted away most of our time together.

My hand moves without being instructed to do so. Brushing her chocolate-colored hair from her face. It traces the contours of her features, taking in every curve and line. My fingers skim over her eyebrows, as my mind recalls how her brown eyes change depending on her mood. Right now, I wish she'd open them so I could appreciate the transformation. Study them closely while her eyes lighten or darken in that unique and amazing way they do.

My eyes shift to her lips. They are usually perfect appearing soft lips. Often covered in shades of pinks and reds, just subtle enough to attract attention. Even cracked and dry, they draw mine. Not just my attention, but they seem to be enticing my lips to want to connect with them. Appreciate exactly how they would feel against mine.

Leaning forward, I find myself running my thumb over hers first. My mind recalls how two of the princes in those fairytales broke the spell that had been cast on their princesses with a kiss. Not just a kiss. It had been one with promise and sentiments that in no way had been faked.

I realize now that over these last several months, I've developed more than just an infatuation for this woman. When I wasn't paying attention, I'd fallen for her fully and completely. Even though she'd done her best to push me far away, it seemed she'd failed royally.

Therefore, I wonder if there is some truth in those stories. Start to let myself believe in the power of something I hadn't considered until this very moment. Funny how when it hits you, you are futile to fight against it, instead you begin letting it suck you in and overtake you.

Which can only explain how my lips land on hers. Clarify why they remain there while I give her everything I possess. I don't move until hers twitch slightly against my hand, the one that is caressing her face.

As I pull back, I am confident I will discover her eyes staring up at me. Unfortunately, that isn't the case, reminding me that real life isn't as neatly put together as a child's fairytale. A kiss can't magically awaken the maiden, no matter how noble the suitor's intentions might be.

I hear the door behind me click closed. Then I begin to wonder if I just made a complete fool of myself in front of one of the nurses charged to care for Violet. As I rotate to face the person standing behind me, I realize I've done one better. I've made a fool of myself in front of my mother, who now looks at me with eyes of understanding.

"Hello dear," she softly speaks as she approaches. "How is she?"

I don't move. I only turn to stare back at Violet as I answer her. "Same, unfortunately. She needs to wake up. Each day she doesn't, causes my hopes of her waking to dwindle more and more. I just found her mother; I can't lose her before we are given a real chance."

"My dear Lorenzo," my mother takes my hand in hers as she too studies the woman fighting for her life. "Time is often the best medicine. Don't give up hope. She will need your strength to get her through when she returns to us. Let God do what he needs to do and trust him to take care of her while he does. I know it is easier for me to say than it is for you to accept or do. But I also believe there is a reason you are here with her now."

I only nod in agreement.

"When was the last time you showered, ate, slept?" She asks me as she takes Violet's hand in hers and gives it a gentle squeeze. "Why don't you let me sit with her while you go and take a few hours to do those things."

"No." There is no way I'm leaving her side until she wakes.

"Allow me to try this again. Go shower Lorenzo. Three days' worth of stale body odor, isn't going to impress her when she finally comes back to us. While you are gone, I promise to not leave her side. I thought I might even help her clean up as well. Take the time to change her gown and fix her hair. Do a little personal hygiene with some assistance from one of the nurses." It amazes me how my mother seems to care equally for Violet as she does for me. "She'd be embarrassed if you were here while we took care of those personal matters, don't you agree."

"Violet wouldn't want you here either, or anyone else for that matter. I've already witnessed the worst while I held her so..."

My mother tugs me against her the best she can. "Lorenzo, you and I both know that is not the same. You did what you had to do at the time when she had no one else there to do so. She now has me to step in and assist you and her until she is well enough to take care of herself again. It would be my honor to look after her like I would any of my other children. Even those children that have come to be mine, only because the ones I've born found them and claimed them as their own. A mother's love knows no limits, dear."

"Thank you," I whisper with a great deal of emotion. "You promise to alert me if anything changes."

"Of course, I do." She draws me back so she can look me directly in the eyes. "Take a few hours away from this. Go home and shower, have someone fix you a decent meal. Return if you must, after that. You can sleep here on a cot; I'll ask the staff to bring one in. But you will sleep, while I continue to stand vigilantly here with you until she is out of the woods completely. You do her no good in this condition."

She's right. I know she is right.

"Fine. I will be back after I've showered and eaten."

Patting my cheek, my mother smiles, "Good boy. Now tell her goodbye."

As mother takes a seat, I do just that. I reach up and run my fingers over Violet's face softly. It nearly kills me to leave her, even though I realize my mother will do exactly as she has stated.

"Violet," I whisper her name as I lean in next to her ear. "My mother is here. She's going to stay with you until I return. I won't be gone long, a few hours at most. Be good for her. Don't give her any trouble, save that for me please."

I then graze the side of her face and shut my eyes, as I try my best to maintain my composure. Violet doesn't need me falling apart right now when she can't make fun of me for doing so. I give her one last kiss on her forehead, and then quickly make my way out the door before I change my mind about leaving at all.

CHAPTER 3
Violet

The Royals

Slowly, I wake and become aware of my surroundings. Hear unfamiliar noises. Voices I don't recognize immediately. They sound muffled and distant, causing my head to pound worse than it already was.

Everything is foggy.

My last clear memory is not a pleasant one. None of my memories involving Ruben Del Markov ever are. He is a man who entered my life when I was a stupid, naïve teenage girl. From that day forward he has been a recurring nightmare that I haven't been able to escape.

Don't ever let anyone tell you that what you do as a teenager will soon be forgotten once those days are long gone. That might be true for some. It certainly has not been true in my case.

I expect that to be because most do not have to live the life I have been subjected to endure. Therefore, the majority don't comprehend how difficult getting out from under the thumb of certain mistakes can be nearly impossible. Once you start down a particular path, you are forever stuck on that path.

If I could do it over again, I'd walk away from those choices and never look back. Except do-overs are not granted in this life.

My mother died when I was twelve. Petra Hill fell in love with

Dolan Blanc, who was gone more than he was home. She found it challenging to remain positive during his absence. While I suspect she truly loved me, her ability to take care of both of us during those spells was beyond her.

My father enjoyed the nomad way of life more than he did the settled down life my mother wanted for them. I was a mistake that pushed him into marrying my mother. After my mother's untimely death, he dumped me on my grandparents, ultimately making me their responsibility. Our relationship never really developed; I was only his daughter by blood. A harsh reality I'd learned to live with during my younger years. As you might imagine, it left me with all kinds of issues.

My grandparents weren't interested in raising another child, so they didn't. I lived with them. They fed me, clothed me, even offered me shelter. What they didn't do, however, was parent me or teach me how to make choices that would get me safely through this life. I was left to raise myself, and in due course got drawn into a crowd that wasn't exactly ideal.

At age sixteen, I dropped out of school so I could travel the world with that group of friends. We considered it cool that someone was paying us to travel to places like Bali, Fuji, and Brazil—just to name a few. All we had to do was make it through customs without getting pulled aside and searched. For a year we did just that without incident. We were living an incredibly exciting life for teenagers. Each one of us felt we were untouchable until the day came that we weren't.

One day the five of us almost didn't make it out of Turkey. We'd been flagged because of all the stamps we had acquired on our passports in such a short time. They hadn't found the diamonds or drugs we were smuggling that trip. However, they held us long enough we were positive we were going to jail.

As soon as we landed in Hermosa Islas, the man we worked for had us brought directly to him. That was the first time I came face-to-face with Ruben, and it was also the day my life went straight to hell.

I'll never forget that day as long as I live.

He confiscated the merchandise we smuggled in immediately, then paid each of us for the job. Afterward, he dismissed everyone, said we were no longer of any use to him. Dumped us back into society. As we were exiting, he studied each one of us remarkably close. It made me extremely uncomfortable and frightened about why he was doing so. Before I was able to make my escape, Ruben stopped me and pulled me aside.

"What is your name?" He snagged my arm, separating me from the others.

"Violet."

"How old are you, Violet?" His eyes did a quick once-over down my body. "You are very pretty."

"Seventeen."

An agitation of his head communicated that wasn't the answer he'd been hoping for. "What a shame. You and I could have had fun. When is your birthday, Violet?"

At that moment, I realized he was not asking out of curiosity. He was asking because he had intentions for me that made my skin crawl. "I just turned seventeen a few months ago."

He nodded and took a step back. Then appeared to be deciding if that mattered to him or not. "I'm not the sort of man who is typically interested in someone so innocent."

"Who said I was innocent?" I'm not sure why I'd blurted that out, but for some reason I had.

It was clear Ruben was lying since he'd pulled me aside and had asked about my age in the first place. He didn't care that I wasn't an adult in the eyes of the law. The law was not important to a man like Ruben. This man's occupation incorporated every imaginable illegal activity you could think of, and a few I suspect you couldn't. He was striving to make me assume it mattered to him, and that I was somehow special. I didn't feel special though.

He raised his eyebrows and then laughed. "I see. Perhaps I should keep you around then, Violet. We could get to know each other. That way I can decide how to best use you."

"Maybe I'm not interested." I'd dared to challenge his authority over me.

A wicked smirk crossed Ruben's face as he stared me down. "I don't believe I asked if you were, now did I? You and I, Violet, will get along better if you do as you are told. Go now, before I break all my own rules, and show you a few things before you are ready. In a few days, someone will be in contact with you and you will do exactly as they instruct or else. Do not mistake me as a nice man because I am letting you go for now. Understand that I always get what I want when I want it."

Two days later, a man dropped by my grandparents' home and instructed me to pack my belongings. I did so while he watched closely. He then drove me to a building in a rough neighborhood, where he set me up in one of its flats. Before he left, he informed me I was enrolled in classes at a local trade school where I was to be trained on how to work in an office. Told me that if I didn't show up and go to class, Ruben wouldn't like it. That it would be in my best interest to not upset his boss. I wasn't sure what to think. Although it didn't seem to be an awful arrangement at that time.

Over the next year, I'd taken Ruben's opportunity for trade school seriously and completed it with high marks. He made frequent visits to check up on me. Taught me all the stuff no one else had ever bothered to. Showed me how to balance my checkbook, where he'd deposited a substantial sum of money in already. Helped me learn how to pay the bills, cook a decent meal, all while encouraging me to study hard. Sent me to a salon that coached me on how to apply makeup and fix my hair, so that later I'd look like a professional. He even bought me clothes to wear in an office, to ensure I'd fit in with the other staff instead of stand out. When I was finished with school, he also helped me acquire a few jobs in companies he had some interest in.

I'd started to assume he was a nice man. Forgot who he was or why he was doing all those things for me. Not because he dropped the act of being attracted to me, but because he never acted on that attraction like I first feared he would.

That all changed once I turned eighteen. Ruben showed up like he often did on that Friday night, except this time he didn't leave until late Sunday. I'd been so excited to see him, so happy to have someone finally remember my birthday. Willingly accepted the cupcakes and champagne he brought with him to celebrate me coming of age. I'd let my guard down just long enough for him to sneak in.

I'll admit, at first, I was flattered when he told me he thought I was beautiful. Let all his friendly gestures soften me up and trusted him more than I should have. Allowed Ruben to get me a little tipsy. Even accepted a pill he offered me when he caught on that I was growing anxious once he started to put the moves on me. He enlightened me it would help me relax just enough so the two of us would be able to have some fun. It was then I realized how naïve I had been for trusting him at all.

From that point on, Ruben controlled my life. I was his to do with as he pleased whenever it pleased him to do so. When I tried to refuse him, he'd show me why I couldn't. It continued like that for two years. And as you might imagine, every day that passed I wished I'd never met the man.

Then it ended for a short time after I turned twenty. That's when Ruben married his betrothed Lady Amber, and he was no longer free to roam like he once had been. I had hoped he'd lost interest in me. Even started to consider he was finished with our relationship. Convinced his new wife was keeping him occupied.

I should have known better though. Men like Ruben don't let their most prized possessions go. That is what I was to him. A possession he'd kept hidden away and used when it pleased him. Once he came back, he did so with a vengeance. He was way more violent than he had been before. Started lacing my food with drugs after I refused to accept his pills. Then when I stopped eating anything he brought with him, he no longer tried to cover up the fact he enjoyed drugging me. If he couldn't force me to swallow a pill, he had no problem holding me down while injecting his drug of choice into my system. It became a game to him. He would test his newest street drugs on me for fun. Doing his best to ruin me, forcing me to become one of his addicts.

It might have worked if he had continued the practice much longer. I was close to becoming a junky when I'd discovered myself pregnant. At that point, Ruben once again started leaving me alone. He still visited, except without the drugs and the awful unpleasant sex. I got to experience a gentler side of him. I should have known it was all an act. Understood he was only doing so to benefit himself. It had nothing at all to do with me.

As my due date approached, Ruben's visits became more frequent. He started stopping by daily, even spending his nights in my flat. When I only had a few weeks left, I learned why that was exactly. He'd planned it all out perfectly. Escorted me to our appointment with the doctor he'd handpicked for me to use. As soon as we arrived, I once again realized my mistake in putting my trust in him.

Lady Amber was waiting for us this time inside the doctor's office. It was clear her thoughts about me were not pleasant by the way she scowled when we walked in.

"What's going on?" I'd stupidly asked.

"Did you really think I was going to let you raise my child, Violet?" Ruben sounded so sure I'd not argue with him.

"Are you so stupid that you'd think I'd just hand this baby over to you?" I had retorted and learned that is exactly what he'd expected me to do.

I delivered my baby girl two weeks earlier than necessary. I was held captive in that dingy office against my will and forced into labor. Once my baby was born, she was immediately passed off to Lady Amber as if she were hers. I'd not been allowed to hold her, even though she was mine. They'd whisked her away and into another room, leaving me behind wailing about how they'd stolen her without my consent.

Ruben made it very clear once I'd calmed down what my role would be in our daughter's life. He wasn't worried he'd not get his way. I'd lived in his world long enough by that point to realize fighting him was pointless.

In the beginning, I'd been allowed to visit with my daughter once a week, as I dropped off the breastmilk I was forced to pump. Once she was old enough to not need my milk, I could only see her a few times a month. Only when it was convenient for Lady Amber, though. When my daughter was no longer a cute and cuddly baby, started to be a handful and they both needed a break, Ruben would bring her to me. He'd even allow me to keep her overnight on the weekends. Of course, I wasn't completely left on my own. Someone that worked for him stayed with us to make certain I didn't try to run.

I always took whatever time with her they would allow me whenever they would offer it to me. A fact Ruben quickly came to use to his advantage, and once again used against me to acquire what he wanted when he wanted it.

And since Lady Amber couldn't be bothered with being pregnant, because it would ruin her body and was an inconvenience. As soon as she decided Charlotte needed a sibling, I once again became his victim. His frequent visits started up again. If I wanted to continue to be a part of my daughter's life, I was expected to comply with all his demands.

Meaning that when I missed a scheduled visit because of the party I'd been invited to, he'd gone completely off the rails. Took my punishment to an entirely different level. Using my daughter once again as leverage to force me to fall back in line and do as I was told.

"Where were you?" Ruben asked when I walked into my flat. After leaving the party, I'd known had been a mistake to attend.

"At a birthday party for Princess Winifred. I was told it was rude to refuse such an invitation." I had done my best to explain, even though I'd come to understand he'd find it hilarious.

"If they only knew you, Violet, like I know you. They might think differently about all that. Perhaps I should come visit you one day at the palace so I can introduce myself to your boss." He'd threatened with a sadistic laugh. "What do you imagine the king would think about that, Violet? Do you suppose he would appreciate that his secretary is my whore?"

I'd refused to answer him. Made a point to not show how hearing him call me his whore affected me. It would only encourage him. He did not need to be encouraged.

"When I summon you, it is not a request, Violet. You drop whatever it is you are doing and you come. I don't care what you have to tell your precious royals. I told you taking that job was a mistake. Explained that you were not good enough to be associating with their type. They will never accept you should they ever discover the truth. Imagine the scandal that would arise if anyone learned the king hired someone associated with the Del Markovs." He informed me as he became comfortable.

"When did you get that dress?" Ruben asked as he examined it closely.

"It was a gift." I didn't elaborate because I'd known he'd only use who gave it to me against me, eventually. "What is it you want that couldn't wait until I returned later this evening?"

I found myself up against the wall with his hand tightly around my neck as soon as I'd mouthed off. "I don't wait for you, Violet, ever. You will pay for making me. And this time you will not be offered something to help you relax. Maybe next time you'll remember that and play nice. Now about this dress..."

The next time he summoned me, I remembered how much better it was when he drugged me. I allowed him to do so without arguing. He'd spent two days with me. Most of our time together I'd been so high to even care that he was using my body, however he pleased to do so.

I'd started to come down when he handed me a syringe while he reminded me of the reason he was there. "My wife has decided Charlotte requires a sibling. So, I will continue to stop by like this until we achieve the results she is hoping for. The sooner we do, the sooner I will be out of your life for good, Violet. If you want me out of your life, then it would be in your best interest to stop fighting me. What do you say?"

I stared at the needle in my hand as I thought long and hard about his words. "What is in here?"

"Do you like how it makes you feel, Violet? Take it, let me do what I need to do; if you do, I promise to let you visit Charlotte. You can even take her for an evening if you'd like. Be a good girl and let's have some fun."

I handed him the needle as I nodded my head in agreement. It wasn't that I preferred to give him what he wanted. I was done fighting for my freedom and hoped that maybe this mix of drugs would end it all for me. As the warm liquid flooded my veins, I prayed God would stop the madness and let me fall asleep and never wake again.

I don't remember much after that. My body relaxed and my mind started floating into a state that was between reality and sleep.

Ruben did whatever he usually did to me, while I let my mind wander and recall the memories of my daughter. Deciding that if I woke from this, I should take her and run. Save us both from this man who had ruined me, and would most likely do the same to her. Understood that he'd eventually realize the reason I wasn't getting pregnant. I had an IUD inserted shortly after Charlotte by a doctor he didn't know I'd visited.

I briefly recall hearing Ruben speaking with someone who sounded pissed after he left me naked on my bed. The high I was experiencing was unlike any I'd ever suffered from before. My body was numb and my brain was making everything appear as if it were moving in slow motion.

A man who looked similar to Ruben, only younger, entered my bedroom and stared at me with concern in his eyes. No man had done that before, so I wasn't certain how I felt about it while I was so vulnerable.

The last thing I remember clearly is being carried into the bathroom after throwing up all over my bed. Then gazing into familiar brown eyes, while wishing I'd met whoever this was instead of Ruben all those years ago. Knowing how different my life would have been had that been the case.

Then my world went black.

Now I am slowly waking up in a place unfamiliar to me. Surrounded by voices I don't recognize. My mind now understanding I didn't die. So that means I am going to have to face Ruben all too soon. Nothing is ever going to get any better for me. I'm doomed to suffer through another day.

I open my eyes sluggishly, dreading the reality I will face.

Blinking a few times, I strain to coerce my eyes to focus.

A shadow moves into view and I do my best to try to make it out. Except my eyes aren't cooperating fully yet.

An earlier muffled voice starts to become clearer, "Violet."

I recognize that voice.

It's the same voice that was at my flat arguing it out with Ruben.

As the voice becomes clearer, so does the shadowy figure hovering over me. I come face-to-face with the one man I have been doing my best to avoid all these months because I couldn't handle how he affected me.

"Hey." His large hand brushes over my head. "Welcome back."

"Go. Away." I try to tell him, except my voice is weak and my mouth is dry.

CHAPTER 4
Violet

The Royals

I want to die right now, for other reasons than I did prior to this moment. My mind is clearer than it was a few moments ago. When I was doing my best to recall what happened and why I was here.

I can't believe my luck or lack of it.

"Please. Leave." My lips move and form words, although I don't believe my voice actually utters them.

How is it possible that I always find myself in situations that result in horrible consequences? Why did Prince Lorenzo have to be the person who found me after Ruben left?

"Shh." The most handsome man I've ever laid eyes on leans closer, "Hush now."

I shut my eyes again, praying I'm hallucinating and none of this is real. I'm probably tripping in my bedroom, and my mind is playing tricks on me in the worst of ways.

"Come on, Violet. Open your eyes for me, honey. Let me admire those beautiful brown windows to your soul. I've missed watching them do that thing they do when you get upset with me." He is so close now that I can feel his breath warming my skin. "Come on, it's time to wake up. You've been sleeping for five days now. Surely that's more than enough time to catch up on your beauty sleep."

I'm confident I've heard him incorrectly.

Did he say five days?

My eyes blink several times as they adjust to the light. It seems almost too bright right now. Nonetheless, I am determined to keep them open this time.

Lorenzo beams down at me, and I can sense the pressure behind my eyes building. How is it possible someone like him could be staring at me in that way I've always wished for?

"That's it," he whispers softly. "Do you have a headache?"

I nod once, and my head feels like it just might explode with that simple movement. So, I raise my hand, or at least I attempt to, but it is so heavy and won't cooperate.

A woman appears on the other side of me. She then shines a penlight in my eyes, nearly blinding me. Moving it around a few times before clicking it off. Next, she forces my eyes open even wider as she stares at each one carefully.

It's then I realize she is talking to me. "Violet, don't try to speak. Just blink once for yes, twice for no. Do you understand?"

I blink once.

"That's it. Do you remember what happened?"

I blink once.

"Do you recognize who this very devoted man is?" She pats Lorenzo on the shoulder, tossing a smile in his direction.

My eyes shift to stare at him and I blink once, even though I don't understand her question completely.

"Good. That's a relief since he's not once left your side since they brought you in. Okay, that's not true exactly. One of the other nurses said his mother forced him to leave two days ago for a few hours. Although I do suspect he rushed back to you rather quickly, even though Her Royal Highness promised to not leave while he was gone." I strain to process her words, not sure I understood because that can't be correct.

"Why?" I whisper through dry lips and a parched throat.

"Why?" The nurse repeats my words, amused at my question. "I believe it's rather obvious, dear, this young man is quite fond of you."

Lorenzo, I swear, blushes at her comment. And I must make an extremely confused face because he shrugs while appearing guilty. "We'll discuss all that later. Right now, I'm thrilled that you've decided to come back to me."

"What?" I mouth, not at all understanding what parallel universe I woke up in.

"What I wouldn't do to be a fly on the wall during that conversation." The nurse snickers, but then moves on. "Would you like some ice chips?"

I didn't realize how thirsty I was until she mentioned ice chips. I blink once.

"Your Highness, could you go get those for her while I continue my examination?" She pats his hand when he hesitates. "Go on. Your lady wants a cup of ice chips. I'm sure she'd be more than grateful if you got them for her."

Lorenzo leans forward, placing a firm kiss to my forehead before he steps back and disappears from my sight.

The second he is gone, the nurse checks all kinds of tubes while she chats with me. "As soon as you are up to holding a full conversation, I'm going to need to hear all there is about that fine man. I thought our King was a sight when I met him once in this very hospital. Woo, I nearly wet myself when he walked in and stood there all king-like. Queen Larkin is one very lucky woman, to get to wake up to that handsome face every day for the remainder of her life. Know what I mean?"

She pauses and glances down at me, so I blink once.

"Yeah, of course, you do. I hear you work at the Palace. His secretary, even. So you get the pleasure of appreciating how God has blessed all the Reyes males. Prince Esteban gives his brothers a run for their money as well. I've never met him like I have now met the other two. But I've seen them all three standing side by side on television enough times to see I speak the truth. Am I right?"

Again, when she pauses, she glances down at me and I blink once.

"But I do believe your young prince might be the best looking of the bunch. Maybe I'm biased since I've gotten to know him quite well these last five days. I've kind of had a front-row seat, where I've had the privilege of watching how much he cares for you." She informs me as she hits a button on my bed and makes it sit up a little. "I've seen my share of men stand valiantly by the side of their love. So I've gotten good at noticing those who know how to do it right. Those who realize touch is just as important as talking to someone who might need encouragement along the way. I'm sure you appreciate what I mean."

She adjusts the sheet and then tucks a pillow behind my head before smiling at me. I notice then she is waiting for an answer. I blink twice this time and she displays her confusion.

"That surprises me. I was positive you all had one thrilling romance going on that none of us knew about." She taps my nose, much like I've seen someone do to a child. "You will, I am positive of that. He has made it quite clear to us all, here in the ICU, that we were likely treating the future…"

"Don't give away all my secrets, Kim." Lorenzo interrupts before she can finish her sentence. "I've got ice chips."

I hold up my hand when he takes his seat and fills the spoon with a few chips. Hoping the gesture will stop him, I then motion for Kim to finish.

Lorenzo ignores me, though. "I don't think so. Open."

I open my mouth to say something, but he shoves the spoon inside so I can't speak. The moment the cold wet ice touches my tongue, I close my eyes as it melts. I've never appreciated ice more in my life than I do right now.

"You like that." Lorenzo scoops more onto the spoon and offers it to me. "Let's do this slowly, for now, to make sure your stomach can handle it."

"More," I voice once the other melts. "More."

"Shh." He chuckles as he scoops up a few more. "Greedy as always, I see."

I open my mouth as I glare at him.

"It's good to see you haven't lost your sass," Lorenzo announces as he feeds me more ice chips, then leans forward and kisses my cheek. "I've certainly missed deciphering your eyes."

Before I can say more, a female doctor walks in and introduces herself. "Hello, I'm Dr. Kroger. Kim had me paged as soon as you woke. We've been patiently waiting for you to return to us."

"Hi," I whisper.

"Has anyone explained what happened?" Dr. Kroger questions as she drags one of the stools over to the bed.

I shake my head.

"First of all, I need to make sure you are okay with me speaking freely in front of Prince Lorenzo. Are you okay with that?"

I'm not sure. So, I ask a question of my own, although it takes me a few seconds to get it all out. "How much has he been told?"

Lorenzo grabs my hand and squeezes. "Very little. In order to gather information from them at all, I practically had to disclose all my intentions I have where you are concerned. You didn't make it very easy on me. Your emergency contact was left blank on your work documents, so I couldn't even convince that person to speak for me. You'll need to rectify that."

I lift my eyebrows and am quickly reminded how painful that action is right now. "What intentions?"

"We'll discuss that later. Tell the doctor there is no reason to not share all of it with me. You need someone here who can explain it again later, should you not catch it all. Plus, I'm not leaving, so there is no use in trying to kick me out now. You, Violet, are stuck with me." Lorenzo brings my hand to his lips and holds it there. "If you are okay with that, that is."

"It's fine." I am in no state of mind to process his words. Plus, he's right, I will need someone to explain it all again to me later. It seems he may have earned that since it sounds as if he's been here all along.

The good doctor starts from the beginning. Explains how I was brought into the ER five days ago after overdosing on a mixture of some very powerful drugs. She names them all, but I can't be sure if I've ever heard of most.

I might have caught her mention something about tranquilizers and muscle relaxers being a bad combination. Heard her reference the name opioids and a few details about bath salt traces being discovered in the syringe they recovered in my flat. Even questioning me if I was aware of how dangerous it was injecting those kinds of toxins into my body.

"I didn't inject." I stammer out as I struggle to process all she has revealed so far. "Did you say cocaine?"

She nods her head in that way that makes one feel guilty. "Along with a countless amount of other illegal substances. It's a miracle you are still with us. How long have you been an addict?"

"What?" I don't believe I heard her correctly, so I repeat her words. "How long have I been an addict?"

"These are not the kinds of drugs one starts with, Miss Blanc. A person has to work her way up to the dosage you took. My guess is that you had been at it for a few days. As soon as one high wore off, you were chasing it with something different. Explaining why your body reacted the way it did when Prince Lorenzo finally discovered you. It's a good thing he came along when he did. Otherwise, you'd have succeeded in overdosing on that last method of high you injected into your system."

"No." I close my eyes, not wanting to hear this any longer. "No. I didn't inject those drugs."

I don't want to explain the horrid details surrounding why those drugs were found in my body. It's bad enough I have to live with the fact I'm shackled to a sick and cruel man. A man who almost killed me for his own pleasure. I'm not even sure that wasn't his objective after hearing how many drugs he continued to feed me. He'd learned I could not tell him no after that first high.

Dr. Kroger goes on without missing a beat, obviously not believing me. She explains how my heart was beating so rapidly when they brought me in. It was close to exploding. That situation, along with the seizures I suffered through, is what caused my body to shut down. Keeping me in a comatose state for five days. My overstimulated body needed time to heal before allowing my brain to wake again.

She went on to explain they wouldn't know the extent of the damage I had done until I fully recovered and they could run some tests. If I came through without any serious issues, I had Lorenzo to thank for that. Lorenzo and God.

Before Dr. Kroger left me in a state of complete confusion, she explained why I had a feeding tube running down my nose. A tube until she mentioned it, I hadn't even noticed. Explained that if I didn't fall back into an unconscious state, it would be taken out. Allowing me to resume normal digestive functions and test how my stomach would react to food again.

The nurse returned to check on me as Dr. Kroger was stepping out. She changed one of my IV bags and emptied my catheter bag, with the promise to remove it as soon as she got the green light to do so.

The entire time Lorenzo stayed close by, only stepped behind the curtain when I required more privacy. He was quiet for a man who always seemed to have something to say. Way quieter than I was comfortable with after listening to the doctor explain her thoughts about my drug addiction. I had to wonder if he had drawn the same conclusions about it after hearing how many drugs they'd found inside my body. If I didn't know the truth about it all, I'd have accepted her assumption as well.

"Violet." I hear him uttering my name as soon as Kim leaves again.

I can't even look at him right now. Does he believe what Dr. Kroger suggested? Does he think I injected all those drugs into my system willingly?

Of course he does. Why would he assume differently? He doesn't know about Ruben or the circumstances revolving around him. Plus, who would believe such a complicated, unfathomable story? I'd have a hard time buying into it if I wasn't the one living the nightmare.

My head begins to really hurt again.

My guess, for the reason it hurts so badly, is that they aren't giving me anything to suppress the pain. It's probably against hospital policy to give a drug addict pain medication. Adding more drugs would be counterproductive when trying to detox a patient and rid her body of the poison.

"Violet." I feel the bed dip and then nearly jump out of my skin when strong arms wrap around me. "We are going to get through this."

"I'm not an addict," I whisper, needing to explain.

Lorenzo rests his chin on my shoulder and draws me closer. I start to wonder if he has done this when I was unaware of him doing so.

"I didn't willingly take those drugs," I confess, not even sure he hears me.

"I know." He informs me. "It was my cousin."

"Your cousin?" I repeat, confused, twisting my head slowly so I can look at him.

"Yes, my cousin. Ruben Del Markov is my cousin. His mother was my father's youngest sister, Princess Marjorie. She married Ruben's father, Viktor Del Markov, a few years before he got mixed up with the Russian mob and eventually took over their criminal organization. Did you not notice the family resemblance?"

I had never really thought much about it. "No. Maybe. I don't know really, but I suppose that would explain why he found it ironic I worked for the king while involved with the likes of him."

"And why were you involved with the likes of him?" Lorenzo tightens his hold on me. "He mentioned something about getting his hands on you when you were sixteen."

I can't have this conversation right now. "Your Highness, if it is alright with you, I'd rather not get into all that at the moment. I'm tired."

"Okay." He doesn't bother to move, though. "Sleep then."

"With you so close?" I'm not sure I can.

"Yes, Violet. You should get used to me being close like this." He shifts and gets comfortable. "I plan on being by your side for a very long time."

I'd have argued with him, but my eyes are heavy again and his warmth is luring me to sleep. So instead of using energy, I don't possess. I try not to think about what he is saying and let my body fall back into a deep sleep.

CHAPTER 5
Lorenzo

The Royals

I wish I could tell you that everything between Violet and me changed the moment she woke. That she took one look at me and confessed her undying love and would be thrilled to have me be the man in her life.

That is so not what happened at all, not even close.

I'd held her while she fell asleep after hearing a very troublesome report from her neurologist, Dr. Kroger. It was clear that Violet found the truth about it all shocking. I'm not sure how Ruben had gotten all those drugs in her system, but I was pretty confident he'd forcefully done so.

Ruben Del Markov was no ordinary man. He was a powerful man who had nearly as many connections as I did, although his reasoning for using them was anything but honest. If he had a politician in his pocket, or even on a loose rope, it meant he had something substantial on them, and all he had to do was tug at it to get their attention. He kept their deepest, darkest secrets and was not at all afraid to expose them if they didn't assist him when he called.

The Del Markovs are the largest crime family in Hermosa Islas. They tolerate smaller criminal organizations that surface, as long as those organizations understand not to interfere with their business.

Should one get in the Del Markovs way, or attempt to take over one of its territories, they were quickly eliminated and made an example of.

Ruben was second in command. He answered only to his father, Viktor. And Viktor made his son look like a poodle when dealing with someone who crossed him.

Our families had parted ways after my father took the throne and declared the Del Markovs a threat to the kingdom. Called the criminal organization a poison that needed to be disposed of before their corruption ruined Hermosa Islas and its relationships with our foreign allies. He vowed to pass as many laws as possible that would tax the hell out of all the industries the Del Markovs had their hands in. Composed laws that made it extremely difficult for them to smuggle illegals in and out of his kingdom. Threatened to come down on those organizations hard. Go after their leaders until each and every last one was behind bars or dead.

He went so far as to strip Viktor's family of their Royal titles. Along with any claims they held because of the Reyes name, including inheritances. To say he made an enemy who was equally determined to take the Reyes family down was putting it lightly.

My father had accomplished most of what he had promised his people where the Del Markovs family was concerned. It was a war he had been putting a large dent in before his death. He had been doing such a great job at it that many had first speculated the Del Markov family had somehow taken the King out because of that. It had been a good conspiracy theory, but false. My father's own selfishness had taken his life, I'm afraid.

Antonio was doing his best to keep up the fight. He had a few setbacks early in his reign when his focus was directed toward economic issues. But over the last two years, he has gained some positive ground according to the reports I'd read. A new Organized Crime Task Force was being erected inside of our armed forces. One that would solely focus on criminal organizations in hopes to eliminate each one from the top down. It would be the most aggressive tactic to date. One that was generating lots of attention, while putting pressure on these criminal régimes to come back fighting as well.

Thus, I was curious about how Violet had gotten mixed up with

Ruben. And when I'd asked for her to explain again later, she did her best to avoid the conversation. Each day that passed, I watched as she pulled further and further away from me. Slipping back into that ice princess persona she wore when around me, avoiding me whenever possible.

At first, it was a subtle move on her part. She'd awakened hours later and asked for some privacy so she could contact her family. Later claiming she was fatigued and not up for talking or company. Even tried to get me to leave. As each day passed and she was getting around easier, she requested I stop assisting her with every little task.

I walked into her room this morning after reluctantly returning home last night. I did so once she all but demanded I give her space. Meaning that I wasn't surprised to come face-to-face with the woman who always greeted me at the Palace.

"You're like a bad penny that keeps showing up. Your presence is no longer required, Your Highness. I'm being released in a few hours to return to my mediocre life. One, that if I recall correctly, you are not a part of." Violet clutches her head with both hands, an indication she is still suffering from those chronic headaches. "I've got enough to resolve without having to deal with the likes of you."

Needless to say, I ignore her outburst and mosey over to where she is standing. I set down the paper bag in my hand so I can retrieve its contents. Open the small glass vial, letting a few drops drip into my palm. I then place it on the back of her neck so I can knead the liquid along the base of her skull.

Violet starts to step forward as she questions me, "What the hell are you doing?"

I snag her waist with my free hand. Pick up the vial again so I can apply more to my fingertips. "Doing my best to rid you of this headache you've been suffering from since waking up three days ago. Now stand still so I can do what needs to be done."

When I release her, I expected her to try to make a quick escape. But am pleased when she doesn't move. Therefore, I begin to massage more around her ears, before moving onto her forehead and temples.

I reach in the bag again and retrieve another dispenser. Pumping it twice before I rub my palms together. Then I run my hands down the side of her neck, over her shoulders, and down her back where it meets her spine. The place she is holding all her tension. As I do, I can sense her relaxing. So, I pump more into my palm, working the oily substance into the base of her skull and up into her hair slightly.

Violet grips the edge of the small table in front of her. "What the hell is that stuff?"

I continue to move my hands over along that spot, then move in behind her ears. When I have to draw her head back, so I can work her temples and forehead again, I explain.

"Some essential oil blends my mother has recently discovered. She swears it relieves her migraines. One of her equestrian club ladies recommended it when she learned how mother suffered with no relief. Shortly after listening to how over-the-counter medication bothered her stomach. When I mentioned you were still having some issues, she brought this to me and then explained how to apply it. I assume by your demeanor that it is offering you some relief."

Brown eyes glimpse up at me, and I swear I could get lost in them if she'd just let me. "Yeah. Thanks."

"Will you talk to me now?" I softly probe. "Let me in, Violet."

Her hands seize my wrists before she removes them and spins around. "Sorry, but no."

"You can't go back to that place you've been living in." I shove my hands in my pocket, wishing I could break through her tough shell. "There are two reasons, so listen up. First being, that no one should have to live in those conditions." The sarcastic grunt that escapes as she rolls her eyes catches my attention. "I'm serious."

"Yet it seems like a number of others have been living there with me now for nearly seven years. I realize it's not up to your standards..."

I cut her off, "It's not up to several standards. The rats were glad to be making their escape even."

"It's fine. Rent is cheap. Commuting on public transportation is convenient. I'm saving my money for a rainy day. Plus, *you* don't get to *tell* me where I live." Violet can be one stubborn woman and I've found I like it when she puts her foot down.

"Second, the building has been deemed unfit for dwelling as of four days ago. Until it is brought up to code, all residents are being relocated." I might have had a hand in that after having stepped foot inside.

"Great. Just fucking great." She drops onto the couch and inclines her head back so she is now staring up at the ceiling. "When it rains, it pours. So, am I to assume that means it's the resident's responsibility to relocate?"

"Yes and no." I clear my throat. "Those who can do so without assistance, have been asked to. Those who cannot have been assigned a liaison in the housing department, they are diligently assisting them to locate affordable housing that meets their needs. Reyes Capital has some real estate waiting to be renovated and has agreed to house those who meet certain requirements. So far, we've provided five families with much nicer accommodations at the same rate they were previously paying."

"How very noble of you, sir. I'm sure those families that don't..."

"Don't. I'm not putting drug dealers and convicted criminals inside complexes where they could endanger the other residents." In my mind, there has to be a standard and I will not be made to feel bad about that.

"And I'm certain the children of those drug dealers and criminals understand, since you had them evicted, to begin with. I bet even the prostitutes, addicts, and questionable riff-raff realize where they stand. It's fine really because people who live in those buildings obviously do so because they have options." Violet's point strikes a nerve.

"I can't win with you, can I? No matter what I do, it will always be judged and measured by standards I can't possibly understand. I'm damned if I do and damned if I don't," I grumble.

She doesn't answer me with her words. Those expressive eyes of hers alert me I've hit the nail on the head.

"Then I'm pleased to inform you I've secured housing for you as well. It's a home rather than a flat, with more than enough breathing space. I had your belongings delivered yesterday and my staff is setting it up for you as we speak. I'm certain the biggest complaint you'll have is that it is on the same property as my personal residence.

"Before you blow a gasket and deny me the privilege of offering you the home, let me explain why I am setting you up there. Since you no longer have a flat to return to, because I might have reported your previous residence to the housing board. I felt it was my duty to do so. Because I have a guest cottage that isn't being used at the moment, it seemed like the perfect temporary housing to offer you.

"Then there is the fact that I'm very concerned about your security. Fear that once you are no longer under my protection, you might be in danger. My home is well guarded with security on location at all times. Plus at least one, sometimes two, of my guards are always in house. Making them available should I need them. Meaning they will also be available to you should you require one.

"Since you have refused to explain your relationship with Ruben. And after the brief conversation I had with him the day I found him inside your flat. I have concluded that the relationship is hostile. It would be neglectful of me to not take the proper measures to ensure the safety of you and little Charlotte."

The mention of Charlotte has Violet's head rising rather quickly. "You know of Charlotte?"

"He might have mentioned her, piqued my interest and hand."

Currently, I have Winifred's sister, Karina, looking into it all very closely. I've also assigned someone to keep a close eye on the young girl. Darius Falcon—a family friend and the Royal Family PI—is doing what he does best. He has even infiltrated the Del Markov home with a plant. For now, his people have been instructed to watch and observe. But should Ruben do something stupid or assume he can use the little one against Violet. It is then they have orders to retract her for her own protection and bring her to me.

Tears begin to fall down Violet's cheeks. "He took her from me and gave her to his wife. I didn't give her to him. He just took her. I died a little inside that day and every day since. Everything I've done since then has been to protect Charlotte. He owns me in ways I cannot explain. None of it will make sense to you or anyone else. But I cannot fight against him or deny him, in fear he'll harm her just to hurt me."

I've always known Ruben was about as evil as one can get. To see how he has manipulated the toughest woman I've ever met infuriates me. I wasn't sure exactly who Charlotte was to Violet until now. I had my suspicions after the conversation I held with Ruben, but I never took his words to be the truth. He was looking to get a rise out of me that day and would have said anything to accomplish it. However, I now know without any doubt that the little girl is Violet's daughter. Therefore, I will do everything in my power to make sure the two are reunited.

"I appreciate you trying to help, but it won't matter." Violet hiccups. "Ruben always wins."

"I'll make him pay for taking her. It will all work out for you this time, Violet, you will see." I inform her with confidence as I get down on her level. "He cannot do that and get away with it."

Violet jumps to her feet and then paces the floor. "Except he can. That's what I'm trying to tell you. As her father, he can."

"It makes no difference that he is her father, Violet. He cannot take your daughter from you and just give her to someone else, just because his wife wants her. You have rights as her mother." I grab her shoulder to stop her pacing so she will listen to me. "Unless you've signed her over to them, then what they did is illegal and punishable."

Violet shakes her head in disagreement, "If only it were that simple."

"Did you sign her over?" I don't understand why she isn't listening to me.

"No. I didn't have to. As one of his wives, I am obligated to defer to him the right to choose which of us he deemed was better fit to raise any child we had." She blurts out, shocking the hell out of me.

"Excuse me," I stumble back and release her. "One of his what?"

Once again tears trail down her cheeks as she stares at me, knowing her next words will change everything that could be. "I'm his wife, Prince Lorenzo. He married me when I was eighteen, a year before he met his precious Lady Amber."

"That's not possible. I know for a fact Hermosa Islas only recognizes one wife legally. I had to study all our laws as a young prince, I always found those the most interesting." I inform her.

"There is an old bylaw, one that has never been grandfathered out and practiced by a very select few. It states that as long as a man designates one wife as the head wife when he takes another, one who will be listed as his official wife. Any others he may claim are his, he can do with them as he sees fit.

"Trust me, I know exactly what I'm talking about. Do you honestly believe I'd choose to live this life? Do I seem like the sort of woman who would want to be married to a man who has another wife he respects more than he does me? I can't even file for divorce, not after he demoted me. I'm basically a slave who is stuck with her master until he decides he is finished with me and agrees to let me go. Barbaric, isn't it?"

I nod once and head for the door. I need to figure this out. Talk to someone who knows the law better than I do. Get to the bottom of this once and for all. But before I walk out that door, I circle to face Violet. "Gayle will drive you to the home I told you about. I need to go speak with someone about all of this. For once, just do as you're told."

Violet crosses her arms and glares at me. "The resemblance is becoming clearer."

I'm not sure what I am thinking when I release the door and stalk back toward her. "Excuse me."

"You heard me. I believe I am starting to see…"

Her words are cut off when my lips crash hard against hers, as I wrap her in my arms. I've never kissed a woman like this, ever. Something about this woman however fires me up and has me doing all kinds of crazy stuff.

"Never compare me to him again," I growl as I pull back so I can gaze down at her.

Violet blinks slowly and swallows hard, licking her lips. "Then don't give me orders as if I don't have a mind of my own or the freedom to make a choice."

It kills me to hear those words, so I run my knuckle down the side of her face and nod. "Point well made."

A slight smile sneaks into the corners of her mouth, but she keeps her thoughts this time to herself.

CHAPTER 6
Violet

The Royals

I can't believe I told Lorenzo I was married to Ruben. It is the truth, but not one I myself enjoyed remembering.

Not only had Ruben showed up on my eighteenth birthday to claim me for himself. He also informed me of what his gift for me was going to be. Not that I had a choice about accepting his so-called gift, or even wanted it. It was bad enough he was there expecting to get what he had been after for nearly a year. To hear what he had decided all on his own, not only was he determined to take what he felt he'd earned by waiting for me to come of age. He was prepared to force it to continue for several more years, possibly never letting me go.

I'd thought when Lady Amber entered his life she was my ticket out. Until I learned otherwise when he visited a few months later to share his devious new arrangement with me. He was keeping me just because he could; making me stay married to him through a loophole he'd discovered years ago. One he was looking forward to taking advantage of. If only to prove to those Royal assholes living in the Palace that he was the true ruler over their precious kingdom.

I didn't get the reference at the time. Ruben often said things about taking down the régime and showing them where the real power laid.

Made it clear how he despised all Royals and those who supported them. I'd assumed it had more to do with the fact they were on one side of the law and he was on the other.

But now it all makes perfect sense. These two families hated each other for so many reasons. And I was going to be caught in the middle if I didn't figure out how to get away from them both.

I'd taken the Palace job when things between Ruben and I were basically nonexistent. He was punishing me at the time for upsetting his precious Lady Amber, all because our daughter took to me easier than she did her. So, I'd gone off and done everything I could to remain busy in hope of distracting myself. Eventually, I landed a job I knew was going to force me to focus while putting in long hours while I learned what I was doing. A job I'd gotten all on my own without Ruben's assistance, and I was proud of that fact.

When Ruben returned, he almost forced me to resign. However, once he calmed down and used me in his own special way, he changed his mind. Decided that having one of his wives inside the palace was to his advantage. Not that I'd ever shared with him any of the details concerning my job. I'd taken my oath to privacy seriously. There wasn't much in my life I could be proud of, but I was determined not to let my king or his family down. Meaning I never brought my work home with me or logged into work using our personal laptops.

I was completely aware of who Ruben was, that he couldn't be trusted to not take advantage should I make a mistake like that. I did all I could to keep it separate. And I had done so until Lorenzo interfered, suddenly making my worlds collide.

Plopping down onto the couch, I place my head in my hands. If I thought my life was a mess before, it is a complete disaster now. I am caught in a whirlwind that is not only going to destroy me but the man I've been doing my best to avoid at all costs.

The first time I was introduced to Prince Lorenzo, my entire world tilted and spun off its axis. His friendly smile nearly knocked me flat on my arse. It was so genuine, offering me so much insight into the type of man he was. Then, being the gentleman he is, he took my hand in that proper way he'd been taught to do. The zing that zapped my central nervous system caught me completely off guard. At that moment, I realized he was a danger to my survival, and I had to avoid him no matter what.

I wasn't a single woman free to let myself be attracted to a man, especially a man like the Prince. I was married with a child. It didn't matter that I didn't feel or even considered myself married. The law recognized it, and the only way out was if my husband agreed to let me go. I'd learned over the years that my chances of that ever happening were slim. So, I'd accepted my life as it was. I did my best to get through each day as they came. Prayed and hoped that there would be a day when I'd miraculously get my freedom back, but at what cost. I didn't want my freedom if that meant Charlotte wasn't with me. She was the biggest reason I had not run. I couldn't leave her behind to be raised by a monster.

My fate had been sealed years ago, and I'd come to terms with it. Made the best out of the cards I'd been dealt and then played the game to the best of my ability. I hadn't expected the game to get sabotaged by a man who invaded my dreams nightly.

It was bad enough I had to deal with facing Lorenzo at least once a week, if not more. Figure out ways to ignore him when he was impossible to ignore. Do my best to not get drawn in by his charm and extremely valiant demeanor. Everything about the man attracted me to him, coerced my mind to discover something new I liked. Putting all my senses on high alert. Meaning it took every brain cell I possessed to not do something incredibly stupid. I'd done a rather decent job of it until he'd thrown his prince temper tantrum. The day he assumed I was blowing off his best friend's party all because of him.

I'd blown off every party I was invited to because I couldn't afford to have Ruben catching wind of it. It was bad enough having to deal with his interrogation when he stopped by for his visits. I was afraid if he discovered I'd been invited to some event where they'd all be attending; he'd demand I take him with me. There was no way I could do that for so many reasons, and not just because I didn't want anyone to know about him.

But once Lorenzo had come back to offer a very sincere apology, accompanied by a token to express how serious he was, my defenses weakened. At least I'd been smart enough to not let him pick me up at my home address. Made up some excuse about a friend having to do me a favor since I had to rearrange my previous plans.

The only thing I needed to rearrange was Ruben's visit, so he wouldn't wonder where I was. If only he'd have just agreed to let me have the evening. Except that wasn't how he worked. When he scheduled time for us to spend together, I was to be there with no exceptions. And since I'd attempted to move that time to a different night, it only spiked his interest and had him making his appearance earlier than usual.

Ruben waited for no one, especially not me.

I'd paid severely for dismissing him.

It was degrading enough to be with him drugged up, but to suffer through without the drugs really messed with my mind. I have never once been with the man willingly. Each time Ruben has ever taken me, it was done by force. Take away the drugs that slowed my thoughts and paralyze my body, all my instincts kicked in full force. The kind that refused to give in until one physically couldn't fight anymore. As a result, that night had been the worst it has been in a very long time. I was beyond broken, on the inside and out, by the time he left to return to his other wife and my daughter.

I often wondered if he treated Lady Amber in the same way. Or did he save it all for me and let it all out then? It felt like he saved it all. Allowed it to build up and then took all his rage and diabolical thoughts out on my body until there was nothing left inside of him. When he left, he always appeared calmer and ready to face the world. Free of the hostility he brought with him. My theory is his precious Amber wouldn't put up with that behavior, which is why she has allowed him to keep me around. That way I could be his outlet when the need arose.

What am I going to do now?

What was I thinking letting Prince Lorenzo kiss me? Goading him like I did prior to his charge, by comparing him to Ruben? Enjoying a kiss from a man, one that wasn't my husband? Not that I'd ever enjoyed my husband's kiss.

I was putting us in a situation that not only was impossible, but very dangerous. All of Lorenzo's actions had been done with false hope. He'd assumed I was an unattached woman who he could save while riding in on his grand horse.

Except that isn't how real life works. A Prince can't ride in on his white stallion with sword in hand. Determined to rescue the poor helpless damsel, being held in a prison built by her own hands. He can't swing his sharp sword, slaying all those dragons surrounding her, without getting wounded in the process. There would be no pivotal moment when he stole her away from it all. Take her to his home far away so they could live happily ever after. A home where he'd protect her and her young daughter from having to deal with those dark forces ever again. All because he is a prince and everyone knows the valiant prince always wins in the end.

Fairytales are pathetic, made up stories that don't mirror the way it works in the real world. Cinderella and Aladdin are fictional characters, created to give children false hope. Annie and Oliver Twist don't exist in this reality, where the rich only look out for themselves. There is no point in hoping my life will turn out any differently than it has.

I grab the Styrofoam pitcher next to me and heave it across the room out of frustration. It hits the wall and explodes at the very same time the door opens.

Standing in the open doorway, looking as prestigious as always, is Her Royal Highness. Her eyes glance down at the destroyed pitcher briefly before finding mine. "It feels good, doesn't it?"

Her words catch me by surprise. Not to mention her presence in my hospital room does as well. I'd heard she stayed with me a few times when I was comatose. However, since I have been awake, she hasn't visited. At least not while I was alert that I am aware of. I guess it is possible she came by. But because I have refused all visitors, besides the prince, who only got to stay due to the fact he'd refused to be denied.

"I'm sorry, what?" I stand quickly, intending to clean up the mess I just made. "I-I wasn't expecting company. Please forgive me, Your Royal Highness."

She waves for the man behind her to remain put as she releases the door, and it shuts. "I myself have thrown a few pitchers in my day. Better to break something that can be replaced, then to hurt yourself or someone else. The first time my ex-husband entertained openly inside the palace, I went through an entire set of our finest dinner china. Dismissed the kitchen staff, then sent the previous evening's dishes flying and crashing into the walls. Picturing how pissed off King Ramon was going to be when he heard of my behavior. And that, my dear, only made it all that much more satisfying."

I stand there momentarily frozen, uncertain how to react until a reaction breaks free on its own. First, it starts as a giggle, but morphs into a laugh rather quickly. It grows stronger until it becomes hysteric, at which point it turns into sobs. Full-blown sobs that bring me to my knees before I can stop them.

"It's alright, dear. Let it all out. We all reach our breaking point, eventually. Some of us handle it longer than most. You certainly have been holding your own for long enough." The former queen and mother of the men I work for tells me. Right before she drops next to me and lays an arm around me. "There is only so much one person can bear on her own. It's time, my dear, to allow someone else to assist you with all these heavy burdens weighing you down."

"You don't understand." I lift my head so I can explain. "I'm married…"

"Shh." She hushes me and then kisses my forehead. "So, I've heard. The best we have are looking into the matter as we speak. My Lorenzo is speaking to a lawyer right now, a woman who knows the law better than most. Let them work this out while I take you home with me."

"I can't. No." I protest. "A hotel… a hotel is best."

Her Royal Highness squeezes my face gently with her hand, much like a mother would, I imagine. "A hotel? No. You will stay with me in the Palace or at the Hacienda Refugio Seguro cottage. My son wants you at Hacienda Refugio Seguro, of course, but I believe you should have a choice in the matter. Too many of your choices have been taken from you, therefore we are going to start by giving you a few."

I cannot impose on this woman. Which means I only have one option for the time being until I am able to figure out another one. At least if I am at the cottage, I will have my own space where I can think.

"Hacienda Refugio Seguro I suppose would be best." I blink slowly.

Knowing I didn't make that choice because of the privacy, but because of the man who will be close by.

She stands and offers me her hand, a gesture I'm pretty confident is not done all that often by someone in her position. "Come on, my dear. It's time we take those first steps to getting your life back."

If only I had a life I wanted to get back to.

CHAPTER 7
Lorenzo

The Royals

Before I left the hospital, I ran into my mother. There was no masking I had something heavy on my mind. My mother has always been capable of reading all her children well. Then in her own loving way encouraged us to talk with her. I'd done that mostly, shared what Violet revealed moments ago without going into very many details.

My mother couldn't hide the fact she was shocked, even briefly, from me. It was transparent she had a great deal of questions; thankfully she held them off for now. Offered to speak with Violet, escort her home once she was released since I was leaving to take care of this business.

Because I realized my mother would be as kind as possible to the woman I have grown to care for deeply, I'd agreed to let her do so. Asked her to make sure Violet got to my place safely, then had everything she needed before leaving her alone. Made sure my mother informed Violet of my wishes and didn't turn away those I'd appointed as her security detail without speaking with me first. My mother would probably handle Violet's refusal better than I would. Understand how to get her to see reason. Plus, I doubt Violet would dismiss my mother or her suggestions, all because of how she had been taught to respect someone in her position.

I've been on the phone since I climbed in my SUV. Javier is with me today, thankfully. I am not at all concerned with him mistaking my mood since he has been with me the longest. He's seen me at my best and my worst; therefore, he knows what I like and how I mean no disrespect when I give short orders.

"Where..." he starts to ask when he gets in the car.

"Just drive. Don't talk." I grumble out as I put the phone to my ear.

I am not in the mood for conversation and have no idea at that moment where I'll be heading. I just want to get moving, we'll figure out the details after I've made a few calls and know exactly where that would be.

It hadn't taken me long to figure it out, which is why I am standing in front of this door, knocking. I've talked to this woman more over the last couple of days than I've talked with her in all the years I've known her.

When her door opens, I notice she has an abundance to say by her expression. "Your Highness, you've gotten yourself into a pickle."

"May I come in?" I motion, not wanting to chat here in the hall. "First, tell me what you've got for me."

"Hello," she waves Javier inside after me. "You and Stew hangout."

"We do, Lady Karina," Javier smirks slightly as if he knows where this is likely going.

"What's his deal?" she crosses her arms and glares at him.

"I'm not sure I understand."

Dropping her head so she can give it to him, Karina makes it known she's not buying it.

Lifting his hands in defense Javier explains, "I can't speak for my friend. However, I suppose I could offer you my opinion."

She motions for him to continue.

"He was with Prince Esteban for the duration of his courtship with your sister. Perhaps seen and heard enough to draw some conclusions, accompanied with an impression on those close to her. Plus, he is loyal to the throne and family. Would never risk..."

Karina interrupts him when she decides it's time. "Please. I'm not interested in all that. I'm captivated by what he has between his legs and how good he is at using it."

I don't believe I've ever seen Javier blush until this very moment as he responds. "Then perhaps that also is part of the problem. Stew may not be an innocent, but his loyalty follows him wherever he goes. Respect is built into his personality, and I've never known him to indulge in brief and meaningless relationships."

"His loss then." Karina is now finished with Javier, so she moves on. "Let's go into my office, so we can discuss this issue you're having, Lenny."

Her sister Winifred is my best friend. Since we officially became family once our siblings wed, Karina has started using my nickname in less social settings. Accordingly, I gave her one of her own, hoping to discourage her. "Sure thing, Rina."

As you might have guessed, it only egged her on. "Have a seat, Len," she motions to one of the chairs facing her desk. "Your friend joining us?"

"No. So what have you learned so far?"

Karina clicks on her keyboard and brings her monitor to life. "I did a quick check on Charlotte. Pulled her birth certificate."

I wait with anticipation, hoping for good news.

"You said Violet is this child's mother, correct?" Karina glances in my direction to see me nod. "How positive are you about that?"

"I don't understand," my eyebrows rise. "Are you asking me if I believe her? Of course, I do. Why would she lie about something like that? Plus, my cousin mentioned the child when I ran into him at her flat."

"I only ask because the certificate names Amber Bea Cornillez as the birth mother. Typically, but not always, in an adoption the actual birth mother is still listed for a point of reference later on. But there are times when that may not be the case when there are other reasons to maintain privacy. Although in those cases it's usually listed as unknown and then added later when the adoption is legalized. Paper trails are important, so that should there be a dispute later, it can all be traced back. There isn't a paper trail. No adoption papers even." Karina hands me a printed copy of the birth certificate.

I read it carefully. Violet isn't mentioned at all. Ruben is listed as the birth father, his wife Amber as the birth mother. Time and date match what Violet shared with me when we discussed it. I take note of the doctor's name, doing my best to recall if she mentioned one.

"Could this be altered?" I have my suspicions.

Karina shrugs. "Sure. Enough money passes through hands and it wouldn't be difficult to falsify. But if that were true, then I'd still expect a trail that gave me more. This, as far as I can determine, is the only one filed and was issued shortly after birth.

"I went a step further because I know you Reyes. Well enough to understand and not leave one stone unturned. Lady Amber was a patient of this Dr. Kuzmin. Went to him every four weeks for prenatal exams. I found that odd since he runs a free clinic in the heart of Aragon inside the Del Markov territory. Someone of her status would not typically be seen by the same doctor who treated those not capable to afford the best."

I believe I grasp where she is going with this. "But someone who lives within a few blocks of that clinic, who most likely has no medical, like Violet, might use a false name. Or perhaps the records were falsified to match hers later."

"I can't say, however, I'd say it's suspicious."

I don't like where this is heading at all. "Anything else?"

"No. It's pretty cut and dry. You said you had more information for me. Care to share?" Karina leans forward, eager to hear what I have.

"This does not leave this room," I warn her.

"You've retained my services, Lenny. I take that seriously. Spit it out."

"Violet claims she is married to Ruben and has been since she was eighteen." I still found that information hard to swallow.

"Shut up!" Karina slaps her desk as she does her best to conceal her amused smirk. "You've gone and fallen for a married woman, Your Highness?"

"I didn't realize she was married, first of all. She claims he is married to both of them legally. Said that was why Charlotte is with him and Lady Amber. That Ruben placed their child with his other wife, claiming that it was his right, as the husband of both women, to do so. I think he lied to her, but I need to be certain. Violet says it's some early bylaw that has remained on the books by mistake, and once my dear cousin discovered it, he took full advantage." I am shaking my head, frustrated. "Is there such a law?"

I also believe Violet is afraid of my cousin. He is a dangerous man who I'm confidant has shown that side to her more than once. Making her understand not to cross him unless she was willing to pay for it.

"There are several outdated laws on the books still, unfortunately. New laws void most, but there are a few that have fallen between the cracks. I guess the only way to know for sure, is to dig it up and see it with our own eyes. How much time do you have?" Karina types frantically.

"As long as it takes." I lean forward and watch her carefully. "How long do you suppose it will take to find such a law?"

While she is typing, Karina decides to offer her thoughts on my situation. "You know, I find it ironic that all three of our dear princes, grew up to discover love in the strangest of places. Our dear king certainly didn't take the easy road. He could have had he chosen my sister to be his. But no. He went and broke her heart, then humiliated her by falling for some unknown from a foreign land."

"He was searching for something real," I defend Antonio's actions. "I understand you find that hard to believe or comprehend, but I however respect him for not falling in line. It wasn't easy for him, you realize, sticking to his idea of there being someone out there that would love him. He sacrificed a myriad of years experiencing loneliness because of that."

Karina glimpses up from what she is doing, letting me perceive her eyes and thoughts reflected in them. "His choice. We know there were several willing lady's ready to fulfill all his needs while providing him with some company."

"His choice indeed. It would have been easier for him in a sense to just give in, but then look at what he would have missed out on. Larkin is his reward for sticking it out and not taking the path traveled by so many others. Instead, he chose the less traveled one that was full of thorns, rocks, and overgrowth, all placed there to encourage him to give up. My brother, however, didn't let that discourage him from clearing the path that led him to the beautiful field where his love was waiting for him."

Karina rolls her eyes. "Such a vivid picture you paint, Prince Lorenzo. I suppose you believe Stan did the same with my dear sister."

"In his own way, yes. His path was different, though. He discovered it as a young lad and kept it cleared. Constructed a locked gate, one that discouraged others from going down that path. Visited it regularly when the time was right to clear it out again and then tried his best to keep it that way. I believe he might have even resided there while watching over the fair maiden he found hidden within. Then when the day arrived, he swooped in and rescued her, before it was too late to do so."

"You certainly have a way with words. Why is it my little sister never fell for you?" Karina prints something and then begins typing again.

"It wasn't like that between us and you know this. Freddy and I were never more than friends. I was there for her when she needed me to be. Watched out for her, because I already grasped who she belonged to. You forget that my family is very close; we know each other well. I was aware of Esteban's infatuation long before he ever acted, as I was aware of my friend's. One only needs to pay attention to pick up on those things."

I watched those two interact. Esteban was always extremely kind to young Lady Winifred. Stopped by when he knew she was going to be around our home in Prieto. Kept a close eye on her and always questioned me about her whenever I brought her name up. Not to mention how my friend always blushed at the mention of his name. Got nervous when he showed up unannounced and then talked to her. Winifred acted differently around him than she did any other guy, so it wasn't hard for me to read between the lines."

"And this path you've veered off on seems like it might be the worst one so far. One that you would be better to vacate, so you don't get tangled in the thorny mess surrounding the maiden you've discovered. She's clearly..." Karina pauses as she reads something.

So, I finish her thought, "She's clearly gotten herself trapped in the thistle. Someone needs to help her remove it without causing more scars, or allowing the poisonous thorns to do more damage. I believe I'm up for the challenge, if she will allow me to, that is. Not fight me more than she already has.

"What are you reading? You seem to have discovered something worth sharing."

She holds up a hand to quiet me. Therefore, I move in behind her to let me read it for myself. I'm well trained in reading laws and deciphering the wording many would not understand.

It seems Karina has discovered the one we were searching for. It goes back to the days when our limited constitution was first established. Appears King Nicolas fathered some children outside of his marriage and wanted to ensure they were named as his. Accordingly, he constructed a law that allowed for men in his situation to marry the mother of his children—mothers in his case, two to be exact—even if the men were already wed. To guarantee matters didn't get out of hand, King Nicolas limited the number of wives a man could legally claim to three. Stated that he didn't want to encourage men into taking too many wives, as it might cause more problems than it did good.

In order to keep all his wives in line, he declared that a man with multiple wives would be the governing head. All wives were expected to submit to him. The husband would appoint a wife to be his voice when needed, known to the others as the head wife. She would also be the wife who would take over in the raising of his children. Should a husband find that necessary to maintain all children were equal and taught properly. In King Nicolas' case, it was his first wife. But he made it clear that it did not always have to be the first if one of the other wives was better suited for the job.

Several other points went into greater detail, points I had a difficult time reading. This law was obviously constructed for the benefit of the husband, so he could control the women in his life. Allowed a husband to keep a few extras on the side, when his first wife wasn't keeping him satisfied, without making it appear as if he were actually cheating. Legalizing his mistresses basically, so others were forced to accept this practice. It had been voted in by one vote. King Nicolas being the tiebreaker, of course.

"Unbelievable," I voice when I've scanned it enough to understand.

"Crafty, really. He recognized he still held a tremendous amount of power. Used it early on to achieve what he desired. Later, his eldest son buried the law deep inside the Institution of Family Act. Had it amended inside, after it had all but been approved. Not giving the Governors enough time to read through it. And since most do not practice this anymore. Many believe it was taken off the books when that act was established in the early 1900s, most have forgotten it once briefly existed. There is one problem, however with this."

I perk up and rest my hip against her desk, "What is that exactly?"

Karina swivels her chair around and stares at me. "One might argue, that if this was performed before The Marriage Act was added six months ago. The one that abolishes all prearranged or unconventional marriages. Any marriage that falls under this category will be grandfathered in."

"Antonio and Larkin fought hard to get that added to our constitution, so everyone had the freedom they did. Both felt it was time to demolish a practice that belittled women." I was extremely proud of my brother and sister-in-law for acting so quickly once they'd stated publicly the time to move forward was now. That this country was ready to join the modern world.

"Yes. Unless one studies the Marriage Act—reads it verbatim—then they assume things they should not. Your brother wanted to free those trapped inside these types of relationships, give women the freedom to get out should one choose to do so. I'm actually overseeing a case right now, that involves a young woman who wants to dissolve a marriage she was forced into. Since there are no children, it is proving to be rather straightforward, but the ones that involve children are more problematic, as you might imagine." Karina informs me.

"So, Violet could dissolve this rather easily then?" I believe that is what she is suggesting.

"I wish I could give you a definite answer. We first need to establish if she is legally married to Ruben. Why doesn't she use his last name?" Karina directs her attention back to her computer.

"I don't know exactly. My guess is because Ruben didn't want others to know about her. He married her when she was barely eighteen, which means he was twenty-five. Lady Amber and him were already involved by then, deep in negotiations, I'm certain. Had he publicly named Violet as his wife, that most likely would have disbanded.

"Do you think Lady Amber would have agreed to marry a man with a young wife he'd kept hidden? I do not. I believe he deceived them both. Probably planned on terminating his marriage with Violet secretly, before taking his vows with Lady Amber. Then he discovered this little hidden gem and decided otherwise." I hate thinking about my devious cousin, knowing he took full advantage of an inexperienced, desperate woman.

"Interesting," Karina mumbles as she searches again. "He is technically legally married to both women. I see that is not what you were hoping to hear."

"No, it is not," I huff out.

"However, it seems his marriage to Violet was not performed here in Hermosa Islas. They were married in Turkey." She glances over her shoulder as if I should understand why that is important.

"Okay," I don't though.

"Prince Lorenzo, I'm disappointed in you and your knowledge of why this is a critically valid point. Turkey is one of the countries Hermosa Islas does not have great relations with. During this time, we were at a standoff and rejected all dealings with them. Meaning, unless Ruben reapplied for his marriage application again a few years ago, when the ban was lifted. Went and paid the proper fees one must pay to file. In the eyes of this country, they are not married.

"His time to do so has passed now that The Marriage Act is in full effect. It indubitably states that a man can only be married to one woman and vice versa. That it must be consensual, and that there be a grace period to allow either party to contest. Just in case one might slip past those enforcing the new law. Meaning, I'll need to get Violet to sign a document that states she wishes to dissolve the marriage. Affirms, it was performed illegally without her consent. It was performed illegally without her consent, correct?"

"Of course, it was," I don't imagine Violet would willingly marry Ruben. "I mean, I'm not completely sure. From what I've come to understand, he got his hands on her when she was barely sixteen. Forced her to work for him after he met her when she and her friends almost got arrested while doing a job for him. Took an interest in her and didn't give her a choice to dismiss him."

Karina shakes her head and smirks, while I do my best to explain. "If that is all true, then I'm sure we can easily argue she felt forced into the marriage. You sure do know how to pick them, don't you, Lenny? Couldn't just fall for one of the many normal easygoing women eager to attract your attention? You go and fall for the one with enough baggage to make Lady Hilda seem like the better choice."

Just the mention of the eccentric Lady Hilda makes me tense. "Please don't. Violet is by far the better choice, even with all the baggage."

My phone vibrates in my pocket. I take it out to read the message. I'm going to need to wrap this up so I can deal with this new situation.

"Are we finished for now? Can you get the ball rolling?" I type in a quick response, letting my team know I'm on my way.

"Yes. I'll send you the paperwork I need your beloved to approve. You do realize you have a very difficult road ahead of you, don't you? Not just the marriage aspect of this entire mess, but establishing maternity and then taking it to court. Are you certain Violet wants to do that? It could put Charlotte..."

"You let me worry about Charlotte's security. You focus on the legality of it all. Darius is handling the other as we speak." I wave my phone at her, explaining my earlier interruption. "We're good."

Karina stands and escorts Javier and me out. I don't miss how she instructs him to let Stew know she is waiting for him to call her. That she won't let it go, just because he has some moral code, even asks he make that clear to his friend.

Javier and I both laugh at her blatant statement as we walk out. "Where to, sir?"

"Home," I tell him as I climb into my SUV. "I need to speak with Miss Blanc."

CHAPTER 8
Violet

The Royals

I'm not sure how I talked Her Royal Highness into leaving shortly after escorting me to her son's home. I guess it could have been that she appreciated I'd be safe here, and since I requested some privacy, she granted it to me.

Lorenzo had been truthful to his statement that all my belongings had been delivered to his nice three-bedroom cottage. I'm not sure why I doubted him. Although I could write it up to the fact that few people in my life did exactly what they said they'd do. I expected some of my belongings to be missing. Those items like my cellphone and laptop. Items that allowed me to be in contact with anyone I chose to communicate with, gadgets that also allowed others to contact me.

I was both relieved and disappointed when I discovered them charging on the kitchen counter. My family's numbers were on my phone. Those numbers were important to me. They allowed me to interact with my younger siblings.

My father remarried a few years after my mother's death. He and his new wife Marisol have two children. I'm not close to my father or my stepmother, however, I am very close to my siblings. I do my best to look out for them, make sure they have everything they need. I send a large portion of my check to assist their parents in paying for their education. I want my siblings to have a better life than I did. To become well educated as a guarantee that they can make smart choices once they are older. I don't want them to have to worry about the troubles I had to worry about. So, having those phone numbers is important.

But as soon as I pick up my phone to check my messages. It's the repetitive number that appears over and over again that has my heart sinking. I could have lost that number and been okay with it. If I never spoke to the person who has sent hundreds of texts and left over thirty voice messages, my life would be better.

I don't bother reading or listening to them. Doing so will only upset me, and afterward, I will still be expected to call. Better to call without hearing all his hatred so I can maintain some composure.

"Where the hell have you been?" Ruben answers without so much as a greeting. "Do you know how much trouble you are in *suka*? *Podgotovsja* my little *suka*, I'm on my way to collect you."

"You know where I am?" I breathe in through my nose and out through my mouth.

"*Nada*. However, you will tell me now so we may get on with it. It's been eight days since I left you in a state of pleasure and pain. Tell me my little Violet; did the prince enjoy your company? Did he steal you away for himself? Is that why you missed your scheduled visit with Charlotte? Is he so superior that you are busy pleasuring him you forgot about her?

"I do you a favor and that is how you reward me. Do not expect me to offer her up again so easily. Next time you will have to agree to me taking you without your pleasure drugs. All your orifices will need to experience my punishment until I decide you've paid yours and hers. Do you understand?"

Removing all emotion from my voice, I answer him, "I understand."

"Good. Now tell me where he's been hiding you?" It's hard to determine if Ruben is truly upset or if he is toying with me right now. Surely, he knows where I've been since he put me there by being so irresponsible with his drugs.

"The hospital."

"Say again?" He sounds surprised and displeased.

"It seems my body was overridden with a number of toxins and I nearly died." Again, I do my best to keep the emotions out of it. I don't want Ruben to see how very pissed I am that he nearly killed me.

"Do you not think that I checked the hospital's first, Violet? There was no record of you..."

I interrupt him this time. My anger flies out of me before I can control it. "Why would I lie about that? Why? Do you think I really would lie and say I was in the hospital for eight days, when I was not? It would do me no benefit to lie to you, Ruben. You'd only punish me more if I did. Were you trying to kill me, or did you just forget how many drugs you'd already forced on me?"

There is a long pregnant pause that isn't at all comfortable. I've accused him of something, and now he is doing his best to decide how to respond. I'm sure Ruben's also noting all the ways he is going to make me pay for questioning his actions.

"If I wanted you gone, Violet, you'd be gone," Ruben answers with a haughty tone in his voice that discloses he is serious. "I don't need to make it look like you took too many drugs. I'd simply put a bullet in your head and be done with it.

"Who would miss you, anyway? Your siblings perhaps, although very doubtful. Certainly not your father, as he barely speaks to you. Not me either really, since I could replace you with a much younger and better *suka*. So, who do you suppose would even care that your pathetic life ended? Charlotte has no need for a drug whore mother, which is why she is in my wife's care and not yours. No one would mourn your death should your number come up."

He's right.

I know he's right.

No one has ever cared for me, not really.

"Now tell me where you are so we can move past all this. The sooner you suffer your punishment, the sooner you can spend time with Charlotte." Ruben knows I can never reject him when he uses my daughter as the reward for stomaching his company.

"Prince Lorenzo put me up in the cottage on his property. Seems my home was deemed unsuitable for living." I'm certain he knows this since he owns the damn building.

"Yes, so I've been informed, which is why I came looking for you in the first place. I believe I've located a suitable flat, not far from the one you were living in. Should I come and retrieve you from the prince's home, or do you want to meet me at your new accommodations? It is a little less cozy than the other, but what do you expect when the rent is free." He chuckles as if he finds his little statement humorous.

Nothing is free. I've learned that lesson so many times from Ruben, that the word actually holds new meaning to me. I'd overpay for something if given the choice before taking it for free. At least then I'd understand the price and not have to guess what it might cost me later.

"You have one hour, my little Violet. I'll text you the address. Don't be late or I'll come retrieve you myself. I don't give a shit about his guards or title. You are mine and..."

"I understand. No need to start a war over little old me. I'll be there." I hang up the phone, not interested in listening to him rant more about how he always gets what he wants.

Immediately a text comes through with an address and a warning to not test him.

I know leaving this sanctuary is a mistake, except what choice do I have? Ruben is ruthless enough to do the unthinkable to Charlotte. She is eighteen months old and already terrified of her father. Thankfully he doesn't enjoy spending time with her, meaning he has little interaction with her at all.

After I've packed a small suitcase, collected all my personal belongings, and shoved them inside my purse, I call for an Uber. The main gate is not far from the cottage. I can walk the long drive and be there by the time my ride arrives.

What I hadn't expected, though, was for there to be a woman in a black pantsuit stationed just outside the cottage. I am accustomed to being able to come and go as I pleased. As long as I obey Ruben's orders, he didn't place a guard on me to keep me in check unless I had Charlotte with me.

"Are you going somewhere, madam?" The woman asks as soon as I step outside with my suitcase in tow. "I can drive you."

"That's unnecessary. I've decided not to take Prince Lorenzo up on his kind offer. I'm going to go stay with a friend instead. I have an Uber meeting me at the front gates." I lie and start heading down the asphalt paved drive.

She steps in behind me like I've seen others in her position do to those they guard. I've had the privilege of observing such behavior since I work for the king.

"You don't need…" I do my best to dismiss her.

"I'm Gayle. Prince Lorenzo has assigned me to you." She introduces herself as if that will make me agree to her presence.

"Well, I'm unassigning you to me. Since I'm not going to be staying here with him, I don't require babysitting." I don't know why I thought that would work. I've worked for the king long enough to appreciate this game. "You can express that to the prince when he asks you why you allowed me to flee."

Gayle nods but says nothing while she continues to follow me to the gate. When we reach the main entrance, she instructs the guards posted to let me pass and then shadows right behind.

I've never been happier to see a stranger than I am right now. I need to get as far away from all of this as quickly as possible. My Uber driver jumps out to introduce herself, confirming my destination. As soon as I do, I climb in the back and start to close the door.

Gayle however is standing there, as if waiting for me to slide over. "Madam, please do not make my job harder than it already is."

"Excuse me?" I rub my head as it begins to throb again.

She physically gives me a gentle push as she climbs in next to me. Before she explains, she introduces herself to our driver with a promise to add a sizable cash tip for her trouble once we've reached our destination. The twenty she hands the woman seems to be enough motivation to encourage her to accept the offer and off we go.

I stutter out my next words because I realize Ruben will have no problem with an audience. He'll find it a challenge to see if he can shock the pretty security lady; show her a few tricks she's likely never seen before. Invite her to join in perhaps, just for shits and giggles. His way to determine if he can get her riled up before he puts his own men on her.

"P-Please listen to me-me. I-I don't want…"

Gayle reaches over and smiles sincerely at me. "May I call you Violet, madam?"

"Yes. And it's Miss if you suffer the need to address me formally. I'm nobody," I express as I extract my hand from hers and fold both in my lap.

"Violet, you work for King Antonio, do you not?" she asks.

"I did. I'm not sure I still do after an unfortunate incident." I honestly inform her. I'm sure me being hospitalized for drugs, violates some ethical rule that results in immediate termination.

Gayle nods once, as if she seems to be able to read my mind. "I've not been informed otherwise, therefore that means your employment is still intact. I am an employee of the Royal Guard, assigned to Prince Lorenzo's detail."

I've never been very good at just listening when being spoken to. "And I'm not a member of the royal family or in any way associated with Prince Lorenzo."

The grin that takes over Gayle's face expresses she has been advised otherwise. "Prince Lorenzo has personally assigned me to you. Until I get a direct order from him, notifying me differently, I'm afraid you are stuck with me. I am to do whatever I have to, to keep you safe and ensure no one lays a hand on you unless it is what you want. Do you understand?"

"Damn," our Uber driver mumbles louder than I believe she meant to. "Sorry. Carry on."

I might find this all humorous too, if it were happening to anyone other than me. However, it is happening to me, therefore I do not find this amusing at all. I wish instead to get swallowed up by a crater so I never have to deal with this life I've suddenly found myself in.

"So, you are just going to follow me. I will only get you to leave if I can somehow get your boss to call you off." I grit my teeth together, making my head pound more.

"I could call him," Gayle offers, and when I nod, she does just that.

The two of them hold a conversation, explaining my situation. It is clear her boss is not at all pleased about any of it. When she tries to pass me the phone, I've already decided I'm not speaking to him. So instead of just telling him my refusal, she places it on speaker, while she notifies him why she has done so.

"Thank you, Gayle. Are you certain you want me to speak so freely over the speaker where all in the vehicle can hear me, Violet? I've got much to say, and I have no issue airing out our dirty laundry..."

I snatch the phone from her hand and take him off speakerphone so we can have a semi-private conversation. "You really are an arrogant arsehole bloke, not all that different from your cousin."

"Careful there, Violet. Do you remember what happened the last time you compared me to my prick cousin?" Lorenzo growls into the phone, making his point.

Of course, I remember. I'll never forget how he stalked up to me and planted a hard but firm kiss on my lips. While it might have been aggressive in nature, it was anything but in my crazy, deranged mind. It has been a lifetime since a man has truly kissed me, intending to prove he was anything other than a monster.

He hadn't forced his tongue inside by biting my lip until it bled and I yelp in pain. Nor had he grabbed a fist full of my hair and yanked it so hard, forcing my head back and causing my scalp to ache.

For the first time since I was a young naïve girl, I received a kiss from a man. This man did so because he had no other choice but to. And when he kissed me, I could do nothing but let him, while every ounce of my will melted away. I couldn't fight him, because my body was unsure how to do so when treated with a gentleness packed behind all that aggression.

"Yes," I whimper and feel my entire body flush. "That won't be necessary."

"I disagree. It will be very necessary to do again once we've settled a few matters. Where are you running off to? I don't think it is wise for you to stay with a friend right now," he sincerely informs me.

I'm not sure exactly why I tell him the truth, but I do. "Ruben has ordered me to come to him. He's expressed I could have time with Charlotte if I play nicely."

Lorenzo growls loudly this time into the phone, while he strongly objects to me going anywhere near his cousin. "Absolutely not."

"You don't get to fucking order me around. Nor do you get to decide how I choose to appease the man holding my daughter in his care."

I don't care about much other than her. I've survived hell so far; one more moment in it won't kill me. Once he is satisfied I am still with him, he'll likely have one of his men bring Charlotte to me for an evening. I've devised a plan I'm certain will work. I just need to follow Ruben's rules until the time is right and I've gained a portion of his trust again.

"I'm not ordering you around, I'm trying to protect you."

"I don't need to be protected," I lie. "Why do you care, anyway? Why does it matter what a woman of my status does? You've not grown up in my world, Prince Lorenzo. You came into this world with a golden spoon in your mouth and more privileges than most ever earn. There are a lot of us out here fighting for the scraps your kind tosses aside. So, don't go judging me or my kind, for doing what is necessary to merely survive. Allowing us to can give those we care for a better life.

"I understand I've made some horrid choices that repulse you, however, they are mine to make and mine to correct. Do you honestly think if I had the chance to make other choices, I'd not do so? I'm not afraid of what will happen to me, I'm terrified of what my daughter will have to suffer if I don't."

Not at all interested in revealing more, I press the red button to end the call and pass it back to Gayle.

We have arrived, so there is no turning back now. What will be, will be. I've accepted that fact many times over during my life.

Gayle is busy paying the extra tip to the Uber driver while also talking her boss back off the edge when he immediately called back.

I decide to get out and not listen. I'm completely comfortable in this neighborhood, more than I would be in the one where the prince resides. I've grown up on these streets. Recognize the people aren't nearly as scary as most of them appear.

As I begin walking toward the door, I distinguish the clicking of hard sole shoes against the sidewalk behind me. I assume it is Gayle following orders, therefore I ignore them. I reach for the front door handle, so I can enter the building where I know the devil himself waits for me on the sixth floor. My hand is seized before it can grip it firmly, and then I'm dragged to the alley between this building and the next. I'd scream, but my voice seems to have decided not to work at the moment.

"You are the most stubborn woman I've ever met," Lorenzo's voice fills the small alley where he shields us from anyone who might be watching. "If you think I'm going to allow you to endanger yourself…"

"That's not up for you to decide," I shove him away from me. Infuriated he believes he can just show up and I'll change my mind.

"The hell it isn't." He points his finger angrily at me while he continues on his rant. "Someone has to talk some sense into you. You've obviously been trapped in survival mode for way too long to think rationally. He tried to kill you, Violet. What makes you assume he won't do so again now?"

I've already thought of that. It would be so easy for Ruben to do what he told me he would do if he wanted me out of the picture. Except I don't presume that is his plan at all; I believe his plan is to make me appear to be an unfit mother, so he can continue to manipulate me. He gets off on watching me yield to his will because he knows as long as he has my daughter, I'll not fight him.

"As he pointed out earlier to me, it isn't as if anyone will miss me should he decide to do so. He's right. I know he's right. I also realize that I have to do what I have to do to protect Charlotte. So that is what I'm doing and you can't stop me." I go to shove him again. Except this time he grabs my wrist and holds my body close to his as he backs me up against the brick wall behind us.

"Let me go," I struggle against him.

"No! He's wrong. You both are so very wrong." Lorenzo leans in closer so I am forced to gaze up at him. "I'd miss the hell out of you and kick my own arse for not doing all I was capable of doing to prevent it. Not just you, Violet, but Charlotte as well. However, I can only do that if you stop fighting with me. I can't keep you safe if you keep insisting on meeting him in neighborhoods like this one."

"Why are you not listening…"

He rests a finger against my lips to stop me from speaking. "I am listening. Charlotte is your top concern, which is why I have put Falcon on her. She had a new au pair show up early this morning after her current one got called away for a family emergency. Her detail was assigned three new guards to the house, once three former guards were arrested during a raid that took place last night. They will not only be keeping an eye on what goes on in that home, but also making sure she is safe at all times, all times." Lorenzo bends so we are eye to eye now. "I realize in order to keep you focused on your safety; you first must trust someone is ensuring hers. My team is on her like they would be any other member of the royal family."

"But she's not royal family. She's one of your sworn enemy's offspring." I can hardly believe what he is suggesting, let alone comprehend why he would even do that.

Lorenzo shakes his head as he places his lips to my forehead and sighs. "Silly woman, how have you not figured it out yet?"

"Figured what out? That you are an annoying man who cannot mind his own business." I question and feel them curve upward to form a smile. "Why is that exactly, Prince Lorenzo? Why do you insist on..."

I squeal out in surprise when my body is once again pressed hard against the brick behind me. I'm caged between his arms that are pressed flat against it, not leaving a great deal of space between us.

Panic begins to set in until his soft words calm me.

"First of all, you will stop addressing me as Prince Lorenzo or Your Highness. It is either Lorenzo, Lenny, or some other endearment that expresses how you feel about me." He apprises me seriously; once again looking at me the way he did that day, I opened my eyes and found him there. "Do we have an understanding?"

Don't ever accuse me of not being creative or not listening. "Let me make sure I have this. I'm to drop the formalities and call you by your given name or a form of it unless of course, I'm feeling another one that suits you better. I believe I understand. Please continue to enlighten me, you *tosser*."

I don't know why I enjoy poking him so much. Possibly because there is something about this man that has always communicated I have nothing to fear. It's not that my mouth hasn't gone off at the wrong time around those who weren't safe, it has, and I've always paid for it dearly. It has more to do with the fact that when I let loose around Lorenzo, there is a light that sparkles behind his eyes displaying his delight.

That light is burning rather brightly at the moment. "Well played, my dear. The rest I'd rather not discuss out here on the street. As you can imagine, my team is working overtime right now to keep us safe and undetected. It is only a matter of time before that could change. Are you going to leave with me peacefully, or am I going to have to throw my weight around?"

My phone rings inside my purse. I already know who it is. It's been an hour and my dear husband is wondering where I am. "I have to take this."

I duck under his arm to put some distance between us, hoping for privacy. "Hello. I'm close. Got caught in traffic and..."

"Seems I have another issue to deal with right now. I won't be able to get there until later tonight, most likely tomorrow, depending on how long this takes." He interrupts me so he can explain.

"How am I supposed to get in if I don't have a key?" I've never been more thankful for unexpected business.

"Don't sound so disappointed *suka*, I'm sure my dear cousin's offer still stands. We can reschedule our reunion at your new place in a few days. Anticipation, after all, is what makes the heart grow fonder, is it not? We will have our fun then. I'll text you with the details, and it would be wise for you not to make me wait. Make sure you don't miss any of my calls or text moving forward unless you are looking to get an extra treat."

My entire body shivers, and not in a good way. "I understand."

"Good." Ruben chuckles and bile rises into my throat. "Violet, don't disappoint me."

"I understand," I respond in rote, doing my best not to let him notice he is getting to me.

I hang up as soon as he dismisses me and stand there stiffly. I have a few more days before I will be forced to face him again. That gives me more time to ensure I am prepared and ready when the time is right.

"Business?" Lorenzo's voice echoes too confidently from behind me.

"You had a hand in ensuring something came up?" I spin to find him smirking while he shrugs.

"Shall we get out of here before we are seen?" He gestures toward the opposite end of the alley where an SUV has pulled in and is waiting for us.

I don't fight him, because there is no point. I don't want to be here anymore than he wants me to be here. Therefore, I allow him to guide me to his vehicle that will likely take us back to his place, where I'll be safe for a few more days.

CHAPTER 9
Violet

The Royals

After returning to the cottage last night, I was surprised when Lorenzo gave me my space without me having to ask for it. I sort of expected him to hover over me, but it seems he understood I required some freedom to gather my thoughts.

I'd done a lot of that actually, so much that my brain hurt and forced me to go to bed earlier than normal. I had expected it to take me hours to fall asleep in an unfamiliar place. It had taken all of five minutes, if that, to my surprise, and I'd slept a solid ten hours. Beginning to wake when the sun started shining through the shades I'd left open, so I could admire the full moon that shone brightly last night.

I haven't been allowed to enjoy the fresh air while recovering in the hospital. Now that I was on a large plot of land in the middle of East Aragon, where homes like this one were all around, it seems like a good idea. So I dressed in a pair of joggers with its matching jacket. Grab a mug of coffee and then begin to take a stroll through the garden between my cottage and the main house.

I couldn't see the main house from the cottage. There were a few rolling hills and a grove of trees that obscured my view. Although I could make out a portion of it, enough to recognize it was larger than the house Ruben and his wife lived in. The one located on his family's large estate, right outside the western region of Aragon. It is on a plot of land that has been in the Del Markov family for nearly a hundred years.

Almost as soon as I step outside, I am greeted by a large dog escorted by the man I've had on my mind most of the night. The beast runs around me clumsily, much like I imagine a puppy might do, except this giant is no small playful puppy.

"Valentina, calm down. Sit and stop with the over-excited shenanigans. Leave the pretty lady be. She won't like you and then force me to find you a new home with less land for you to roam." Lorenzo yells good-humoredly as he bends down when the dog sprints back to him and flops down so he can rub her belly. "Crazy *perro*. Why do all the women in my life seem to require extra attention and not listen to me?"

I watch him love on his beloved dog and begin to appreciate a different side of the prince. When I've seen him, he is always dressed in suits with an air of confidence beaming off of him. This man, on his knees in the grass, is a more relaxed version of that man. He is displaying a portion of his vulnerability only those closest to him are privileged enough to witness.

When he stands, he tosses a red ball across the lawn before advancing toward me. I start to wonder how old Lorenzo actually is so I ask, "How old are you?"

A genuine smile takes over his face, displaying the deep double dimples I hadn't dared notice until now. "Twenty-three. Fourteen months younger than you, my dear. Does it bother you that you are attracted to a younger man?"

I nearly spit my coffee all over his handsome face. "I'm sorry. What makes you so sure I'm attracted to you?"

He shrugs as he leans in and places a sweet peck to one of my cheeks, one packed full of sentiments I'm not ready to accept. Which is why I take several steps backward, giving me more than enough room to regain my composure.

"Good morning. Did you sleep well?" He asks, still wearing that smile.

I have to look away so I can answer him. "Yes. I was getting some fresh air. Thought I'd take a stroll in the garden if that is okay."

He whistles loudly to secure his dog's attention and then motions for me to lead the way. The large animal darts past us down a paved pathway, quickly discovering a butterfly to chase and bark at. "She's still only a pup, will be two soon. Larger breed dogs remain pups longer than smaller breeds. Are you familiar with dogs?"

I watch as the large dog leaps over a small hedge to run after a flock of birds she spotted in the meadow. "No. We never had enough money to afford a pet. When I was about seven, I found a nest of mice in my closet. Tiny baby mice, that were in my mind very cute, so I used an old shoebox to move them into and left scraps for the mother to feed them. When my mother discovered what I had done, she belted me and forced me to clean our small flat from top to bottom for the next week." I take a sip of my coffee, not sure why I just shared that story with him, embarrassed really. "What breed is your dog?"

"Saint Bernard," his voice is softer than it was. "You grew up in a place similar to the one you were recently living in, didn't you?"

I choose one of the many footpaths heading for the grove of trees. "I did. My father is a seaman and was rarely around while I was growing up. My mother and I didn't require much, and it was all they could afford. She worked in the corner store for minimum wage once I was in school. Most of that money supported her destructive habits. If there was money left, we ate better, if not we did with what we had."

"I'm sorry." Lorenzo steps up next to me and takes my hand. "I didn't realize that. What happened to your mother?"

I stop walking as I tug my hand free of his, then tread over to one of the many fountains. "She mixed the wrong pills with alcohol. My mother suffered from bouts of depression, and when she got low, it was hard to bring her out of it. I knew that day when I left for school she was in a bad frame of mind. I found her passed out cold on the couch. The paramedics could not revive her.

"I'm not like her, Lorenzo. I hate drugs. Not a huge fan of alcohol either, although I do appreciate a glass of wine with dinner sometimes." Again, I'm not sure why I disclosed that, but I guess I don't want him to think I am an addict like my mother.

Lorenzo moves to the left of the fountain where I can see him in my peripheral, then leans his frame against a stone pillar. "I never once doubted that, Violet."

My eyes move so we are staring into each other's, even though there is a significant amount of distance between us. It's then I realize he needs to hear all there is to know about my life. He's done more for me than anyone else ever has, put his reputation on the line for me. Which means he deserves to understand the mess that is I.

"I know you believe you are helping me by offering me a gracious home and some security. I do appreciate all you've done. I don't want to sound ungrateful for all the wonderful gestures you've carried out." Hoping to make this easier on him, I start there.

Surprisingly, he remains quiet as if waiting for me to continue, instead of arguing with me.

"Not long after my mother died, and my father dropped me at my grandparents, that is when my life took a spin down the commode. I stopped making excuses years ago and take full responsibility for the reason my life is how it is now. I could have easily chosen a different path, but I didn't.

"When I was sixteen, I decided to not continue with my education. One of my friends started working for the Del Markovs and suddenly had more cash than most of us had seen growing up in our neighborhood. When he got offered to do some overseas trips to deliver and retrieve packages for them, he invited a few of his friends along.

"I wasn't stupid. I understood we were most likely transporting drugs and other illegal items they couldn't ship openly. After our first trip was successful, we all got paid substantially, making the next several trips become much like a drug. Adrenaline pumped through us, had us all believing we could do whatever we wanted, and get away with it.

"That's how Ruben first trapped me inside his world. After we'd gotten stopped in Turkey, he pulled us off those jobs. Two of my friends ended up dead, one ended up getting busted for a job Ruben sent him on, and the other three of us found ourselves imprisoned. I was the luckiest of them all, really. They put my other two female friends to work in one of his clubs, where they have been forced to do way worse acts with some very ruthless men. At least I only had to suffer one man's debauched behavior." I take another sip of my coffee and do my best to keep it down.

"The drugs are his reward to me, so I don't have to suffer while he does all the things he likes. I accept none of them willingly. When he wants to really punish me, he refuses to even offer the drugs while he gives me his absolute best." I swallow the bile that rises in my throat, taking a sip of my coffee to wash it back down.

"At least when he does drug me, I'm not forced to think. My memories of his visits are foggy. Later, I don't suffer the nightmares that follow when my mind is clear. My husband has made it very clear that this is the life I've been granted; therefore, I should do my best to not piss him off, unless I want to encounter the devil himself."

"He's not your husband," Lorenzo announces, as if that will make me jump for joy. "Your marriage was never legalized here. I have my doubts it's legal, even in Turkey. Nevertheless, I know for a fact it isn't here and never will be."

"Do you think Ruben gives a shit?" I shout, outraged by this news. "Am I supposed to be ecstatic about that?"

"I thought you'd be pleased to learn you weren't his wife in the eyes of the law." He actually sounds shocked that I might not be.

I look down at the mug in my hand, and before I realize what I am doing, I launch it across the stone pathway. It lands and shatters into sharp shards, making me appear like some crazy raging woman. It doesn't help that I let out a loud angry shrill, one that makes my throat raw and my head pound.

"Why the hell would I be pleased to learn that? So instead of being his wife, I'm simply his fucking whore that he controls. His slave. He stole my daughter and holds her captive, forcing me to bow to his every need to keep her safe!" I yell in his direction. "Should I call him up and demand he return her since I am not his wife? March right up to his home and take her back. Certainly, he will give her to me without a fight since that is the case."

Rising to his feet, Lorenzo struts up to me slowly and cautiously. "If only it were that easy."

Tears I didn't expect blur my vision. As soon as he is close enough to me, I raise my fist and begin pounding his chest. All that anger inside of me comes out, and I take it out on a man who does not deserve it. Which only infuriates me and has me pouring out all the vile inside of my soul loudly.

"Why? Why do you care so much? I'm nobody. I'm a whore who has allowed an evil man into her life. All my ugliness will only ruin you and bring shame to your family. You should have left well enough alone, so I could remain as stupid as he always said I was." I continue to pound his chest harder with each word out of my mouth. "Why?"

Lorenzo seizes my wrist gently, then presses my hands against his solid chest. He waits for me to calm before he wraps those sturdy arms of his around me, hauling my body against him. Holding me there like I've never once been held before.

"Shh. Shh." He whispers into my hair, as he presses his lips against the back of my head. "Do not speak of yourself like that."

"It's true," I whimper into his shirt.

"No. Had you freely chosen him that would have been different, but you didn't freely choose him, did you, Violet?" He runs his hands through my hair and stops when he reaches my ears to tilt my head back. "Did you?"

"No," I hiccup.

"No, you did not." He stares at me with eyes that seem to see so much. "Which is why, when I look at you, I don't perceive you in that light. When I look at you, I see a woman searching for a way out. I know it's hard for you to understand that someone could see you differently than you see yourself. That a man could ever look past all those toxic scars you live with and notice the lovely woman you are underneath.

"However, that is exactly how I see you, love. I detect a beautiful stubborn woman, one who is fighting with all her might to get out from under all those who are trying to hold her down. Which is why I am determined to stand by your side and fight with you. Teach you that not every man out there is hoping to keep you from reaching your full potential.

"A real man would do all he could to protect you. Will support you while you fight all those demons blocking your way. He would fight proudly with you, beside you, for you when you are unable to fight for yourself. I hope to be that man for you, Violet. For you and Charlotte."

I have no words. No one has ever wanted to stand and fight with me before.

"I have a surprise for you when you are ready." His smile is back in full force.

"What kind of surprise?" I ask, taking a deep breath, knowing I need to focus on something other than what he is suggesting.

"Do you feel slightly better after getting some of that off your chest?" Lorenzo asks as he wipes my face off with his fingers.

"Slightly," I honestly tell him.

"I bet I know how to make you feel even better." He takes my hand and begins pulling me up the walkway to his home.

I do my best to compose myself, not sure what he has done. When I glance up, I notice a middle-aged woman walking toward us. At first, I wonder who she is and what she is holding securely against her. When we get closer, I catch the bundle in her arms move and a curly head appears.

"Charlotte?" I pick up my pace. "Charlotte, sweet baby girl."

Her head turns towards my voice, and it is then I see she has been crying. When she spots me, her sobs increase as she stretches her arms fully at my now running form.

"Baby," I snatch her from the woman's arms and bring her to my chest. "Shh. Shh, little one, Mama is here now. Shh."

The woman smiles up at me as she rubs Charlotte's back softly through the blanket. "Hello, madam. I'm Olga. You have a very sweet little one. She's been under the weather, which we've established is simply a cold."

"How did you get her here without protest?" I ask as I squeeze my sweet child to my body, giving her all the love that I have stored inside me.

"The Del Markovs are both away and won't be back for several days. I've been left to care for her as I see fit. Her personal guard escorted us here so we could see the doctor." Olga sounds unruffled and I have to wonder why that is. Why isn't she worried Ruben will discover what she has done?

"This is the woman I told you about, Violet. The guard is also a member of my staff, so there will be no need to worry. She brought Charlotte here because I ordered it to be done as soon as the coast was clear." Lorenzo steps up next to me and does his best to peek down at my daughter, who is hiding. "Hello, Char. You look like your mama. A beautiful little one."

Charlotte hides her face from him and starts shaking. Her discomfort around men has to do with what she has been exposed to during her short, brief life.

"Shh. It's alright, baby. Lorenzo is a nice man, like Bruno. Nicer than Bruno, even. Say hello." I assure her as I run my fingers through her curls as she listens to my voice. "Go on, baby. He is, after all, a prince."

Charlotte peeks up and studies him carefully, still uncertain, but follows my instructions. "Hi," she whispers. "Miss. Mama, no go. Mama stay."

Lorenzo places an arm around my shoulder to drag us both into his arms, using me as a barrier between him and Charlotte. He is not at all afraid to show this little one some affection, displaying his kindness. "Yes Char, Mama is staying. You are staying with her too. I promise."

I can't take his words as absolute. There is too much at stake to trust him. Therefore, I take them as comforting words he is speaking to a child who needs reassurance about this temporary situation of being reunited with me.

"Shall we go have breakfast?" Lorenzo squeezes my arm. "Do you like pancakes, Char? Banana and strawberry pancakes with maple syrup drizzled all over the top. I love them. Why don't we go inside and I'll whip us up a batch while you and Mama cuddle?"

I allow him to lead us toward his home. Right now, I'd go anywhere he suggested I go, as long as I get to take Charlotte with me. Perhaps if I can talk them into a sleepover, I will be able to do what I have to do to keep my baby safe.

CHAPTER 10
Lorenzo

The Royals

I dismissed my staff for the day so we would have privacy to discuss everything openly. Unlike my brothers, it isn't uncommon for me to send my staff away when I'm home. I don't enjoy having people around to wait on me hand and foot. I am partial to my solitude and only permit staff inside my house when necessary.

As soon as we are inside, I lead Violet to the kitchen and motion for her to sit down at the table overlooking the garden. "Coffee? Tea? I have both."

"Coffee." She glances around as if expecting someone to appear suddenly to fill her request.

I retrieve a mug from the cabinet and go about getting the single-serving machine started. While I'm waiting, I begin to gather all the ingredients I need to make us breakfast. Start slicing the bananas and strawberries thin, setting them aside when I hear the sputters of the coffee maker.

After I wipe off my hands, I grab her cup and set it down in front of her, then point to the sugar on the table. Next, I retrieve both creamers from the refrigerator and place them, along with a spoon, there as well. Then I'm back to making breakfast, only peeking up when I become aware of Charlotte's soft babbling. Both are studying me closely, as if unsure about what they are witnessing. It's rather exceptional to notice how they resemble one another. The way they stare in my direction with the exact same expression on their lovely faces. There is no doubt in my mind, after seeing them together, that Charlotte is Violet's daughter.

"What?" I mix the pancake batter, then check the griddle to determine if it's hot. "Do I have something on my face?"

"No," Violet shakes her head as she sips her coffee.

I spin to grab a spatula, flip in it my hand a few times as I turn back to face them. While I'm pouring the batter on the now hot griddle, I do my best to figure out why they are staring so intensely.

"Is it that you've never witnessed such a stunning male fix breakfast before?" I tease, hoping to break some of the tension in the room.

Once again Violet coughs after choking on her coffee. "What?"

I flash her one of my brightest smiles and watch her blush. "It's clear you aren't certain I'm capable. I'll have you know I cook most of my meals."

"Don't you have staff to do that for you?" She glances around again.

"I don't enjoy having extra bodies hovering. My security detail has a guardhouse they hang out in. My house staff only works during the week when I'm gone. At the time they are only responsible for all the chores I would rather not do, really. However, when I'm home, I value my privacy.

"We are alone, Violet. It's just the three of us in the house." I flip the pancakes before I lean my hip against the counter. "Even Olga has gone on her merry way since her services are not required anymore."

Violet makes a face and looks at Charlotte suspiciously.

"I poop," the little girl announces. "I stink."

I snicker at the sweet little one's honesty. "Olga left a diaper bag by the main door, I believe. More of her belongings will be delivered later today to the guest house, ensuring she is more comfortable."

Violet stands and takes off to where I pointed, saying nothing. She returns several minutes later, right in time for us to enjoy a nice breakfast. I suspect she is trying to figure out exactly what is going on and if there is a catch.

We eat in silence for the most part. I watch her interact with her daughter, feeding the little one off her own plate until she has had all she wants. Then Violet stacks a few more pancakes on the plate and begins feeding herself, all while Charlotte cuddles into her side. It cannot be easy attempting to eat one-handed, especially when her daughter nods off and becomes dead weight.

"May I," I gesture to Charlotte. "She's asleep now, and it might be easier to eat if you had the use of both hands."

Violet jiggles her head, glancing down at her daughter, "She's fine."

I don't argue, because clearly, she doesn't want to let her go just yet. She needs to hold her as much as this little girl needs to be held by her. It doesn't happen as often as it should, and that is something I vow to rectify as quickly as I can.

I sit back in my chair and decide it's time to give her the complete rundown of what I have in mind. "I have a proposal and I want you to hear me out fully before you object. Can you do that?"

She shrugs.

"To be clear, what I am about to suggest has more to do with me keeping Charlotte and you safe. Although it's not the only reason behind it. And should you agree to do things my way, you are under no obligation to assume I expect anything from you at all."

I can decipher by her raised eyebrows, she's not following my line of thinking.

"We will keep matters low-key, platonic for as long as you wish to do so. If it never moves into something else, something I'm hopeful eventually it will, something it could have been, had we simply met like normal couples. I will never hold it against you. Should you ever want out, all you'd ever need to do is say so. I will grant you your freedom, no questions asked."

"Just spit it out, Lorenzo," Violet gets a little annoyed by my talking. "You aren't making any sense."

We stare at each other for several drawn-out minutes before I do as she suggested. "Marry me."

"No." She doesn't even hesitate with her answer, almost looks disgusted even by my offer.

"Why not?" I ask, stretching my long frame out so I can get comfortable. I get the impression we will be here for a while, hashing this out.

When she fails to respond, I explain more on why I am suggesting something so radical. "If you legally were married to me, it would make this fight we are about to embark on, so much easier. Ruben wouldn't have a leg to stand on, giving you the power back, because you'd have all my resources available to you. A title that would instantly make you one of the most..."

"Are you crazy?" Violet keeps her voice low, although her irritation comes across loud and clear. "First of all, how do you know I'm not really married to him already?"

I explain what Karina shared with me the other day. Hand her a folder that has all the paperwork inside. The voided copy of the marriage certificate which was never filed correctly, dated back five years. Meaning in the eyes of the Hermosa Islas government, they were never legally married. So, he has no claim to her whatsoever, taking a huge part of what he has always held over her head away from him.

Inside, it also has the marriage license that informs her Ruben and Amber are legally tied together. Married exactly like he had always rubbed in her face when he wanted to make her suffer being rejected.

Charlotte's birth certificate is even included. It is obvious Violet has never seen it before, by the way she cringes as she reads. Attached to it are the documents Karina intends to file after we perform a maternity test to prove they falsified this. An offense that can be prosecuted, especially once she explains her father abducted the child, used her as a pawn to keep her biological mother in check.

Of course, that will mean exposing years of his abuse involving Violet, forcing her to testify against him in a court hearing. A hearing will also allow him to do his best to discredit her, bringing up all those secrets she has been able to hold silent so far.

I can perceive the pain in her eyes as she flips through the explanation Karina attached. Know that for us to move forward, what it means, and the uncertainty about how she suffers exposing the ugly truth.

"Violet," I whisper her name, taking her hand to show her my support. "I understand this is scary for you."

"You couldn't possibly understand. You have no real concept of what it was like." Her eyes are looking past me, allowing me to stare at her without her being completely aware of how diligently I am taking it all in. "I'm afraid if you ever really understood how it all went down, what kind of woman I really am you won't..." Violet doesn't finish her thought, instead, she blankly stares off into space.

I wish there was something I could do.

She tightens her hold around the precious bundle resting in her arms, and I get the pleasure of watching her breathe in her scent, treasure it. It is something she shouldn't have to do, putting that scent of her sweet baby to memory.

When she regains her composure, she glances down at Charlotte while she asks me a few questions. "Does that mean if I reject your offer, then I'll be left to fight this on my own? You'd..."

"No. No, I'd never do that."

How could I have not realized that would be a concern of hers? She has been all but forced to do as my cousin ordered her to do, and if she didn't, then he most likely reprimanded her for it. Possibly threatened to leave her with no resources, kick her out of the home he'd put her up in. Later, I don't even want to consider all the ways he got her to comply. If I thought too hard about all of that, I'd in all likelihood kill him the next time I saw him.

"Why then offer me something I know your family holds sacred. Marriage is a sacred religious vow that the King and Heir Apparent have taken a stand for. One that changed how this country viewed the sanctity of marriage, no longer permitting others to arrange them years ahead of time. I realize not everyone is on board with the way the country is shifting, but I thought you all felt the same." She pauses and glances up at me briefly.

"We do. I do."

Her face contorts into confusion. "But you just offered me a marriage without love, platonic in nature. That sounds more like one of convenience, opposite the types of marriages your other two brothers have entered into. So, which is it?"

I make sure that when I answer her, I have her complete undivided attention. That she can distinguish I am being completely honest with her, opening up to her, giving her what I believe no one else has ever done before.

"The only reason I'd ever marry is for love." I don't elaborate, because I want her to recognize the truth in the way I am regarding her.

Words are often an easy way to manipulate someone into believing what you are trying to sell. Without words, it is much harder to get the other person to believe you. You have to be willing to let them see the truth with their own eyes, the raw truth you are freely putting out there.

Until this very moment, I've allowed no one to read me so freely. So, I am hoping with everything inside of me that Violet recognizes I'm an open book only for her.

"You don't... You can't possibly...", she stumbles over her words. "How do you know?"

Now that I can answer. I believe she needs to hear the words to that question because I'm certain no one has ever verbalized the details I'm about to share with her.

But before I do, I want to shorten the distance between us. I need to be as close as she will allow me to be. Which is why I maneuver my chair around the corner of the table and sit next to her, instead of across from her. That way when I lean forward, resting my one arm on the table and the other along the back of her chair, it becomes more intimate.

I don't miss the fact she slightly inclines away from me as soon as she senses me invading her personal space. Noticing how her posture straightens or how her arms tighten around the babe she is hugging. It kills me to ponder why she always tenses when I get close, a triggered response she cannot prevent. Being alert when someone is this close is a defensive response, one I look forward to breaking when it comes to me.

"How do I know?" I let the hand behind her brush against her shoulder. "It's simple, really. Something I myself was unaware of until I spent all those days sitting vigil, wondering if you were going to live or die. When I held your hand and prayed that you'd open those beautiful eyes and smart off like only you can. How with each passing day, I worried I'd never get the chance to say all the crazy thoughts running through my mind."

"Like what?" Violet whispers and then blushes, as if she only meant to think those words.

My fingers tug gently on her silk hair as I scoot my body closer, sliding off the chair some. "Like how I love it when you laugh, it's such a joyous sound, and it brings a smile to my face. You should definitely laugh way more than you do. Or the way your eyes change color when you get a little upset. I've wondered often if they change for other reasons. That since meeting you, I can't walk by a flower shop and not stop to smell each and every one. Begin searching for the one I'm certain smells like you. I've yet to pinpoint it, although I calculate it's somewhere between roses and gardenias."

Violet blinks slowly, and I am blessed to witness her eyes changing color. Not only that, but her cheeks brighten faintly as well. "But how do you know it's not just infatuation?"

"Because I've been infatuated with a few women before. It fades rather quickly and doesn't keep me awake at night. I've never once dreamed about a future with any of those women before either. And my sentiments for them never grew daily until it took all I had inside of me to keep my mind from wandering. It's an emotion that runs deep, so deep, that the moment I saw this little one, everything I feel for you, immediately transferred to her as well. That is how I know."

My hand on the table lifts so I can brush it against Charlotte's tiny head. Her wayward curls are wet from the sweat seeping out while she sleeps. Everything inside me wants to keep her safe, as if she were my own to protect. The same way I desire to protect her mother, even though I'm almost certain she will be way more hostile about the process than this little one.

"I'd like to amend my previous offer." I run my hand down the baby's cheek before I move it to her mother's. "It's clear to me now how foolish I was about not understanding I was not offering you what you also needed. Call me selfish if you must."

Violet's eyes flutter closed as my knuckles caress her skin. "What is your amendment?"

"Allow me to be here for both of you. However, you come to work out what is best. We can simply be very close friends if that is all you have to offer me right now. I'd however like it if we could eventually be more." I allow my thumb to tickle her bottom lip and groan.

"How much more?" Her words are soft and breathy, nearly destroying my resolve to not lean forward and kiss her senseless.

Instead, I slant toward her, so that my cheek brushes hers, causing her to shiver and make the cutest little humming noise. With my lips near her ear, I tell her what I believe she needs me to say. "As close as you are comfortable allowing me to get. I'm not going to lie Violet; I want everything with you. If you decide to change your mind about my previous offer, I'd give it to you without hesitation. But I'll take whatever you will give me, hoping eventually I can persuade your heart to accept mine."

CHAPTER 11
Violet

The Royals

I've been staying in the cottage with my daughter now for two days. They have been the best two days of my life. We've been left to our own accord mostly, something we've never gotten the chance to experience until now.

Charlotte has been extremely clingy; therefore, I've rarely left her side. Even when I have, she has never wandered off too far, quickly returning to being only a few steps—if that—away from me. Wanting me to hold her most of the time, as if she is afraid our time will come to an end the way it always does.

I've given Lorenzo's proposals a great deal of thought. Both of them.

His first one didn't sit well with me. Not only for the reasons I told him, although they weighed heavy on my mind. But because marrying him seemed like the coward's way around an already impossible situation. Just because my marriage to Ruben was not recognized as being legal, never had been apparently, didn't mean the man would just let me walk away without making it extremely difficult. And it wasn't only me I had to consider here, I had Charlotte to look after as well. I couldn't put her life at risk all because I'd learned a few truths that in the long run didn't change my situation. Not in the eyes of the man I was shackled to, married or not.

The second one sounded more feasible, although it too was risky for both of us. Once Ruben caught on to what was transpiring between Lorenzo and me, he'd make my life hell. There is no way he'd sit back and allow another man to take what he believed was his. Not only would he once again use our daughter, but I feared he'd also take it one step farther. Go after the man determined to give me and her what he never could. Not ruin him, although I wouldn't dismiss that either, but get rid of him once and for all. He wasn't afraid of anyone; I'd heard of all the awful ways he'd dealt with those who crossed him. He enjoyed sharing all the methods he'd used to take care of anyone who dared take a stand against him. His means of keeping me aware that he could very well be the devil himself.

So, while I'd love to agree and allow Lorenzo into our lives, I wasn't about to risk his to do so. Meaning I'll never really get my chance at knowing how he claims he feels for me. There would be no moments shared where he'd get the chance to convince my heart to accept his. Although, I'm pretty sure my heart has already done that. It was my mind that wasn't quite ready. We were too different. From different sides of the spectrum. And I'd learned long ago where my place in this world would always be.

I made my final decision on the matter early this morning, not long after I received a very descriptive text from Ruben. It was then I decided the only way my daughter and I would get our chance to be free, was to do the unthinkable.

Everything I needed to hightail it out of the country was here, thanks to Lorenzo. When he relocated my belongings, he had left nothing behind, including my passports and important documents, hidden in my lockbox at the bottom of my closet. He'd also provided me with a birth certificate for Charlotte, which is all I required to take her on a plane. I had to alter it, of course, since I clearly wasn't Lady Amber, the woman named as her birth mother. It was a skill I'd learned from Ruben, altering documents so well it was practically impossible to detect unless you took the time to do so. I was counting on no one taking an extra minute to study it so closely.

I knew we'd have to take the bare minimum with us and do so in the darkness of the early morning. A time when no one would suspect us to be moving around and allow me to hopefully slip through one of the back gates without setting off any alarms. Thanks to our afternoon strolls along the grounds, I believe I have located the spot that would allow me to do just that.

And when Ruben's second message came through around bedtime, I knew I was making the right decision. He would return in three days. I'd been instructed to get my arse to the new flat by noon the day of his return so he didn't have to wait. One of his men would meet me there and let me inside. If I didn't show, he threatened to come and retrieve me himself, storm his cousin's precious East Aragon home. Proving once and for all that I was his property to do with as he pleased.

With a small suitcase filled with mostly Charlotte's necessities, I mustered up all the courage I had and then snuck out in the wee hours of the morning. Scared to death I'd get caught and then have to suffer the disappointment I was sure to uncover in Lorenzo's eyes.

Except we'd made it out without setting off alarms. Walked safely to the corner where our Uber was waiting, precisely as I had requested. And this time there was no one following me, or joining me when I climbed inside the back.

I didn't relax until we had been cleared through customs and seated on the plane. Even then I was on edge, knew I would remain that way until we were in the air.

We were heading to the States first. Once there, the plan was to take a bus to one of the smaller cities. A place we could get lost in, but one that wouldn't necessarily be on Ruben's radar.

He rarely travels to the States because of issues he's ran into in the past. They have him on a list that denies him entrance. Not that that would stop him, but he'd have to be rather crafty to make it into that country undetected. And while he has more than one passport—illegally, of course—he only uses them on the rare occasion he needs to escape quickly.

I'd learned just enough in the eight years I've been associated with him, to have a few tricks up my sleeve as well. Enough money stowed away in online accounts that aren't traceable. Enough cash to get me through an emergency. Along with a fake ID that declares I am a citizen of the United States. The last will allow me to be able to rent a place once I get settled. I should be good to secure work online as well, meaning I wouldn't need to leave Charlotte with anyone while I did my best to give us a decent life.

I have it all worked out in my head, a plan I am certain will keep us far away from Ruben and safe. Safer than we have been at least, in all the years I suffered being under his thumb. I know it's a risk, but it is one I'm willing to take. One I have to consider if I want a better life for my daughter and me, otherwise, I fear eventually I won't be around to protect her. When I'm gone from this world, my daughter would be doomed to a life where wrong is right and morals are tossed out the window.

Charlotte started crying as soon as we got in the air. The cold she is suffering from is making her head throb, I'm sure. And since she's only eighteen months old, there is no reasoning with her. No matter what I do, nothing seems to calm her down or comfort her. I can tell the other passengers are getting a little frustrated about it. Thankfully, she isn't wailing, but she is whimpering just enough to disturb everyone around us.

I overheard one man disclose to his seat mate. She is the reason why children under a certain age shouldn't be allowed to fly internationally.

I was doing my best to quiet her, pointing out all the clouds floating by. I was so busy trying to distract her, that I hadn't been aware someone had taken the seat next to me until I heard him speak. Now Charlotte wasn't the only one crying. Because I was right there with her as his voice washes over us.

"May I offer my assistance?" his ever level voice asks calmly.

My daughter hiccups and then smiles at the familiar face. "Hi, Len."

"Hello, Char. What's a matter, sweetheart?" Lorenzo reaches over and runs his fingers through her curly hair. "Still not feeling so great, are we? Why don't you and your mummy join me in first-class? I'm rather lonely up there as it is, need my girls to keep me company."

He extends his open arms, palms up, toward her. He's done this several times over the last couple of days, without success. But that didn't stop him from trying, offering her what he believed she desperately needed.

For the first time, my daughter stretches out her chubby arms and leans for him. She practically leaps out of my lap actually and falls against his solid shoulders, resting her head there. Completely comfortable in his arms, soaking in all he is offering her. She's never looked so comfortable in a man's embrace, not that she's been held by many men. But when she has, it never looked the way it does at this exact moment.

"*Meu anjinho, eu amo-te tanto. Descansa precioso, deixa o papá abraçar-te por uns tempos.*" (My little angel, I love you so much. Rest precious, let Daddy hug you for a while.) Lorenzo whispers in her ear while he rubs her back. "Hush now, *pequeno anjo.* Shh."

I stare at the vision he is presenting, while I listen to him soothe her. Charlotte's eyes are heavy and fading fast. She startles like she often does when she senses herself falling to sleep, only nuzzles in closer instead of fighting it. Even turns her head into his neck as she tucks her arms under her to get comfortable.

In that sweet little voice, she repeats his words. "*Eu amo-te, Papá. O meu Papá.*" (I love you, Daddy. My daddy.) Then a soft snore replaces her whimpers, speaking so very much on how she feels about the man now holding her.

Lorenzo turns his head and kisses her soaked curls as his eyes lock with mine. I can see how she caught him off guard with that honest, brief statement. From the mouths of babes, I do believe it is what they say.

"Will you join me? Or am I stuck here for the remainder of this extremely long flight? Not that I'm complaining, I'd suffer through, of course. Char is certainly making it less uncomfortable." Lorenzo finally speaks, still in a voice almost too calm, considering.

The lady across the aisle is staring at Lorenzo now. She nudges the woman next to her as she signals in his direction. I watch as recognition takes over the other woman's face and her mouth nearly drops to the floor.

"You're..." she starts to announce.

Lorenzo is quick, though. "I'm often mistaken for the person you are about to blurt out. I'm Lenny. An everyday businessman, traveling with my secretary and her daughter, to a conference in New York. And so, we don't cause a riot, let us leave it at that, shall we? I'd be more than willing to..."

The lady next to her, the one that first noticed him, waves him off. "No need, sir. I thought my eyes were deceiving me at first. Your secret is safe with us, mum's the word. Although I do believe I'd come up with a better storyline. One might get the wrong impression should they witness the way you gaze dreamily at your secretary." Then both of the women laugh as they fan themselves.

A genuine smile takes over his handsome face before he stands and takes a step back. "Point well made, my lady. I'll work on that."

Then he looks at me as if they have made a point, one that should get my feet moving. "Violet, love. It might be wise to conduct this conversation somewhere a little more private. I hear first-class has been taken over by a very greedy aristocrat. It cost him dearly and possibly upset a few passengers who were reassigned to less accommodating seats."

I stand, start to grab my bag from the overhead compartment, but am nudged forward.

"Leave it, Laney will retrieve it for us."

I don't argue. I move forward to where I notice an extremely chipper stewardess is standing. She isn't at all eyeing me; her attention is on the man following me. As soon as we are closer, she takes the staircase that leads to what I am assuming is first-class. Leads us down a corridor to a door she slides open.

"Sir," she addresses him and steps to the side. "Is there anything I can get you? Anything at all?"

We enter a private lounge area that looks nothing like what I expected. Two seats are facing each other, a couch, and even a bar where a large television is hung. I spin once, taking it all in.

He must have dismissed the stewardess because when I turn back around the door is closing.

"This is first-class?" I am doubtful, but what would I know, I've never sat in first-class before.

Lorenzo chuckles as he takes one of the two seats, adjusting

Charlotte slightly before he speaks. "Not exactly. This is an executive lounge area, reserved for those who have more money than they know what to do with. It was what was available on such short notice. This, along with a few seats in regular first-class, where my guards are taking shifts. I rarely fly commercial, too much work involved to secure it properly, but I made the exception this time."

My head lowers shamefully, "About that. How did you?"

"It was actually something we anticipated you might do. Once word came that Ruben had finished his business and was heading this way, with Lady Amber arriving one day ahead of him. Once you learned of his return, assumed your time with Char was coming to an end, I warned them you might run."

I drop onto the couch, defeated. "I was granted an opportunity. One I'd never been presented with before. There has always been someone with us during our visits. A man standing guard who answered only to Ruben."

"I'm not angry at you, Violet. In fact...", Lorenzo pauses, staring at me like no one ever has. "You are the bravest woman I know. Because to you, there was no other option, you took an incredible risk."

"I appreciate how stupid you must think I am for running. If I get caught... when you turn me in, I mean, they will most likely take her from me. Give her back to the people listed as her legal parents, people who..."

"I'm not turning you in. If you don't know that yet, then we have more work ahead of us than I realized. I'm running with you, my dear. My team is working with Darius, formulating a solid alibi and a few aliases for us if necessary.

"Karina is working equally hard. She's petitioning the court to fast track the custody hearing of Charlotte by awarding her to her biological mother. She will use the reason for the Del Markovs' detainment upon their arrival home, as a solid case on why she would be better off with us."

"Us?" I ask.

"Yes, us. Since you are currently living on my property." He sounds so confident that I hate to burst his bubble with reality, but someone has to.

"And when they bring up my recent hospital stay; you expect a justice will grant custody to a drug addict."

"You are not an addict!" He says louder than I suppose he meant to, then immediately glances down at the still sleeping child in his arms. "You are not an addict; you are a victim. His victim. You've passed every drug test required of you since working at the palace. A trustworthy employee of the king himself. Never been late to work. Never showed up drunk or high. Given no one a reason to complain about your work ethic. That in itself should speak volumes."

"And me running doesn't make me appear guilty." I'm on a roll and know very well it does. "And how will you explain how I got my hands on her? She was not left in my care, yet somehow..."

"Simple. I learned the child was ill. Your child. Spoke to the au pair and requested she bring her so I could have a doctor look her over. Accepted that it was my duty to look after the child of the woman I love since there was no one else around to do so. Then to help the little one get better quicker, I allowed her to stay, so we could keep a close eye on her." His hand brushes a few curls away from her face. "A mother's love after all is the best recipe for an ailing child. No one can take care of a sick child better than her own mother, providing a comfort that cannot be replaced."

I don't miss what he said, but I choose to not focus on those three words. "But then I ran off with her."

"Did you, though? I do believe I got called away on business. In need of a personal assistant with palace knowledge. Requested my brother loan you to me during this month-long circuit. Since the youngster was no better, and I didn't feel comfortable leaving her behind, I received special permission from the king himself to allow the child to travel with us."

"You cannot be serious?" I sink back against the seat and all but give up. He seems to have an answer for everything, even if it sounds ridiculous.

"It's good, right? I believe I will share those thoughts with my team. Make sure they lead with that one. No one ever dares question the king, after all. That should buy us some time to come up with a plan." He stands and takes the empty spot next to mine.

I do my best to ignore him until he slips his arm under me and drags me closer. It's hard to overlook him when he's this close. Especially when he leans his head next to mine, at the same time he runs his hand up and down my side. It's the closest he's been since the day he climbed in my hospital bed, a day I have relived so many times.

"This plan of yours may not have been ideal, but we can work with it. Time away from it all might do us both some good. Give you some time with your daughter, she so loves spending time with you. And that has allowed me the chance to prove I'm not like anyone else you've ever known before. I'll always have your back, always. You only need to trust me, as much as I trust you."

"You trust me?" I make the mistake of repositioning my head so I can look at him. His eyes alone speak volumes.

"Completely." Lorenzo doesn't hesitate. "I know that is difficult for you to understand. But when I look at you, what I see is all I need to know. You'd never do anything to hurt me purposely. You'd give me up, in fact, were willing to actually, I believe. You have some idea in that stubborn head of yours, that in order to keep us all safe we can never be.

"I however believe differently. I'm not afraid of him, Violet. He's a smart man. Unless he wants the wrath of my brothers to come down hard on him, he'll see reason."

"That word is not in his vocabulary." I flat out tell him.

"Then perhaps his father will be able to convince him." He confidently speaks with a clear understanding of how very true he believes what he is suggesting will happen.

"I'm not worth..."

My words are cut off by the pressure of his lips against mine. With a growl, he kisses me, and I'm not at all frightened by it. In truth, I find myself submitting to his aggressive behavior, kissing him back even. He doesn't deepen the kiss, not this time.

"I'd suit up for battle for you in a heartbeat, Violet. Many wars have been fought over a woman. Women who I'm certain probably thought they weren't worth it either. But the men fighting knew better, both sides were willing to fight for her, you see. Proving throughout history, that there were way too many women who didn't recognize their worth.

You are worth it, don't sell yourself short. You are so very much worth it."

I don't have the strength to argue. We may never agree about my worth. But Charlotte, however, is worth it, and she deserves a man like Lorenzo willing to fight for her. So, I stop fighting against the inevitable and decide to allow this man to do his best.

In the back of my mind, the doubt lingers. The fear of what Ruben will do. The sadness of how my life always seems to find the hardest and most difficult path to travel down. And until now, I've always traveled that path alone, getting stuck in the thorns and thistle, always having to fight my hardest to get loose. Perhaps having someone to assist me might make the pathway clear and less bumpy.

CHAPTER 12
Lorenzo

The Royals

For the last three weeks, I've done my absolute best to keep Violet and Char out of harm's way. We moved around the United States more often than I liked, but I had a cover to maintain. I needed to play up the CEO role for Reyes Capital, continuing business as usual. Talking to all our contacts and making deals like I would on any other business trip. All of it would provide us with a proper cover later, should we need one.

It didn't take long, however, for Ruben to cause major issues. He was a smart man; knew he couldn't simply accuse me, a prince, of kidnapping. Being a member of the royal family had its perks, and one of those was that we are revered as honorable citizens. His reputation was not even close to my family's. That fact forced Ruben to use all his resources to get back what he assumed was his. Attacking me and my family head-on would not be the best way of doing so. Instead, he started reaching out to those in his world. That is when I decided it was time for us to find a suitable hiding place where he couldn't find us.

There was only one person I could think of to turn to when I am a little uncertain about my decisions. She has been there for me so many times before. Always supporting my major decisions. So, calling her seemed logical.

"Hello, dear. It is good to finally hear from you." My mother's voice is as soothing and calm as always.

"Sorry I took off without warning." It seems like I should apologize.

"I get it, Lorenzo. You had to do what was necessary, and I will forever stand behind you. I learned a long time ago that everything isn't always as it appears."

I do my best to catch her up on everything I've learned since leaving home, along with my plans moving forward. She never once interrupts me. Like every other time, she listens carefully so that when I do finally ask for her opinion, she can give it to me. My mother has a way about her that can, at times, be hard to explain. There is so much about her life I'm not sure I fully understand, things she has kept private. One day maybe I'll get a better understanding of how she gained so much knowledge. For now, I am happy she has it and takes every bit she has to offer.

"You've put some serious thought into this. It sounds like you understand what it is you need to do. I'll make sure you get the support you require and do what is necessary to calm Sir Edward down. I expect after I explain it all to him, he'll agree that it is best to go into hiding for a while. If not, then I'll simply remind him he works for us and not the other way around."

I almost laugh at the thought of my mother standing up to the man in charge of the King's Guards. He has been a member of the guards for as long as I can recall. I know they have a history that goes back many years. It helps when she steps in and speaks to him on our behalf. He often may not agree with her, but he takes her opinion seriously.

"I appreciate that," I tell her.

"So, now tell me how things are going between you two." I knew this question was coming. My mother doesn't let things go unsaid.

"As good as they can, considering the circumstances. I'm doing my very best to not trample in and make her see things my way." I start there and hear my mother snicker. "Why do you find that funny?"

"Oh, my dear Lorenzo, you must be having an awfully grueling time, not trampling. You've always been wise beyond your years, seen things others may not. You have an old soul, and it is in your nature to step in when you see something you dislike or disagree with.

"I've been around Violet long enough to also understand the kind of woman she is. To say she is headstrong might be an understatement. It is why she was so good at the job your brother hired her to do. Only a brilliant person can deal with all the arrogant people who come and go, making demands. She has remarkably thick skin and has never been afraid to take a stand against some extremely intimidating men and women. I believe she did her best to prove that very point to you, even."

Now I'm the one snickering because she certainly did. "Only because she liked me."

I've heard my mother laugh a lot at me over the years, but I'm not sure I've heard her laugh this hard. "Lorenzo, may I offer you some sound advice?"

I don't hesitate. "Please do."

Once she has composed herself, she does just that. "While I know you want to jump in with both feet and take over, you will not win this woman over by doing so. You need to let her be the one to decide you are what she wants. I realize how hard it is for a man to do that. You all wish to be the noble knight who sweeps in and saves the day. However, Violet is not the kind of woman who wants a knight. She is a woman who needs an equal partner who will stand by her, not in front of her. You must let her decide when she needs you, what she desires from you even. Be the man she can confide in, lean on when the time calls for it, hold her up when she is feeling defeated. Do not be the man who takes over for her, that will get you nowhere."

"I'm trying, mother. I'm doing my best to be all of those things for her." I sigh, knowing I've had a tough time holding back. "I only want what is best for Char and her, they mean the world to me."

"I know they do. I saw you sit by her side when no one else was there. You have found who you trust is your forever."

"She is without a doubt that," I say confidently.

"Then, you need to be patient and let what is meant to happen, happen."

We say our goodbyes, and I lean back in my chair to take it all in. It takes me only a few seconds to realize I'm not alone. I should probably be embarrassed, but it isn't as if I've not been completely open with her. "How much of that did you hear?"

"I didn't mean to eavesdrop," Violet responds. "Charlotte wanted to come say good morning. You know how impossible it is to keep her from you when she is determined to do so."

I smile at the thought of little Char. She and I have become very close, and I love every second we spend together. I never tell her no when she wishes to see me, I want her to always feel I will be there for her whenever she wants or needs me.

"Where is she now?" I sit up so I can receive her should she come running.

"Gayle brought cinnamon rolls up a few minutes ago, you lost out due to the sugar fix she instantly required when she smelled them." Violet walks toward me. "That was your mother? Does she hate me?"

I spin in my chair and pat my lap. "No."

Instead of taking a seat, Violet leans against the desk and crosses her arms. She is not so sure I am telling her the truth, and her posture gives her thoughts away.

I stand and step in front of her so I can help her understand that it is true. "She doesn't hate you, not even close Vi. My mother is a knowledgeable woman, she sees things we often miss."

It is hard for me not to touch this woman when she is this close. My hand automatically lifts to push her hair away from her face and cups her cheek. I do my damndest not to pull her into me and kiss those soft lips, or I try at least. We don't have all that many moments alone, so when we do, I usually take advantage. Plus, she has started letting me kiss her without complaining. I'm breaking through those walls she has built, and each day I try my hardest to knock them down completely.

"She told me not to trample," I whisper against her lips. "God, you taste good."

The feel of her mouth curling upward makes me want to kiss her harder. I hold back, though, knowing if I do, it could be the end of my resolve.

"It is so hard for you not to take charge, isn't it?" This time she leans forward and kisses me. "What else did she tell you?"

I pull back so I can look into her eyes. "All the things I already knew but needed to be reminded about. So how do you feel about getting away and finding a place where we cannot be bothered?"

The tension builds in her body, and I can sense it. "He's causing more issues."

I step closer, letting my arms wrap around her back, so we are now particularly close. "Shh. Maybe I only want to sweep you away so I can have you to myself without all the other distractions. Call it a holiday if you must. When was the last time you went on one?"

"I cannot recall," her eyes sparkle as she stares up at me. "Are you going to be on your best behavior, or are you planning to drive me crazy?"

"I think you want me to drive you crazy, Vi." I tug her closer because I love her as close to me as possible.

"You may be growing on me just a little." She rubs her nose against mine. "But that doesn't mean I like you; you are still very annoying."

Her snarky attitude is causing my body to stir. I have never had this response to any other woman, not the way I do for her at least. Simply her being around, giving me attitude, seems to do it for me.

Her eyebrows lift slightly when she notices. "Do you like hearing that, Your Highness?"

I don't answer her with my words, I kiss her harder than I intended to, not at all helping my predicament. When I pull back, I find her flushed and beautiful. Making me wish we were on the same page so I could do all kinds of other things to her.

"What?" She asks me a little breathless.

Before I can answer, we can hear the pattering of little feet running down the small hallway. Violet gives me a slight shove back. She still isn't comfortable letting others see us so intimately. I release her before we get caught. I've learned to steal the moments I can and cherish them.

Char comes running and heads straight for me, arms wide. "Papa."

I catch her as she leaps into my arms and plant a kiss on her cheek. "You smell yummy."

"I eat sweet roll. Yummy. You ungry?" She asks as she grabs my face. "You eat?"

"Did you save me any?" I ask as I carry her to the door.

"Yes," Char replies. "Gay, not me eat all."

Violet looks over at Gayle, "Thank you."

"No problem. It is always a pleasure to hang with her, give you two some time." My team is no dummy, they notice everything.

Violet cringes as she glances my way. When our eyes meet, she relaxes slightly, as if remembering what we discussed. "I appreciate that as well."

Her response warms my heart, so I reach for her hand. "So do I."

When she takes it freely, my heart warms more, knowing this is an enormous step in the right direction. It also makes me even more confidant that getting away from it all is exactly what we need. Not merely to keep us safe, but to help us secure some time where we can focus on us and not everything going on around us.

I speak to Gayle as we make our way to the kitchenette. "Have Rico make the call. We move today. It's time."

She nods and then heads for the room the others will be in, to inform them of the plan. I'm done playing games, letting others call all the shots. I recognize what is best for Violet and Char. They need time away from it all, and we need to get away as well. If what my team is feeding me is correct, Ruben has put the word out, and that puts us all in danger. Finding a secluded place off the grid will be good all the way around.

Hopefully, this break away will do two things. First and most importantly, I hope it keeps my girls safe and far away from Ruben and his plans. Second, I'm hoping it will give us the time we need to grow closer. I know how I feel, and each day my feelings grow stronger. I don't want to trample her; I want her to be the one to do a little trampling. Not that she will have to, but damn if she even tried, I'd be thrilled.

CHAPTER 13
Violet

The Royals

I f you are ever forced to run, and you have a choice who you would like to be on the run with. I strongly recommend you do so with a man similar to the one I've been stuck with for the past five weeks.

Never underestimate the power a man holds when he displays his true colors while on the run. It's so powerful that it is impossible to resist, and can open the eyes of a woman like myself to an unexpected world.

Not because he flaunted his life or wealth as a way to impress me. I've been around the Reyes men long enough now, that I learned a long time ago there was more to them than all of that. We stayed in the finest hotels, ate at several five-star restaurants, were driven around in luxury vehicles, and shopped at boutiques whose specialties were women and little girls' fashion. The last only because he insisted on buying us enough clothing to last the duration of our time together.

I understood the reason for most of those before mentioned places had more to do with the lifestyle he was accustomed to. It had nothing to do with him showing off for us. He knew those marques of establishments were discreet, never asked questions when unusual requests were made—like closing a shop for privacy. They were well trained in what to do and gladly always accommodated.

Lorenzo is a private man, way more than either of his brothers. There was so much I didn't even understand about him, I had always assumed I did. For example, the way he presented himself to the rest of the world, compared to the manner he acted when no one else was watching. Our time together gave me a proper chance to appreciate who he really was.

Most people would describe the third prince of Hermosa Islas as outgoing, a flirt, the free-spirited brother. I've heard others label him as a womanizer. The one who can charm any woman in the room and have her eating out of his hand before the evening is over. Rarely being seen with the same woman more than once, and even known to interact with several at one time when attending a social event without a designated escort. I've even overheard some more prominent heads of government mention how they speculated him to be more like his father than his strait-laced brothers. Some have even expressed how he'd be better suited for office than either of them. How it was a shame that his skills were being wasted on the family business when his kingdom needed his point of view more.

I was finding they were all so incredibly wrong about him. He was most certainly outgoing, enjoying with this contagious attitude. He also walked through life beating his own drum, while understanding how to fit in almost anywhere without really fitting in at all.

I know that sounds strange, but allow me to explain. Think about the one person who always seems to be the life of the party. The one who appears to get along with everyone. The person they all look forward to seeing and claim to be friends with. This person makes his way through the party—so to speak—chatting it up with everyone. High fives those from all the social clusters, wearing a smile that seems almost genuine while he does. But when the party is over and everyone has gone their separate ways, who does he leave with. He arrived alone, which means he most likely left alone as well.

Now granted, Lorenzo has his core group of friends he is extremely close to. Dinger, Cris, and Freddy are the only ones who appreciate him at all. Darius Falcon has been accepted into that core unit now since he married Dinger. Whose name, by the way, is Ingrid; she acquired the nickname one wild night after they all had a little too much to drink.

I've not actually met these people, but he's spoken with them several times these last five weeks.

Well, I've met Freddy, otherwise known as Winifred Reyes, Prince Esteban's wife. She often sends treats to the palace that are so tempting it is all I can do not to overindulge. I've never actually had a conversation with her or spent time in her presence outside of my palace duties. Even though I attended her birthday party, I had done so as the King's secretary, not a true friend.

These people are the ones he speaks to regularly, often laughing unashamedly during those times. Opens up completely with them about everything, knowing he can absolutely trust each one with all of his secrets, just like they trust him with theirs.

Besides his small group of close-knit friends, it's all a game. A smoke and mirrors magic trick, where he presents himself, how he believes others want to perceive him. I do not doubt that he once enjoyed the company of the females he spent time with. That he has danced with his share of women. Invited several to dinner for entertainment purposes. Escorted some to those prestigious events that they expected him to attend because of who he is. Those ladies were never more to him than his way of pleasing the masses. Meaning he doesn't fit in like everyone assumes he does, not really.

Prince Lorenzo Gabriel Reyes enjoys his solitude. Didn't enjoy being in the public eye, really. Would be happy to walk away from it all and live in a world where no one knew him. A life where he could walk around without guards. One where he could stroll down the street and no one would recognize him or even care. Which is why, when he could dismiss his detail, he did so.

These last two weeks we've been taking it easy in a cabin somewhere in Wyoming. A secluded one in the mountain region where civilization is miles away. It's peaceful. I've experienced nothing like it before. I've never lived anywhere but inside a crowded city surrounded by people. Although I'm starting to appreciate why someone might choose such a life.

We are hiding out. Maintaining a low profile. While matters cool down back home, we are staying off the grid. We'd been advised to do so by Darius and Karina. It seems what we did has caused some waves back home. Ruben is in an uproar about how it all went down and acting out. From what we've been told, he has gotten so out of hand that his father has even taken a stand against his son's actions. And to make sure we don't get caught in the crossfire, everyone in charge of our security considered it best if we quietly disappeared for a while.

I do feel bad that I've dragged Lorenzo into this war I caused. But I'm not sure I'd have survived it on my own. That I'd have been able to keep Charlotte safe without Lorenzo's assistance.

Plus, whenever I bring it up, the man reminds me he was the one who stepped in and inserted himself into my life, not the other way around. That even when I provided him the chance to wash his hands of me, brings up that he refused to let me go, us go. This is why, even though I feel bad, I am so very happy to have him with us. Glad he is the one calling most of the shots.

Right now, I'm standing on the front porch watching him interact with my daughter. Only moments ago, I spoke with my younger siblings to check in on them. Something they have allowed me to do once a week using a burner phone. While I spoke briefly with their mother, I learned tuition had been taken care of for the next school year. I was happy to learn she's been able to keep why I've not been around from them. Has communicated with them I've been working overseas. And even though I know she has many questions, it was nice for a change to not have to speak about any of it. We kept things simple, and she caught me up on the activities my siblings have been doing. It was freeing to forget, if only for a moment, and to hear they are doing well and unaware of all the drama surrounding me.

I should probably be uneasy about that financial burden being taken care of, without anyone asking me about how I felt. It wasn't as if I'd ever mentioned that I supported them because I wanted a better life for them than I had. Except I couldn't find it in me to be upset with Lorenzo for knowing how important they were to me as well. And like he has done several times, he simply stepped in when he saw a need to ease the burden.

Therefore, I find myself watching him right now, taking it all in while I watch him and my daughter doing what they have done most afternoons. They are both crouched down, looking at something they've discovered on the ground. He reaches down carefully and picks up whatever it is, then places it on his palm. Laughs, when Charlotte squeals loudly, as whatever it was escapes. Catches her when she all but leaps for him, almost knocking them over in the process. Then stands with her in his arms, while reassuring her she is okay. Leaning over with her, safely secured tightly against him, so he can pick it up again to show her that whatever it is won't harm her. Only to laugh again, when what I realize is a frog, leaps out of his palm and lands safely on the ground, making her shriek and then giggle.

I've seen him interact with her like this hundreds of times now. Sit with her on the floor so they can play. Hold her in his arms when we take a stroll through a park or down a hiking trail. Watched him cuddle with her lying flat on his back while she slept on his chest. Have been witness to him becoming an essential part of her little life, getting her to trust him. Listened to him express his sentiments to her freely and then heard her repeat his words. Noticed how whenever she did that, it shattered him in much the same way it did me when she verbalized those same words.

We've spent almost every waking hour together. While he conducted some business early on when he was determined to provide us with the proper cover. Once matters started getting questionable, he took a leave of absence and made this more of an adventure. Began moving us around inside a country where we could stay safe while being inconspicuous and well hidden.

During all those countless hours together, something has developed between us. We've become friends. I didn't have friends before, not really; it wasn't something a person who lived the life I'd been living had. Not the kind of friends others had at least, not the kind of friends Lorenzo had. Certainly not the type of friend he was quickly becoming. A person who I knew saw beyond all my past mistakes, not once judging me for them. One who I enjoyed being around even when we had nothing at all to say. Just being with him in the same room provided me with a peace I'd never felt before. When it was just the three of us, I could relax, breathe. I can't even remember the last time I could do that. Maybe when I was just a kid, but even then, I'm not sure that is true.

The thud of footsteps trekking across the wooden planks, followed by tiny clomps, has me rotating my head. My daughter is babbling so quickly it's difficult to understand her. Although I catch the highlights easily, the words like frog, jump, and daddy. At the mention of the man she has been calling daddy or papá since he intercepted us, has me taking my eyes off her so I can stare at him.

My breath catches at the sight he presents. A much more rugged appearance than normal, one that is lethal to a woman who is finding herself captivated by him. Lately, whenever he is near, I get that tingly sensation deep in my belly. I watch his lips while he speaks, thinking about all those times he's kissed me.

And yes, he has kissed me a few times during our time together. All done respectfully, and at times when it was clear, he just couldn't stop himself. Although it's been nearly a week since we've found ourselves in a situation like that. Too long, if you ask me.

"Hungry?" I ask him as I scoop Charlotte into my arms. "Dinner is ready if you are ready to eat."

We stare at each other, letting our eyes speak our thoughts.

"After dinner..." he leaves the rest for me to freely interpret as he leans down and brushes a kiss to my cheek.

"After dinner," I repeat softly and almost get a little giddy about it.

The night goes on like it has since we arrived. He cleans up after we eat, while I get Charlotte ready for bed. We meet in the lounge area and sit on the couch together where we watch television.

When my daughter finally crashes, as soon as she stops wiggling, he takes her from me and carries her off to the bedroom she and I have been sharing. Settles her between the mountain of pillows that will surround her until I join her in a few hours. Our way of ensuring she doesn't roll off the bed that is way bigger than she is used to sleeping in alone.

As soon as he returns, I decide it's time to share what I have been thinking about most of the day. "I'm not sure how to start this."

Lorenzo shifts so he is now facing me, bracing to argue with me if necessary. We've done that many times, so I know this move well.

"I think I might be ready to offer you more than just my friendship." I decide to just blurt it out and pray I've been reading him correctly.

"How much more?" He reaches over and takes my hand, something he has done several times as well.

I shrug, unsure what he is asking exactly.

"I need you to tell me what it is you're thinking, Violet. More than friends is a vast and vague description." Lorenzo isn't about to let me off that easily.

It would be so much simpler if he would. I have my ideas, except I'm certain our viewpoints are massively different on those types of intimacy. I'm way more worldly in my views than I imagine he is.

Before Ruben ever entered my life, I'd had a few boyfriends. I hadn't gone all the way with any of them, but we'd done things. I'm not sure why I had held onto my virginity. Probably because I had some crazy fantasy that when I lost it. I wanted it to be with someone I actually loved. At seventeen, none of the boys fit into that category. I liked them, but I didn't love them.

And since Ruben entered my life shortly after my seventeenth birthday. I'd never gotten the chance to fall in love and then offer it to that person. It had been taken from me by a man I loathed, one that has controlled me ever since.

So now that I was away from him, not free of him yet, not completely, but have been given a portion of my freedom back, even if only for a little while, I'm still not convinced a life without him will continue to be. I've experienced spells without him before. Those ended abruptly. So I guess you could say I'm merely waiting for the shoe to drop. Therefore, while I can, while this man is in my life, one I have most certainly fallen in love with, I'd like to at least know what that would be like.

"Violet," Lorenzo reaches up and brushes his hand against my cheek. "What is it you want?"

Knowing I'll chicken out if I wait, I stare into his brown eyes and just say it. "Make love to me. I want you to make love to me."

I watch his face closely. Notice how his eyes get this hunger inside of them, that until this very moment hasn't been there. Detect the rouge coloring that appears on his cheeks, and even how his nostrils flare when he takes a deep inhale of air. Catch the lump in his throat as he swallows, while he processes my words. Then realize how tense his body grows as he blinks his eyes slowly several times.

I've clearly said the wrong thing, made a mistake. "Never mind. I'm sorry."

I start to get up, so I can make my escape for being so foolish. Asking a man like Lorenzo to do something I'm certain he has been saving for the love of his life, the woman he will eventually marry. What was I even thinking?

He snags my wrist though and holds it tight, "Where are you going?"

I refuse to look at him, knowing I'm on the verge of dying here. "I shouldn't have asked you that. That isn't what you meant when you asked me what I wanted. You were expecting a much simpler answer, obviously. Please let me go."

He doesn't of course. Instead, he tugs on it, forcing me to sit back down next to him. Then he takes his other hand and encourages me to look at him while he speaks. "You're right, I wasn't expecting you to say that."

"I'm sorry. I was out of line. I forget sometimes that we think differently about those matters." I sit there, stiffly. Disgusted with myself for even suggesting something like that to this lovely man.

"How is that exactly? What do you imagine my thoughts are about what you ask of me? I'm not sure we do." He loosens his grip on my wrist and takes my hand again. "Talk to me, Violet. We cannot move forward unless you talk to me."

What do I have to lose now? I've already done my worst. "You probably have always imagined only being with one woman, the one you planned on marrying. Am I right?"

A devious smile takes over his face and I have to roll my eyes.

"I'm right. And you were probably expecting me to tell you earlier, how I wanted to do the whole relationship thing. Allow you to treat me more like a girlfriend than a friend. Be more affectionate and all. And I jumped from friends straight to lovers, leaving out the other stuff completely. My mistake." I divert my eyes to look away, ashamed at my behavior. "I'm sorry." Those stupid tears build behind my eyes. Soon they will spill down my cheeks, making me come across as some wounded, desperate soul.

"Violet, may I ask you something?" His hand drops from my face and lands on my arm. "Tell me how you always imagined it would happen. Please, since you've shared your thoughts on my views concerning the matter."

Whatever.

"Sure, why not?" I huff. "I sort of thought I'd always give myself to the first guy I fell in love with. Except I never got that chance, thanks to Ruben. I wasn't completely innocent before him, but I'd never done that. And now that I've... it doesn't matter. Just forget I asked, okay."

A chuckle arises from the man next to me. "That's an impossible detail to forget first of all. And it matters to me." His hand rises and lands under my chin, lifting it so we are once again looking at each other. "Now that you've what, Violet? Be brave, tell me."

I scowl at him as I swat his hand away from me, before standing abruptly. This way, as soon as I've said the words, I can get the heck out of here. Arms crossed, I once again go for broke. "Now that I've fallen in love with you, I thought..."

Lorenzo is on his feet, wrapping his arms around me, preventing me from running like I had intended. "You love me?"

Still wearing a scowl, I respond a little harsher than I meant to. "I said I did, didn't I?"

Grinning like some young boy, he gives it right back to me. "I love you too."

"What?" I'm confused.

I mean, it's not like I didn't suspect he did, he pretty much said so a while back, when he suggested we get married. But he has never actually spoken those words, and I didn't realize how hearing them would affect me.

"I love you, surely that is no surprise to you. I realize I've not said it until now, but that had more to do with you not being ready to hear it. Now that I see you are ready, I am determined to remind you of that fact multiple times a day for the rest of my life." He drags me forward and I don't miss the fact his body is aroused.

In the past, I've always felt sick when an aroused male body brushed up against mine. Not this time, however, not with this man.

"What?" I'm struggling to process it all, his words along with his arousal.

"I love you. Will forever love you. Tell me again what you want, love. Tell me how you feel and then ask me again." He leans in only inches away from my face.

Can I do this? Can I drag this man down with me, into my life that is nowhere near as perfect as his?

"Don't think. Just say it." He kisses my cheek. "You are wrong about me, Violet. I only ever imagined loving the person, knowing they also loved me. When and how that happened was never a part of it. I mean, of course, the ultimate goal would be to marry her... you, marry you. And I will do that as soon as you are ready, I believe we've discussed this before. But loving you like no man before me ever has, would give me great pleasure."

Then he kisses me like he hasn't kissed me before. His lips move across mine softly. The abrasion of his beard scuffs the skin around them.

I open when his tongue encourages me to and am blessed with the taste of him. It is the most intimate kiss I've ever been a part of, one that has me experiencing all those things I've missed out on before him. A kiss that makes my eyes spill all my emotions onto my cheeks and down my face.

"Don't cry." He tells me, then uses his lips to wipe them away. "Don't cry."

I grab his neck and drag him closer so that his ear is next to my lips. "I love you, Lorenzo. I will love you and only you for the rest of my life. Make love to me, show me what that is like."

CHAPTER 14
Lorenzo

The Royals

I didn't lie to Violet when I expressed how I always envisioned my first time. Unlike my brothers, who were more worried about getting trapped. It was different for me.

My life differed from theirs. I wasn't around our father all that much growing up. He came to visit us in Prieto, stayed in one of the many guest rooms. Respected my mother's wishes while there and left his playmates behind. So, I never really encountered that side of him until I was older. Old enough to understand that it was his choice to act the way he was acting, and by then my mother was long over him.

And unlike my brothers, who both hold extremely important titles, at one time were considered likely heirs to the throne, I never had to worry about all that. My pecking order was far enough removed, that no one even bothered acquiring me a tutor to teach me how it all worked. I grew up like most with privileges did, having way more freedom than either of them ever did.

And while there are many women out there who only want to be a part of the Reyes regimen, those who were only interested in my title, none of those women were ever the ones I found myself attracted to. I was remarkably good at playing the game, but always appreciated I'd never settle for someone like that.

Lady Hilda had sealed the fate of all others like her. Not all that long after my eighteenth birthday. I'm still uncertain how she managed to sneak past our highly trained palace guards, but she had. She'd somehow snuck into the living quarters I was staying in while visiting my brother the king. Greeted me like no one had ever done before. I found her sprawled out on my bed naked. Handcuffed to it even, with an offer to let me do every imaginable wicked act I wanted to her. If I told you I'd not been marginally tempted to do so, I'd be lying. But I quickly remembered she was only fifteen, way too young to be taken advantage of like that. So instead, I walked right back out and had the guards deal with her. That little stunt had banished her from further access to all events where any royal was expected to attend. It also taught me where to draw the line when dealing with the ladies.

When I went away to university, I thought maybe I would come across a woman who didn't know who I was exactly. I had, although none who held my interest all that long. I had a few girlfriends, some who even offered me the freedom to sleep with them. I'd declined for a couple of reasons. Mainly because I didn't love them, understood they didn't love me either.

The act wasn't referenced as making love just because it sounded nicer than the other word some people used. And because I wasn't interested in unattached sex, a meaningless act where two people used the other person to satisfy a need, it seemed wrong to do the very act if there was no love involved. Call me old fashioned, but love I do expect makes the act of sex so much more meaningful. I've seen my share of those who were free with their sexuality, and they always seemed unsatisfied. I thought the point was to satisfy, so it seemed counterproductive, hence the reason I had refrained.

I had decided during those earlier years that I would only give in to my desires when I was certain it was love. Real genuine love, the kind that grabbed you and refused to let go.

That's how I felt about Violet. She was the first woman I'd ever loved, the only one I intended on loving. And loving her fully and completely is exactly what I so very much want to do.

So when she whispered those sweet words in my ear, I immediately scoop her into my arms and begin carrying her toward the room I've been sleeping in. My heart is pounding so hard I can feel it in my ears, hear it even. The blood pumping through my veins is moving at a rapid pace, making my pants tighter on my groin.

Our lips lock when my feet cross the doorway and I blindly find my way to the bed. Pull back only enough, so when I lay her down on it, I am blessed to watch the way her hair fans out around her. I stretch out next to her, gazing down at how beautiful she is right now.

And because I'm certain no one has ever told her so, I do just that. "*Es muy bonita. Eres la mujer más hermosa que he visto. El amor de mi vida, mi futuro, mi alma gemela, la mujer con la que elijo compartirme. Te quiero, Vi.*" (So beautiful. You, flower, are the most beautiful woman I've ever laid eyes on. The love of my life, my future, my soul mate, the woman I choose to share myself with. I love you, Vi.)

The smile that overtakes her face warms my heart. Her eyes are a soft brown right now, almost glowing. I only want to give her my best, my all, everything I am.

I place my hand on her stomach and caress it, while I gather the material in my fist. "May I?"

She lifts her hands above her head as an answer, so I tug it up and over. Toss her top on the floor, then run my fingers down her arms until I reach the upper valley of her breasts. My thumb spreads out and catches the strap of her bra and slides underneath it, following along the lacey material, brushing against the side of her breast. Giving me my first experience of how soft these globes are. The smooth protected skin she keeps hidden under her clothing.

Violet's other hand slides between us, and I hear a click as her bra falls open. Then reaching for my hand, she places my palm on her now unprotected flesh. Her warm soft breast fits almost perfectly in my hand and it has me giving it a gentle squeeze.

Her eyes flutter closed, so I don't feel guilty about glancing down so I can stare at them. They are more stunning than I imagined they'd be. Pale peach, perfect globes, with rose-colored nipples that point upward.

I lean down and take her lips with mine. Get lost in the kiss we are sharing. The way this woman tastes is addictive, and I'm not sure I'll ever get enough of her. I only break away when I feel her tug on the back of my t-shirt.

Our eyes lock again and I nod. Only losing contact when the material skates over my head. I take over for her when it gets stuck on my arms. Toss it off for her, landing not all that far from where hers is on the floor.

Feminine hands knead my hard, muscular chest I keep concealed under my clothing. I'm not as fit as my guards, but I like to use the gym they have in the guardhouse basement. Those soft hands trail down the center of my chest to the beginning of my tight stomach. A whimpering sound originates from her, and I am privileged to witness her bite that bottom lip as she agitates her head.

I decide to suck on that lip and draw it into my mouth, nip it gently, raking my teeth along the plump skin. Then I kiss her hard and feel those hands wrap around my back, encouraging me to press our bodies together. The feel of skin on skin has me growling like an animal.

Violet snickers into our kiss, making me pull back so I can look at her. The glow of her skin is so intoxicating, she is intoxicating. Which is why I find myself kissing her jaw, neck, and eventually that spot just below her ear.

When her hands dig into my hair and encourage me to move south, I do. I kiss my way along her collarbone, the swell of her breast until I reach her nipple. I draw back so I can glimpse up at her the moment my tongue darts out to circle the stiff tip. Her hooded eyes are watching me, while her nails are scratching my scalp, sending all kinds of tremors down my spine. I pay homage to her breasts, before deciding I want to kiss every inch of her skin.

My lips are enjoying the softness of her stomach, lost in her scent and sweetness. Once I reach for the clasp of her shorts, I feel her tug on my hair. I then let my eyes find hers. She seems a little anxious about something, therefore I pause for a moment and slide back up her body.

I kiss her lips again until I sense her relaxing, then my hand skims back down to her waistband and I catch her tensing again. "Vi, I do believe these must go if I'm going to make love to you, darling."

"I know. It's just..." she doesn't finish.

"It's just what, love. You can tell me." I kiss her softly, doing my best to encourage her to just say whatever it is she is thinking.

"I'm nervous. I've never done this before. I don't want you to be disappointed. Plus, there are scars." She diverts her eyes to the ceiling. "I have scars that are more visible down there. On my thighs, my hips, along my... and I hate them. You are going to hate them. Maybe we should stop. I don't think I can do this." Her voice shakes, in a way that tells me I need to take this as slow as she needs me to. "I'm sorry."

I get on my knees and hover over her. Straddle her body but don't put any of my weight on her. Getting into her line of view, I do my best to gaze down at her with eyes of understanding.

I remember how she looked when I found her on the bed naked and drugged, right after my cousin had done his absolute worst. The ugly bite marks, both old and new. Nor had I missed the ones that were still visible on her breasts, although I had chosen not to focus on them. The scars did not make her any less alluring in my mind, they proved her impressive strength to endure and survive. Making her even more beautiful in my eyes, the eyes of a man who loved her, all of her, scars and all.

"It's fine, Vi. If you wish to stop, then we will stop. I'll never make you do something you don't want to do. Never. No matter what. That is what love is. Love is allowing the other person equal power over all things. Not being selfish to one's own needs, but understanding the needs of the person you'd die for. You've given me what you can for now, and that is all I will ever ask of you."

Angry, tearful eyes meet mine. Then she voices her true thoughts about it all, using words that express how furious she is. "It's not fucking fine. None of this is fine. I'm not fine. I'm a goddamn broken woman, who will never be anything but broken. And I have no one to blame but myself. I did this to me, to us. I'm the one who made stupid choices that led me to some arsehole who knew exactly what he was doing. I'll never be rid of him, not with all these fucking scars he's left on my body, both inside and out. The only way out of this nightmare is to put a bullet in my brain so I won't have to face the reality I've created."

It kills me to see her in so much pain. To hear that she believes she is broken beyond repair. That's not how I see her at all. What I see is a woman fighting for her freedom, for her life back, for the life she believes her child deserves. She is the one that I will stand firmly by her side and fight right along with her, never letting her give up that fight. And when fighting for herself feels impossible, like it must right now, I'm determined to fight for her.

I suddenly get this idea in my head that I believe might actually help. I know she is likely to think I'm crazy. But I also know how I feel after a round, how the adrenaline pumps through me like a drug. Making me believe I can defeat the biggest of all giants out there, slay them.

"Get up," I instruct her as I crawl off the bed. "Take your bra off and slip my t-shirt on. I'm calling Rico to bring me a gym bag. I don't want him seeing you like that."

She rolls her eyes but does as I ask. Then takes one look at me and decides to make her own observation. "What about seeing you like that?"

"If he were gay, I might be worried," I tell her as I get on my phone and explain to my guards what I am in need of.

"I meant the tent you are sporting, Your Highness. And why the hell do you need boxing gloves?" Violet spaces off for a second and I have to wonder where she's gone.

I should address her for using my title, but I let it go for now. She does that from time to time when she gets a little frustrated. When that smart mouth of hers needs to go off, it usually has me backing her into a corner and ends with me kissing her.

Before I can answer or pounce on her, Rico is at the door. The grin on his face when I open it expresses that he didn't miss my predicament. He hands me the bag and turns to leave without saying a word, exactly like I expected him to do.

I close the door and toss the bag on the floor, bend down and start to remove the items I need. My text tone pings in my pocket, so I pull it out and chuckle. He may not have said it to my face, but it didn't stop him from having a little fun.

> RICO: I've heard of all kinds of foreplay, but this is a first. Might want to make sure she doesn't aim below the belt or you could be out of commission for a while.

JAVIER: Do you need Rico to dig through his supply? We are not judging, but I'm not sure you've thought this through completely. Or maybe you have and... just checking.

GAYLE: Seriously gentlemen. Why are we group texting this shit? But if you must know, the lady has already taken it upon herself to secure an ample supply.

LANEY: Oh yes, that was a fun little run we did for her. Sneaking them into the diaper supply so as not to give her away. So does that mean? I like her for the record. Excellent choice. And mum is the word.

ME: Wow, this isn't awkward at all guys. Can we just drop it? And thanks, I guess for all your concerns. Now mind your own damn business, or shall we discuss why Rico needs a supply to begin with.

I receive two ha ha's, one thumb down, and one angry face. They are not the only ones who know what is going on behind closed doors. I have eyes and ears too.

I stand with the gloves and tape in my hands and come face-to-face with Violet. She is both embarrassed and confused if the expression on her face gives her away. Agitating her head, she points at my phone, rubs her hands over it, and then laughs.

"Something funny?" I ask, smiling.

"Uh... about that. Sorry, I'm a good snoop, read all that. I tried to talk them into letting me go to the store with them. Said I needed to get something personal and didn't want to explain. I even tried to use the excuse that it was a gift I wanted to pick up for you. Said it would be easier if they just let me do it instead of having to describe what it was exactly.

"Laney told me I'd have to speak to you first, and clearly that was not going to happen. It would have been worse bringing that up to you at the time. So I just wrote it down on the list and handed it to them, then briskly walked away." A lovely blush rises from her neck.

"When they dropped off the diapers and you took them, I just about died. Then I died a thousand more deaths once I opened the box and realized what they had done."

"What did they do?" I don't know why I asked, but when it comes to my guards, who knows.

I can only imagine how much those two women enjoyed depleting the condom supply of the local country store about fifty miles away. Those two haven't been with me all that long, just over a year, I guess. But in that time, they've made life interesting. Not just for me, but Rico as well. The man has had to take several long walks to cool down. Then when that didn't work, he... well, let's just say he has his hands full.

"Let's just say we won't run out anytime soon, with so many choices..." She waves her hand around to dismiss the rest and points at my hands. "Why do you have those? Plan on doing a little boxing? Sexually frustrated after I stopped us, so you thought you'd punch something."

I drop the gloves at my feet and motion for her to step forward, then grab one of her hands. "They are for you. No. Maybe a tad frustrated. But if all goes as planned, then once you've had a chance to beat up a few demons, I'll need you to share with me where you stashed that supply."

Her eyebrows rise high on her head. "And who exactly am I supposed to box? Are you going to call one of your trusty guards back so I can give them a good beating?"

Something I enjoy is boxing, but I rarely am allowed to get in a ring. The few times I've amateur boxed, have been when I've slipped past my detail while on a business trip. Entered under a false name and even got knocked around some, although I didn't lose, was able to hold my own. However, the next morning was always interesting. No one goes unscathed when fists are flying. And that is the reason I'm not worried about stepping up tonight to help my woman fight a few dragons.

"Me." I tear off the tape after I have her hand protected correctly and reach for the other one. "And don't worry, I won't hit you back."

She says nothing while I get her ready. I can tell her brain is processing it all carefully. When I slide on the gloves, she just stares at them.

I raise my hands in front of her, flat with my palms facing out. Then I instruct her to give them a blow. She shakes her head and drops her arms to her side.

"Violet, come on. You won't hurt me. I spar with Javier all the time. He's done a little cage fighting, you know MMA. I've even done some amateur boxing myself. Won, in fact. So, I'm not afraid of taking a blow from you."

There is a fire that lights up behind her eyes. "Are you saying I'm just some weak little woman, therefore, I couldn't possibly hurt you?"

My hand drops to protect my still semi-aroused crotch. "Not at all, dear. I'm only saying I can take it. I have no doubt that you will have one hell of a punch. I'm counting on that even."

Lifting my hands again, I place them in front of me and instruct her to hit them.

Violet looks at me like I'm crazy. Maybe I am. Crazy about her, enough to believe that if she does this, then it will at least give her an outlet. I'm not sure she's ever released any of her frustration, tackled it like I plan on doing. Sometimes the best way to move past something you feel is holding you down is to let it out. For so long she's been holding it in, and when she did fight back against the source holding her back, she paid. She needs a safe place where she can let it all out, so I'm offering it to her now.

"Come on. Give it a try," I encourage her.

She lifts her hands and punches. Not like I want her to, or even with any force behind it. She does it again, except there's no drive, no heart to it.

"Come on, Vi. Hit me." I take her hand and slam it into mine. "I can take it, babe. Let me have it."

I let her do it her way a few more times before I try something different. Because her way isn't cutting it. She's only going through the motions; I need her to dig deep and let it out.

Moving in behind her, I lift her arms, position her hands in a good fighting position. I place my hands over her gloves and show her how to throw a solid punch at the air. Then I move in next to her, encourage her to mimic me, teach her how to put her entire body into it. When I see she is doing better, I move in front of her again and direct her to hit me.

But she's not willing to let go like I think she needs to. Therefore, I go about it differently. Revert to my days when I first started boxing. Remember how I finally got past my father's untimely death. How I had to face those demons in my mind and then beat the ever-living hell out of them.

"Do you trust me?" I place my hands on her shoulders.

"With my life. You know that right. That you are the only person I've ever trusted." Violet's eyes begin to glisten. "I love you, Lorenzo. Deep down inside of me kind of love, the kind of love that you have to put all your trust in that person. So, you bet your sweet arse I trust you."

I so love hearing her say those words, that I almost forget what I was going to do. Once I kiss the hell out of her for putting that kind of trust in me, I hold her at arm's length and give her a few instructions.

"Close your eyes. And listen to me."

As soon as she does, I start by telling her a story about myself. "When my father died, I went through a rough time. I was angry, really angry at the person who took him from me. Angry at how his wife took it upon herself to poison him, her revenge so he couldn't toss her aside. That she not only stole him from me, but Isabel as well. From all of us, really. I couldn't go to her and let it all out because she then took her own life shortly afterward. Nor could I rage at my father for being a selfish son of a bitch. I had to figure a way to get that all out so it didn't eat me from the inside.

"Your life has handed you one crisis after another. It started early on with your parents. That's not your fault, nothing you can do about that. Then you got sucked into a crowd at a vulnerable age. Didn't have the right kind of people around to steer you away, warn you that your choice was going to send you down a very long hard road. And while, yes, it was your choice, those who were supposed to be looking out for you failed to do so, so again not entirely your fault."

I know it hurts her to hear this. The tears running down her face proves that. But I believe she needs to hear it so that what I ask her to do next will be beneficial.

"And to top it off, a man who knew exactly what he was doing to a kid of only seventeen. A kid he refused to touch until she was of legal age for his own benefit. Trapped her in that life, by at first making her feel obligated to his kindness—which was all simply a mirage, allowing him to worm his way into her life. Set her up with some schooling, a dry place to sleep, even covered her expenses. So that later he could remind her of all the things he did for her when he could have just as easily tossed her out on the streets."

Violet interrupts me with a voice full of rage, exactly what I want. "I would have been better off on the streets. Safer. So much safer out there on my own."

"I know, baby." I lean forward and kiss her forehead. "I know."

Taking a deep breath, I continue with my story of her life. "Then he did even worse by you. And he continued to do so for many more years until you reached your breaking point. It was around the same time you met a handsome man who drove you completely out of your mind. And you found yourself not knowing how to get out, away from the one, so you could be with the other. Not only that, but you had a baby girl you had to think of. You felt torn in half, divided and broken, with no clear direction of how to break free without dire consequences. And when you got really brave and thought you'd left it all behind, made your escape from him and your past, you came to realize you brought all of it with you and got really pissed about it."

Violet hiccups as she begins to cry harder. "So, pissed."

"Feel that, Vi. Use that. Focus on it." I advise her while I lift her hands and once again stand in front of her.

This time I leave my arms down. So that when she strikes me, she will hit my chest. I'm not worried she'll hurt me; I can take it. But I want her to strike something solid, and since I don't have a bag, I'm more than willing to stand here and steal her pain away from her.

"Hit me, Vi. Take all that rage you feel inside of you and let it go." I order her and then brace myself. "Picture all those people who let you down and let them have it."

She opens her eyes.

Blinks a few times.

Then let's go.

CHAPTER 15
Violet

The Royals

I 'll admit, I thought this was a really stupid idea. Something a guy would come up with so he could use his fists instead of his words. Most of the guys I'd grown up around were always looking to do exactly that. They would much rather punch the heck out of someone rather than trying to talk through it like a civilized person.

This is why when we first started this ridiculous exercise, I didn't take it seriously. Why I only punched him halfheartedly, so we could get it over with and move on.

But I should have known that would never be worthy of this man. Nope, he didn't give up when he was certain his way would work. He'd proven that over and over again to me. It was why we were here now.

His words did exactly what he intended for them to do. They brought all that rage I'd been holding onto for so many years, right to the surface. I had a lot, by the way. Years that went way beyond the eight years when I was trapped under Ruben's fist. There was no way I'd be able to cleanse it all tonight, but maybe I could deal with the one that was angering me right now.

When I opened my eyes, his face is the first one I see.

Not Lorenzo's. If I'd seen his first, I'd never have been capable of doing what I did next.

No, the face I meet is Ruben's. That evil, smirky fucking grin he wore when he showed up to serve up a punishment he suspected I deserved.

I pulled back and threw a solid punch. Felt my hand hit hard male flesh, and it felt good, so I threw another.

"That's it. Again." Lorenzo encourages me. "Let it all out. Let him have it."

So I did. I started throwing solid punches at his chest. Began striking him in the ribcage, leaving behind red marks I focus on. Doing my best to see how red I could make them. Then I did one better and started using my words.

"Arsehole. How's that feel? Not so tough now, are you, now that you can't fight back. You want some more. How about that?" I hit him hard in the gut.

I hear Lorenzo grunt, but he doesn't stop me.

"Pussy." I punch him again in the same spot. "*Podgotovsja, madak.*"

Three more solid blows, and then I spit on him like Ruben had done to me so many times. "You disgust me. I'm done with you. Done. Finished. No more."

Punch. Punch. Punch. All done in rapid jabs.

"You could only get it up when you were angry with me, no more. I'm not going to be your *suka. Pizdets.*"

And then I lose it. I mean seriously lose my control. I beat the hell out of his chest with the sides of my gloved hands. My fists pounding into him hard. The tears from all the hurt that arsehole ever caused me washes free of me and streams down my face.

Ten minutes is how long I carry on, until there is no more fight left in me. I collapse against the chest I was pounding on and begin placing soft kisses all over it. It is red from the blows I took out on it, and I hate that this man is the one suffering when it should be another. I kiss them, hoping to soothe the pain I caused him, the pain he freely accepted without complaint.

I take a step back and lift my hands. "Get these off of me."

Lorenzo nods, leans down, and kisses me first. "Better?"

He pulls off the gloves and begins removing the tape. I notice my knuckles are slightly reddened, although they don't hurt.

My eyes find his. I'm no longer apprehensive about the ugly scars that mark my body. All I care about is having this man. I want it all with him. Everything that he is willing to give me, I want it.

Words cannot possibly express what I am experiencing at the moment. So, I forego them and jump him instead. I'm not sure exactly what comes over me, I've never gone through so much before. Never felt so raw, while at the same time experiencing a deep, intense emotional draw toward this man.

I want all of it. I want to touch him. To welcome him to touch me. Everywhere and I want it right now.

I am kissing his chest again, where he still wears my blows. His hands are stroking my hair lovingly. Always with him, it is only ever done lovingly. He doesn't guide me but allows me to decide all on my own what my next move will be.

I've never willingly done what I am about to do. My eyes skate up his body, to find brown aroused ones gazing down at me in awe. And that's all I need to see, so I can do what I desire to do for me. I have to do this to take back my freedom. Plus, it is something I want to give him, something I'm certain he'd never ask me for.

I kiss his stomach as my hands find the snap to his shorts. I undo them and then release the zipper, shoving them over his hips.

"Vi." His voice is deep, deeper than I've ever heard it before.

"Shh." I kiss the trail that disappears behind the waistband of his briefs.

One of his hands grips my hair tighter, while the other continues to stroke it. He involuntarily pulls it when I slide my fingers under the band, tugging his briefs carefully down his thighs. And to my surprise, I find I like how it feels, probably because he's not doing it to cause pain or guide me, only doing it instinctively.

This man puts all other men to shame, by the way. At least the men I've had the unfortunate favor of seeing. I nearly chuckle, but don't because I don't want to give Lorenzo the wrong idea. I keep it to myself and just admire him.

"Beautiful," I whisper before I kiss the tip of his prince size crown, letting it slip between my eager lips.

Both hands dig into my hair now, tugging gently. Suddenly he begins speaking beautiful words in Spanish, Portuguese, and what I suspect is French. All while he watches me work him over like I am confident no other has ever done before me. It is something I never was willing to do until this very moment.

I recognize when he is about to lose it, spill into my mouth. I always hated it when Ruben made me swallow his. Would force... you get the point. My plan had been to get Lorenzo to that point, but not necessarily swallow.

"Vi, you don't... I'm..." he places his palm on my forehead, encouraging me to release him.

I swat at his hand, take him deeper. And am rewarded with his words, along with the taste of him. I don't release him until he stops pulsing in my mouth. I am immediately scooped up off the floor into his arms and kissed aggressively.

My back lands on the bed close to where we started. A large body presses into me shortly after my body settles. Before I realize it, his t-shirt is being torn from my body so he can do his best to drive me insane. Lips so soft meet my flesh, heating all of me in ways it never has experienced before. My breasts are worshipped, not tormented like those previous to this man always treated them. He is showing me how different it is to be loved by a man rather than owned by one.

I don't protest this time when he dislodges my shorts. Instead, I watch as he continues worshiping my body like only he can. Nearly melting when he runs his nose along the seam of my center and inhales. It's such an intimate act, a personal act that I shouldn't enjoy so much.

What Lorenzo is doing to me, I've never had the pleasure of experiencing before. No man has made my flesh light up in such a way. My pleasure was never a concern until him. I didn't even really understand what was going on with my body. Didn't understand why my brain was advising me to stop fighting against it and just let go. And when his tongue licks me like I'm a delicious treat, hitting a hot spot repeatedly, my body wins the battle. I fall into a spiral of desire, as my flesh tingles in places I never knew it could. It continues until he stops his vicious worshipping. I'm vibrating from it all and breathing heavily, gripping the sheets with my fist to keep me from withering away.

His lips are once again kissing up my stomach, making their way to my lips. When he kisses me, I swear he's never tasted better, felt better against mine. Nothing has ever felt this incredible, and I'm not even close to being done with him yet.

"Top side dresser drawer," I pant out when he comes up for air. "I'll help you put it on."

He grins down at me like he's never been happier than he is right now. "Help me? You think I'll need help?"

I kiss his chest when he stretches out to grab a condom out of the drawer. "I have more experience than you, so I just thought..."

Lorenzo slides back to settle over me, I can detect his large erection nudging my leg. "I'll have you know that my very promiscuous father taught all his teenage sons how to apply a condom by the age of fourteen. He regularly supplied them even, made sure we changed out the one he insisted we carry in our wallets once a month. Didn't want us getting caught without one, or with one that was damaged. He was very vigilant about that.

"Now granted, he died when I was seventeen. I stopped the practice as soon as I realized I'd not need one at a moment's notice. But that doesn't mean I've forgotten all those lessons he gave us." He displays the strip of condoms he grabbed, waving them playfully. "Although he had one rule I'm about to break."

I yank the strip from his hand and tear one off. "What rule was that?"

"Never accept a condom you didn't purchase yourself." He leans down and kisses my lips softly. "He told us that women couldn't be trusted, ever."

I nod. Blink slowly.

"He was wrong, though. Mainly because he himself couldn't be trusted, therefore he didn't trust either." Propping up on his knees so he can suit up, he removes the package from my hand. "Didn't understand that the reason he never trusted one was because he only loved himself. I however love you, therefore I trust you completely."

And then I watch him roll it on expertly, a sight I know shouldn't make me feel what I'm feeling. "Lenny, I love you."

He growls as he leans in to kiss me. "I love hearing you say that name. Only those closest to me ever call me that, and no one will ever know me like you."

After a slow, intimate kiss, he sits back on his heels. Drags my legs over his spread thighs so he can see what he is doing. His fingers are the first to intrude my warmth, moving in and out slowly while he explores.

"Lorenzo, please," I beg as he drags his long fingers along my walls, sending all kinds of heat to my core. "I need you."

He doesn't make me beg again. After he spreads my lubrication onto the condom, he aligns himself and gazes up at me. As he enters me this very first time, he watches while I watch him. Blessed to catch the tension in his neck, the way his nostrils flare. How he rakes his teeth over that bottom lip of his, making it turn almost white. An incredible vision that has me bucking my hips upwards.

A sharp gasp escapes him as his head rolls back. "*É magnífico*. It feels like home. Warm, cozy, welcoming. I do believe this is the last place I want to be when I die. Making love to the woman I love more than life itself. You are my home, Vi, the place I will always return to and cherish. My sanctuary. My comfort. My forever."

He says all those lovely words while looking at me, right before he begins moving at a slow torturous pace. In and out, slowly. Not even all the way in, only as far as this position will permit. And I need more, I demand all of him, every last inch.

I've never taken the initiative before, never on my own took over so I could get what I craved. Every other time, until now, it was never about me. I was usually so drugged out of my mind that I didn't feel much of anything. And the times I wasn't, the last thing I cared about was pleasure, there was no pleasure in it for me.

This thankfully was different. Everything was different. I wanted to do this for me, for him. I needed this for us because this is how I always imagined it would be when I made love to the man I fell in love with. We'd give and take, both of us giving everything we had, wanted, and not once stopping to reflect. Just enjoying the moment as we expressed our love using our bodies.

And in case you were wondering, that is exactly how it feels right now. Like the rest of the world has disappeared and all that matters is us.

I let everything else fall away while we did something a little selfish for once, greedy for how much closer this was making us.

"My turn," I warn him as I sit up and push him back.

He laughs but doesn't fight me. Falls onto the foot of the bed, readjusting us so he is comfortable until I am hovering above him. He's still partially inside me, his hands now on my hips, holding me there while we rearrange.

"Was I not doing it right?" He teases, knowing good and well what he was doing was fine.

I gather my hair over one shoulder. Place my hands on his strong biceps before wiggling my hips so he will loosen his grip, allowing me to move. Without saying a word, I lower my body onto his slowly, painfully slowly for both of us it seems. Then I find a steadier rhythm, one I can also tell he appreciates. And when that rhythm doesn't seem to be doing it for me anymore, I move faster, take him deeper. Until I sense myself losing all control and it becomes wild, frantic, and we are grasping for the ultimate high together.

We reach it at the same time, staring into each other's eyes when we do. All I see at that point is him. All I feel is him. It is as if we fade into each other, giving a part of ourselves to the other, interweaving our souls.

I fall forward onto his chest and bury myself in his scent. Soak in the fact that I'm humming in the best of ways, not at all suffering the need to escape. My mind is reveling in how he knew exactly what to do so we could share this. Thankful that I found him, giving me the chance to experience this.

Suddenly I start laughing when the man below me speaks. I can honestly admit I never dreamed I'd laugh after sex, that I'd be so happy or relaxed to do so.

"Well, it's a good thing I employ guards looking out for my best interest. We are going to deplete that supply they provided for us rather quickly." He informs me as he rolls us over and slides out, removing the used condom.

Again, he is back in front of me, smiling. He is stroking my hair, my arm, my face. His eyes staring at me like no other man ever has before, and it's the last thing I see or experience before I fade off.

A FEW HOURS LATER, I startle, nearly jumping out of my skin when I notice an arm draped over me. I've never woken up next to a man before, not in this way, at least. I don't want to reflect on all the other times one has woken me.

Once my brain realizes the difference, I sense the tension leave my body. The arm wrapped around me tightens, and a light snoring sound invades my ear.

What the fuck have I done? I mean holy mother of all that is, that was the best damn sex of my life. It was everything I ever dreamed it would be and so much more. But I've dragged this lovely man into the darkness with me, stole his virginity that he surprisingly has held on to for twenty-three years. He was saving it for the woman he...

"Stop," his voice mumbles sleepily. "You are overthinking again."

A small smile grows on my face. "How do you know that?"

"Because Vi, I know you. You think you defiled me. That you've corrupted a prince who was saving himself for the perfect woman. Newsflash Vi, I was saving myself for you." He squeezes again and then lets his hand slide between my thighs. "Do I need to prove that to you again?"

My legs open voluntarily, and a small moan escapes before I can stop it. "Maybe you should."

Lorenzo laughs, "Maybe I should."

I'm on my back before I know it. All thoughts shoved aside. I'm sure I'll revisit them from time to time, and if I'm lucky, he'll read me like a book and remind me why I need to stop. God, I hope I have those thoughts daily so I can experience this.

CHAPTER 16
Lorenzo

The Royals

I've woken every morning staring at her face for the last three weeks. Admired her while she slept soundly next to me. It gave me the chance to memorize just how stunning she was. Count the freckles faintly under her eyes, speckles that could barely be detected unless you were looking for them. Began to understand why they called that little brown mark above the left side of her lip a beauty mark. Loved how her hair was all messy, due to the fact we'd rolled around together in the sheets before falling to sleep.

Three weeks have passed since that first time when we allowed our bodies to dance together. And each time after has only seemed to get better, more desperate actually. It was as if we couldn't wait for the day to pass so we could fall back into each other's arms again. Love the other completely, in ways neither of us has ever felt or loved another before.

Last night, we had to forgo the actual act itself, because we had depleted our supply. So, we'd found other ways to satisfy that hunger. I'd enjoyed her body, every inch of it. Just like it seemed she enjoyed mine.

The only reason I am climbing out of bed now is because I hear Charlotte's tiny voice calling. She now sleeps in the other room alone in the big bed. Wasn't really comfortable clambering out of it on her own, thankfully. Had no problem letting us know when she was ready to get up though, or even if she needed something.

As soon as I step through the doorway, she stands up and calls for me. "Papá, I up?"

I never realized how priceless that one word was until her voice first said it. Now every time she calls me papá or daddy, my heart swells, and a lump forms in my throat.

"Good morning, Char." I scoop her into my arms and those little arms hug my neck.

"Mummy sleep you?"

She has asked me that every morning since Violet joined me in my bedroom. I'm not so sure she is happy that I stole her mother from her during the night. Although she sleeps fine without her, equally as well as she did with her. There is just something that tells me she misses her snuggle time, which I get. Until now, their time was extremely limited, only stealing moments when Ruben allowed.

We have our own routine in the mornings while we wait for Violet to wake. It involves a little cuddling on the couch while I catch up on the morning show. Later I browse through a few emails marked urgent, while we sip on our drinks of choice. Breakfast may or may not be served, depending on how the morning plays out. But no matter what, the little one stays glued to my side. Soaks in as much of the time we have together, in that way that makes me understand she has experienced way too much during her young age. She is starving for the kind of affection she is now receiving, waiting for it to all disappear and go back to how it has always been.

Violet usually strolls out a half-hour later, making a beeline for the coffee first. Once she has sucked down a cup and refilled it, she typically joins us on the couch. Immediately reaching for her daughter, who is more than ready for mummy time. They snuggle for a good ten minutes before I even get a proper hello.

And I don't mind, because I love watching them, witnessing the love they share. The bond between mother and child is strong. One thing my cousin couldn't break, even though he tried to do so. It was a bond that was made during those months the little one was growing inside of her.

And since this morning we haven't made it to the breakfast table, I stand and start making it for us. Just like all those times before, I can sense them watching me, hear them softly mumbling.

"You need help?" Violet asks when she joins me in the kitchen.

"Nope." I point to the table, the same as I do most mornings. "Usual or something different this morning?"

"Usual is fine. You know I don't mind helping, although I must admit, watching you does things to me." She drags her hand along my arse on her way to the table, sending a jolt directly to my crotch. "We should make a run into town this afternoon."

"Behave," I tell her as I adjust myself, catching the smirk that does nothing to calm my libido.

I get Charlotte's breakfast first, so Violet can get her started. Then I begin fixing ours, which consists of a few eggs, toast, and ham. By the time I'm bringing our plates to the table, the little one is doing her best to feed herself. She is the cleanest eater I know, and I have to wonder if that has more to do with the way others have trained her to be. It's a slow, meticulous process that she is determined to get through without assistance.

I've had a few matters on my mind these last couple of days. And while I watch my girls closely, those thoughts only grow and turn into something I decide needs to be taken care of immediately.

Rising to my feet, I make my way back into the bedroom, retrieve what I have been hiding for quite a while now. Long before Violet and I changed up the dynamics of our relationship. I've known what I wanted since the days I sat with her in the hospital.

When I sit back down in my seat, Violet does a double-take. Her eyes fixate on the small white box. The fork drops onto her plate as they slowly rise to find mine. Expressive eyes that tell me she believes I've lost my mind.

I don't believe I have; therefore, I open the box and wait for her to fully understand just how serious I am. Although she refuses to even glimpse down again, not until her daughter speaks.

"Oh, petty. For Mummy. Mummy, like?"

Violet nods slowly as tears fill her eyes once she catches what Char is talking about.

It's nothing really special. Not something I imagine others would assume a prince would buy for his betrothed. They'd expect the works, something that made a statement and was eye-catching.

My brother, the king, caught all kinds of static for not buying his wife something bigger, or even giving her the family heirloom. But he knew Larkin, bought her exactly what would be the most fitting for her, what she would love. And she had loved it, wears it with pride in fact to this very day. Stares at it often as if she is remembering the day that he gave it to her, a memory only they share.

I found myself in a jewelry store I strolled by while the ladies were shopping. When I saw this ring in the display case, it spoke to me. Its twisted white gold band looks like a vine, almost holding up the round purple stone embedded within it. An amethyst I learned was its name. While it wasn't necessarily elegant or high-priced, it was something I could picture Violet wearing proudly. A ring she'd not be overcautious about wearing, feel comfortable with it on. And that meant more to me than the price. A price tag cannot determine something's value, much like a title does not determine a person's worth.

Clearing her throat, she does a quick scan around the room, herself, her daughter, and even me. I recognize what she is going to say before she says it.

"I don't think this..." Violet gestures with her hands.

"Please don't think. Hear me out." I reach for her hand, taking it in mine. "Tell me how you always imagined this moment happening. I know how I imagined it, let me share.

"The woman I love, which happens to be you, would be with me. We'd be sitting around spending a day together when it hit me right here." I tap my chest with my hand, precisely where my heart is. "And I'd just know. Know that from this day going forward, life without her just wouldn't be enough. That living without the other half of myself, the woman who completed me, the one that knows me better than anyone else, wasn't an option any longer. So, I'd decide to do something about it. Let her know, just in case she didn't yet. And later I'd pray that she feels the same, because if she doesn't..."

Violet whispers, "She does, she most certainly does."

I know I must be beaming like a teenage boy, one who just found out the girl he likes, likes him back. Probably bigger, maybe like a man who recently learned the love of his life feels the same as he.

I pick up the box, do what every man does when he realizes it's over for him. Dropping on one knee in front of her, I take her left hand in mine and kiss it. I gaze up at her with hope, hope that she saves me with the correct answer to my next question. "Vi, will you do me the honor of becoming my wife?"

She doesn't though. Nothing is ever black and white with this woman, and her words prove that. "You can't be serious. I mean, can you imagine the..."

My finger presses against her lips. "Hush. I can imagine it, not just imagine it, but see it plainly. You, Charlotte, and me as a family. A family that was always meant to be. Does it look perfect? No. But I was never looking for perfect, I myself am not perfect. So how could I expect a perfect family without faults? It's the imperfection that makes this family unique and strong. What bonds us together has to do with the way we have accepted each other's imperfections, love them."

"You don't have imperfections." She discloses and I find myself laughing.

"Trust me, I have them. I'm not perfect, Vi. Not even close. Don't let the title fool you into buying into the myth that those of us who live a privileged life are superior to the rest of you. We in fact are quite the opposite, most are way worse than the average citizen. So many of us are so far removed, that we don't even realize how truly messed up we are. I've made mistakes."

"People expect..."

"Don't get me started on what I think about what people expect. I never once cared what others think or expect. I've marched to the beat of my own drum, always done things the way I wanted to do them. All of us have, in fact.

"My mother was the first. She showed us the way to a happier life, wasn't always doing what was expected of you, it was doing what you considered was best. It took courage for her to step away and make demands to the most powerful man in our country. She did so because she was tired of people expecting her to quietly accept an adulterous husband, all because of his title. She did so, so that my siblings and I didn't have to live up to all those expectations. Making it so we could pave our own paths, with a few expectations of our own.

"Both my brothers followed suit. They didn't fall in line when those around were pressuring them to do so. Went after what they wanted, in the way they wanted it, not caring what others around them thought.

"Now it's my turn. And you, Vi, you and Charlotte, are that for me. It doesn't matter what others will say. They will say it no matter what I do, have opinions they shouldn't voice. Why should my life be so different from everyone else's? Why should I not be allowed to be with the woman I love, just because she doesn't fit the mold they've constructed. I'm not interested in their ideas of how I should live my life, I don't want the life they want for me. I want this life."

I encase her in my arms and get as close to her as I can. "Have I not shown you that these last three weeks? Have I not expressed it well enough for you to understand how much I love you? I love you, Vi. Love you so much, that without you both, I do not exist."

Violet jostles her head deliberately as she speaks, or more like stumbles through her words. "I have never felt more loved in my entire life, Lorenzo. Never. I know you love me, us. I don't understand how or why, but I know it. You've done an adequate job, more than adequate, at expressing yourself in more than one way in fact. Not only when we are alone." The way she blushes brings up so many intimate memories. "But also, in all the things you do for us, how you take care of us. The fact that you are here with us now, when in reality you probably should be anywhere but with us."

"I am where I am meant to be, where I will always be from this day forward." I remind her.

"I know. And I am grateful for it."

"Don't be grateful." I realize I sound a little irritated, that my voice is giving away the fact I am getting a little scared she is about to turn me down.

"Will you let me finish? You can be so very irritating, you know when you believe things are not going your way." She sasses, coercing a grin out of me. I do so love her sass.

"By all means, please forgive me."

"All is forgiven. I'm sorry to inform you, but it seems you will forever be stuck with us because I too cannot imagine facing this world without you next to me."

"Is that a yes?" I ask hopeful.

"Yes, it's a definite yes."

I grab her face and kiss her, almost forgetting that we are sitting at the table with little eyes watching us. But her little giggle reminds me quickly enough, so I pull back and find the box with the ring, then I slide it on Violet's finger, admiring how lovely my ring looks there.

"How long have you been holding onto this?" Violet asks, her eyes fixed on the ring as well.

"A while," I tell her as I take my seat again, feeling a little happier than I did when I woke.

Charlotte is ready to get down and begin playing, so Violet lets her. Watches her run off to the area where several toys have been placed just for her. Bought specifically for her, even though her mother didn't consider it necessary. However, I did, and I may have gone overboard, but so be it. She loved everything I had gotten her. The dolly, the little kitchen, the riding toy, the blocks, and a few other items I won't bother to mention.

After a few minutes, Violet stands and gestures for me to move so she can sit in my lap. Without a thought, I oblige, settling in for whatever she has in mind.

"You do realize we can't actually get married, not until this mess has been properly dealt with." I can identify what she thinks about that fact in her voice, she's not exactly thrilled about the reality she is sharing with me. "Last time Karina called..."

I don't need her to remind me what my sister-in-law shared with us a few days ago. The situation back home wasn't getting any better, not really. Ruben and Lady Amber were only allowing us this time because they had no other option but to do so. They had learned rather quickly how easy it was for me to cause them some issues where business was concerned. Not to mention the fact his father wasn't at all pleased with him at the moment. But our time was running out, and soon we would have to return and deal with it all head-on.

"As soon as this mess is dealt with, though. Before the ink can dry." I squeeze her. "Don't worry about all that. As far as I am concerned, we are already a family, one that cannot be torn apart. As solid as any family that has that slip of paper legitimizing it. Stronger even really, because we also have love, there are so many that do not possess the bond of love to hold them together."

"There will be those who do not agree with you. Those who will fault us for living together before taking the vow. Frown on me as the one who corrupted a member of the royal family. Accuse me of manipulating you during my time in the king's office, so I could get out from under an equally powerful man. They will say I saw an opportunity and took advantage of your kindness, saw it as my way out of a life I myself had created."

I hate hearing how all those things others will say makes her feel. Not everyone is used to this life inside a fishbowl. It is hard handling all the faces staring at them from behind the glass, judging every move they make. Violet's entire life will be dug through and exposed for all others to rummage through. Many will judge her, even though they have no right to do so. And if I could, I'd not let it happen, I would keep her and Charlotte inside of a protective bubble.

So far, only a small portion of the truth has come out. The people are aware she is tied somehow to Ruben Del Markov. That she and I are involved, and that he is unhappy with me about the fact it seems I have stolen her away from him.

Most are speculating she is one of many mistresses, one that he placed inside the palace as a spy. They have it in their minds that during her time there, she discovered how much animosity our families held against the other. Somehow got to me and then swayed me into believing a few untruths about their relationship. Suggesting even, that she misrepresented herself and her situation, just so she could gain the support of my family and myself. All of which had allowed her to live a new and improved life.

The truth, all of it, is what I see as the only way to convince them how very wrong they are. If we come clean. Use it to our advantage, before Ruben spreads more lies or does something unthinkable. Then we may possibly gain a few allies. I know it's a risk, but I also understand how gaining the peoples' trust in us, my family, her. I understand what that can do.

"Then we make them see the truth. We expose the man who has been holding you down for so many years. Use their compassion for all the oppressed women of our country, who have been forced into a course of life by the powerful. Force them to understand that your situation does not differ from those women of high society. Perhaps even worse, because you had no one to help you fight against it. You were not even given the respect every person deserves. And tormented not only by him but also his wife, who knew what her husband was doing and didn't put a stop to it. Even agreed to his behavior by accepting the child he shared with you as her own. Allowed him to hold that child over your head as a way to keep you in line. We share it all, from the very beginning up to the day when I found out the truth.

"Give them a true Cinderella story. One that will grant them no choice but to appreciate all the reasons I fell in love with you. Recognizing that you are the strongest woman I've ever known. A woman willing to live a life on the run, alone, in hopes to save her child from a madman and his equally unstable wife. It was I who decided you shouldn't have to do it unaccompanied. That you needed a little assistance, someone eager to fight with you and for you. A prince in my own right, who was eager to assist in slaying the dragon trying to destroy you."

Through the tears, I am privileged to one of the best eye rolls yet. "You do have a way with words, Your Highness."

"I do my best when it suits me. It is the easiest way to get ahead of them Vi. Do you trust me?"

Her eyes express that she does, the words only confirm it for me. "With my life and that of my child's."

CHAPTER 17
Violet

The Royals

A week later we are on a plane that will take us back to Hermosa Islas. We are hitching a ride with the King and Queen since they came to the U.S. for a visit with her parents in the DC area.

The tension in the air can be felt physically. Not so much regarding me or Charlotte, but between the brothers. And I hate that I am the reason for the strain circling this family when I never once intended to come between any of them. Even though I have apparently been in the middle of a war without realizing it. Having a relationship with a long-lost cousin they deemed the enemy had secured my place on the battlefield I didn't even know I was standing on.

Isabel is with them, of course. She travels with the king during the summer months, always has according to the young chatty princess. It's the first time I have ever really spent any time with the youngest Reyes. And while I know she is their half-sibling, none of them treat her as one. She is just as much a part of their original family unit. Raised predominantly by King Antonio, even though all of them have taken a hand at raising her after her parents' deaths. And are all noticeably very close, despite the sizeable age gap.

She is also very willing to step in and assist me with Charlotte. Sat

144

down on the floor and played with her like an older sibling, or perhaps in her case like an aunt might do. And of course, my baby girl is soaking it up, eager to secure Isabel's attention for as long as she can.

When it becomes apparent a nap is required, Lorenzo takes over much like he has while we've been together. Settling his little Char in his lap after turning on a movie, cuddling her right in until she passes out. Then nods off as well, since he is stuck where he sits, with a very clingy child attached to him until she wakes. Not that he minds, I know he does not. He has expressed that so many times whenever she has chosen him as her snuggle buddy. Plus, I do not miss the smile he shoots me as soon as she is passed out and snuggles in.

And neither did my queen.

"The young prince seems taken by your lovely little girl. I'm not surprised, really. These men, they are in a class all their own. The first time I met them, they made me feel right at home." Queen Larkin sits down, her rounded belly barely noticeable, making her look lovely.

"He is very good with her." I stare at him because I can't help myself.

"And you both are good for him. If I am overstepping here, please feel free to tell me." When I glimpse her way, she smiles and glances down, as if I am supposed to know what that means. "Is the baby Lorenzo's or were you already... sorry, I should've just left it alone. Never mind."

I wobble my head, confused on why she assumes there is a baby at all. "I'm not... why would you think..."

But before I can get my words out completely, a wave of nausea washes over me. All day, I have been writing these spells off as my nerves. Anxious ones that arose due to what I was about to face once we returned home. Topped with the fact, I was in the company of the King and Queen, after running off without a word of my departure to my boss, a man I respect completely. He hired me to do a job I was failing at currently, all because I had been living a double life. Between the feelings of guilt and uncertainty, they both seemed reasonable explanations on why I felt a little off.

I swallow hard to keep it at bay, then try my best to offer a solid defense on why that isn't possible. Not realizing that I could be revealing more than I actually planned to. "I have an IUD, so that's not possible."

Another woman I don't know takes a seat next to mine, hands me a ginger ale. "When was it put in?"

"I'm sorry, what? And you would be?" I place a hand on my forehead, experiencing the start of a headache to accompany my sour stomach.

She only smiles, not at all offended by my attitude or question. "Dr. Devon Wilson, the queen's physician."

Larkin huffs out a sarcastic sound. "She is traveling with us because my husband insisted that I could not possibly travel without her. I didn't argue since she comes whenever we call at the oddest of times, even. Figured she deserves a free vacation at the expense of the king if only to keep him from driving me insane." Just when I expect she will leave it at that, Larkin adds, "So, it's not possible because of the IUD?"

I'm not sure I like what she is insinuating, although I don't have time to address it. My stomach alerts me that if I don't make my way to the lavatory soon, it will be too late to do so. Therefore, instead of debating it out with the queen, and providing her with way more information on the subject, I rise to my feet and hurry off.

In case you were wondering, private jet lavatories are much nicer than public airline lavatories. Roomier thankfully, so that when I do empty my stomach into the toilet, I can do so with a little dignity. Not much really, but a little.

I stand and grab one of the washcloths from the stack and get it wet. Use it to clean off my mouth and damp the clammy skin on my neck and forehead. I grip the sink and stare at my reflection, all while I do the math in my head.

One thing I know for certain is that if I'm pregnant, there is only one man who can be faulted as the father. I've had my usual cycles to all but eliminate Ruben from having been successful after he put me in the hospital following our long traumatic weekend together. Plus, according to my doctor, they administered the morning-after pill once a rape was suspected. A precaution practiced on all victims of rape in our country, to prevent a horrible situation from possibly becoming even worse.

The possibility is low with the IUD, accompanied by our vigilance about using condoms. So many freaking condoms. One might reason we should have invested in those companies that manufacture them.

We'd had a few mishaps, of course, like I'm sure several other people in our situation have had. One broke—more like split right down the middle, starting at the tip. It happens, and because I wasn't worried about a pregnancy, more concerned about him catching something from me because of Ruben, I'd even joked with him about it. Said that was probably the reason his father had been so adamant about not accepting one from any of those eager girls so desperate to trap him.

He'd responded with a shrug and one eyebrow lifted, kissed me like no one else ever had, then spoke the right words to calm me down again. *"I'd love to be trapped by you, Vi. Trap me if you must, so I can never be free of you."*

I'd slapped him in the arse and then squealed when he flipped us over so he could grab another condom. We'd moved on after that, forgotten all about it. Not even a mention of it later, as if we were invincible and beyond capable of getting caught with our pants down.

"Fuck," I declare loudly. So loudly that I'm positive someone probably overheard me. So, before I say it again, three more times, I cover my mouth and let it all out.

And then I stare at myself, noting how sickly I look. Bloodshot eyes with dark bags underneath. A pale complexion that presents that puny appearance, suggesting I'm just not myself. It reminds me of another time when I was in denial about being pregnant. When I wrote all these same symptoms off as a stomach virus that was moving through the city at the time.

This is not happening.

This cannot be happening.

Why does my life always have to revolve around drama, accompanied by these situations where I always seem to fall flat on my face? I have no one to blame again but myself, really. And this time, I've dragged a man not deserving into it down with me.

I even know what he'll say about it. He'll claim he is just as responsible for getting us into this newest mess as me. That he could have said no. Stopped it from happening.

But had I not been the aggressor...

A knock on the door cuts short my train of thought. The voice that follows has me sinking onto the seat of the toilet, so I can drop my head in my hands and cry.

"Vi, is everything okay?" he asks so concerned.

"No," I mumble out between sobs, not meaning for him to hear.

He tries the flimsy handle, then gives it a good shove when he discovers it's locked. Easily busting in to find me in the worst way possible.

I have so many emotions circling inside my brain right now. I'll list them for you.

I've ruined his life, his family's reputation, put them back a hundred years.

Know what people are going to call me. Slut. Whore. Gold Digger. They will assume I did this on purpose. Planned it out. Trapped him.

Corrupted the royal family with my DNA. An unworthy bottom feeder, who mixed it up with one of the most elite families out there, and have now ruined centuries of a prestigious bloodline.

I hate myself for my next thoughts. Thoughts admitting how I am a tad bit excited to be carrying this man's child. Knowing how different it will be with him.

I've witnessed him loving the daughter I already have these last few months. Me witnessing that was one reason I fell in love with him.

And I hate that I know with this news, if there is any news, would mean we'd forever be tied to the other person. It's what I wanted, why I agreed to marry him, right? Although I didn't intend for it all to play out like this, in this order.

"Hey," his hand caresses the crown of my head. "It's going to be okay."

"I have to tell you something. The queen pointed it out to me. I never realized how observant she is, until now." I glance up at him to find those ever-supportive eyes gazing right back at me. "I love you."

"I love you too. What is it? Does it have to do with something my brother said or did? He asked me when you'd be allowed to return to the office. Seems he and Esteban have been doing some plotting while we've been running around. Not to mention, he claims none of the replacements they've had step in, during your absents, have been adequate."

"No. It's not about work, it has to do with us."

Lorenzo nods slowly, almost as if he isn't surprised. "She mentioned that we seemed to have grown rather close during our time together. I didn't deny it, but I also didn't elaborate."

"She wanted to know if you were the father of my baby." I see no other way around the subject, so I decide to blurt it out.

Lorenzo laughs. "Oh, wow. Did you tell her that would make matters easier if I were? Nearly impossible, but easier nonetheless. I'd claim Char as mine, plan on doing just that, very soon in fact."

I already knew his plans where Charlotte was concerned. It would not be easy, but he was not about to allow a man like Ruben to have anything to do with her. He'd become a father to her, felt protective of her, was determined to take that role over for him, with or without his permission.

"Not Char." I watch him blink as he processes my words.

"What baby then?" He innocently asks before it hits him and his eyes glance downward. "Are you? Why didn't you say anything?"

I shrug, shake my head, make a few motions with my hands as I wave them around. "I told you I have an IUD. The chance is extremely slim, but I guess nothing is absolute in preventing one, except abstinence. And we haven't been practicing that for nearly a month now. We had a mishap a few times, ones we laughed off. I'm sorry."

He takes several noticeable breaths while he thinks. "There is only one way to be certain."

Now I laugh sarcastically, not sure he's thought this through. "Yes, I guess you are right. But that will have to wait until we land. Unless there is a chemist nearby, one we can pull over to along the way, so we can buy one, that is."

He doesn't laugh though, instead, he stands and tugs on my hand. "Or we could ask the expert onboard."

"What? No. No, that isn't necessary." I don't want to make a big deal out of this with his brother and wife with us. It's bad enough she is the one who pointed it out to me. "I'm sure it's just my nerves."

"I'm not willing to take my chances, Vi." And that is said in a tone that leaves no room for me to argue, not that it stops me.

"Well, excuse me, Your Highness. I was mistaken, thinking this is my body we are discussing here." I spit out, sounding almost hateful.

I find myself shoved inside a stateroom and pressed against the wall just inside the door. "A body I've been buried inside for hours."

I shiver in a good way at his statement. "I remember."

"Then you know how much I adore this body of yours. And that is why I refuse to take any chances with it." I realize his words shouldn't hurt, but for some reason they do.

"You adore my body? So, therefore, you refuse to take chances with it, because it's my body that you're after, what you care about most then." I slide my hands between us to shove him back.

"Don't do that. Don't put words in my mouth, or twist them. I do adore this body; love all the things it does to mine. But you know very well what I meant was that I won't take chances with you. You, Violet, are the most important person to me, only a sliver above Char, and any child we might create together. And I do believe, should you become pregnant with an IUD, there is a risk involved. To you and the unborn child, you might be carrying. I'm not willing to put it off in case I'm correct. The sooner we know, the sooner we can devise a plan to minimize all risks."

All my earlier fight is now gone. There is nothing to say after that brief speech.

He leaves to retrieve the doctor. Upon his return, he explains to her his concerns.

She listens carefully.

When he is finished, she takes a seat on the bed next to me. "When was your IUD inserted?" Dr. Wilson asks again.

"A few months after Charlotte was born. A copper one, I believe, so I could continue supplying breastmilk." I was waiting for her to ask me to explain, but she doesn't.

She asked me who inserted it and if I had yearly visits to ensure it was in place. Explained that sometimes IUDs are expelled out by the uterus without a patient's awareness. Then she shocks me by questioning how sure I was that I had one inserted in the first place. Or how much I trusted the doctors I'd visited annually, not to remove it without my knowledge.

Honestly, I didn't trust anyone, not until Lorenzo. So, of course, I was unsure and told her so.

With my permission, she reviewed my recent hospital records I had allowed Lorenzo to make copies of. He suggested I have a copy in case I ever needed to know my medical history, something I learned his family did. They had personal documentation of medical records in a safe place, should they need to access them quickly. Meaning as soon as she had my permission, Lorenzo was able to provide her access to them rather quickly.

"They didn't notify you that the ER doctor removed a partially inserted IUD. One that appeared to have been tampered with?"

"No. No, they did not." I blink slowly, knowing I'd remember that news had they shared it.

"It is buried amongst a great deal of serious medical jargon. Mentioned in one brief sentence, that could quickly be scanned over or forgotten, as soon as one began reading the lengthy report." Dr. Wilson has that look I hate, a sympathetic expression on her face I have to divert my eyes away from.

"A mistake, that in the midst of it all seems rather minor, until a situation like this presents itself. Then that mistake becomes a problem." She reaches inside her medical bag and hands me a cup I know what to do with. "Only one way to know, and I always have what I need for these types of tests with me."

I excuse myself and come back a few minutes later. The good doctor and Lorenzo are chatting quietly, stopping as soon as I return. She takes the cup from me, opens what looks like a test strip, dips it inside, and nods.

"Well." Lorenzo takes my hand in his.

"It's positive." She stands and walks toward the bathroom to dispose of the cup, I'm guessing.

"Fuck," I whisper. "I'm sorry. I'm so sorry. I thought we were at no risk. Although I should have known, if it weren't for bad luck, I'd have no luck at all."

I'm certain I know how it got dislodged. Ruben must have

discovered it and tried his best to remove it, left it behind as a warning. He probably planned on punishing me once I'd recovered. It would have given him another excuse to visit and then take out all his aggression on me, not that he needed an excuse.

An ornery smirk forms on Lorenzo's gorgeous face. "You've done it now for sure, Miss Blanc. Ensured my permanent place will forever be standing proudly next to you. There is no way you will ever get rid of my annoying self now. You should just give in and marry me, stop putting me off."

I wish that was possible. "I believe I've agreed to marry you as soon as we get my messy life in order."

"I like your messy life, more so when I am the one making it a little messier. The uproar a scandal like this could cause might give a few of those eager bureaucrats in high places a stiffy."

"You did not just say that." I scold, but can't help but laugh. "Did it give you one?"

He takes my hand and places it over the one growing behind his zipper. "Would be a shame to waste an opportunity to get exactly what I want, along with a good stiffy."

I hear the door to the stateroom close and cannot keep from erupting into laughter, knowing we've sent the good doctor running. She was probably afraid my horny prince was about to show her how I ended up pregnant to begin with.

"Her job is done; she won't let the cat out of the bag." He sits next to me and tugs me into his side. "What do you say, Vi? Shall we allow my brother to perform his very first ceremony? Or if you'd rather the vicar do it..."

"I'm not a member of the church. I can't get married in a church or by a vicar unless I have special permission to do so." I'm sure he's not thought this through. "I wasn't raised anywhere near a church, Lorenzo. God and I, we don't really talk. I'm not against all the things you believe or practice, it just wasn't ever a part of my life. And after Ruben had Charlotte baptized in the church, knowing exactly who the man was, I guess my views about a..."

"I get that. It's something we have been striving to change. While God and I do talk daily, you've surely come to realize my views don't necessarily align fully with the church's views. I believe there is more to it than rules that only make a person feel bad about his or her faults. God wants us to do his work, but he also expects us to use those faults we all have, as a way to do it.

"And as we all know—or maybe not all, but I can show you if you'd like—even the greatest men of the bible were never perfect. David cheated on his wife, as did Abraham. Samuel had more than his share of wives and concubines, yet he was considered the wisest man God knew. And while we are to have learned from these men's mistakes, it has been proven time and time again throughout history, how man often repeats the same missteps. God only asks that we serve him the best we can, look to him for guidance along the way. And when we do that, then he will be there to assist us in our times of need.

"So, getting married in the church is out. Meaning, the other option we have is just outside those doors." He brings my hand between both of his. "I'm not asking because you are carrying my child and I believe..."

"I know. I do." I twist my head so I can look at him. "But like you said, there is no way to rid myself of you now. You will forever be a thorn in my side, so I might as well just suck it up and accept my fate."

I squeal louder than I meant to when I end up on my back with him over the top of me. "Is that a yes?"

"Yes," I whimper. "Are you going to make me wait for this to be legal before you use that weapon on me again?"

"Only because I know we have listening ears out there," he leans forward and kisses me. "Otherwise, I'd ravage you now with my loaded and lethal weapon."

"You aren't planning to hold my mistake over my head," I ask, hating to think he might believe I did this on purpose.

Placing a hand on my stomach, he spreads it out and squeezes gently. "A baby is never a mistake, Vi. Never. So no, I will not hold it over your head."

"What about your family?" I have to ask.

"Do you love me, Violet?"

"You know I do."

"Are you only marrying me because I was a selfish man, who took what was not rightfully mine to necessarily take before you were my wife, and therefore we got caught?"

"Do you believe that? That what I offered you wasn't yours to take until..."

He shakes his head. "No. Had I forced you to do so, then yes. But we both freely and willingly made our decision. My only restriction was that I love the woman I gave myself completely to. If that is wrong, then I am prepared to deal with my actions, but I will not apologize for them. I always intended to marry you, sooner rather than later. I believe that was your intention as well, why you accepted my ring, even before then."

"It was." I hope he believes me. "So no, I am not marrying you because we got caught."

"Then there should be no argument from them. Love was always the only reason Antonio claimed he would marry. Love is the only incentive for me to ever get married. We fell in love first. Maybe we expressed our love earlier than some might agree we should have, but that's on us, not them. I don't care how it all came to be, just that it will be. I love you, Vi, and you love me. That is all my family will want to know, all they will truly care about."

I hope he's right because I like his family. I've always respected them for hiring me and giving me a chance when others hadn't. It changed my life in more ways than I realized at the time. Brought me to the only man I ever truly trusted, who I cannot imagine living without. So, it is important to me they believe I never intended on any of this, but that I also do not regret it, because I love Lorenzo deeply.

CHAPTER 18
Lorenzo

The Royals

I leave Violet to clean up, taking a moment to gather my thoughts before joining my family. There are many, by the way, so many that I have to try to slow my mind down so I can process them all. First. She's pregnant.

How do I feel about that? Scared shitless. Ecstatic. Worried. Those are my first thoughts on the matter.

Scared, because damn, I believe every man panics a little when they hear those words. Being responsible for another human being, who will forever look to you for guidance, while he/she figures out this great big crazy world. Knowing that you will be the man in this little human's life, who sets the bar for all other men who follow you. Should you screw it up, set the bar too low, that falls on your shoulders later when this kid turns out to be an unproductive member of society, or an idiot, or just lazy, or insecure. The list is endless, really. And well damn, that's a lot to take on at twenty-three, when I'm still figuring out exactly what kind of man I am.

Ecstatic, because again, I believe every male also feels this once the panic fades. I got her pregnant. Me. I loved her just right and snuck one past the goalie. I will get the pleasure of watching her belly round as my child grows inside of her. I did that. We did that.

And after having gotten to experience a part of fatherhood with Char, I cannot wait to know how it feels to do it from the beginning. I love that little girl as if she were my own, have since the day I met her. Just like I already love this child who I know nothing about, and it almost feels weird, experiencing that kind of love so soon.

And no one can understand that really until it happens to them. Which explains why Antonio and Larkin took the loss of their first child so hard. Why my brother is being extra cautious with his wife this time around. To ensure he keeps both mother and child safe, in hopes to prevent harm from falling upon his family again.

Which is where the worry sets in. I worry for the safety of both of them. Maybe more than others might worry about that, considering the situation surrounding my family. Violet ran because her ex—if you can even call him that—is a mean son of a bitch. I have no doubt that he is going to come after her again once he learns we have returned. Come for his child, then do his best to once again use her to make her mother fall back in line. And I can't let either of those things happen, because as the head of this family unit, it is my job to keep them safe, to protect them from the wolves circling us.

And while I felt protective before, now that Violet is pregnant, it is as if my protectiveness for them has increased tenfold. And I worry I'll fail. That the most aggressive wolf will discover our weakness, attack at just the right time, and all we've worked so hard for will disappear.

And that gets me back to being scared shitless.

I feel a male hand grip my shoulder; one I know well. "You look like shit, brother. Want to talk about it?"

I nod and he leads me to the office he keeps on the plane. After we are both comfortable with a tumbler of bourbon in our hands, I give it to him straight. "Violet is pregnant. I realize what you are probably thinking."

"Do you?" He takes a sip of his and stares at me.

"You've made it very clear on when you believe two people should come together like that."

He nods and then shrugs. "That was for my sake, brother. To prevent getting trapped by a woman before I knew where we both stood. Imagine had I given in where Dalia was concerned, that could have been detrimental to everything I stand for. I could have been forced into a marriage that would have done more damage than good. Affected Esteban's relationship with Winifred even, and what a shame, to think three lives could have been ruined with that one mistake."

"And you don't think this will affect the lives of others in much the same way? That I've all but trapped Violet into a life I'm not sure she completely understands or even wants?" Wow, now that is a new outlook into this craziness.

Antonio chuckles as he asks, "Was that your intention, little brother? Did you sleep with the beautiful firecracker of a woman, so you could trap her? Or did you do so, because once you found her, knew that you loved her, you only wanted to show her how much she meant to you?"

"Taking into consideration that we went through a significant number of condom boxes this past month, I don't believe trapping her was truly my objective. I love her, have for a while now. When the beautiful firecracker confessed her love, I had a moment of weakness, I suppose. Not that I regret it, I do not. I believe she needed to understand how different it was to be with a man who loved her. One who took his time with her as he washed away all her previous ideas about intimacy. I always planned on marrying her, when she was ready that is, I actually suggested it before she ran."

My brother shakes his head, wearing a smile. "I'm sure that went well."

"No. She called me crazy and then she ran." I remember how she looked at me when I first brought it up, and cannot help but grin.

"Sounds about right. She has obviously changed her mind since then." He stands and walks over to the bar to add a little more bourbon to his, then offers me some.

I nod and join him. "I charmed her the best I could. Let her see the real me."

"And that worked?" Again, he laughs. "You are a good man, little brother. I've always known what type of woman you'd fall flat on your face for. Violet's constant unimpressed attitude toward you, drove you nuts. She didn't fall all over you like so many others before her did. Instead, she ignored you most of the time, making you only work that much harder to figure her out. I'm sure she did not realize by doing so, she was sealing her fate, however, I did.

"Which is why I expected you to do right by her, didn't give you too hard of a time when you ran off with my secretary. But do not think I'm letting you keep her all to yourself. I need her back in my office, if only to show her replacement how to do the job correctly."

"Does that mean you will let us be your first?" I ask hopeful.

"If that is what you both want," Antonio leans back. "But do you not think that maybe it would be better, in the long run, to allow our people to witness such an affair. They are probably tired of hearing about it after the fact."

"No, I do not. I need to protect my family, Antonio. The best way for me to do so is for Violet to lawfully be tied to me. Not to mention, I don't care what the people are tired of hearing. They do not come and ask us about personal aspects of their lives, and I'm thankful for that. So, I shouldn't have to go seeking approval when it comes to mine."

Apparently, that was the correct answer, since he nods in agreement and slams down the remainder of his tumbler. "Shall we go inform the others then, or are we keeping this quiet?"

"I want the world to learn Violet is mine. I don't plan on keeping it a secret. However, we might want to get Karina on the phone. She will need to know the status between us is about to change, giving her time to plan accordingly. She is in possession of a statement we intended on releasing shortly after we land. She might want to do so before, now. Or she might want me to read it within the hour of our arrival."

Violet and I sat down and scripted what we wanted to say. I thought it would be better this way. If she had it all written down, instead of trying to do some interview, where she might stumble over her words, leaving room for others to question the authenticity of her story.

A statement allowed her to tell it the way she wished to tell it. We opted not to take questions about it, since there was going to be a ton of information she wouldn't be comfortable discussing.

Once matters calmed down, and she had time to determine how the people were with the truth about her, then and only then, would she decide if she was up to doing an interview or wanted to comment further. I was leaving that part up to her because it was her story after all. I would only comment on my part if I chose to do so, not allow others to disrespect her wishes or her.

"Then let's call her." Antonio takes a seat behind his desk and dials the phone.

It takes several rings for her to pick up. And by the sound of her voice, I'm guessing we might have interrupted something. "Your Majesty, this had better be life or death."

I answer for him. "Did we interrupt, Rina? You sound out of breath."

"Hold on," Karina responds, sounding annoyed.

I can hear her doing her best to negotiate with whoever it is. We then hear a door slam shut and catch her voice her opinion about that before she gets back on the phone.

"Lenny, you have the worst timing ever. What is it this time?"

I give it to her straight and she doesn't disappoint when she responds. "Oh my. Now that is a pickle you've gotten yourself into, Prince Lorenzo. You are the black sheep of the family, aren't you? I guess someone has to be. So, what is it you want from me exactly?"

"Just assumed the person in charge of the legal side of this should know what is about to come raining down on them once it becomes public." I can so picture her snarky face while she enjoys all this drama way more than she should, but that is also what makes her so good at her job. She understands how to get ahead of it all, use every bit to her advantage when building a case.

"So much for my wild night of dirty sex, it looks like I will spend it drowning in briefs. Not even close to the kind of briefs I was looking forward to drowning in." Karina just can't not say what is on her mind, I do believe it is truly just a part of her. Kind of like how Violet mouths off. And I know from experience that the right man will one day appreciate that side of her as well.

"I thought you were interested in a specific pair of briefs, Rina. A word of advice, if you will allow me."

She snorts, "Sure, Lenny. Lay it on me."

"In order to catch a man like Stew, you are going to need to change

159

your game plan. I believe Javier mentioned he wasn't an innocent, so you need not adjust all of it, but you might want to dial back on the one-night stands. Start thinking about what it might be like to be in a relationship, a monogamous one.

"I understand this might be a foreign concept to you, Rina. But I do believe in order to get your hands on those particular briefs, that is going to be the correct route to do so. Otherwise, you may as well forget about it. Watch him find all you could possibly give him in another woman, one who is willing to be monogamous with him."

I watch Antonio judder his head in disbelief and cannot help but smile at his reaction.

"Are you willing to watch that, Rina? Or am I wrong in my assumption, that imagining him with someone else, bothers the hell out of you?"

"I might get a little testy thinking about it. Have thought of a few ways I could get away with murder when I see another woman with him. But I'm really bad at relationships, Len, terrible." Karina taps something against what I believe is her desk. "So, you're suggesting if I clean up my act, so to speak, that could draw his attention. Is that what I'm hearing?"

"Yes. Not all of us are into women who sleep with you on a first date, we don't all let our dicks do the talking." I attempt to talk her language the best I can.

"But your dicks usually speak better than your mouths, at least that is what I've come to realize. When most of you start talking with your mouths, the level of intelligence that escapes diminishes all the other aspects I was first attracted to."

"Perhaps, that right there is your problem Karina, you've never looked past the outer shell. You've relied on it only, and therefore you have been missing a number of amazing men, whose intelligence sets them apart." Antonio must have decided to remind her I wasn't the only person listening to her.

"Oh my God. Your Majesty, I totally forgot you were on the line. Outer shells, however, are the first thing us ladies notice." Karina has never been one to back away. "Are you suggesting I put on some sort of beer goggles?"

"No, that is not at all what I am suggesting." Antonio chuckles. "Forgive me for being blunt here, Lady Batista, but I suspect you've been wearing those goggles all along, perhaps it's time you remove them."

"Did he just make a joke?" I hear her gasp teasingly. "I don't know that I've ever heard our king crack one before."

"He's not completely a fuddy-duddy. Since his wife, he's loosened up slightly. I believe she removed the stick that was lodged up his arse. The right one can do that, you know; make you want to change."

"I must be extremely desperate, to be taking advice from a man in your current position." She replies, although I can hear her laughing.

"I'm not ashamed of the position I am in. I love Violet. She is the woman I was planning on having a family with. Our family may be coming sooner than I might have expected, but I'm fine with that. I'm fine with that because I don't mind being tied to her for the rest of our lives, not even a little bit. And while I know that others are going to claim we got married because she ended up pregnant, that is not entirely true."

"But partially true. And I'm not judging you by the way. I am fully supportive of you and Violet. I'd even support you, should you have decided not to get married, but since you both planned on doing so eventually, it only seems right to do it now."

"Thank you, I'm actually very excited about making her, my wife." I feel my face breaking into an enormous smile. "It has an amiable tone to it. Plus, it will allow me to protect her, Charlotte, and the baby, without having to explain my reasoning."

We discuss a few of those details surrounding her side of all this that will need to be done immediately. She sends Antonio the paperwork she will be required to properly file with the government come morning to make our marriage official. She also lets me know how other matters are going on her end. Explains what she is still waiting on to move forward, and what she will file as soon as word about our return is released. The key objective being to keep Charlotte out of the reach of Ruben and Lady Amber. Now that maternity has been proven, we are planning to sue for custody, permanent custody.

When we hang up, I know it's time to join the others. Violet has surely joined them by now and is probably wondering where I disappeared to. I'm more than ready to find her so we can share our news, all of it.

"Ready?" Antonio stands.

"Extremely." I stand and lead the way.

CHAPTER 19

Violet

The Royals

When I walk back into the main area of the plane I expected to find Lorenzo there. He wasn't, so I am forced to take a seat and try not to act awkward, which is impossible. What saved me from completely feeling uncomfortable while waiting is my baby girl running up the second she spots me, then climbing into my lap. She must have woken while we were gone and now needs a little cuddle. I never mind cuddling with her. I only hate knowing how starved she has been for affection most of her short life. So, whenever I get the chance to hold her, no matter what I am doing, I take the time to do so. We've eaten dinner a tad later a few times. Spent a few extra minutes getting ready in the morning sitting at the breakfast table. Even fallen asleep in the evenings together. All because she didn't want to let go. Most might not understand why I allow the extra time, but those people have never missed out on their child's love, therefore they don't understand how precious these moments are.

I don't miss it when Queen Larkin takes a seat in one of the chairs next to us. She is carrying a sippy cup, a bowl filled with fish crackers, and two unopened bottles of sparkling water. When Charlotte peeks up at her, she winks and places the bowl on the empty spot by us. As soon as she grabs a cracker, Charlotte reaches for the sippy cup in the Queen's hand.

"You forgot these when you ran off to see mommy," Larkin says as she lets go of the cup. "I hoped we were making progress. I understand though; no one is as special as your mommy."

Charlotte smiles up at me before she collapses against my chest, sucking down the milk inside her cup.

"Thank you for looking after her while I was sorting things out." I run my fingers through her still damp curls. "I hope she wasn't any trouble."

"No trouble at all." Larkin leans forward to hand me a water. "She is an adorable little girl, who is very attached to the two people she trusts most.

"I was about her age when my parents were granted full custody of me. It was the reason my father stepped down and became a full-time parent. One of them needed to make sure I understood they weren't going anywhere, to help me understand I was safe and finally home.

"That's what she needs, why she clings to you and Lorenzo. And who can blame her, or even fault you for allowing it? In time she will accept the rest of us, the more we are around and she'll come to understand we are trustworthy."

I often forget this incredible woman came from a background not that different from mine. Well, not true, she was saved from it when her parents stepped in. Demanded it stop once her birth mother overdosed in her father's ER. Nonetheless, she carries the scars she once had to overcome. A few a direct result from having one parent addicted to drugs. Proof that with the right support, even a child born into dire circumstances can come out of it way better than from where they started.

"I'd like to apologize for earlier." She tells me while we watch Charlotte try to decide if she wants to get down or stay. Isabel is moving around the cabin, catching her eye.

"Stay." Charlotte wiggles out of my lap as she gives me her order. "I back."

I almost laugh, because it is rather cute. "Go and play, honey. I will stay right here with Queen Larkin."

Charlotte pauses and glances over at Larkin before turning back to me. "Aunt Larkin, Papá say. Who Queen?"

Larkin answers for me, almost amused she caught on. "I am both actually, Charlotte, although I don't go by Queen very often. To you, I am Aunt Larkin, exactly like your papá said I was. Go play with Aunt Isabel, she has been waiting for you to wake enough to play again."

A wide smile takes over my daughter's face. "Aunt Izzy, her." She runs off like an almost-two-year-old runs, all clumsy, making you want to shadow her so she doesn't topple over. As soon as she reaches Isabel, she leaps for her, as if she knows her aunt will catch her, which she does.

We watch them for a while, enjoying how good Isabel is with Charlotte. "Isabel will be a wonderful assistant once your little one gets here. She is a natural."

Larkin agrees, "I believe she had some outstanding examples growing up. Antonio is old enough to be Isabel's father with the twenty-one-year age difference, yet he did his best to keep as much of that sibling vibe between them as he could. Which being her legal guardian wasn't always easy, isn't always easy, and will probably get even more difficult as she approaches the teen years.

"Each of her other siblings has done well offering him support; a village I suppose is the best way to describe how it worked early on. Antonio and Esteban co-parented, kind of like a divorced couple who shares custody or had visitation. I realize that sounds weird, but it was Isabel who first explained that to me."

"She's well-adjusted for having gone through so much. I mean, I realize they have had au pairs who helped as well." I wonder what that would be like.

"Yes, we still have Beatriz and Helena with us. But they don't play as much of a role now that I'm around. I enjoy doing things for my family when I can. During the week we see them more. Helena helps with keeping the house in order. Beatriz keeps Isabel's schedule and also helps out with Alejandro and Triana's little one while they are both hard at work. She will help with this one during working hours when it gets here. But the rest of the time, we are on our own, and it's been good for us. I believe it has brought us closer as a family.

"What will you do? I'm sorry. I'm overstepping again." Larkin waves and mumbles something to herself as she takes a drink.

"I don't know." I take a moment to gaze in her direction. "I've always worked because it kept me busy. Kept my mind off everything going on in my life. It was how I stayed sane, or marginally sane."

We sit in silence for a few, and for some reason, I do something I never have before. I open up to another person I don't know, with the knowledge she won't hold it against me. "Seems you were spot on. I was in complete denial. And I realize I should probably not be at all happy about it."

Larkin cuts me off, "Why shouldn't you be happy about it?"

"I realize what everyone is going to say about me." I almost laugh, but don't. "It won't be the first time I've been the hot topic of gossip."

"There is one important lesson I learned during my courtship with Antonio. The gossipers will forever gossip. The ones who assume they know better than anyone else, won't change their minds, even after they have been proven wrong. And the rest of them will believe what they choose to believe. You can either let it bother you or let it go. If you let it get to you, it will eat you alive from the inside out. There is no way to please them all. So instead of worrying about them and what they think, I only worry about Antonio and me, and what we want. Leave everyone else out of it, because what it all comes down to, in the end, doesn't concern anyone else but us.

"Which is why we got married the way we did. I was tired of all the drama circling us. I didn't care any longer if they liked me, or thought I was suitable to be their queen, I was done with all that. I wanted to be Antonio's wife first and foremost. Whatever else that meant, I was willing to figure it out along the way. Knew he wouldn't let me fail, would make sure I was knowledgeable enough to at least be able to fake it."

I find myself laughing for the first time since we stepped on this plane, probably for the first time since I realized who was giving us a ride home. "Do you still fake it, Queen Larkin?"

The way her face lights up when she smiles, allows me to appreciate a side of her I've not seen yet. "Every time I'm forced to step in front of a crowd with that title attached to my name. I fake it so good, I myself am even fooled.

"Violet, I need to ask you something. Since I'm certain we are going to be family soon, I'd appreciate it if you'd just call me Larkin. That is who I am, who I am most comfortable being. And while I understand in this country, not using that title might seem disrespectful, in my mind, I'm simply an American girl who fell in love with a Hermosa Islaians boy. We are living the dream every couple who falls in love hopes for. The rest only happens to be a part of it, mainly because the boy I fell in love with also happened to be the king."

"I believe when you and I fell in love, I was far from a boy." A booming male voice echoes from behind us.

A deep red blush appears on Larkin's face. "Yes, you were."

"Sorry it took me so long to join you," Lorenzo sits down and immediately places an arm behind me. "We were letting Karina in on the plan, after having a heart-to-heart talk about everything."

"Like what exactly? Did you feel the need to explain all of this? Go into how it all came to be, the reason we're in the situation we have found ourselves in?" I don't know why I care, or even why I am giving him a hard time about it.

King Antonio's rumble of laughter catches my attention. "He might have revealed a little more than necessary at one point. Although, I do believe I coerced the truth out of him with the way I worded my questions."

"I'm almost afraid to ask," I reveal, as I pray, he didn't give away too much.

"The point is that we talked, and he has agreed to do as we discussed earlier if that is still what you want." Lorenzo's eyes tell me how much he hopes I still do, and I do.

As soon as the words are out of my mouth, he is calling the others over. And by others, I mean Isabel and Charlotte. Everyone else seems to have disappeared into another room, giving us some privacy.

And right there on a plane, over the Atlantic Ocean, I get married. We stand together and pledge our lives to each other. I didn't realize how emotional I'd get while speaking those words. That I'd also get to witness him getting emotional, which only made me that much more so. A vicious cycle we found ourselves stuck in.

By the end, I'm pretty sure the only two people not crying were Antonio and Charlotte. Those two were actually laughing at the rest of us. He was holding her in his arms, chuckling while she kept asking him why we were all crying. He is only the second man she has taken to so easily, allowed him to pick her up when everyone else was too weepy to do so. Letting her help him at the end when he made it official, by telling her to give us permission to kiss to seal the deal.

"He say kiss. You kiss. No cry, no more. Silly people. Kiss Mommy, Papá. Kiss her. Be happy." Charlotte then claps her hands when Lorenzo does what she tells him to do. "Yea. Now what?"

Before we can answer, the stewardess announces over the speaker lunch will be served in ten minutes. We all gather in the appropriate seats, then accept the trays once they are delivered. I help Charlotte as much as she will allow me to. Speak with Isabel, who seems extremely interested in the love story surrounding her brother and me. More than all the other stuff.

When the trays are taken away, she stands and motions for Charlotte to come with her. Once secured on her hip, Isabel lets me know that while she may be only ten, she is well educated on matters concerning love. "My parents, they weren't really in love when they married, even though I was cooking already inside of my mother. Had been for a while, actually. I don't believe people should get married just because they created a life. Any man and woman can do that, and not all of them should be married, mine shouldn't have. Perhaps had they not married, both would still be alive today.

"What I'm trying to say is, I don't think you guys fit in that category. I see how he watches you, how he has been watching you since we sat down to eat. He loves you, really loves you. Like my other brothers love their wives. And I trust you love him as well. And that is why the two of you getting married, after learning there was life growing inside of you, is for the best. He was never going to let you go. Eventually, you were one day predestined to be one of us, even if that hadn't happened. That's just my ten-year-old opinion on the matter, and I wanted you to know, in case you were wondering what I thought about it."

Isabel hurries off with a giggling Charlotte as she bounces her around. She stops to chat with Lorenzo. His eyes shoot up quickly at her once, as if he is almost shocked by her bluntness, and that makes her giggle. In a few moments, he laughs as he stands and wraps both girls in his arms tightly. When he releases them, the girls head in one direction while he heads straight for me.

"What did she say to you?" He questions as he reaches for my hand and tugs me to my feet.

"Just that she sees more than you probably are comfortable with. Gave me her blessing and then welcomed me into the fold." I yawn unexpectedly.

Lorenzo spins me around and begins guiding me to the staterooms.

I yawn again, "Where are we going?"

"Bed." He leans down and nips my ear. "I'm going to put my tired wife to bed."

I try not to get a little excited about that, but I can't help it. We've been together enough times now that my body hums at the idea of him and bed. He doesn't disappoint me either. As soon as we enter the room, he locks the door and scoops me into his arms. Those delicious lips of his find mine and we kiss softly at first, but like always, it turns to a frantic hungry one.

Once he removes our clothes, I remind him, "Condom."

"No," is his one-word response to that.

Certain he isn't considering all the reasons I've insisted on using them, I shove him backward and walk over to where my bag sets. Reaching inside, where I hid a strip in case we needed it.

Lorenzo's hand grips my wrist and tosses them back inside. "We are not..."

"Do you want an STD?" I lean back over to retrieve them.

I yelp when my body is hoisted up and over his shoulder, as he carries me back to the bed, without the condoms I might add. "Lenny, you are being unreasonable."

He growls as he tosses me on the bed and crawls over me. I get distracted by his perfect shirtless physique. My eyes devour him hungrily, like a woman who knows exactly how it feels when pressed firmly against hers. And he responds like a man who knows how to use my distraction to his advantage.

He is good, I'll give him that, but he is not so good I forget my argument. Even as his lips make a fiery trail down my body, lighting a fire straight to my hot zones. I am still able to process my thoughts on how unreasonable he is being.

"Lenny," I also understand the use of that name always grabs his attention. "Lenny, stop." And that one word is never ignored, ever.

Lorenzo stops his crash of kisses, stands while he stares at me defiantly. Similar to the way a disobedient teenager glares at his parents when they tell him his behavior is unbecoming, and to think before he acts. And like a toddler, he reaches for the snap of his pants and lowers the zipper, removing them as if daring me to object.

I want to laugh at him and his pouty face that displays how much he disagrees with what I'm trying to say. But like the smart man I know he is, after he steps out of his black briefs. Standing buck naked in front of me, he does what he knows is the right thing to do. Grumbles about it, but does it anyway.

"This is stupid. A husband is not supposed to have to suit up when taking his wife for the first time." He mumbles angrily, reaching for that strip of condoms. "Tomorrow, I am having Dr. Wilson run all those necessary tests so we can dispose of these, once and for all. Your earlier test came back clear, so you realize this is unnecessary."

He tosses the strip on the bed, grabs my ankles, and yanks me to the edge. Removes the remainder of my clothing, still wearing that pouty face. Once my feet are placed on his shoulders, he runs his hands down my thighs. His eyes move up my body until they land on my face.

"My husband, those two words never sounded so good before. Lenny, I am only trying to protect you, us." I stare into his eyes and watch them burn with desire. "Make love to me, Lenny. I want to know what it feels like to have my loving husband make love to his wife."

Those words are the ones that erase the scowl from his face, replacing it with a smirk. One that gets closer as he slides forward until my knees are resting on his shoulders, his lips just above my breasts. The brush of his moist tongue darting out to lick the tip of one has me bucking my hips toward him.

And like almost every other time he has taken me, he does so extremely slowly. Worships every inch of my body with his lips, hands, and tongue. He gives me so many orgasms, I lost count after three. The rip of the condom wrapper, after an incredibly powerful one, alerts me the next one I have will put me out for a few hours.

"Lenny," I whisper his name as he enters me. "Wait, I need to tell you something." I grab his face and hold him there while I stare into his eyes. He is the most gorgeous man I have ever laid eyes on, and he is all mine.

Those lips lower to take mine sweetly, "Hurry up, love. Your walls are about to send me into a blissful eruption, and I don't want to let go until I have you floating."

Tears roll down my face, as I appreciate the way my life has turned out with him in it. I never once imagined I'd have this, not really. But I do, and it is all because of him.

"I love you. I love you so much." I hiccup out as his hips start to move, and I know soon my mind will shut down. "Thank you for loving me. For giving me so much more than I ever once deserved."

Those hips move faster now, hitting me just right in that hot spot, as he drags his length along it. "It has been my pleasure, Vi. After all, I do believe you make one remarkably beautiful princess. Princess Violet Amethyst Reyes, now that sounds lovely to my ears. Feels lovely even, for some reason, when I make love to her, to you. Let go, Vi. Let me hear your cries, Your Highness, while I love my wife."

I cry out and pray the others don't overhear me. His words don't completely sink in until afterward, when he rolls me over after removing the used condom. It's at that moment I realize what he said exactly, and a dose of reality washes over me.

"What is it?" He whispers in my ear.

"Nothing." I close my eyes, doing my best to not think about it.

"It's not nothing when your entire body goes tense, love. Tell me." He will not let this go.

"What are my duties as a princess? I mean, I have no idea how to act even. Am I... oh geez... this is so fucked up." I hear him chuckle behind me. "Don't laugh at me. I'm serious."

"You are only to act the same way you have always acted. I don't expect you to act any other way. Don't want you to. I love you for who you are, Vi, not because of what I one day hoped you would turn into once you came to be a princess." He nips my ear teasingly. "Not to mention, I cannot wait to introduce you and watch their faces."

"So, I am the entertainment?" I groan, displeased by that thought.

"No, not at all. For one, I would never let you be anything but perfect in front of them. Nor would I tolerate anyone belittling you. Should you have concerns, you can ask me, or even Larkin or Winifred. I know both would be more than happy to assist you, make you feel comfortable, not allow you to fail. None of my family would. My mother will be the biggest advocate of them all, watch and see."

I laugh, recalling my earlier conversation with Larkin. "You realize Larkin told me she fakes it. Fakes it so well, sometimes she has herself believing."

Lorenzo's arms tighten around me, making me feel safe. "Then you can fake it together because our queen is damn good at faking it. Now stop worrying and rest. Or did I not love you enough to wear you out yet?"

I squeak and then squirm when I sense him growing hard against my back. Perhaps I should start faking it now, so I can experience more of him before I pass out from exhaustion. "You were rather disappointing earlier."

That did it for sure.

"Disappointing?" He is above me again. "Well, we can't have our first time as husband and wife end in disappointment, now can we?"

And before I can argue, not that I was about to, he is sending me back into that blissful place only he has ever been able to send me too.

Have I told you how much I love this man?

CHAPTER 20
Lorenzo

The Royals

W hen we land back on home soil, we do so in Sevilla. I didn't want Violet or Charlotte near any place my cousin might be. Our home, for the time being, will be Fort Serna. That is until I know exactly what we are facing.

The uniqueness of the Fort's security has to do with where it is located. It was built by one of our former reigning Queens, guaranteeing she could be with her husband, who also was a military man. The fort itself was surrounded by three bases. One from each branch, making it the most guarded of all the properties the Royal family maintains.

There are some structural issues with a portion of the large fortress. The reason Larkin isn't exactly thrilled about my plans to keep my family here while we evaluate the situation surrounding us.

"I really think you all should come and stay with us." We are standing in a hall of one of the wings that has been deemed safe. "I'm not comfortable with the idea of your family living here."

I lean down and kiss her cheek. "So, you have told me now for the fifth or sixth time. This section, the north wing, is where you and your family stay when forced to visit the area."

"Visit the area, being the significant part of that sentence. I would not allow them to stay here permanently or long-term. There are so many hazards one could find accidentally if they wandered off into one of the other wings. I'd constantly be worried about that with Isabel. She does enjoy her exploring. It's the reason I was so very thorough with Maximiliano Chateau's hidden gems. The thought of anyone getting lost or hurt inside wasn't something I was willing to risk. When I finally get my hands on this disaster, reinforce all these walls and hidden corridors behind the walls, not even hurricane-force winds will be able to destroy it. But until then, the west and south wings might tumble down if a gentle breeze blows just right."

I know she is exaggerating, for the fact I have learned she would allow no one near this place if that were true. While they have deemed those structures unsafe for occupancy, they aren't going to fall over without something helping them do so. Otherwise, they would have moved this higher on the list when they created it. The fact they didn't, conveys what I need to know.

"I will make certain Violet knows to not wander off, keeps Char close at all times," I reassure her again. "Plus, I don't plan on living here permanently. I like my home in East Aragon. We just happen to be safer here at this time than we would be there, even with those areas you are concerned with."

Larkin reaches down and pats her tummy, smiling. "I know. He is just as stubborn as your father."

"Are you talking to the future sovereign?" I point at where she is holding her belly. "Because if not, and this place is haunted as they all imply, I just might take you up on your earlier offer."

Larkin reaches for my hand and places it on the same spot she was recently holding. "Are you afraid of a few ghosts?"

"Growing up listening to all the ghost stories about Aragon Palace, Esteban's Castle, this place, when visiting the grandparents in Juliana, you can damn well believe I am scared of ghosts. It's why I chose to live in a newer residence that's history didn't go back hundreds of years when people were killed inside these spaces regularly.

"Is that?" I grab her belly with both my hands and hear her snickering at me. "Hush. I can't feel her if you are laughing."

"Her? You don't know it's a her, it could be a him." Larkin laughs harder when I drop to my knees and stare at her rounded center. "Plus, I didn't realize you needed quiet to *feel* a baby moving."

"Shh." I grin up at her, totally mesmerized by the movement tapping against my hands. "It's a her. You are going to have the third firstborn princess; I just know it. We are after all becoming a scandalous family, one who likes to revolutionize all the rules. Have you not been taking note?

"First king to rule as a single man. The first to marry for love rather than status. First to do so in secrecy, giving those in charge the middle finger. First prince to court a lady without the knowledge of her family. Marry her in secret as well. On the following night, the king married. First royal family to allow their women to hold jobs outside of the office of the crown. First prince to run off with a woman and her child."

"Are you sure you are the first on that?" She teases, one of the many things I so do love about her.

"Maybe not. Definitely not the first whose child will be born in a limited time frame. Those who love math will figure that one out easily enough. The scandal it will cause could affect your husband's reign, have them all pointing fingers about how we do and say as we please."

I smile up at her when the child kicks again. "I cannot wait to feel my child moving around inside of Vi like this. I might even be tempted to strip her naked and ravish her, solely to see if the baby moves more."

A lovely blush blossoms on my sister-in-law's face, as if she herself has possibly been ravished by her own husband. "It can be a little weird in the moment."

I throw my head back and laugh at her honesty. "I'll live for weird moments then."

Antonio rounds the corner, looking a bit too serious for my liking. His eyes find mine in front of his wife where I am kneeling, and he shakes his head as if amused. Although the somber expression doesn't dissipate, it remains there and has me rising to my feet quickly.

"Is there a problem?" I find myself asking.

"Not one you can help me with," he enlightens me, reaching for his wife's hand. "Ready to get this over with."

I watch them walk down the vestibule hand in hand, back to where I know the press is waiting. He will field a few inquiries about his trip. The recent announcement Esteban made about running for Governor of the Southern Region. And whatever else these reporters expect, he should fill them in on. He isn't a fan of dealing with the press; they are high on his list of least favorites, right below all those highborn nobles.

When they are finished with that business, Antonio will announce I would like to make a statement. Shortly afterward Violet and I will enter the chamber and provide them with the rules I expect them to follow. At that point, I'll turn it over to my wife where she will read what she has scripted out. When she has finished, we will exit without fielding any of the questions I am certain they will have. There is no way I am allowing them to tear into her. No way I will put her in that position after being brave enough to so freely let them in on her deepest, darkest secrets.

As I follow my brother and Larkin, I find her pacing the corridor right outside the chamber. The same one we will enter in approximately thirty minutes. She is staring at the paper in her hand while she trudges a weary path.

Karina is off to the side talking with one of our PR representatives, one we invited to make sure all goes smooth. They are coordinating what we will allow the other woman to comment on afterward.

When Violet paces closer to where I am standing, I snag her wrist to yank her around the corner. Shove her against the stone wall, while I cover her mouth with my hand so she doesn't scream.

"It's just me. Shh." I enlighten her, peeking back to determine if anyone noticed.

Karina is wise to me, glimpsing up and smiling as she continues her conversation. No one else seems to have realized that the newest Princess has been nabbed by her own husband. Or if they do, then they are choosing to ignore us.

I take the paper from her and shove it in the back of my pants. "Why are you so nervous?"

"Oh, I don't know." Her voice has that same tone to it she often gave me during those early days when I would bother her while she was working. "I guess it could be due to the fact I'm about to expose my entire life for all to judge. You have no idea how that feels."

I place my hands flat on the wall next to her. "You don't think I know how that feels?"

"No, I don't. People look at you and see a handsome prince. Men want to be you. Women want to be with you." She slams her head against the wall and I realize that must have hurt.

I lift one of my hands and run it along her jaw, watch her eyes flutter close from my touch alone. Then I lean in until my lips are only a few millimeters from hers. My breath when I speak warms them.

"Then those men are idiots, and the women are wasting their time. I cannot take a shit inside this place without it becoming public knowledge. My very first day on this earth, I was carried down to the pressroom so everyone could get a look at the newest prince. My first birthday had members of the press present, just so they could snap pictures of me eating cake. I decided however that I would give them a much better show. When my mother placed me down so she could do who knows what, I stripped out of my clothes and ran. I made the front page of the Hermosa Islas Post, with my willy waving in the wind and my bare little arse taking up most of it."

That makes her laugh, really laugh. So, I continue sharing all the times they put my life on display for others to see. I never got a say about it. They didn't ask me if they could print it, or considered if maybe later it might not be something that I'd want everyone to remember. So much of my life can be brought up in a google search with a timeline attached. Offering most of the public an idea of what my life was like growing up. Now granted, there were a great number of events no one knew about, and as I got older, I recognized how to keep myself out of the press.

"When I was seventeen, a few days after my father's death had been announced, I went out and got pissed with one of my best friends, Crispin. We went for a joyride in a classic car my father owned. Picked up a few ladies and drove around Aragon like we owned the place."

Violet nods as if she remembers it well, even though she wasn't there to know much about it. "You made the front page again, and the news. I recall Ruben sitting in my apartment laughing as they played it over and over again."

I'd been dumb and parked the car on a hill overlooking Aragon. One of the young ladies recorded the entire event and then sold it to the media later. I stripped down to my skivvies, stood on the hood of that expensive car. Offered my dad a toast from his own special stash of liquor, while I gave a God-awful speech that I wish I could forget. I jumped up and down on this car until it started rolling forward, all because my drunken arse had forgotten to put the damn thing into park. Cris had been up there with me, and as soon as he realized we were moving, tackled me to the ground, right before it took a nosedive off the edge.

"I remember thinking how sad it was that everyone else considered it was acceptable witnessing a young boy falling apart like that, all because of who you were. Had someone like me done that, they'd not have shown it at all." She clarifies to me. "I ended up leaving the room in tears for you."

"You cried for me?" I ask, surprised.

"And got the shit kicked out of me later for it." She reaches up and caresses my face. "It was worth it, because someone should have wept for you. I wanted to find you, hold you, comfort you even. Then I watched the funeral, saw your family was doing that for me, felt better knowing you had someone."

I am truly touched by that. We didn't even know each other or understand that one day we would be connected, and yet she cried for me on one of the worst days of my life. Broke down for me. A boy whose life was not anywhere near as awful as the one she was living. Not even on my worst days did they compare.

"That was the last time I let them catch me with my pants down." I joke to break the tension I can sense building.

"Until now," she grabs my shirt and tugs me forward. "In a manner of speaking, that is."

"My point was that I get it. Understand how letting them see all those stupid things you did before you knew better is grueling. I wonder if we started digging into all their lives, what we'd uncover. Until one becomes a public figure, they do not realize how lucky they are." I kiss her lips gently at first.

"Lenny," she whispers my name, making my kiss turn into more.

A female clears her throat while tapping her heeled foot. "Oh, how the mighty doth fall. I suppose a snog before something so serious is acceptable when you are hoping to calm your wife's nerves."

"Rina, your timing sucks." I groan as I pull back some from Violet, noticing she is completely flushed by my ravishing. "Tell them we need..."

"Pull it together. And for goodness' sake, put that away, or they will have more pictures of you showing off." Violet takes a deep breath and agitates her head to clear it. "Once again, all the men will want to be you, and all the ladies will want to be with you. And since I don't share, there will be so many disappointed women out there, and men unable to give them what only you could have."

"I like her Len. She has spunk." Karina motions for us to move.

We enter the chamber and are immediately bombarded with questions. The PR rep steps up to the mic, asks everyone to hold all questions until after both of us have spoken. Explains that at that time, should we decide we want to answer we can, otherwise she will field any questions they might have the best she can.

Once the room quiets, I start. "I know you are wondering what is going on exactly. If you will allow us to explain, we will. Should you choose to interrupt us with questions or statements, then you'll be left to continue wondering."

I pause, waiting to see if they can keep their mouths shut, surprised to learn they can. "Good. Before my wife gives her statement..."

"Your wife?" Someone shouts. "Sorry, so sorry. I'm keeping my mouth shut, Your Highness."

I appreciate how hard it is not to ask questions with all the uncertainty surrounding us. They have questions, I'm sure, on why Violet is with me. What her connection is to Ruben Del Markov? Where Charlotte plays into it all, and why there is so much drama surrounding the little girl. And we will eventually get to that. Maybe not today, but eventually. Today we are here to provide them the background story, before hell and brimstone rains down on us. We are using it as our protective force field that will make Ruben's counter-attack sound more defensive, and sounding defensive I've learned rarely sets well with most.

I don't go into significant detail about how it all came to be. I only explain that Violet and I are married and that I expect them to treat her as they would any other member of the Royal Family. Again, I take a side step and invite her to come forward.

Her hands are trembling something fierce, so I do the one thing I have learned will help. I stand directly behind her, wrapping my arms around her tightly, all while I encourage her to read from the paper she is holding.

"My name is Violet Blanc or hmm..."

"Her name is Princess Violet Amethyst Reyes, wife of Prince Lorenzo Gabriel Reyes. The best looking of the Reyes brothers, and by far the..."

She drives her elbow into my side. "Do you mind? I believe you had your chance to speak."

That gets a few chuckles from the media and I realize now she is ready to do this. "Just trying to help, dear. By all means, please continue."

And she does.

She reads the entire statement. A few times having to pause to keep from losing it, she does an excellent job despite how hard it all was. And when she is done, she looks up at me and appears relieved it is over.

We somehow make it out of there without a single question being tossed our way. They seem to be processing all they recently heard, it's not an easy story to listen to. Even for me, one who has heard it multiple times now, I still have a grueling time listening to it.

Violet takes a moment to visit the restroom right outside the room, while I watch and wait. I'm shocked when my mother is the person who walks back in instead of our PR rep. She takes her place behind the podium and introduces herself before giving a statement of her own.

"What is she doing?" I hear Violet gasp when she joins me.

And we both stand there and just listen.

"As the self-appointed spokesperson for my family, I'd like to say a few things about what you have recently heard. Our family stands proudly behind Princess Violet and supports her fully. We will continue to do so, and will not tolerate those who might question the authenticity of her statement.

"I have asked the captain of the Royal Guards, Sir Edward, to conduct a full investigation into the Del Markov family, specifically Ruben Del Markov. Advised him to turn over anything he uncovers, that would suggest Ruben is recruiting underage children into his criminal organization, to the authorities. I believe a man does not do what he did only once. That a person this depraved develops patterns to this type of behavior. And that this brave woman, who spoke only moments ago, is one of many we will likely stumble upon that he is responsible for ruining.

"We as a kingdom should be disgusted by what we heard this woman went through. We should unite together to stop this from happening to other young girls, no matter their background or social status. No child, no boy or girl, no man or woman, deserves to be treated the way Princess Violet has been treated for eight years. Instead of pointing fingers at the innocent victims out there like her, as we often do once the accused makes excuses for unacceptable behaviors, I challenge you all to stand with us, support her for being brave enough to report this unbelievable tale she thankfully survived.

"Thank you."

And like she walked out there all on her own, she exits. Once again, the room is silent, as if unsure of what just happened. This time I'm right there with them. My mother certainly shocked me with her words.

Maybe that's not right, I didn't expect her to take a stand like this. I'm not sure why, because my mother, after all, is the first of us to stand up and do what was right for us, her kids, and herself. So why I'm shocked she decided to appoint herself as the family spokeswoman seems silly. That she all but took charge of how our family would handle this situation surrounding the woman I love. It has my mind trying to figure out why I didn't expect that.

"Why did she do that?" Violet puts her hand on her throat as she stares at the now black screen. "She didn't have to do that, say all that. Why?"

"Because it was the right thing to do," my mother informs us when she enters the area we are waiting. "Because no one gets to treat my family that way. And no matter how much Ramon and I often stood on opposite sides of the fence, we always agreed on how men like the Del Markov's should be dealt with.

"I always had my suspicions about Viktor and how he got his hands on Marjorie. She went through a phase when she was a teenager like most do, I suppose. And that is when Viktor showed up and everything about her altered, she withdrew within herself, started getting involved with people that before she would never dare. Then she ended up pregnant with Ruben, at barely eighteen. Sound familiar?"

"You think..." Violet can't say the words, but we all can read between the lines.

"We could never prove it. And unlike you, Marjorie was at least able to give Viktor what he needed to gain access to some very powerful allies. The apple does not fall far from the tree. Sins of the father are often passed on to the son. Behavior is often learned and repeated throughout generations. History shows us how deeply true that is. Violence often produces more violence. Until someone breaks the cycle, by taking a stand and doing something about it, just like you did." My mother lays a hand on Violet's arm, and when she does, my wife completely loses it.

"Oh, my sweet child," she wraps Violet in her arms and holds her. Exactly like I have seen her hold my sister. The way my wife holds Charlotte when she is upset and needs her mother. "It's time you understand, that we are all here to help you with this heavy burden. You are no longer alone. We are all here for you, we are your family, and as you are about to discover, we don't let anyone mess with our family."

"Thank you, Your Royal Highness." My wife snivels very unladylike all over my mother, trying to regain her composure. "Oh, wow. I'm so sorry."

My mother takes Violet's face in her hand and squeezes gently, not at all bothered by the mess left behind. "Angela or Mother, not Your Royal Highness. My other daughters-in-law had to learn and you will as well."

"Okay, I'll do my best to remember. I believe this is the second time I've rubbed snot on you like that. I should start carrying a handkerchief with me, these hormones will surely cause more meltdowns." She takes the one I offer her and cleans her face before blowing her nose.

"Second time?" I ask, not recalling the first.

"The hospital." My mother quickly answers and then crosses her arms. "Hormones?"

Oh shit.

Yeah, we didn't get around to sharing that little news with her. I wanted to tell her myself so Violet did not have to suffer the lecture I knew would follow.

"Perhaps we should move this to a more private setting," I suggest as I grab my wife's hand and start moving. "Mother. I believe you haven't met your granddaughter yet. Come with us, and while we talk, you can get acquainted with her."

Antonio falls quickly in step with me and chuckles softly. "Using the granddaughter card already, little brother?"

I nod once. "Damn straight I am. One look at that sweet little face and all will quickly be forgiven."

CHAPTER 21
Violet

The Royals

Why do I suddenly feel like I want to go hide in the bedroom far away from Lorenzo's mother? I saw the look of disappointment on her face when realization set in and she discovered she hadn't been given the complete story.

It's been years since I've been made to feel as if I am about to get sat down and expected to explain my actions. I expect the last time that happened I may have been about fourteen. My grandmother, who mind you, pretty much let me do whatever the hell I wanted, found a joint in my jean pocket. She waited for me to come home from school, placed it on the table in front of me as soon as we were seated for dinner. I stared at it, not really sure what to say.

"Is it yours?" She'd asked me point-blank.

I could have lied, but I didn't, "Yes. What's it matter? It's just a joint Gran, no biggie."

She'd slapped me, pointed that crooked finger of hers at me, while she ranted and railed about how it was a gateway drug. One that led to all the other drugs floating around out there. Something about how that joint was how they pulled me in and blah, blah, blah.

I don't remember what she said completely or recall if she punished me even. I do remember she made me empty my pockets every time I came home for the next year. I also came to realize later she hadn't been wrong about it being a gateway drug. Pot was the least of her worries a year later when I returned home after letting some of my friends talk me into swallowing a few pills. I don't remember what they were exactly, but I remember how they made me feel. Those friends introduced me to the ones I took off with shortly after I turned sixteen, and we all know how the rest goes.

My grandmother should have taken a more proactive role in my life when she found the pot. Found me something more useful to do with my free time than hanging out with my loser friends. Maybe gave me a curfew or focused on my school work. Took that as a sign I needed more supervision. Instead of yelling at me when I stopped coming home at all, because who the hell needs to listen to that bullshit.

The way Angela was staring at Lorenzo, as he asked her what she wanted to drink, made me want to apologize. I hadn't apologized to my grandmother back in the day, never. So, this awareness of guilt was new to me. Had the mother inside of me taking notes on how effective a stare could be, even when polite words were coming out of one's mouth.

"Tea is fine, dear. Hot preferably, if it's not too much trouble." Her words sound so sweet and proper, but her eyes declare she will not wait forever for him to explain.

"No trouble at all. Take a seat and I'll start the kettle." He motions toward the lounge area, while he scrambles off in the direction of the small kitchenette. "Violet will keep..."

"I'm going to join Lorenzo in the kitchen." I flash her the best smile I can at the moment. "Make yourself comfortable. I'm sure Isabel will be here soon with Charlotte."

And then my feet are moving faster than Lorenzo's. I am so thankful there is a wall between us so I can chew him out quietly and she can't see us.

As soon as he steps inside the small kitchenette, I whisper shout at him. "You didn't tell her?"

He whisper shouts back while digging around for the kettle. "When was I supposed to have that conversation with her, Vi? Was it when we got off the plane and she made her presence known? Or perhaps I should have done it when she was out there making her statement. Hey mum, one more thing. That woman you are defending so greatly, she is also carrying your grandchild. How do I know that already, you ask mother? Simple really, we've been going at it like rabbits for the last month, while hiding out in a cabin, deep in the mountains of Wyoming."

I find the kettle first and chuck it at him when he looks up, almost hitting his stupid head with it. "You said you were going to talk with her. I thought that was what you were doing while I was getting Charlotte settled. What the hell were you doing all that time? Hiding from her because you knew she wasn't likely to approve. Do you realize the position you just put me in?"

He gets that stupid smirk on his face, as he says the dumbest thing yet. "I can tell you what position I'd like to put you in."

"You're an idiot." I spin around so I can look for something to go with the tea. "I thought she knew and was okay with it. Only to blurt it out, after making a complete fool of myself yet again. First, she walks in on me after I threw a Styrofoam pitcher at the wall when I was in the hospital. Which was bad enough, by the way. Having a woman like her, witness me having a meltdown after her son got the entire truth, as I knew it at the time, out of me. I mean, I was embarrassed enough as it was, that only added…"

His arms encircle me from behind, as he enfolds me inside the safe cocoon. "We've come so far since then, Vi. Calm down. Take a second and breathe. You are stressing over something that is already done. Trust me. My mother will forgive you, long before she forgives me."

"I don't want her mad at you either." I lean into him. "I'm sorry I've caused all this animosity between you and your family."

He spins me around, lifts me easily, and sets my arse down on the counter behind me. Stepping between my legs, he drags me as close to him as he can with us like that.

"One thing you are going to need to understand is that I know how to handle my family. You haven't gotten between us and you never will. I'm a grown-arse man, who hasn't answered to anyone since I left for university. The last time I lived at home was when I was nineteen. After that, I have been on my own. My mother's influence on my life, her control over it, stopped around that time as well.

"I've been living in Aragon for over a year, in a home I own with my dog, and a staff I control with no one's assistance. I'm not one of those Momma's boys who lives to please her. Granted, I would like her to be pleased with me. But like I have said time and time again, I am not ashamed about putting my child inside of you before we got married. And if my mother has an issue with that, then that is her problem, one she is going to have to get over all on her own."

The tea kettle whistles, directing both of our attention to why we are in the kitchen. Apparently, while we were so wrapped up in our arguing, his mother decided we were taking longer than necessary. Or maybe it was the little girl she is holding in her arms began wondering where we were, so she thought she'd bring her to us.

Mortified once again, I throw my hands in the air as I jump down to intercept. "Thank you, Angela. I see you've met my daughter."

Charlotte makes a face as she glances at the woman holding her. "Mummy her Gram, no Angela. Aunt Izzy say. Gram Papá mummy. He her baby boy. That silly." Charlotte lays her head on Angela's shoulder. "Her nice. Smell like flowers. I like her. She stay."

Angela rubs my daughter's back affectionately, clearly touched. "Isabel dropped her off shortly after you two ran off to make tea. Since Charlotte seemed comfortable with me, she headed back. We thought maybe you needed some assistance in here, so we came to offer it."

I don't say anything, I can't. I've never once seen my daughter take to someone so easily. The au pair Ruben has for her is the grandmother type, but Charlotte was always more afraid of her than anything else. That's the impression I got, at least. And even though I saw her with the woman Lorenzo hired secretively to replace the other one, I could tell Charlotte still wasn't at ease. Leery of her, much like I always am when I meet new people.

"You okay," Lorenzo's voice is closer than I realized, startling me. "Wow. What's wrong?"

"Excuse me," I tell them and get the heck out of there before I lose it in front of her for a third time.

As I go to pass by Angela, her words stop me. "I suspect I need to apologize."

"What? You need to apologize? Why is that exactly?" I sense that wave of nausea that never fails to show up at the most inconvenient moments.

"Lorenzo, run down to your brother's and ask for ginger crackers and cinnamon tea." Angela wraps one arm around me and guides me to the nearest lavatory.

"Why am I doing this exactly?" He asks as he follows behind.

She doesn't put Charlotte down as she pilots me to sit on the edge of the tub and grabs a washcloth, all while giving her son instructions. "Because a good husband makes sure his pregnant wife has what she needs to settle her tummy. Your brother makes sure to always have those with him after Larkin learned how well they worked for her."

I feel Charlotte grab onto my leg, meaning Angela must have put her down. She runs a cool cloth against my clammy neck after my hair is brushed to the side.

"I always hated the first trimester. The bouts of nausea, the headaches, the emotional ups and downs that have you not sure if you want to kill the man responsible or thank him. Maybe both, but not necessarily in that order, can't thank him properly if you kill him first."

Her hand rubs circles on my back and I sense the need to cry. I've never had anyone, other than Lorenzo, sit with me. Show any regard for my health or that they actually cared, and I don't know how to deal with that.

"Hi, Momma." Charlotte lays her head on my leg while she hugs it.

My hand immediately goes to her back, and I do exactly what Angela is doing. There will be no stopping the tears now. They fall from my eyes in rapid amounts, dripping down my cheeks, landing on my thigh before hitting the floor.

A tissue box is displayed before me and I tug on a few. "Thank you."

The hand on my back continues to rub, as the other reaches for my hand on Charlotte and pats it. She squeezes my forearm as if trying to decide if she should speak or let her silence do it for her.

"I'm really bad at letting others in. Your son, he snuck in without warning really, and then basically refused to go away. His kindness, compassion, caring demeanor to someone like me, someone not accustomed to that, was what had me falling so hard and fast for him. The way he wasn't afraid to show my daughter she didn't need to fear him. How he loved her, cared for, makes her feel safe. That only sealed the deal for me.

"Once I came to realize I'd fallen in love with him, I was afraid it would all slip away almost as quickly as it came to be. And before that could happen, I wanted to appreciate what it felt like to have a man love me, wanted that man to be Lorenzo. So, it's my fault this all happened, that you're disappointed in him, that I've brought disgrace..."

"Stop right there." Angela turns my face, so I am forced to look at her. "You've done no such thing. My son would not appreciate me making you feel like you've brought anything but happiness to our lives. Do you love him?"

"With all that I am."

She smiles widely. "And he loves you in much the same way. I have only ever wanted my children to find the person God thought was best for them. The one who would love them for who they are on the inside, one who could look past the other stuff. So far, they have all been very successful at that, even Lorenzo.

"I'm sorry if I gave you the impression that I was upset with you for..."

I do my best to help her when she pauses, "Trapping your son by getting pregnant."

When she offers me another tissue, I take it. Blow my nose and wipe my face so I don't look like some sappy woman who is completely insecure. Although that is exactly what I am, an insecure woman who is terrified that my husband will wake up very soon.

"If that is how I made you feel, then yes. That was not at all my intention. If you were anyone else, one of the many who have been hoping to be in your current situation, then I'd have said something that day in the hospital. But I knew even then you were different, and that you had bigger issues to concern yourself with than my son. Trapping him was never something you ever wanted to do because I suspect you realize the danger that puts him in. And the very last thing you want is to put one more person inside the life you have been suffering in."

"I am so scared of that, yes," I whisper through an additional set of tears. "I know the evil that surrounds Ruben. Know what he is capable of."

"And the people protecting this family do as well." She tells me standing, offering her hand. "I believe I heard him walk in a few moments ago."

I lift Charlotte and follow Angela to the kitchen.

Lorenzo's eyes land on me first when we step inside. He is doing a thorough inspection of me to make certain I wasn't railroaded by his mother. I can tell he is having some trouble determining that, so I let him see all is well.

"Your mother is very wise. She suggested I not kill you until after I thank you for planting your seed inside of me." I hand him Charlotte and grab one of the ginger crackers, taking a nibble. "But after that, all is free game, so you have been warned."

"I'll sleep with one eye open then." He grins as he leans over and places a kiss on my forehead. "Larkin said to keep these with you at all times. Even when you assume you won't need them anymore. They helped her early on and have saved her a few times since. The tea she says helps around bedtime when she has trouble sleeping.

"Dr. Wilson will be coming by soon. She was doing one last exam on the Queen, before heading back to Aragon. So, if you need to do anything before she gets here, you have time to do so."

"Like what exactly?" I ask as I take another nibble.

"Whatever it is you ladies do before letting a doctor examine you, I guess." Lorenzo hands his mother a cup of tea and then gives Charlotte her sippy cup. "What?"

He's asking this because I'm giving him this look that I'm certain he's not received before.

"Are you suggesting I wash up? That I might smell like clam or tuna, perhaps down there."

Poor Angela coughs on her hot tea as she tries not to laugh. Then I believe we both blush something fierce when her son drops to his knees and buries his face between my legs and inhales.

I grab his hair and try to step back from him and his sniffing. "What the f... hell, are you doing? Your mother, Lenny, is standing right there. Are you crazy?"

"About you, yes. In general, no. And you smell..."

I cover his mouth with my hands and try not to laugh at the idiot giving my crotch the sniff test. "Perhaps we should not discuss that at the moment. Stand up, please."

His mother shakes her head slightly as she suggests she take Charlotte for a walk. Letting the two of us meet with Dr. Wilson privately and without the interruption of a needy toddler.

While he gets her ready, I decide maybe I had better do a little freshening up. After that little stunt, my knickers were feeling wetter than normal, and I didn't want to have to explain why that was.

CHAPTER 22
Violet

The Royals

S
o, it's been a week since I exposed my secrets to the world. A week where I've had to listen to all sides discuss their thoughts on Lorenzo's judgment.

That's what it has come down to, really. I was either the woman he felt sorry for and took pity on. Or I was a woman who figured out how to use my circumstance to work best for me. Some were even insinuating I'd flipped sides once I realized the grass really was greener on the other side.

What hadn't been brought to light was Ruben's opinion on the details that had been released. His camp so far has kept very tight lips, while they seemed to be doing a little scheming. And that was worse than them simply denying everything.

The only action they have taken was to file legal lawsuits with the court. One dealt with the custody of Charlotte, asking the justices to return her to the only home she has lived in since birth. They weren't suggesting I took her without permission; they were only asking the court to not allow me to keep her. It was a crafty way of pointing fingers using documents, all of which had suggested I was a drug user and abuser. They were even pointing out that I had never once filed for custody or demanded visitation through the justice system. Until recently, I seemed comfortable with the arrangement we'd privately agreed to.

Thankfully, the court wasn't so eager to turn a child over to a man facing a number of legal battles of his own. They were at this point in time trusting the Royal Guards to report if the child was in imminent danger. Even assigned a liaison for Charlotte, one who was required to evaluate her current living conditions and report back. The liaison had recommended the child stay put for now after one visit. Stated that she was in no risk of harm and being well taken care of. Well-adjusted and attached to Lorenzo and me.

Two days after that decision had been made, the aftermath of what I had done hit and hit hard. I had expected retaliation, the worst he had, but I hadn't expected this.

We had prepared for a number of fights. Custody, kidnapping charges, even bigamy accusations against me for not divorcing Ruben first—no matter that our marriage was never legal in the eyes of the law. We even planned for the abuse of power allegations, aimed directly at the royal family, suggesting they were stepping in on a situation that was no concern of theirs.

Except the first attack had nothing to do with any of those matters. Nope, Ruben knew how to hit, throw a punch, catch you where you were not expecting it. Make it hurt in ways you didn't realize you could, and then have you sinking into the depths of despair, where life just couldn't possibly get worse.

I hadn't even been aware that he'd done some of the horrid acts he'd done over the years. Didn't grasp how awful it had been until that day.

We were woken by a phone call during the wee hours of the morning, by Darius Falcon, the family's lead investigator. He was requesting we get online and check out a video his team had received an alert on less than thirty minutes before. Warned us it was a graphic video, one we might have trouble watching, but one he needed me to verify that I was the person being victimized. His words, words that later I'd appreciated, because the purpose of the video was to prove otherwise.

I'm not sure how old I was, or when exactly the video had been taken. At least eighteen, that was the best I could do. Because before eighteen, nothing between me and Ruben had gone this far. Taking into account the style of my hair, the way I wore it prior to the days I started working, it made me look every bit of a naïve teenager. Exactly how he liked me to always look those early years.

What was even more disturbing, besides the fact it was a video of me and him having sex, his kind of sex. The kind where I was drugged out of my fucking mind and he was doing whatever the hell he wanted to me. Seeing me like that was awful enough, but the fact Lorenzo was also witnessing me at my worst was so much lower. And then to consider others had or were soon going to also be watching it, had me throwing up for the first time.

Before we even finished the first video, three more had been uploaded to a few different sites. I was older, but not by much. Early twenties, before Charlotte. I knew that much because I was missing a few scars, ones I distinctly remember acquiring the first time he returned once I'd been released to go home without her.

And these are worse, so much worse.

Apparently, Ruben wasn't the only man I'd ever had sex with. And just to be clear, I'd not given my permission for any other man to touch me, hadn't agreed to this type of behavior. Wouldn't have ever agreed if he'd bothered to ask, but Ruben never asked. Not even when he took what he claimed was his right to take. He never asked, he always just took.

When I was so far beyond high, it seems he allowed some of his closest men to do the same horrid acts to me he liked to do. He wasn't only allowing it, he was overseeing them, participating in the acts with them. Sitting back and watching, laughing, talking, while giving them a few orders on what to do and how to do it.

When I got mouthy or tried to voice my disapproval, they'd gag me while they fucked me. Sometimes they'd gang rape me while I was tied up and tripping on the drugs they'd forcefully injected into me, to ensure I wouldn't fight them, couldn't fight them. Two at a time, even. They used my body until they had had enough, and then they'd leave me for Ruben to abuse some more.

While I was watching, I'd thrown up so many times I felt as if I was dying. Nonetheless, I refused to stop watching until I'd made it through to the end. I had to know what I hadn't known, just so I had all the facts for once. I so was tired of being lied to and being kept in the dark.

My being so physically ill had concerned Lorenzo so much that once we'd made it through all four, he'd insisted someone call a physician to calm me down. He wanted to make sure both the baby and I were okay, that physically I was going to be okay at least. Once the doctor was done examining me, administered a light sedative, one he assured my husband was safe for the baby. He suggested I rest and drink plenty of water.

After Lorenzo had walked him out and returned to our bedroom, he laid with me on the bed. "My sister Gabriela is here. She came as soon as she heard about the videos. Char and her are going to hang out together."

"Heard about the videos? Doesn't she have class? I don't want her..."

Lorenzo places a finger over my lips. "She said this was more important, and I can't say I disagree. It was one of her schoolmates who'd alerted her of the first one. She called it in immediately. I don't know much more than that."

I can only blink my eyes at that knowledge. I mean seriously, did I want to learn the details, probably not.

"I love you, Violet." He whispers softly and sweetly as he stares deeply into my eyes.

That's when the tears start for both of us. We cry so many tears in that bed together, that later I can't distinguish whose tears are whose when we finally stop. Afterward, he leaves me to rest, so he can get us some food, check in on his sister and our daughter—that is what he's started calling Charlotte, his daughter. Once he has forced some soup and water down me, we continue to lie there a little longer. Talk about it all. More tears are shed, but they are not as severe as earlier, just leftover tears.

"I didn't know about all that," I admit, ashamed I'd been so stupid to not realize that was why he often had his men accompany him. Why they looked at me like they knew my body as well as he did. The reason several of them made me extremely uncomfortable. Why I hated it when they were around me without him when Charlotte was left in my care.

"What they did to you Vi, it was wrong. It makes this, what we have…" His words trail off while he tries to compose himself. "I love you so much. What I saw on those videos could never change that, if anything, it has strengthened the bond holding us together. Reinforced it. Makes me glad I went with my gut and chased after you when you tried to run without me. We are going to take them down, expose them, make them pay. When you are ready, we are going to slay each and every one of them, until we obliterate them."

He pulls us out of bed and forces us into the shower. Washes me with hands that take their time to display his love. Soft hands move over my once misused body, doing their best to remind this body who it now belongs to. And while he does all that, his eyes express the love he endures is still strong and present. It hasn't been diminished by all the vile he's seen. In fact, I expect it is even stronger now than before. Not because of what we'd been forced to watch, but because of how we have fallen into the other person and soak up all they have to offer.

And maybe you won't understand how this next part materialized, but I don't care. After he has washed the day away from both of us. I make a conscious choice to relish in the man I am coming to depend on as my rock. I stare into his eyes and then carry out that decision. "Lenny, make love to me."

Those words begin to affect him the way they always do, his eyes get that sultrier appearance. His facial features alter just enough, as he rolls his neck, readying himself for one hell of a performance. "Are you sure?"

I love that he asks, while at the same time I hate it. I hate that he is questioning why I may not be.

"I'm sure." I reach down and stroke the length of him and he grows harder in my palm. "I want you to take me in here first, with nothing between us."

He has been dying to get inside of me with no protection. Even after Dr. Wilson examined me and gave me the all-clear, I'd wanted to be absolutely positive before risking it. She'd taken some blood, sent us to a lab the following morning, where they collected what they needed. The results were due any day now, and we had no reason to conclude they would be any different since I wasn't displaying any signs.

Which is why my words seem to propel him from almost there, to completely there in seconds. I'm lifted off the ground and pressed against the tile wall, my legs wrapping around his waist, securing me to him. One hand slips between us, where he touches me, working me like only he ever has. As soon as he realizes I'm more than ready for him, he wastes no time to give me what I need. He is pushing inside of me slowly, dragging that wonderfully large head of his through my channel. It is firing off all those sensitive nerves along the path he has put on alert.

"Vi," my name falls from his lips. "Incredible. How is it possible for this to be so much better? Let's do our best to abolish a few of those damn dragons now, shall we? Are you ready?"

I am more than ready and I tell him so. I want it soft and sweet, then I want it hard and fast and rough. After he takes me in the shower, I want him to take me on the bed, against the wall. Afterward, I want him to take me from behind, with me on all fours while he is driving into me hard.

Later, once we'd recovered from all those glorious acts, I ask him to tie me up.

"I don't know about that one. It might trigger something." It isn't a no, so I take that as my chance to explain.

"This is about me trusting you, Lenny. Before the reasons they had restrained me, had nothing to do with trust, it was about control. I am freely giving you control along with my trust. Proving that I know, even though I won't be able to stop you..."

"Speak the words and I'll stop." He interrupts.

Reaching up, I cup his handsome face, "Even though I physically cannot stop you, I have no reason to fear you. Tie me up however you want and then make love to me."

Using the tie he'd yanked off after a meeting yesterday afternoon, he secures my wrist together. Lifts them above my head and orders me to keep them there. Again, he heats my body with one delicious ravishing.

When I lift my arms to touch him, he stops and pushes them back above my head. His playful attitude as the dominant one in charge has me laughing, and that only encourages him to continue. Before long, we are both laughing and playing around while he ravages my body. He is convincing both of us that this was the right thing to do, possibly something we might even be up to doing more often.

The rest of the afternoon, we touch on almost everything. We cried some more, but not because we were sad, because not all tears have to be sad ones. Shared a lot more laughs, some that had us crumbling against each other, accompanied by more joyful tears. We even screamed out in pleasure so many times that both our voices were displaying signs of strain.

And before it was all over, I made one last request I wasn't sure he'd agree to. I need him to take me anally because I want him to wash away all the horrible acts done to me without my permission. I know this time he will need to wear one of the condoms we have left.

He is reluctant to give in. "Violet, that seems a little over the top, don't you think? I've never really thought about that before, I'm not sure I can or should. I don't want to hurt you."

"Just this once. I need you inside all the same places he once invaded, without ever caring if it was what I wanted. You need lots of lubrication and to go slow. Even he was smart enough to know that. It was the one time he took his time with me. Please, just this once."

Lorenzo agrees finally, makes certain I am well lubed, and that he is able to maintain eye contact while doing so. Like all the other times, he does his best to make sure we both enjoy it, that I don't feel the least bit ugly or sick about it. It is tender and from the heart, equal to all the times he made love to me. He does his best to make certain I orgasm more than once during the act, keeping my mind on those. Instead of allowing it to wander off and ponder on other things.

Once he is inside of me fully, our final climax ends up being one that is so powerful, I nearly blackout from the pleasure. All I remember is him roaring like an animal, as he pounds into me like I had demanded. And me being right there with him, matching those roars with a few of my own.

After we are done erasing all the ugliness from both our minds, we slow it down one last time. He makes soft, sweet love to me, sending us into a blissful slumber.

When I wake hours later, sore and stiff from it all, from everything, my mind felt renewed. I know I need to get up and come up with a plan of attack. And because he is snoring softly next to me, exhausted from the events of the day, I leave him there. He's done more than enough for now, had earned this moment to sleep it off.

I sneak off to the bathroom, clean up quickly, and get dressed. Later slip out unnoticed into the main living quarters where the small kitchenette is located. After I've made myself a cup of hot tea, I make my way down to the bedroom I know Charlotte is likely sleeping with her aunt.

Pushing the door open quietly, I am blessed with the sight I uncover. Once again, I'm blown away by this family we are so blessed to call ours. I've only met Gabriela once, and that was at Winifred's birthday celebration. The very same day this seemed to turn into something I couldn't stop.

Lying together in the bed sleeping is how I find them. Charlotte is as close to Gabriela as she can get, practically sleeping on top of her. The younger woman must not mind though, because her arm is wrapped around her in slumber.

Even though I want to join them, wrap my arms around my daughter, and hold her just because I can, I don't. It's almost midnight, and I have so much I need to do before tomorrow gets here. So, I blow an air kiss across the room before I close the door quietly.

I trek back down the hall and scrounge through the refrigerator until I find something that sounds good. Once I have a plate, I go into the small office Lorenzo has been using. Log onto the computer with a pen and paper in hand. I locate the first video that has someone besides me and Ruben in it and start taking notes.

I'm not sure how long I have been sitting here analyzing these videos. The stiffness in my back and neck warns me it's been a few hours. The cramp in my hand screams the same warning. But it's the male voice that echoes from the doorway, that is what finally makes me pause. "What are you doing? You shouldn't be watching those again. Why are you? I swear if I ever get him in a room alone..."

I turn the monitor off so he isn't forced to stare at the image currently on display. "I'm writing down names. I thought Karina might like to identify who she needs to file charges against. I'm also using a video noise elimination software Darius sent me, that way I can enhance certain sounds. I'm even recording all the times I said *no, please stop, you're hurting me*, along with anything else that suggests I was not on board with any of this.

"And before you ask me why I'm doing this instead of someone else, it's because the thought of anyone else analyzing these so thoroughly, makes me sick again. Someone has to do it. And while I understand another person will have to verify all this, at least I know that they won't be watching it a thousand times to do so."

I toss the pen down and stretch. Yawn even, now that I've stopped.

Lorenzo flips the screen back on. "Have you watched it a thousand times?" Then closes the window and does whatever is necessary to save my progress, before shutting it down.

"Probably. I've only made it through the first and second videos so far. Darius told me they've been removed and the accounts have been suspended. His team is working extra hard to prevent any more from popping up. I'm not sure how, but it sounded technical and like it was something they did a lot."

I don't fight him when he tugs on my arms to pull me to my feet. Or complain when he scoops me in his arms and begins carrying me down the hall toward the bedroom. I only lean my head against his shoulder and allow this man to put me back to bed, now that I've at least got a head start. The rest can wait until morning.

"That's because they do. Before you go back to sleep, is there anything you need?" When I shake my head, he tucks me into the bed next to him. "We rest now. Both of you need sleep. We can slay more dragons tomorrow together. No more slaying them alone, okay."

I yawn again as I snuggle into him. "Okay."

CHAPTER 23
Lorenzo

The Royals

My wife has proven to be one of the strongest women I know. She has spent hours analyzing new videos that were constantly popping up. Writing down names, documenting each time she made it clear she wanted it to stop. Doing what she could to ensure these men paid for what they had done to her.

It was always hardest for her the first time through, even though we always watched them together. That was a rule I made once we realized this was going to be a regular occurrence for a while. And most of the time she would throw up immediately afterward. We'd talk about it sometimes, depending on how debauched they were, we might even shed a few tears.

My absolute preferred method of moving past the ugliness of it all, was when she allowed me to love her. Mainly because I loved making love to my wife. Love how her body feels against mine. Enjoy all the noises I am able to coerce out of her, while I do my best to drive her over the edge. In my mind, there is nothing better in life than loving a woman who appreciates all the ways you love her.

But I also love it, because something always seems to materialize during those times together. We often connect on a higher level as we open ourselves up completely to each other. Not afraid to be vulnerable when we are in the thick of it all so we can heal together. We didn't judge what the other person might need, and we didn't push the other person to give something maybe they couldn't. We merely loved each other however we wanted to and cherished every second.

I know there are those who would probably judge us for the way we choose to deal with it all. But that is the beauty of being in a relationship with only one person. There is only one other person who matters, what others think doesn't. And that has become our motto we live by. As long as we are on the same page, keeping the lines of communication open, everyone else can shut the hell up.

As a couple, we decided to make another public statement a few days ago. Once again, Violet was the one to speak, with me standing proudly next to her. It was short and to the point. She mentioned the recent videos being posted on the web. Explained how sick they made her feel, because she had not been aware of the acts now being made public, had even been done to her. Mentioned how she planned on bringing charges against the men responsible, not for just posting them, but for raping her. Encouraged those who were so sure of her consent, to take a closer look at them again, listen closely to her voice and words when she had been allowed to express them. Pointed out that no matter if a woman is drugged or drunk, or even at first has given her consent. As soon as she says no, says the word stop, pleads for them to leave her alone, all while she then does her best to fight her attacker off, it is not okay for it to continue.

Using my mother's words, she challenged the public to not tolerate this type of behavior, and to become outraged that there were men like this out there, abusing young girls. No man, woman, or child should have to suffer from the hands of men like this, no matter their status. It was time to take a stand against this behavior. Time to become the voice of the silent and oppressed victims.

Social media had blown up after that. People started the hashtags *#WeStandWithPrincessViolet* and *#VioletProud*. Posting those all over the web, revealing how they agreed with her, that it was time to stop blaming the victims and start standing up for them instead. She'd become an instant advocate for all those women out there without voices. And she was not about to back down now that she had the men responsible in a corner.

It was Karina who came to us with something neither of us had taken into consideration. She wasn't sure exactly how to bring it up, but once she did, both of us were glad she had. And there was only one way to get what we needed to test her theory. There was probably a better method to collect what we required, but there sure wasn't going to be a more exciting means of getting it.

Ruben was an amateur fighter, much like me. He enjoyed cage fighting, MMA, best. Was often invited to the different establishment that held monthly matches and paid the winners well. Some were legal, most were not. But in his world that didn't matter, the illegal fights were where a man like him walked away a winner either way. His hand was most likely in the pot first, since the Del Markov's organization never permitted other criminal groups to outsmart them.

Tonight's, however, was taking place in a legal and more respectable establishment. We couldn't take any chances at the moment, give his side a reason to make us look bad in the eyes of the public—or the courts, for that matter. We were definitely winning that battle. According to recent reports, it was actually starting to hurt several of his business dealings, both legal and illegal.

Keeping our noses as clean as possible right now, was not only a smart move, it would also aid with the court cases that were soon to follow. We had a few coming up. And tonight, we were hoping to get the biggest one thrown out completely. We needed proof, and since we'd sent a request that had been denied by their camp, we were going to obtain what we needed another way. Two can play this devious game, and I for one was really looking forward to this match.

I wasn't exactly thrilled my wife was here with me, but there was no way to leave her behind. I knew her well enough, that if I'd even tried to do so, she'd eventually show up. This way at least I didn't have to worry about who was with her when she did.

Our best men and women, our sharpest guards, were with us tonight. Not just the best from my staff, we'd borrowed Stew from Esteban. As soon as Karina had caught wind of that, she offered to accompany us to keep Violet company. So, there was Stew, along with

Hillary and Vincent, who were part of Winifred's team. They were posing as the other couple we were out with.

Right now, we are all walking in, about to take our seats in the VIP section close to the cage. Javier is scheduled to fight tonight. That's why we're here, to watch him kick the shit out of the man I'd rather be kicking the shit out of. I've been to a few of his fights before, but have always kept a low profile when doing so. Tonight, the plan was to make it very well known that I was not only here, but here with my wife. Visible from the cage where the men would be fighting, letting Ruben know we weren't hiding anymore, not even scared to be in the same room as him. What happened after he spotted us would be up to him.

While we waited it out, we are well entertained. Karina is not about to give up on Stew. And by the way, she is dressed tonight, it's a wonder the man can maintain his focus at all.

If you've never been to an MMA fight, you may not be aware of what goes on. I've never seen so much skin on display. Women dressed in clothing that barely covers all the essentials. Bikini tops, halter tanks, t-shirts that have been cut into tiny strips that don't hide the fact they left their bras at home. That's just the top half. The bottoms are no better, though. Shorts that only cover the parts not allowed to be shown in public, skirts that if they bend over, will put all those parts in plain view. Not everyone is dressed like that, mind you, but there are enough that it paints a pretty descriptive picture, suggesting sex and fighting often go together.

I will at least give Karina some credit. She went for the classier sexy look. Her red dress covers her, mostly. It's cut a little low and incredibly tight, not leaving a great deal to the imagination. But that doesn't stop her from putting on one hell of a show for Stew. She is sitting in his line of sight, so he doesn't miss a damn thing. Giving him some rather sultry eyes that express all her thoughts directed at him and only him.

And when some dude gropes her arse, while she makes her way to the bar area, none of us miss the expression that takes over Stew's face. A murderous look that says he's taking notes for later.

"How much longer do you imagine it will be before he finally gives in to her advances?" My wife giggles next to me when another guy grabs Karina's waist and drags her to him.

Stew growls loudly at the sight of that. Shortly after he is chuckling, because Karina can take care of herself. She nearly twists the guy's balls right off.

As soon as she sits down Violet asks, "What did you say to him while you did that?"

Karina shrugs nonchalantly and stares directly at Stew. "I asked how he likes getting those grabbed without his permission. Then I pointed out the large man glaring murderously at him. Told him he was lucky I took care of him myself but warned him he might not want to stick around."

Violet laughs and shakes her head at the woman's honesty. "I'm sure my husband may not exactly be thrilled about this fact, but well, I like you. When this is all over, I think we could be friends. The kind that gets into a lot of trouble together. While I adore your sister and Larkin, I'm not so sure they'd appreciate all I have to offer. But you, you and I are like kindred spirits."

I might have laughed if my attention hadn't been drawn to the familiar face staring at me from across the arena. Realization washes over hers, and before I can make my demands, she begins making her way toward us. The guards don't even stop her, they allow her to pass and walk right up to our table.

"Before you blow a gasket..."

I don't let her finish. "Way past that point Gabby, way past it. Where are your guards? Please tell me they are here and only being inconspicuous." I stare at my sister, already knowing her answer.

"I might have snuck out without them knowing. You remember how to do that, right? It wasn't all that long ago when you used to ditch yours so you could pretend to be half-way normal."

She holds up a hand when I nearly lose my mind. "Hold your horses. Don't you start acting all barking mad and causing an unnecessary scene. I knew my shadow wouldn't let me down. He'd alert the Calvary. And like always, I'd have someone making certain I remained pure and untouched, at least until I'm old enough in his mind for him to finally make a move. Although I'm getting a little tired of all this cock blocking, I'm not..."

Violet tugs on Gabriela's arm and into the vacant seat next to hers.

"Using the term cock blocking, when speaking with one of your brothers, might not be wise. Who is this mystery man we need to keep an eye on?"

Gabriela grabs Karina's fresh martini, aims it at the shadows directly across from us. "You know what I really hate about all this?"

I squint my eyes, but can't make out the man standing there, posed against a wall. "That someone is onto you and knows that we will pay him greatly for keeping you safe?"

My sister rolls her eyes as she downs Karina's drink, causing the other woman to laugh. "You already pay him greatly."

"I do?" I squint more now, trying to figure out which male on my staff is about to get either a promotion or an arse-kicking.

"Well, not you directly, but he's on the payroll." Gabriela waves the now empty glass in his direction and points, then flashes two fingers at him before snapping her fingers. "Might as well take advantage of the fact he can now relax and enjoy himself, right? I mean, since I have all these other fine men to keep my arse safe, he'll be my cabana boy."

Violet is trying hard not to laugh outright, "Who? You haven't exactly given us a name."

"That's because he's a chickenshit and I..." she pauses with a devious smile, taking over her face. "Well, would you look at that, maybe he's not so chicken."

I'm a little surprised when I see who emerges from the shadows. He's been with my brother Antonio for almost five years now. One of his personal guards he works closely with.

There is another man with him, I've never seen him before. My wife however appears to recognize him. "Please tell me you do not mean Bruno, Gabby."

"Bruno, no. So that's his friend's name. The man who seems to show up and ruin all my fun when Gino isn't capable of doing so himself."

I reach for Violet's hand, noticing how uncomfortable she gets when the men get closer. "What is it?"

Before she can answer, both men are standing at the table. The man I recently learned is Bruno smiles fondly at Violet, and I decide I don't like it.

"Who's your friend, Mr. Leblanc? I'm not sure I like him." I glare at the man next to me to make my point.

Bruno extends a hand my way, "I'm Bruno Leblanc. I work for..."

My wife interrupts him, "He works for Ruben."

"Not exactly. I mean, yes and no. I do work for him, yes, but because I was ordered to do so. Infiltrated the organization to gather information. I didn't realize... you must recognize, had I... please know I'd not have allowed any of that had I known. My job was not to ask questions. I was never really privileged to all things concerning you, that beautiful little girl of yours, or the comings and goings. My position deals with, or more like dealt with, other aspects.

"Please forgive me, you have no idea how horrible I feel for not asking more questions, or stepping in when I felt something was not right. I am so very pleased that you and the little one, are now safe. It will be my pleasure taking him down, making him pay greatly for all his crimes."

"You don't work for him any longer?" Violet's hand grips mine harder. "And for the record, I always thought you didn't fit in all that well. You have kind eyes, an actual conscience, always showed too much concern for my daughter's safety. It, I believe, got you in trouble a few times."

The man nods slightly. "Got me fired, actually. Seems I allowed the nice new au pair to take her with one of the newest guards, and we all appreciate how that turned out. They dismissed me after a good beating and then told me I'd never work in the business again."

"You are related to Gino?" I ask as I look closely at them both.

"I am his younger brother. I work for the National Investigative Agency, in the Organized Crime Unit. Until recently I was one of the undercover agents, now I work with those agents, help train them for fieldwork. Eventually, I'll get back out in the field, when it's safe to do so again. My cover hasn't been blown; I do trust it still hasn't.

"And since I seem to have a little more free time, I've been doing some recon work for Gino. Keeping tabs on someone dear to him, dear to those he works for..."

Gabriela voices her opinion loudly. "I call bullshit. He's just afraid I'll actually find a guy who isn't concerned with who I am or who my brothers are. And frankly, I'm getting bored with all these childish games."

"Then perhaps you should stop acting like a child." Gino finally speaks, in a voice that says he's close to losing it. "If I was one of your guards…"

"Like that will ever happen." Gabriela rises to her feet. "I'm done here."

Gino blocks her from leaving. I'm not sure what he says, but it has my sister taking a seat again with her arms crossed defiantly.

"Now keep your arse in that seat for the remainder of the evening. Otherwise, you are going to get to know a side of me I do not believe you are ready for yet." He storms past Stew, who by the way is chuckling, and heads straight for the bar with his brother shadowing him.

Violet and Karina are both fanning themselves as they watch.

Karina is the one this time to raise the question we are all wondering. "What did he say that put that blush on your cheeks and made him go all alpha male on you?

I can't hear her but Violet can, she is laughing outright at my sister, along with Karina's reaction to her words. She hands her the fresh drink that was just delivered to the table and offers her some advice I'm not privy to either.

When she is done, I lean toward her. "What did he say?"

"Are you sure you want to know?" Her eyes find mine and I can see amusement bouncing around. "You have to promise not to kill him if I tell you. It was meant to get her attention, not as a threat or some sort of punishment. He's a man who is a little frustrated about a few matters, letting off some steam. Can you do that?"

She's my little sister, who I am extremely protective of, I'm not sure if I can or not.

"Whatever, I won't allow you to harm a man I believe actually has your sister's best interest in mind." Violet grins as if she knows I'm not going to like it, but at the same time can hopefully be reasonable. "He told her if she did it again. He promised to treat her like a disobedient child and spank her arse with his bare hand and enjoy every swat she earned."

"And you're okay with that?"

I find the man we are discussing and notice something I never have before. He's fighting a serious battle with himself right now, one he is eventually destined to lose. For Gabriela's sake, he's fighting hard to keep it together for as long as he can, giving her time to grow up. I have to appreciate that. His strength to hold off shows me just how much he cares for my little sister.

"Yeah. If I thought he meant to harm her, I'd take care of him myself, but he's not." Violet slides her hand onto my thigh and squeezes. "Playful spanking, as we've learned, can be a lot of fun."

I growl for two reasons. One, remembering how spanking that arse of hers, that she wiggled in my face a few nights ago, was a lot of things, fun being one. The other being, "She's my sister, Vi. Those thoughts can get a man killed when put into her brother's head."

CHAPTER 24
Lorenzo

The Royals

We sit there almost an hour before the fights begin. By then the crowd has been well primed to cheer on the blood battles taking place in the cage not all that far from us. We aren't in the front row where the sweat, blood, and spit lands on you. The VIP sections are a level off the floor, even with the main stage. It is however close enough to the action you miss nothing, but far enough away you also don't end up needing to get tested later.

Javier's fight is the featured event, so it is the last one scheduled for the evening. All the other fights are meant to rile up to the crowd. They do just that. One fighter ends up having to be carted off after his opponent did a number on him. Another's leg snapped when it got twisted in a very painful position while he tried to kick his challenger in the head. Several more were unrecognizable by the time they called their matches.

The crowd was loving every crack, pop, snap, and splat that sounded. Filling the air as fist met flesh, knees contacted with bones, and blood landed on the mat.

It is one of the most violent sporting events around, one that explains why it was so popular with a certain brand of crowd. Why so many of these fighters are known to be associated with criminals. Often recruited by them when they are struggling to make a name for themselves.

"Why does Javier fight again?" Violet doesn't seem at all impressed by what she has witnessed throughout the evening.

"He says it gives him a chance to use all those skills he needs as a guard. Let's him throw a real punch and kick, in a controlled environment, but one that feels every bit as real in an uncontrolled situation. Sparring with the other guards isn't even close to the same as fighting someone who has no reason not to give you everything he has. The guards need to be able to work, these guys couldn't care less if you can work or not, they just want to fight and win."

"Aren't you afraid he won't be able to work if he gets hurt fighting? Why do you let him fight? It's so violent. He doesn't seem like a violent man." I can tell she is seeking to figure out why anyone would ever want to do this.

"He's not. He's a protective man. And I'm more concerned about the men he fights against than I am about him. He only fights a couple of matches a year. So far, he's only lost once, and that was in the early days when he was still learning about the rules of MMA fighting."

"You said you've done some fighting, boxing. Is it like this?" I notice the concern and I know why. "I don't know if this is such a good idea, Lenny."

I lean over and kiss her. Not a simple brief kiss, but not like I kiss her when we are alone. Although it is a kiss that is meant to do a few things to her, mainly quiet her mind.

"Boxing is a lot different. Less violent, in my opinion, but it's still fighting. Requires stamina and strength, being quick on your feet while predicting your opponent's next move. Different, but still the same." I grip her face and stare deep into her eyes. "Javier wouldn't allow anything to happen, he needs me as much as I need him."

The lights go dim and the crowd roars. The announcer is doing all he can to get them excited about the fight ready to take place. I slide in behind Violet and wrap my arms around her. We are eye level with the cage, have been recognized several times this evening. Fighters talk, so I'm confident that news has been shared with the one man we are hoping to get a reaction out of.

"Ladies and gentlemen. We are about to start our main event." The crowd roars. "You are in for a real treat. Both of our fighters tonight usually draw a crowd. But that isn't why I believe this night will end up being one of the greatest fights you'll see this year."

I recognize the moment he enters the arena by how my wife's body tenses. Every muscle she has goes rigid, and the hold she has on my hand tightens to an almost painful grip. Which is why I lean over and place a kiss on her shoulder as I drag her body closer to mine.

That is when our eyes lock and I realize what he is thinking, just like I am sure he knows what I'm thinking. Turning to the man standing next to him, he mumbles a few words, glares in our direction again, and nods toward the announcer.

One spotlight, that has been spinning around the arena, stops spinning and lands on us.

"Tonight, we'd like to welcome Prince Lorenzo and his lovely new wife. I'm sure most of you are aware of the controversy surrounding him and one of the men about to fight, Ruben Del Markov. There has been some bad press, some accusations tossed around that have put both sides on the defensive.

"We don't normally like encouraging two men who hate each other to get inside a cage and go a few rounds." The crowd seems to realize what might actually transpire, it's as if they can taste the thrill of witnessing something so primal play out. "However, tonight we have a challenge being offered to do just that. To guarantee this is a clean fight, we've agreed to allow these men to have their chance to brawl if they'd like. What do you say, Prince Lorenzo, are you up for the challenge Ruben is extending your way?"

Let it be known that the men running this place would not have asked if they didn't already know my answer. Of course, I wanted my shot to make Ruben pay for all the sick and cruel acts he'd done to my woman. And I wasn't about to look like a pussy in front of this crowd.

I stand.

I loosen my tie and start to unbutton my dress shirt, letting that be my reply. The entire room goes ballistic. People chant my name, not exactly making Ruben's day.

Gabriela is on her feet. "You can't be serious. This is crazy. Violet, don't let him get in there. Ruben will..."

I grab my sister's arm and gently push her back down into her seat. "Watch and learn, little sister."

Gino is suddenly back amid our little group, taking control over Gabriela when she protests. "A little faith in your brother and his men will go a long way, Ela."

My sister glares at him but seems to settle for now.

I nod, step in front of Violet as I remove my shoes and socks, slide my belt from my pants, and then empty my pockets. We stare at each other, agreeing silently how far I will allow this to go. We've talked extensively about this, I promised her I'd let it go only so far, and that nothing he says will make me break that promise.

The announcer broadcasts that while I'm getting ready in the back, warming up and changing, there will be a thirty-minute intermission. While he does this Violet escorts me, along with my guards, to where Javier and his team are waiting.

I've changed into my standard, tight dark green and red fighting shorts, the kind most of these fighters like to wear. Completed my warmups, so my muscles are ready to do what I need to do.

Violet has mostly paced nervously the length of the small locker room. Mumbling to herself. If I'm not mistaken, I believe those mumbles are in the form of a prayer. She's been doing that a little more lately, praying. We've talked about where I stand religiously. I'm not a big fan of religion, she's learned. I'm a fan of God, though. Believe in him. Pray to him. Study all points of view about what others who also believe in him think. Do my best to live my life aligned with how I believe he wants me to live it.

And with all this stuff she's had to deal with, we've turned to him for comfort and guidance. By doing so, I've noticed the peace she seems to experience about it all. I'm not saying she's completely calm or doesn't have moments when despair sets in, it just seems to silence those responses quicker so she can think.

When I'm ready, I ask for a few minutes alone with her. The room clears and we stand there staring at the other person for a bit until we don't. Then we're wrapped up in each other, providing comfort in our own special way.

The loud clapping has us pulling apart, just enough to notice the man standing in the doorway smirking.

I slide an arm around her protectively. "What do you want?"

"Aren't you two the sweetest?" His voice has that sadistic tone to it. "I bet you fuck her just as sweetly too, don't you?"

I jolt forward, except Violet presses her hand against my chest. "Don't. That's what he wants, for you to react while he gets in your head."

Ruben throws his head back and scoffs mockingly. "She really has you fooled, doesn't she? I bet you even believe all those lies she's been feeding you. How I forced her to do all those..."

"You did," Violet this time is the one to lunge forward. "Proof is right there in all those videos you've posted. You..."

"Oh, please. Did I also force you to shoot up all those times when I wasn't even around? Awe. You didn't think I knew about those, did you? Does he?" His voice sounds so confident that I don't know, so when neither of us respond, he goes on. "Does he know the reason I never left you with Charlotte? That you were a danger to her, and yourself, threatened to kill both of you when you didn't get what you wanted. That the original plan, when you ran, was not to just start over fresh, but ultimately to end both your lives, just because you could. Does he realize that?"

We'd discussed all of that, yes.

She told me that early on, when he'd left her alone with her daughter, in a moment of weakness she'd planned it all out. Added some sleeping pills to one of the bottles and then shot a lethal amount of Ruben's special blend into her veins. The plan had been to go together, except hers kicked in faster than she'd intended, making her incapable of offering Charlotte the laced bottle. Ruben returned hours later to a screaming infant, evidence of crushed pills, and Violet passed out, lying in a bed of her own vomit. She'd awakened to a note left by him, explaining what he was going to do to her when he returned.

That had been her wake-up call, and the last time she'd ever willingly used the drugs he left for her. She cleaned herself up. Eventually applied for the job at the palace. Did her best to figure out what she could do to keep her daughter safe, what she would do if she ever got the chance to run. Her plan about ending both of their lives was long forgotten. While she knew if he ever caught her, her own life was over, she'd figured out another way to protect Charlotte, one he clearly wasn't aware of.

"I know everything," I answer. "My wife and I don't have secrets. I even know what you don't know. Her intention was never to end their lives, it was to end yours."

If ever there was a laugh that made a person's skin crawl. "That *suka* could never pull something like that off. How did you plan on ending my life? Were you going to shoot me yourself? Please. I find that idea ludicrous. There is no way you would ever get close enough, I'd end yours first."

"In the eight years I was with you, did you not think I had learned a few tricks along the way? That I hadn't picked up on what it was you liked most, where your weaknesses are, the best places an enemy of yours could strike..."

Ruben this time advances, "You fucking bitch. I'll fucking kill you, kill him. Make you watch while I fuck your sister first, then your brother. Turn those little brats over to my associates, ones who like them young. And then I'll raise that little bitch and teach her the Del Markov way."

As soon as my guards heard his shouts, they stepped out and made their presence known. Rico immediately places himself between the raging man and us.

"Are we going to do this? Or are you going to back down like a pussy?" He shouts and tries to move Rico with his body, but the man is a brick wall that cannot be moved.

"I'm ready when you are, arsehole. I'm planning to enjoy kicking your arse first, then I'm going to enjoy watching everything fall in around you." I nod my head toward the doorway. "Lead the way, Ruben. Let's do this."

He turns and storms out the door he entered moments earlier. Speaks in Russian to the men standing just outside in the hall, and they lead him to his own staging area.

"Sir, when you are ready. It is all set." Rico need not elaborate; I understand his words.

"I'm ready," I tell him, rolling my neck. "I'm ready."

"Lenny," Violet steps in front of me. "This isn't necessary. We can find another way."

"I know we can. But I don't know that I'll get another chance to knock that smirk off his face. Trust me."

I haven't exactly told her the entire plan; I'm holding a little back for just me. Although I don't imagine when she realizes what I have done, she'll be all that mad. In the end, we will get what we came for, and I'll get a little revenge in as well.

Even though Ruben left first, we make it back out to the arena ahead of him. I'm not surprised, old habits are hard to break, I'm counting on that, actually.

I know the moment I see him, I'm not wrong. His eyes are dancing around wildly, exactly like I knew they would be. He is already experiencing the high, and it is falsely empowering him.

The announcer explains the rules. Since I'm not an MMA fighter, more of an amateur boxer, we have modified a few of them. Kicking and hitting will be allowed, but no pinning or restraining. And to ensure this is a fair fight, and that Ruben follows the new rules, an extra ref has been allowed inside the ring.

What no one understands but me and my staff, is that both refs tonight are on the payroll of Darius Falcon, plants of his when we arranged this. I'm not willing to take a chance that Ruben will try something, or that something will go wrong, putting Violet and my daughter at risk. No, this has all been meticulously planned and executed by a highly trained team who never takes unnecessary risks.

The reason Gino hadn't sabotaged us earlier was because he knew how seriously the men in the Royal Guard were about protecting those they happened to be assigned to protect. Chances were how things went south fast, and that just didn't happen.

The bell sounds and we dance around a little. I have an approach on how I like to fight. One a lot of people don't understand, but one that hasn't let me down so far. Because I didn't want my wife freaking out about it, I made sure she understood my strategy ahead of time.

216

Ruben strikes first. It's a good solid punch that rings my bell a little. When I don't strike back, he does it again. I block him this time. He doesn't let up, and I don't try to attack him, I only defend against him for now. It's my way of learning and how I size up my opponent. Then when I believe I've gotten a solid read on him; I devise my strategy.

The first round ends and I take my spot in my corner to do just that. Javier is there with water and some advice. I listen as I continue to watch the man across from me getting more and more hungry. Feeling invincible. Thinking he's gotten to me, figured me out as well. Feeding on the disapproval of the crowd who is favoring my side over his. He's never really been a crowd favorite, always the guy they love to hate, and usually, that works for him.

Rounds two and three go a little differently for him, though. His punches don't land exactly the way they did that first round. I strike back, land solid blows to his gut and face. Block a few of his kickboxing moves and show off that I'm no rookie, know a few moves of my own. Perform a roundhouse that knocks him on his arse while it pisses him off all at the same time.

By round four, we have done a decent job of giving the other person all we have. Both of us are suffering from a few solid blows. When the round is over, we take our corners.

And that's the moment I witness the transformation. When the adrenaline jump kicks those drugs, he injected earlier into overdrive, and he recognizes something is wrong.

I find Violet, who seems to be aware of it now as well. Our eyes lock, and realization takes over. She laughs and nods her affirmation.

I am back on my feet now, rejuvenated for this last and final round. We agreed to go at least seven, but he won't make it past this one. Him being a greedy son of a bitch was what I was counting on. It always pays to know the habits of a man you plan to take down.

"Feeling okay?" I ask as we meet in the center of the ring. "Tell me, do you imagine this is how she always felt?"

I dance around with him, and when he tries to punch me, I strike first. Knock the shit right out of him, making him stumble backward.

I know what some of you are thinking. This is cheating. I'm cheating.

But am I really? Did I inject his body with drugs? Did I hold him down and force them into his bloodstream?

No, I did not.

He did that all on his own. He just didn't take the time to realize that what he was about to shoot into his system wasn't the shot of adrenaline he was expecting. It was one of those special mixes he enjoyed giving Violet when he wanted her alert enough to fight back, but unable to do a damn thing about it. Granted, we had to estimate the dosage needed for a man his size, trust he'd go back in for a second shot once he realized we were doing this.

A loud roar originates from him as he lunges forward and wraps me in his arms, slamming me into the cage. "I'll kill you for this."

I wrap him up in mine as well and force him back, then drive him into the ground. "You'll try, but you'll not succeed."

We roll around a little, blood from the cuts over his eye drips onto my skin. Exactly what I need from him, and so I tell him just that. "Thanks for the blood. It will be enough to prove you aren't Charlotte's father, and that you wrongfully held her hostage. How long have you known?" I ask as one ref pulls him off of me.

"What the hell are you talking about?" His words are blending and becoming slurred. "Fucking know what exactly?"

"That your swimmers don't work. God knew better than to give you the ability to reproduce. One of you was more than enough for this world." I stand and then ready myself.

Ruben doesn't disappoint, he shakes the men off of him and barrels forward like a raging animal. I meet him with a solid kick to the chest, one that sends him peddling back. Ending him with an uppercut under his chin when he tries to charge me again. He finally collapses to the ground similar to a rag doll, moaning.

I give the signal and one of my team members rushes in. They kneel beside Ruben, do what looks like the traditional vitals check, but in reality, he is collecting what we need to run the test to prove I'm right. Once he has it, he passes it off to one of my guards, who shoves it in a bag and walks it out of there. Long before someone from Ruben's team even realizes what we have done.

We didn't need to fight. I could have just as easily had them take an extra vile of blood before the match. Its standard procedure for a doctor to test the blood of a fighter before they allow him inside the ring. But what would have been the fun in that?

CHAPTER 25
Violet

The Royals

I didn't trust Ruben to not try something. It wasn't in his nature to follow the rules laid out before him. He was the kind of man who made the rules up along the way.

Watching the two of them fight it out in that cage was unnerving. It was a good thing Lorenzo had warned me on his brand of fighting. Otherwise, I might have demanded they stop the fight long before it ended.

I hated watching him take punch after punch. Knowing with each one, Ruben believed he was getting the upper hand. Relieved when Lorenzo finally threw his first, landing it so hard, I got the pleasure of seeing the effect it had on the man who once loved hitting me.

Blow after blow, I stood there and listened to the crowd. They were cheering for their prince thankfully, encouraging him to do as much damage as necessary to his opponent. They would roar each time Lorenzo got the upper hand and hiss when Ruben seemed to be fighting his way back.

The moment I heard the loud crack of Lorenzo's foot connecting with Ruben's face, I had a flashback and had to sit down.

It was the day after I'd almost made a fatal mistake and done something I would regret for the rest of my life. I knew even then that killing Charlotte and me was not the answer to all our problems. But I was so far beyond depressed, deeply demoralized, that I wasn't thinking clearly, hadn't been for months.

Ruben had left me to die once he'd discovered what I'd almost done. Told me if I died, that it would probably be best for me in the long run. Because once he was finished with me, if I didn't, I'd be begging him to kill me. Praying for death to come, with the understanding that it would never reach me.

He hadn't lied either. When he returned a few days later, death would have been welcomed. Instead, I'd been forced to suffer through his kind of torment, without the assistance of the drugs he normally offered me. Not only while he was doing his best to punish me, but also afterward when I was recovering. I hadn't been left anything to relieve the pain, physically or mentally. All the drugs had been removed from my home, and I'd been told I wouldn't get anymore. Not until I'd learned that the only person allowed to kill me was him.

The withdrawals alone had nearly killed me. But in the end, once I had cleansed my body of all the toxins, I started perceiving it all differently. Had an epiphany in the trenches of my despair, I realized that there would be only one way to ever get free. In order to get out, I was going to have to play his game his way and learn all I could while playing it. Then when my chance presented itself, I'd be ready. I'd know what to do, where to strike, and just how hard to do so.

I hadn't expected my chance to come as quickly as it did. I'd always expected it to take several more years before the opportunity appeared. And I never thought when my chance came, it would also come with a bonus attached to it. One that would provide me with the strength I never knew I possessed. Never realized how the power of two standing together, not only meant you were never alone in a fight, but that the fight took on an entirely new meaning.

Alone, I was fighting for a new life for my daughter, one I'd been determined to get for her. But now, together, we were fighting for the new life we'd uncovered for all of us. Not just for Charlotte, but for Lorenzo. For the life growing inside of me. For all the other little lives, that should we be successful in this fight, would get the chance to enjoy life. I'd never dared to dream so big before, never looked beyond the present into the future. And now that I had, I wasn't about to let it slip from my hands.

My eyes focus again, and I'm on my feet searching the cage. I find Ruben sitting in the corner, swatting frantically at those trying to give him some water and clean up his cuts. His eyes have that glossy gaze to them I recognized instantly. Jumpy eyes that won't allow the person to focus and have one feeling off-balance, at the mercy of the drug pumping through the body. Making every nerve sensitive, every sound a little too loud, the voices inside your head sound as if they were screaming at you. So, you did what you had to do; you fought against it and tried to gain back control. Only to realize the more you fought, the less control you actually had.

As soon as he stands, shoves all those around him out of his way, my eyes drift to the other man in that cage with him. The instant our eyes connect, I realize what he has done, why he has done it. I'm not sure how he did it, but I'm certain he had a few willingly aid in his plot. And while I know I should probably be upset with him for taking that kind of risk, I can't seem to give a shit.

All those times I was forced to suffer from the hand of the man now stumbling around. They come rushing forward as I watch. Knowing how he feels right now, with absolutely no sympathy. I have no doubt he has done the same to several nameless and faceless souls. That given the chance, he'd gladly do it again without remorse. So, it brings me some satisfaction to know he's getting his for once.

I watch as my husband finishes him. Notice when a man enters and collects what we need, before turning him over to the proper people there to help.

Finding my feet are almost running for the door of the cage when it opens, with a good deal of personnel surrounding me. He no sooner steps onto the main floor, when I all but leap into his arms, wrap my body around him like a monkey and hold on tight.

"Need something," he chuckles into my hair as he secures me there.

My nose buries into his neck and I breathe him in. Sweat never smelled so fulfilling before. This man has never smelled better, as far as I'm concerned.

"I'm good now," I mumble as I cherish the way it feels to be right here.

As soon as we enter the locker room, he peels me from his body explaining, "I need to clean up so we can get out of here."

I want to tell him we can do that at home, but know he is right. He is a mess. Sweat, blood, thick globs of goop covering him. Some of it is now covering me, but I don't care.

"Need help?" I ask hopeful he says yes.

He tosses the tape around his wrist into the trash before he removes his shorts. "No, I won't take long."

I don't hear if he says much more, my eyes are focused on that fine arse moving toward the open shower. He presses the button and steps under the stream of water, and the way it cascades down his backside has me disregarding his earlier words.

My dress is ripped over my head and tossed aside, as are my knickers, bra, and shoes. They are all stripped off my overheated body so I can join him. As soon as I am directly behind him, I press my naked form against his. Reach around the front of him and begin stroking his long fleshy member until it shows some signs of life.

"I really hope that's you, Vi." He moans as his hands land against the tile wall to hold him upright.

I rake my teeth down his back until I reach his firm arse and take a bite of it. It's not the first time I've done that, it won't be the last. "Turn around."

"Vi," he tries to protest but stops when I run my tongue down the seam of his arse. "Woman, I swear."

As he is turning around, I suck on the water running down his glorious body, lick at the rivers until I am right where I want to be. "You have one beautiful cock, Your Highness. I'm going to suck it dry."

My words alone, have it releasing a stream of creamy liquid.

"Don't tease me like that," he mutters as his hand caresses my hair, then he gathers it into one of his hands, wrapping it around his palm. "I love it when you... yeah... I really enjoy that."

I allow my lips to slide over his warm flesh and start sucking on him like I know he likes. He's not picky, really. I could only take in the very tip, pump the rest with my hand, and he'd love it. But when I take him deep, when I swallow him past the closure in my throat, when his length slides down into my tight esophagus that clamps down. That move always makes his legs go weak, has his hand tugging the hair he is gripping just hard enough to make my scalp tingle.

"You're asking for it later, Vi." He warns before he is no longer able to stop, and I am now swallowing as fast as I can, to make sure nothing spills out of my mouth.

As soon as I release him, I'm forced to my feet, and he is kissing me, tasting himself on my tongue, growling like an animal in heat.

"Are you done with him yet, princess? The doctor would like to have a look at a few of his cuts and give him a once-over." Javier's voice echoes off the walls. "I swear you two are competing for the top spot, on the number of times your guards can catch you all in the thralls of sex. What are we at now? I know I've passed the ability to keep track using my hands."

Lorenzo reaches for the soap as he answers. "Get the fuck out of here. I've told you all to stop walking in uninvited. Yell if you must, before entering from now on."

I however only laugh, as I help my husband wash off what hasn't been rinsed off by the water. "Javier, I think you all take bets on what response you will get from him when you catch us. Am I right?"

"You are not wrong," the man chuckles back. "Five minutes, and then we are all coming in. Unless you want to give Gabriela a lesson on what she will be in for eventually, I suggest you hurry it up. You can finish the rest later in the privacy of your own home."

"Vi needs something to slip on. Can you manage that for me?"

He points at the bag on the floor we both missed. "Already taken care of. Now towel off and get dressed. That's an order."

"Did he just give me an order?" Lorenzo lets the water stop and reaches for a towel. "I thought I was the one who gave the orders around here."

Large male hands caress my wet body, as I remind him why we need to get dressed. "Your sister is coming inside this room soon. Is this how you want her to see us? I do believe she's seen more than enough of me..."

"Please do not mention those. I'm feeling murderous enough as it is, and the man I'd like to kill is only through that door and down the hall." He grabs a handful of my arse and squeezes. "I'm so riding this hard, later tonight. Hurry up, princess, before I decide I don't care if I give my sister a lesson on the proper way to love one's wife."

I reach inside the bag and find a pair of shorts and a t-shirt for both of us. I toss him his before I slip into mine. As soon as I've secured my hair into a messy bun, the door opens and a white cloth waves, as a familiar voice announces his entrance.

"I've seen enough of his pretty arse over the years, please tell me it is covered." I've not met the man yet, but I've heard his voice many times over the speaker.

"Crispin, what the hell are you doing here?" Lorenzo rushes toward him and wraps him in a tight embrace. "And I think I saw that arse of yours way more often than you ever saw mine."

The other man laughs and walks right up to me and does a slight bow. "Lord Crispin Oliver at your service."

"Stop showing off. She's not available and will never be again, so you can put those fake manners of yours away." Lorenzo shoves the man to the side as he steps up next to me. "Why are you here, anyway? Don't you have some boards you should be studying for?"

"Even medical students get a break." He laughs and studies Lorenzo's face. "You're going to need a few stitches over that left eye, otherwise you will have one ugly scar. Then again, it might help that face of yours, take the pretty boy look away, make you look more like a man."

That's when I notice the bag he sat down, a medical one, and I can't help but ask. "You aren't a doctor yet, are you? I thought..."

"No, I'm still deep in the books. But I have a nursing degree, have my certification, and freelance when I get the chance." He points to the exam table in the corner. "Hop up there so I can keep you from scaring the little ones."

"Nursing?" I follow them and watch carefully.

"Oh, yes. Lord Crispin acquired that degree against his father's wishes. Worked in the field for nearly a year before applying for medical school." Lorenzo is laughing. "You have to understand Vi, Cris' family has expectations, and it has become his goal in life to upset those."

"But you're in medical school. How does that upset expectations?" I have to ask.

After sticking a needle in that cut to numb it, Crispin gives me my answer. "Even a pathologist is required to go to medical school."

"Pathologist? The doctors who determine why a person died, correct?" I'm pretty sure I am right, but then again, I could be wrong.

"They do that, yes. They also examine the tissue to determine disease. Lab rats. Many people don't realize they hold a medical degree. Good for you, Violet.

"My father says a person who works with the dead isn't really a doctor. A doctor heals people, tries to prevent death from coming. A pathologist's patients are already dead, so what's the point in a degree that will be wasted on the hopeless. I should, in his mind, have higher standards."

"Can I ask why you chose that field over the others?" I take my husband's hand when he offers it. "Did I say something wrong?"

Lorenzo shakes his head and gets scolded for it. "Do you want me to do this right or not? No, Vi, you asked the right question, actually."

"I did?" I smile proudly. "Why did you choose that field then?"

He glues a few more cuts on Lorenzo's face closed while he answers. "Because the dead need a voice as well. They have a story to tell us, and if we don't listen, don't get it right, then their death has no meaning."

I lean against the table and study him carefully before I speak my next words. "Someone you were close to died, didn't they? And you believe that their story didn't get the ending it should have gotten."

"She's very perceptive. Yes. I had someone dear to me die." He doesn't elaborate and I don't press. This is clearly a sensitive topic for him.

"I thought my sister was coming in." Lorenzo must decide it's time to drop the subject.

"Awe, yes." Cris chuckles. "Her previous party she was with, decided they needed to go, so she took off with them. Told me to tell you to forget all you saw and heard tonight."

"Like hell will I forget that. I'm calling Antonio tomorrow and having him assign better guards to her detail. I'm going to suggest he put Gino Leblanc in charge, actually."

I point my finger at him. "You'll do no such thing. He has no business being in charge of her team, not when he has intentions."

"He has intentions?" Crispin asks. "That explains it."

"Explains what?" We both ask at the same time.

"Why he was glaring at me while we talked. She's not a kid anymore, I can look, just not touch. And your little sister, Lenny, she's one beautiful young woman." He takes a step back and lifts his hands. "I said I was only looking. The outfit she had on made it kind of hard not to look."

"You need to leave now, Cris. I'm still very pumped with adrenaline and would have no problem kicking your arse." Lorenzo warns as he grabs the t-shirt next to him and yanks it over his head.

"Nice to meet you, Violet." Crispin is laughing as he walks out the door.

"You weren't very nice," I tell him as he takes my hand and starts dragging me behind him. "He had a point, and we both know Gino wasn't about to allow another man near your sister."

"I was as nice as I am required to be when discussing how my sister was making him think impure thoughts. Plus, I'm ready to get out of here. I believe I owe you yours, and since this will be my very first sexual act in the wake of a fight, I'm looking forward to getting on with it."

It's not mine, but I don't plan on sharing that with him. For one, I do not want to be reminded of all that, just like I'm sure he doesn't prefer to hear about it. Then, of course, I'm certain the two experiences will be completely different. This time I'm going to be begging and screaming for totally other reasons than before. My pleasure will be just as important as his, and that right there is why I'm pushing him out of the door.

"In a hurry all of a sudden, Vi." He wraps his arm around me and drags me to his lips. "I'm thinking we've not made use of having a driver, private partition, and a spacious backseat."

I am grinning against his lips while I remind him. "I'm not so sure our guests would appreciate it as much as I would."

He growls and grabs my arse possessively. "Damn guests. I forgot about them. You are going to cop it for allowing Karina to tag along, I'm going to own this arse before the night is over."

Now it's my turn to growl and moan just thinking about it. "Yes, please. Exactly like you did the first time. I'm definitely game if you are."

When I stare into his eyes, I get my answer. My man is recalling how it felt, remembering the intimacy of the act. I believe we are both surprised about how something so taboo, can be one of the most sensual acts you'll ever be lucky enough to share with the only person who truly gets you. It won't be something we practice regularly, but I get the impression it will be something we dabble in from time to time.

"I love you," I whisper, meaning it.

"I love you too."

CHAPTER 26
Violet

The Royals

The results of the DNA test confirmed what Karina had suspected. Ruben Del Markov is not Charlotte's father.

I didn't really know how I felt about confirming that truth; it was yet one more I'd not been privy to. It had taken me completely by surprise, brought me to a low I'm not sure I've ever experienced before. And as you know I've had some pretty deep lows, but this one for some reason was the lowest I've ever felt.

We have moved back to the Hacienda Refugio Seguro, our home in East Aragon. Lorenzo needed to get back to work as the CEO of his family's company. It was his contribution to the family who supported us all those months while we were on the run. Life needed to get back to a more normal way of living, and that consisted of my husband returning to a job he was actually very good at.

And because it had been almost five months since his abrupt leave of absence, the hours he was required to put in were longer than usual. He needed to get caught up in all of his business handling and whatnot. Go over reports, figure out exactly what his role was going to consist of now that he had a family counting on him. All those were keeping him away from home and not helping me come out of the depression I'd sunk into.

I was really good, in case you were wondering, about withholding that from him. I'd perfected not allowing others to really see me when I didn't want them to. And each day that passed, each day that I sank a little lower, it seemed to get easier to not say what I needed to say. Pretend that all was right in this mess of a life that has always been mine. A life that always ends with me not knowing what hell was coming next.

Even the beautiful gardens, the bright sunshine, the birds chirping, the crazy dog chasing them causing my daughter to laugh, none of those were enough to bring me real joy. I missed feeling the joy, the happiness that had entered my life not that long ago. I hated that all the good that was now in my life couldn't even be appreciated like it should be. Instead, there was this dark gloomy cloud hanging around that refused to leave.

"Papa," I hear my daughter squeal and then run as fast as her little legs will take her. "Mummy, it is Papa."

My head follows her path until it lands on the man striding our way. He's dressed in the same suit he was wearing when he left this morning, sans the tie and jacket. The waistcoat is still there, unbuttoned and hanging loosely off his shoulders. It should be a sight that sparks all those feelings inside of me, the ones that burn for him and have only ever burned for him. But that's how low I am. Not even the sight of the most handsome man I have ever laid eyes on reaches me like it once did.

He scoops her in his arms and swings her around. Kisses her cheeks and tickles her little body, forcing a giggle that has them both smiling. Then he sets her on his shoulders and continues his progress to where I am seated on the lawn, trying my best to shake off these fucking blues.

"What are you doing home?" I ask when he gets closer.

Lorenzo drops dramatically next to me, with Charlotte still safely in his hold. Drops his head back and stares up at the canopy above us, trees and a bright blue sky that appears so peaceful. "I've been thinking."

I raise my eyebrows and wonder if maybe I've not been as good at hiding my mood as I thought. "About?"

"Us. This little one." He tickles Charlotte again and listens to her laugh. "The other little one. You."

Charlotte hears Valentina bark, so she jumps up to go figure out what the beast could possibly be barking at. She is safe to explore this area without me hovering, it's why I chose this garden over the others. We are surrounded by a fenced area that will keep her contained while allowing me some time to try to get my mind back.

"You aren't fooling me, love. I worry. What can I do to make you better? Talk to me." He turns those eyes that perceive everything on me, and it is as if the damn breaks.

"I hate when you do that." I sob and let all the sadness I've been keeping bottled up pour out of me. "It's not fair."

Yanking me down next to him, Lorenzo tucks me into his side and just holds me. Rubs my back and shoulders, releasing the tension that has been building. And while he's done this almost every night, held me against him while we slept, there is something different about it at this very moment.

"Tears are not a bad thing. They allow you to release emotion, cleanse the soul, and let all the dread you've been feeling out." He whispers against the top of my head. "We have a few errands to run when you are done cleansing your soul. No rush. Let it all out and when you are ready, I have some surprises for both my girls."

"What surprises?" I hiccup against his chest.

I feel a pinch against my hip that has me squirming. "No. You are not going to use these tears to get answers. Surprises are meant to be just that. Not to worry, I only believe in the good kind of surprises. The kind I hope will assist in bringing a little of the light back into your eyes."

"I'm sorry," I whisper sadly.

"I get it, Vi. You've had a lot of shit to shovel through. And I believe I've allowed you to do just that, given you time to feel what it is you need to feel or not feel. Now it's time to put it all behind us and move forward. I understand this is a process. That you might even require speaking to someone. But I also believe you might need to be reminded that you are no longer alone. That I'm here to help you when the darkness creeps in. I'm armed and ready to slay those damn dragons holding you down. You only need to allow me to help you do so, however it is that I can. Even if that means getting you the assistance you require, that can teach us both ways to hold them at bay. I'll do whatever it takes, love, whatever it takes."

I have no words. It can be so hard for me to understand I have someone like this man willing to go the distance after being on my own for so long. To actually let someone else take care of me when I've never really felt like there was anyone who cared enough before to know how to do that. He has proven to me time and time again, in the short time we've been together, he means every word. It's just old habits are hard to break.

When my tears have dried, a small amount of the weight I've been carrying has lifted. Shortly afterward, we head back to the house. He feeds us lunch and helps us get ready for whatever it is he has planned. I'm only told how to dress and that we will be gone for several hours, other than that he's keeping very tight lips on it all.

After making a few phone calls, the three of us load into the town car and begin the journey he's organized. Charlotte babbles with her father while we drive. I sit quietly next to them and listen while he keeps a tight grip on my hand.

We pull into an underground parking lot somewhere downtown. Lorenzo gives his men the time they need before getting us out and on our way.

It takes me five seconds in the elevator to know where we are. I've ridden in it a hundred times if not more, every day when I came to work in fact, at least twice each on those days.

"Why are we at the palace?" I ask, knowing he will not give me an answer. "Never mind. This is your party and I won't ruin it for you."

"Thank you." He says leaning over to kiss my cheek.

We get off on a very familiar floor and head down the hall to an office I will forever be grateful for. It was my haven during one of my dark times. A place I felt safe. Worth something. It is where my new life started actually, and that brings a smile to my face.

"Why are you smiling?" Lorenzo questions me as he squeezes my hand. "I really like it when you smile."

I haven't smiled very much lately, and it feels good. "Just recalling the good times that I had here. I miss it a little."

"It misses you a lot." A booming voice echoes down the corridor.

"Your Majesty." I can sense my smile growing, even more, when I catch the king standing there in all his glory. "I'm not so sure that is true."

"Then you would be wrong. Anytime you want to come back, say the word and the job is yours." He tells me as we follow him into his outer office.

Sitting at the desk I used to sit is a woman who always made me feel I didn't belong. She appears out of sorts at the moment, frustrated about something. The moment she spots me walk in, I don't miss the scowl that takes over her face.

"Is there a problem, Lady Cora?" The king must have caught it as well. "I assume you've fixed the issue we discussed earlier."

"I'm working on it," she barks out in that voice that I always hated. "It takes time to get a man like Governor Hanson to respond."

"Ask to speak with Natalie, she has a way of always getting things done," I blurt out.

"Who's Natalie?" Cora is flipping through all her contacts, coming up empty. "There isn't a Natalie listed anywhere..."

I walk over to my old desk, pick up the phone, and then dial the number by heart. "Hi Natalie, this is Violet. I'm great, thanks. So, it seems the King is trying to get a hold of Governor Hanson."

The other woman is asking me a few questions and I motion for Cora to give me what it is she needs. I then explain to Natalie and get an immediate response.

"Thank you. I will let Cora set that up, she's the one running the office for the king now." I hand her the phone so she can do just that.

When she hangs up, Cora tells King Antonio what he wants to hear and then turns to me. "Now who is Natalie?"

I can't believe I am about to share this with the current crowd standing so close watching, but what the hell. "Natalie is one of the younger secretaries in the governor's main office who also is sleeping with him. It's been going on for a little over a year now. When you want something that no one else can get you, she's the one to turn to."

"How do you know she's sleeping with him?" Cora sounds shocked I'd know something so scandalous.

"I just do. It pays to know all the secrets of those who try to stall the King from getting things done. I've always been excellent at reading people, and it took me less than five seconds to figure that one out. You just have to pay attention." I'd overheard a conversation I wasn't meant to overhear when the governor's line was left open by mistake.

King Antonio is shaking his head. "So, when are you coming back?"

"I'm not." I stare at my husband who is holding my daughter, our daughter. "I am needed at home for the time being. But I'd be glad to come in and share my knowledge about all I've learned if that would help."

"No need to do that." King Antonio motions for us to precede him into his office. "I'm sure Lady Cora is crafty enough to figure it all out."

He closes the door and takes his seat behind the large desk, then gestures for us to have a seat. I'm still not sure why we are here, but I take my seat anyway and hope someone will fill me in soon.

"How's Larkin?" I ask, hoping to move this along.

"Working like a madwoman and driving me into an early grave." He huffs. "So did my brother enlighten you on why he dragged you here?"

"No. He only said he had a few surprises lined up." I answer, wondering why he is smiling so big. "Why am I here?"

"As you know, Lorenzo has petitioned the court to adopt Charlotte. What you might not realize, is that because he is a member of the royal family, once the court approves such a petition, it falls upon my shoulders to make it all legal."

I scrunch up my face confused. "I wasn't aware of that, no. Although we haven't heard from the courts yet on whether they approved his request. With this recent development about her father being a..."

"I am her father." Lorenzo interrupts me.

I roll my eyes. "Since the man who provided the other half of her DNA hasn't been located as of yet, we were told it might take a while."

Antonio leans back in his chair, looking very much like a king at the moment. "I know. I might have ordered them to forgo that process and move forward. It does no one any good to drag this out any longer. The man who provided his DNA would never get his chance to be Charlotte's father. He'd given that right up when he raped you. Aware that what he was doing was illegal. We will prosecute every one of those men, right alongside their fierce leader, for what they did to you. Along with anyone else willing to come forward as you have done."

"But I thought the statute of limitations to file was three years," I once again ask, confused.

"Without the evidence of a rape occurring, it is three years. However, it seems we have more than enough evidence thanks to Ruben. He handed it to Karina as soon as he posted that very first video on the web, then continued to do so with each new video that got leaked. He can deny it all he wants, as can the men captured on video with him, but a video does not lie, does it? It doesn't even matter who posted it. It is enough evidence to prove he raped you more than once."

After a long silent pause, I say what I am thinking. "I guess that is about the only positive that came from having to endure all that publicly then."

I don't miss the sympathy in Antonio's eyes. "I'm sorry you had to suffer through that. No one should ever have to go through what you did, but doing so in the public eye was unfair and unjust."

Ready to discuss something else, I ask again. "So why am I here again?"

The smile returns to the king's face. "To officially make Charlotte a member of the royal family. The court sent over the papers this morning. All we need to do is have you both sign the documents. Afterwards, I will sign it and then seal it with the King's seal. Once that is done, Charlotte will officially become a Reyes."

"Are you serious?" I blink several times and dare to glance over at my husband. "You knew about this? This is your surprise?"

He kisses Charlotte's head and nods. "One of my surprises. It's time to slay one of those dragons for good."

"Okay." I agree. "Can I change her name? I never got to name her, so would it be okay to do that? Or is she stuck with Charlotte Renée?"

"You can completely rename her if you'd like," Antonio informs me as he slides the folder toward me.

"It would be confusing to change her first name now. But I'd like to give her a family name." I've been deliberating about this for a while now.

I fill out the correct spot and beam, knowing how much better I like it. She deserves a fresh start and a name that will provide her a strong history behind it, one she can be very proud of.

Lorenzo takes the paper from me and I notice when he realizes what I have done. "You didn't have to do that."

"She needed a solid name. I can't think of one more solid than that one."

He swallows and speaks to his daughter. "What do you think, Char? Do you like the name, Lorenza? Charlotte Lorenza Reyes does sound very pretty, I believe. Do you like it?"

"I like. Like you, Papa. I name like you. Please?" She grins up at him, tilting her head.

"You got it, kid." He signs the paper and hands it to his brother. "Do what it is you gotta do so we can do this next surprise officially as a family."

King Antonio signs and seals the document, and a little more weight lifts off my heavy shoulders. I never knew how worried I was about that not happening until it happened. Funny how a piece of paper can change everything you once thought you'd never have.

CHAPTER 27
Lorenzo

The Royals

I've sat back and watched Violet suffer in silence for way too long. Her screwed up relationship with my cousin was never even close to what he led her to believe it was. From the very beginning, he lied to her, made her one of his playthings, humiliating her every chance he got.

Here is what I've learned since the day we confirmed Ruben wasn't Char's sperm donor. Ruben Del Markov was sterile, one of the very few men in this world whose sperm wasn't able to survive outside his body. Even inside the count was so low that the possibility of him being capable of fathering a child naturally was considered impossible.

The only reason I know so much about this is because Karina and Darius were that good. They hired only the best to dig up dirt and uncover all records deemed confidential. Only a handful of very well-paid associates had known his secret within the Del Markov organizations. It is a miracle they were even able to discover it at all. Although, I've quickly learned that Darius Falcon is worth every penny my brother Esteban pays him.

That information was the final nail that ended all ties Ruben once held over Violet and Char. It removed him from her life permanently and drove him into hiding. Because like my brother the king had pointed out earlier, he was now one of many listed in one of the biggest sex crimes to date for Hermosa Islas. They were going after every person in those videos, not only the ones where my wife had been exposed but all the others that had recently been popping up. Ruben had unintentionally shined a light on a portion of his illegal business by what he did out of anger. Handed the authorities a few pieces of a hidden map, one that led them to one hell of a treasure chest they'd been searching for. It would help them take down some very powerful men. Everyone was scrambling to save themselves, willing to turn in those in charge for leniency. Forcing Ruben to get the hell out of the country before he would never see the light of day again.

But none of that mattered when my wife was sinking into the pits of despair. It was as if something was grabbing onto her and dragging her down, pulling her slowly away from Charlotte and me. And if I didn't figure out how to save her from it, I was afraid I'd lose her forever.

So, I'd made a few calls. Knew I had to show her she was no longer expected to do it alone. That when the pressure became too great, she could count on several people now to help her get through. Not just because of me, but because they cared for her as well. And the only way I knew to do that was to show her.

In fact, it hadn't even been my idea, not that I expected her to believe me. If anything, I anticipate her to throw out a ton of accusations.

After we left the Palace, I took my girls for a celebratory treat. Allowing everyone time to complete what needed to be done, time to do so before we returned home. I could tell Violet was a little confused when we pulled back into the driveway an hour later.

"I thought you said…" she starts, but then stops and goes in a completely different direction. "Why are there so many cars here? Are you throwing a party? Did they all come to welcome Char into the family officially?"

I wink at her and smile. "Something like that, yes. Shall we go see what is going on exactly?"

"You mean you don't actually know? Or are you just not telling me because it will ruin the *surprise*?" She does that squinting thing with her eyes.

"All I know for sure is that they are here, by the looks of things. I'm not exactly sure what it is they have planned. I have an idea of course since they called and ask if it was okay, or if I had planned anything myself. When I told them I had not, that I wasn't certain you'd be up for it, they asked if it would be okay to do it, anyway. I didn't see why not, so I gave them permission to do so. That is the extent of what I know." I inform her as we climb out of the car and hear laughter echoing from one of the garden areas.

Charlotte wiggles out of my arms as soon as we are on the path heading for the noise. My daughter—really, truly mine now, God that sounds so good—isn't as shy as she once was. She's come to accept the new faces that reappear quite a bit since our return home. And has begun to recognize voices even, like the one laughing, ready to greet her as soon as she spots us moving toward the gathering.

"I go. Grammy here. I go." Char charges as fast as her chubby little legs will take her.

My mother meets her and scoops her up in arms full of love. She squeezes her tightly as they have a private conversation Violet and I aren't privy to. But from the expression on my mother's face, I believe I know exactly what she is sharing.

Shifting the little one to her hip, my mother, very ladylike, greets Violet with a proper kiss on the cheek. "Am I correct in understanding she has a new name, Charlotte Lorenza Reyes?"

Violet displays her confusion. "I thought this was a party to celebrate that? Am I wrong?"

My mother blinks slowly, doing her best to maintain her composure. "This certainly has become a double celebration, but it's intent from my understanding, wasn't that. She's really ours for keeps? Bears your name?"

I almost laugh at my mother's uncertainty that it really happened, like we all had hoped it would. "They are both ours to keep. The name was Violet's doing, and a surprise on a day full of them, I suppose."

Violet shrugs, a little uncomfortable at the moment. She is still adjusting to all the affection my family is throwing her way.

My mother has most certainly taken her newest daughter-in-law under her motherly wings. Protected her from the press by releasing more than one statement requesting our family be given time to adjust before bombarding us with questions. She's even called daily to check in on my wife, just to make sure Violet understood she only needed to say the word and she'd come. In fact, I believe she's stopped by a few times when she felt that maybe a little company would be good. Used Char as an excuse, but spent a great deal of her time focusing on both my girls' needs. That is what my mother is very good at, knowing how to step in without being overwhelming.

"It just felt like the right thing to do. Lorenzo is the only father Charlotte has had. I know I probably should have asked permission..."

My mother smiles as she corrects her like only she can. "No reason to ask for permission, my dear. It is clear my son is honored, as am I, as the rest of the family will be. She is after all family, was in my opinion, always meant to be family, just like you Violet. Family does not need to ask permission when naming a child."

"Thank you," my wife softly mumbles. "So, if this party isn't for Charlotte, who is it for?"

My mother smiles as she walks toward the gathering. "Perhaps we should find out."

"Or you could just tell me, Angela." Violet sighs, a little frustrated.

It's actually good to hear her use my mother's name, using it like she would any other name. Scolding my mother for not just telling her instead of trying to play it off.

"I am simply a guest, invited by those who arranged it." She isn't going to let a scolding get to her. "How are you feeling today?"

"Frustrated that no one will tell me anything." Violet blurts out, before giving her the answer she knows my mother is looking for. "One day at a time is the motto. I'm fighting the best I can. Trying to focus on the happy elements in life and doing my best to forget the rest. However, that is a lot easier said than done."

"I know, dear." My mother sets Charlotte down so she can run off to see Isabel. "Perhaps a little fun is just what the doctor ordered then. Excuse us." And then she follows my daughter, providing Violet with a break.

Violet's feet stop moving while she takes in the décor and crowd. Larkin, Karina, and Winifred have gone all out, it appears. Lanterns, streamers, balloons even. Everything one might expect when celebrating a birthday for the newest princess. She covers her mouth as she blinks slowly.

"Okay?" I ask as I rub her back.

Her head bobs up and down slowly as tears stream down her face.

I tug her closer, forcing her to turn into me. "Happy Birthday."

"So, you did know what it was?" She hiccups.

"I told you I had an idea." I bring my knuckles under her chin and lift it. "You okay? These are good tears, right?" I then wipe them off with my thumb.

"I've never... no one... I'm too old for a birthday party." She rolls her eyes.

I chuckle. "No one is too old for a birthday party. My mother insists we throw her one every year. I do believe that is to force all her children to visit at the same time."

"This was your idea?" She accuses and I shake my head. "Whose then?"

Two of the culprits have now joined us, both smiling, clearly pleased with themselves.

"I hope this is okay," Winifred speaks first. "We thought it might be a nice way for you to get to know all of us."

"All of us?" Violet does a quick study of the garden.

"Don't worry. It is just a small party. Family and friends." Winifred assures her. "We wanted it to be a fun, joyous occasion, not one where we all had to smile when we didn't feel like smiling. You will get to experience that soon enough, probably when my husband wins Governor and we are forced to entertain the masses."

"You could sound happier about that, Winnie." Esteban squeezes his wife's shoulders.

"Family and friends? I don't really have friends." Violet announces.

"Ouch," a loud female voice announces. "What am I then? I thought you said we could be great friends, cause a lot of trouble together."

That has my wife smiling again as she turns to the voice. "Okay, I stand corrected. I have one friend."

Karina in her truest form marches up to Violet and links her arm with hers. "Well, when you have a friend like me, one is all you need. Now, come with me. I have something for you, it's something I think you are going to like."

"You bought me a birthday present?"

Karina hip bumps Violet as she drags her to where they are headed. "Oh yes. I couldn't resist. It's nothing big but after our little talk the other day…"

"I'm better now, I am." Violet squeezes her arm.

"That's good to hear, but every girl needs an outlet. After listening to you tell me how freeing it felt, I just thought maybe that this is just what you need. And if it's okay with you, I think I'll join you. Let's just say I have my reasons for wanting to do so as well."

There is an exchange that takes place between the two women. I have to admit, I'm a little scared Karina has befriended Violet. I realize she is not exactly that same person she once was, but she's also out there in her thinking. That being said, I'd never discourage this friendship between these two. She seems to be exactly what my wife needs, understands how to reach her when I can't.

"What do you suppose she got her?" My brother sounds apprehensive. "You sure you want those two hanging out. Karina is a handful."

"Rina is just misunderstood," I tell Esteban. "I'll admit it scares me, but at the same time I expect it might be good for both."

"She's trying, Stan. Old habits are hard to break, but she is trying." Winifred watches the other two women talk. "Plus, I guess Lenny is right. Sometimes we need a kindred soul, someone who just gets us without tossing judgment, to befriend us. It's clear by looking at them they are that for each other. Who knows why, and who really cares."

"Holy shit!" Violet shouts, holding up a pair of padded gloves. "Kickboxing lessons with a professional fighter. Are you kidding me?"

I step up and stare at the name, a little shocked myself. "How did you arrange that?"

Karina blushes a bit before she answers. "Let's just go with we are old acquittances. He owed me a favor after I got him out of a jam. I'm not sure this is actually the favor he was hoping I'd ask for, but he agreed anyway once he knew who I was requesting his assistance for."

"What favor did he hope you'd ask for?" Violet snickers.

"Exactly what you are thinking, don't be coy. I however made it clear I was trying something new, looking for more than he was willing to offer me. Plus, even if he was offering it, it seems I'm only interested in attracting a certain male." Karina then grumbles out a little of her frustration. "I seriously hope all this is well worth it because let me tell you I'm extremely sexually frustrated. Which is why I'm joining you during your sessions. Perhaps it will help me get some of the frustration out so I don't mess up."

"We can kick the shit out of everything together then. I'm pretty sure it will help. I guess if anything it will supply you with the skills to maybe do a little sparring with the man causing all this frustration." Violet suggests, and I can see the wheels spinning inside Karina's head.

"Perhaps I could." She waggles her eyebrows. "Or I could just jump him, forcing him to use all those skills he's learned to restrain me. Once he's gotten me pinned, both of our bodies humming after a good fight, maybe the adrenaline will be to my advantage."

They both laugh and I get the impression that this might help Violet. Not just the gift Karina gave her, but this party my family decided she needed. We all often need to be reminded of the positive aspects of life, the parts that make it all worth living. And Violet has so much to live for now, so many who are here for her to help her when it may not seem perfect.

CHAPTER 28
Violet

The Royals

It took some convincing, getting Lorenzo to permit me to attend this session Karina bought me for my birthday. He wasn't convinced I needed to be learning kickboxing while pregnant. After a long conversation with Dr. Wilson, where she provided me a list of the do's and don'ts, he'd reluctantly agreed. Only allowing us to attend with Gayle and Laney tagging along to guarantee we follow her guidelines to the T.

Karina at first voiced her thoughts on that. Once she understood how serious Lorenzo was about it, decided it was better to let him have his way this time. Although she insisted we drive separately with the two female guards following behind.

"Don't you tire of all that?" Karina quickly ask once we are alone. "I mean, can you even go anywhere unaccompanied anymore? That would drive me insane. I'd likely try to ditch them as often as I could."

I will admit it isn't something I enjoy, and I pretty much tell her that. "If it weren't for all that's currently going on, I'd probably suggest you give it your best shot. But for now, it's perhaps best we don't."

"Still no word on where the arsehole is hiding?" She probably knows more than I do, but that's what I like about this woman, she never assumes.

"Not. One. Word." And that is frightening, Ruben has never gone completely silent before. Even when we were on the run, he'd made his presence known. Sent me messages weekly, even though he knew I'd left my phone behind. He appreciated that eventually I'd be back and get bombarded with them. Read and listen to all his hateful words and threats.

And he wasn't wrong, I'd done that with one exception he hadn't counted on. When I finally read them, Lorenzo was right there with me. He'd expected me to be alone like I'd always been, without the support behind me when that day came. He'd assumed one way or another he'd get to me, the same way he'd always gotten to me. It had never crossed his mind that I'd end up being the one calling all the shots. But that is what had happened. He no longer had control over my life or Charlotte's. All the methods he once used to rule my life had been quickly taken away the second I exposed the truth.

One thing I appreciate about Ruben and men like him is that they don't like not being in control. Control is power. Power is what fuels them. Without either, they often become a threat that needs to be dealt with swiftly. They are unpredictable and often act without thinking, which could be dangerous for all involved, even him.

"He can't hide forever," Karina finally says. "I mean, he can surely try. However, one thing I've learned while working this job, is that eventually, someone will turn him in. Someone will decide it is in their best interest to make some deal to save themselves, and then he'll get what's coming to him."

"Ruben has been in this game long enough to know that as well. And while I'd like to agree with you, pray you are right. Something has always warned me there is more that none of us understands. More that will likely be used to either end us or him."

We pull up in front of a warehouse looking structure. "And that is why we are doing our very best to be ready for the unknown. Why we are keeping very close eyes on all involved. So, are you ready to do this?"

I roll my neck and throw a few jabs before answering her. "I was born ready."

That makes her laugh, "I do not doubt that. Too bad you've got a bun in the oven because I'd really love to see you give someone..." Karina does a quick punch and marginal kick after she gets out. "You'd knock some poor unsuspecting chick right on her arse."

As soon as we step through the dark glass doors, the smells of testosterone, sweat, and adrenaline in the air bombard us. At first, it brings back too many unpleasant memories, but after a few deep cleansing breaths, I banish those from my mind.

I instead choose to focus on a memory that isn't at all unpleasant. It is about the man I love. On a night when I recall him smelling much that same way, a night where he took me home and did wicked pleasant acts to me. My man is extremely talented and knows exactly how to reprogram my brain, making sure there isn't room for the bad. Every day all those hostile thoughts have to be shoved out to make space for all the precious ones we were now making.

"If you were a man, you'd be sporting a boner right now," Karina snickers as she shoves me. "God, I am so jealous. How the hell does Lenny always seem to put that look on your face."

"I have a look?" I realize I do because I can sense it.

"It's one that cannot be mistaken, it says you are well fucked and loved." Karina makes a gagging gesture. "Do you understand how long it's been for me?"

"Longer than you've ever gone before." I understand because she has brought it up often. The poor woman is suffering from a decision she made, one she has questioned a time or two.

"We could take care of that problem first," a deep male voice nearly has both of us jumping.

I have to be honest here. Damn! Damn! Damn!

He extends his hand while I stare at him, dazed. "Rupert Castiano. Everyone calls me Cast. You must be Princess Violet."

I go to shake his offered hand, except Karina swats it away. "Cast, you are so behind on protocol. You can't just shake a royals' hand, not unless they make the first move."

He only laughs and then wraps her in his arms instead, lifting her off the floor. "Lady Karina it has been way too long. Apparently for both of us. We should make some time later so we can catch up, possibly help each other out as well."

"Put me down. I believe I've explained this all to you once already." Karina straightens herself and appears annoyed. "It better be well worth the sacrifice, is all I have to say."

I wrap my arm around her shoulder while I do my best to assure her it will be. "The right man is by far better than just a fuck. There is nothing, and I do mean nothing, like it. Even if Stew ends up not being the right one, maybe he is getting you ready for the right one."

"I'll die a slow death waiting should that be true. God, I'm dying as it is. This is like the worst torture." Karina grumbles.

"Stew?" Cast snaps his fingers and laughs. "DeBeers is the prick getting in my way?"

I don't believe I've seen Karina blush until now. "You know him?"

He waves for us to follow him, and right as we enter the main area he yells out, "DeBeers. Get the fuck over here and help me out. I knew there was more to your story when you showed up today. I'm passing this one off to you while I give the princess a private. And don't try arguing with me, you're the reason she's turned me down twice now, so deal with it."

Gayle and Laney don't bother holding back their laughter when Stew catches sight of Karina. She is dressed to hit it hard today, tight workout capris, and a sports bra. Nothing left to the imagination for either of them, really. Since he is wearing only a tight pair of those shorts most fighters like to wear, like the ones Lorenzo had on when he fought Ruben.

"Why are you at my gym?" Stew accuses sounding a little perturbed.

"Your gym? I thought this was his gym." Karina crosses her arms and nods towards Cast. "And don't bother, I'm sure someone else here would be glad to show me the ropes. Or better yet..."

I swear my mouth drops to the floor when Stew does the only thing that he can to shut Karina up. He kisses her briefly, but it was enough to leave her speechless and gave him the advantage. He then grabs her arm and drags her to one of the bags. Once there, it seems they are now at a standstill and unsure what to do next.

I miss what happens because Cast begins moving, leading us to a private room while he talks. "So, you want to learn how to do kickboxing? I've been instructed that we have to limit our training, but I imagine we can start with the basics. Teach you some defensive moves so you can protect yourself. Move on to the proper way to hit and kick from there. Learn where you want to strike first."

"I know how to do all that," I enlighten him.

"Alright. Let's see what you've got. Which one of you ladies is up first?"

"I thought we were doing this?" I hold up a hand to keep Laney and Gayle where they are. "No offense, ladies. But if I'm doing all this for *self-defense,* don't you believe it would be best I learned it on someone similar to the enemy. Height, physique, and stature would make you the best choice. Or are you afraid I'll kick your arse?" I shrug and wait for him to decide.

"It's just that your husband..."

"Isn't here for me to kick his. And while I'm pretty positive he called and warned you off, he's not the one in charge right now. I am. And if you aren't interested in doing this my way. I can find someone who is." I don't know what has come over me, but for some reason, I feel the need to start calling the shots.

Cast does a quick glance at the two ladies with us. It's obvious he's making sure they are fine with that. When they both seem to get comfortable while grinning, he takes that as a yes and we get started. It's a light session. He's been schooled as well about all the dos and don'ts to keep me and the baby safe, all while allowing me to have some fun. Not once putting me at risk, letting me do most of the hitting and kicking on him and the bag he has.

An hour later, I'm feeling like I've made a step in the right direction. I've scheduled a session daily moving forward, at a time I know will work best for all of us. After I talked it over with Lorenzo, of course, and told him how I felt and why I realized I needed this. He listened like he always does, then agreed to allow me this for as long as it was deemed safe. Eventually, I'll have to stop, resume again once the baby comes, but for now, I am excited about it.

The weight I've been carrying around has lessened tremendously since my husband forced me to talk about it. Showed me I wasn't alone any longer. I had many willing to stand by my side and support me. While I wasn't completely back to where I had been, I was well on my way, better each day. Able to see the light that had been dimmed. I've even come to realize that I am the one who has to decide it is time to begin appreciating all I now have. And while I realize I have a very long challenging road ahead, I also understand I'll never move forward if all I ever focus on is that.

One day at a time. And today I plan on doing something I've never done before. I intend on taking care of myself first. If I don't do that, then I will be no good to Charlotte or Lorenzo or even this little one growing inside of me. My mental health, along with my physical health, has to be a top priority. Making sure I release some of that stress I've been holding onto for way too long is important. And that is why I'll come back every day, it will be therapeutic and help me be the best I can be.

"Ready?" Karina looks better even.

I find myself smiling at that. "Yep. So?"

She stares at her nails and shrugs. "So what?"

"Don't so what me?" I shove her and she breaks.

Tears I'd not noticed start to fill her eyes as she clears her throat. "I don't know what to think."

I glance over my shoulder to find Stew glaring at us. It's hard for me to read him. Clearly, he is fighting a battle within himself as well. Proof of that comes when he mouths, *'She okay?'*

Interesting.

I mouth back, *'You tell me. What did you do to her?'*

He points at himself, shrugs, and turns around to make his escape before I ask more and force the truth out of him.

"Let's go get lunch. I'm starving." I rub my stomach and it growls loud enough for Karina to hear.

Shaking her head as a way to free her emotions, she grabs my hand and drags me out the door. "Yes, lunch. Lunch and drinks. Well, drinks for me at least, you will have to pass. I guess I'll have to drink for you because I so do hate to drink alone."

We both showered and changed earlier, so she leads us a few blocks to one of her favorite Cantinas that serves good food as well. After we order, we sit back and do something I've rarely done; we talk. We sit and talk about everything and nothing at all. We laugh, seriously laugh, like I know I haven't done in so long. It feels good. Laughter is the best medicine by far, and I can once again sense the gloom fading.

Right as we are about to wrap it up, I suspect someone watching us. You know that sensation you get. It isn't the first time I've had it. It's a familiar one that puts me on alert, and that seems to spark the ladies keeping watch. I catch right away how they perk up and scan the restaurant, which means I also catch when they spot something they don't necessarily like.

Lady Amber is seated across the room with a few other women. They all seem to notice she has suddenly directed her attention my way. None of them however seem to wear that sour face she has perfected. Instead, they seem more interested in if I am here alone or with someone, not just someone, but Lorenzo. As soon as they spot Karina, they seem disappointed and all but forget about me, start talking amongst themselves again.

Lady Amber however can't seem to do that. She appears to be in a trance. Even when someone says her name, she waves them off right before she stands. It takes me all of five seconds to figure out where she is heading, straight for me.

When she reaches in her purse to retrieve something, Gayle is on her so fast I'm not sure she even saw it coming. "I'll take that. You should go before you do something you'll regret."

I expected it to be a gun or knife. Instead, it looks like a small booklet, an album maybe. Gayle inspects it thoroughly before giving the woman in front of her a suspicious look.

"I have no need for it," Lady Amber scoffs. "I've been meaning to mail it to her."

Gayle passes it off to Laney, who flips through it rather quickly and then hands it to me. "There. Now I suggest you turn around and return to your party."

Not surprisingly, she doesn't move, and that sparks Karina to voice her opinion while I stare at the booklet carefully. "I thought you were a smart woman Amber; thought you knew when to back off."

"And here I assumed you were better than befriending a criminal," the other woman isn't about to not get a few words in as well. "Kidnapping was once a punishable crime until it benefited the royal family. How convenient."

When Karina starts to reply, I stop her by shaking my head. "Thank you for this." I hold up the album filled with baby photos of Charlotte. I was never privileged to any until now. Ruben wouldn't allow it, always found and destroyed any I tried to keep or take.

The sour face is back when she answers, "I have no use for a bastard child's photos. I'd only agreed to take her on when I assumed the little brat was my husband's. Now that it seems the child is fatherless, no bloodline worth the dirt on my shoes, I saw no point keeping such trash to clutter my home."

This time it is Laney who speaks up, stepping directly in front of her. "I believe that is Prince Lorenzo's daughter you are speaking of. A child nonetheless, one I am fond of, with a very solid bloodline I might add. Watch what you say or I'll be forced to remove you from the premises, then have you arrested."

"For what exactly? Speaking the truth." Lady Amber mocks before she turns. "I have nothing else to say. Nor do I care what you or anyone else associated with that family thinks. In time they will all get what is coming, you will see."

When the women start to take off after her, ready to defend the family they have sworn to protect, I stop them, "Leave it. She has the right to be a little upset. I'm sure she was lied to as well, probably way more than I ever was. Bitterness, I do believe, is a step she must go through. And at least she was kind enough to not just toss all these into the bin. Thought well enough to give them to me, that means she's not completely heartless."

"You do realize that she's always been a class A bitch? The queen of all the bitches I know. And that is saying something since I was raised to be a class A bitch myself." Karina downs the last of her drink and smiles. "Bitterness is a step she must go through, seriously?"

I shrug and laugh again. "Well, it is. That has to explain why her face has soured the way it is."

And just like that we are both back to laughing, pushing away all the bitterness that woman tried her best to bestow upon us.

The only thing that bothers me is her last statement. Although I know Laney and Gayle won't let it slide, they'll report it and have Darius and his team on it. But for now, in this moment, I refuse to dwell on something I can't do anything about. I choose to focus on the here and now, that's my new motto.

CHAPTER 29

Violet

The Royals

I am a nervous wreck standing here. So afraid I will mess up. Say or even do something that will embarrass my new family. Tonight is a celebration, and it seems the entire city of Aragon, along with most of the Southern Region, has come to do just that.

"At least you aren't expected to give a speech," Winifred joins me as we study the crowd. "The last time I spoke in front of a group was during speech class in college. I don't even remember what I said. The only thing I could focus on was not passing out, not throwing up, and not reading my speech without ever once glancing up. To this day, I still have no idea how I managed to get an A in that class."

The two of us haven't been able to get together like I had hoped. The poor woman has been extremely busy with her husband's campaign and her booming business. According to my husband, she often crashes in the evenings once her day ends. He has spoken to his brother more these last few months than he has her.

"Have you tried picturing everyone naked?" I'm not sure why I said that, but it draws a giggle out of both of us.

A bright red blush appears instantly on her face, "No. I do recall trying that once. All that did was keep me from moving my eyes off my notes. Thankfully, it was a practice speech we had to do in a small group, but still. Is that what you'd do?"

I scan the crowd again and smile, all while I do my best to figure out what I might do in her situation. "Maybe not naked, because—and I mean no disrespect or anything—if I had to see this crowd naked, it would be a very sad sight. Lots of droopy bits, wrinkled up little willies, and floppy skin that hangs loosely in places it should not."

When I glimpse down at Winifred again, I catch her smiling while shaking her head. "An image I may not get out of my brain now, thank you."

Since it seems to work, I decide to continue and hope it is the right thing to do. That it will help calm her before she is forced to make a formal introduction to this crowd.

"Instead, I'd probably picture them in their undergarments." I point to a woman draped in something that looks more like a costume than a gown. "What the hell was she thinking when she dressed in that? Someone like her is probably tucked inside the tightest shapewear they make. You and I both appreciate how unattractive most of those are."

"Lady Maribel has a unique taste, always has."

"Freddy, can I call you that? Lorenzo often does and…"

She nods while she explains, "If you want to, sure. There was a time it bothered me. Not when he used that name, mind you. However, I'm over that. It's just a nickname that has less meaning to it now."

"Would you prefer Winnie or Winifred?" I understand how a nickname can stir up memories you'd rather forget.

The smile that appears tells me she would, even though she doesn't actually give me an answer.

"Winnie, it is then. Winnie, there is unique…" I point out a woman dressed in something a little different from everyone else, even one of the male guests whose tux is not the traditional black and white.

We both have a friendly laugh at the expense of a few. And perhaps that is wrong of us, but it seems to put us more at ease for now.

"And then there is unique, off the wall, one of a kind. Not that I'm saying she shouldn't be allowed to dress how she wants, or him even for that matter. They would certainly make a pair, wouldn't they? I bet he has the most exceptional colorful thong covering his meat and veggies."

No sooner do I get the words out when Larkin joins us. "Oh, this is an interesting conversation. Please do tell."

Winifred tries to explain as she laughs her way through most of it. "Violet, you are not allowed to skip out on any formal event moving forward."

"Well, that sucks," I blurt out. "I so was hoping I'd make a spectacle of myself tonight and you two would ban me from them permanently."

"Nope," Larkin rubs her protruding belly. "If the two of us have to endure, you do too. Trust me, I'd skip out as well if I could do so. I did my best to convince my husband to let me sit this one out since I look like I've stuffed a basketball under this dress. Do you realize how difficult it is to dress for an event like this when you seem to be daily adding on the pounds?"

Winifred places a hand on her flat stomach and groans. "It's bad enough getting ready for these things as it is."

I take a moment to glance down at my own slight bump that I can no longer conceal. It is just big enough to not be mistaken as a fat pooch, but instead a growing bump that will surely get this crowd gossiping.

"What do you imagine the odds are that we would all be pregnant at the same time?" The question slips out before I can stop myself from asking.

"What?" Winifred drops her hand. "I... oh... well, shit."

Larkin laughs first. I'm not sure if it's because Winifred said shit or if it is because she let her secret slip.

"Well, at least you all have been married long enough to not raise all the wrong questions." I do my best to hopefully make her minor slip up, not seem so bad. "Plus, I do believe your husband already outed you a few days ago. Lenny came home after a meeting with his brothers and shared."

"He did?" Winifred once again pats her stomach. "I'm still a little shocked about it, I guess. Stan is over the moon and driving me bonkers. Insisting I eat and sleep more already. My ass is going to grow again..."

"I believe we've established that I love your ass in all shapes and sizes." Esteban declares as he steps in behind his now blushing wife. "Shall we get this show on the road?"

"Do we have too? Can't we just pretend I introduced you and…" Winifred's nerves are back and I seriously suspect she might puke.

"Would you rather I make the introduction?" I'm not sure why I opened my mouth and volunteered like that.

"Would you be willing to do that? Although my speech probably would sound rather odd coming from your lips and not mine." Winifred gets very pale and immediately heads straight for the bathroom directly behind us.

"Your wife is not going to be able to go out there and speak, not unless you want them to all watch her blow chunks on the front-row. And while I'll admit I'd pay good money to witness that, I also don't suppose it would be the best way for you to make alliances."

I gather all the strength I have and begin to walk toward the podium before anyone can stop me. The silence that seems to take over the room is quite intimidating, but there is no turning back now.

"Good evening and thank you all for coming. Princess Winifred is a bit under the weather this evening, so I've volunteered to take her place. I've only been a member of this incredible family for a few months now, but during that time they've shown me nothing but love and support. Everyone here is aware of all the sh … you are all aware of the struggles I've faced."

I stop and take a deep breath, reminding myself I cannot curse in front of a crowd like this one. What the ever-living hell was I thinking trying to do this without a speech to refer to? Then I almost start laughing when I notice the teleprompter displaying Winifred's prepared one. There is no way I can use it.

"I however have had the privilege of working for them prior to all of that. Those months I spent in the King's office allowed me to appreciate a side of this family most never get the chance to. I can tell you from experience that the man you have chosen to govern the southern region of this incredible kingdom will serve you with all he has. He will not be intimidated by the King or allow his brother to push him around. I've seen those two men stand their ground many times, neither backing down and eventually realizing that they don't always have to agree on everything. After all, different views and opinions are what makes the world a more diverse place to live. It would be boring if we all thought the same. Don't you agree?"

Applause breaks out, making me pause again while they show they do. "So, without any more delay, I'd like to introduce you to your new Governor of the Southern Region, Prince Esteban Carlos Reyes."

I take a step back as I join them, applauding for a man I hold a substantial amount of respect for. He was always nice to me when I worked for the king, took time each day to say hello, and spent a few extra minutes to simply chat. I've missed seeing his smiling face daily, missed my work that I once did to help me make my days less stressful. There are those who may not understand that. Assume working in an office like that one would be very stressful. To me, however, it was exactly what I needed to keep my mind off all the other crap that was my life.

Prince Esteban waves at the crowd as he steps toward me. I expected him to take my hand and possibly kiss my cheek. I did not expect him to wrap me in a warm embrace, forcing me to do the same. Nor did I predict he'd keep one arm around me as he stepped forward to address the crowd.

"Thank you. You all have no idea how amazing this woman next to me is. Her strength and ability to overcome is an inspiration to me and my family. We are truly blessed to welcome her into the family, and all of us look forward to watching her and my brother show us all up. Mark my words, this woman is going to do incredible things while changing the world."

I'm speechless. I never expected him to say such kind words. All I can do is smile and say thank you. As soon as he releases me, I quickly make my escape. More than ready to take my place behind the stage where everyone is waiting. I'm greeted by the King and Larkin first—no matter that he is my brother-in-law, he will always be King Antonio to me. They offer a thank you and hug, which I understand is something they do not take lightly. I've seen the king only hug those closest to him, mainly his wife, sisters, and mother. Therefore, when the emotional train hits me, it hits me harder than I anticipated.

I've blubbered all over this family so much more than I am comfortable with. Hormones or not, I refuse to fall apart one more time for them to witness. Therefore, I quickly excuse myself as soon as possible after I've allowed each one of them to say how grateful they are to have me in their family.

I'm not sure I will ever get used to hearing that without experiencing some emotion. Knowing my daughter, this little one, will always have this because I caught the attention of the most amazing man. Then unintentionally fell hard for him, securing our place in his family. All of it.

Aware I'm going to lose it soon, I excuse myself. The only problem I didn't account for was the one I ran into like a brick wall when it stepped in my way. One that didn't give, but engulfed me in large powerful arms where it was always impossible to keep my emotions from spilling out.

"No running." His voice washes over me. "Unless you are running toward me, remember?"

I bury my face in his chest and nod. "I just need some air."

Lorenzo tucks me under his arm and turns us to a set of doors that lead outside onto a terrace. I assumed he'd release me as soon as we stepped through them. Seems I was wrong.

This man knows me better than I often know myself. He spins me around and presses me up against the stone wall just to the left of the doors. Then devours me like only he has ever done. Making us both breathless and hot, so fucking hot.

"We need to be quick," he gathers the material to my dress.

"What?" I am finding it difficult to believe what he is suggesting.

Taking my hand and placing it on the crotch of his pants, he gives me his most wicked, sexy smile. My hand instinctively cups the length of him and gives it a nice firm squeeze, sending heat down my spine.

"We can't have me standing in front of a room like this," he groans.

"No, we cannot," I agree and nearly squeak when one long finger slides between my wet folds and rubs my clit. "Fuck."

"I so do love it when you talk like that," Lorenzo adds another finger and I whimper.

I rarely allow myself to speak so freely. Although it seems to slip out when we are both so ramped up that my filter stops working. "I want you to fuck me with that big cock of yours. Hard. Long. Cock. Now."

And that is exactly what I get. A quick fuck that I needed to calm down and focus minutes before facing all those people inside. One that reminds me I will be facing none of them alone. This man will be right there by my side.

"I'm so proud of you," he whispers as he fixes my dress.

Laughter falls from deep inside of me. "Because I allowed you to sex me up out here before we have to pretend to be some stuffy couple."

Now Lorenzo laughs, "We will never pretend to be a stuffy couple. I plan on keeping a firm hand on your arse most of the night."

"The scandal," I snicker, knowing he's not kidding.

His face becomes serious. "There is nothing scandalous about it. I want you to watch my brothers as they lead their women around tonight. I promise you they too will do whatever is necessary to keep them feeling comfortable."

He runs his hand down my cheek so lovingly, letting his touch say so much. "Vi, I'm proud of you for what you did in there. Stepping in like you did without hesitation. That's what family does, Vi. Tonight, you proved your place in this family in front of everyone."

"I did, didn't I." I hadn't thought about that when I just stepped in, all because it was the right thing to do.

"Yeah, you did."

It's kind of funny how I never realized that maybe I did that because this was my family. A family I've waited so long to have. My family, who I'd do whatever I had to do to make sure they shined always. While they have done their best to prove they were here for Char and me, it seems they've also wormed their way into my heart.

The tears from earlier rise again, for different reasons now, I think. Maybe not, maybe that is why it touches me so much when they display their gratitude. I'm still convinced these hormones are making me all that much more sentimental, not that I'm complaining.

Lorenzo shakes his head and kisses away one of those fallen tears. "Why are you crying?"

"It's your fault. You did this to me." I slap him playfully.

His hand lands on my stomach, "I certainly did."

"That too. I mean, you gave me this family. Made me care about each one of them. Pointed out that they are just as much mine as they are yours. So, forgive me if I get a little emotional about that. I've never had a family until you came into my life, not a real one.

"Brigham and Juliet are the closest I've ever had. While I care deeply for them, help Marisol and my father make sure they are taken care of. Speak with them as often as I can, it's not the same. We aren't the kind of family others have, not really. They live on the island, North Hermosa, a place I cannot just drive to, making it more difficult to visit. And even when I did, I always felt like an outsider, not easily fitting in. It's not my siblings' fault my relationship with my father isn't great, and Marisol has never tried to get close to me. She saw what my life was like and didn't approve. I can't blame her for that. She was looking out for her children. I wasn't exactly the ideal role model for them, although she never seemed to have issues accepting my financial assistance.

"Your family, however, accepted me without hesitation. Even when all the ugliness of my past came out, they never once let that be a reason to write me off. I never realized how much that meant, I guess. That they accepted all of me. Ready to battle it out even when so many others would have used that as a way to walk away, have used it as a reason to do so. They have shown me what it means to be a family, a real family. And now that I have this family, I'll vow to do my best to make them proud of me. To help others see how I see them. I will let no one disrespect them, do whatever is necessary to prove my worth."

Grabbing my face, Lorenzo smiles, "You do not need to prove your worth."

A tear falls again, "I know, and that is why I love them all so much."

CHAPTER 30
Lorenzo

The Royals

T he evening continues to go well, for the most part. I keep Violet close to my side while I prove that she has nothing to fear. Tonight is more of a celebration than it is anything else, for everyone except Esteban, that is. These are his people, the ones who supported him to get elected. Those he will represent, a few that are even hoping to steal some of his time for political motives.

For the rest of us, we are only present to show our full support. Meaning this is the perfect event for my wife to become comfortable with what it can be like when placed in the spotlight. Because even though we are not the key focus tonight, we are never out of the public's eye.

This is a formal event. Most events we are invited to are. And those that are not still have a dress code we abide by. Meaning we make it a point to never be out dressed because after all we are Royals and take that as serious as everyone often expects us to.

After the welcome speech, we take our designated seats at the tables we are assigned. Unlike many of these events we've attended in the past, our family for the first time has found themselves separated. My brothers are seated with other leaders, justices, along with their spouses or significant others. My mother and Gabriela are at a table with other women who don't have a male companion. We happen to have found ourselves with some unexpecting couples close to our age.

It takes everyone a while to become at ease with the arrangement. It's not every day our people get the privilege of being seated at the same table with a member of the royal family. There has always been a protocol, but it seems as if we've moved into a new era. One that will make us a little more accessible to those my brothers represent.

Half-way through our meal, I am asked a question I've been waiting for; one I had an answer for without having to give it much thought.

"Prince Lorenzo, do you also plan on becoming a politician?" Lord Brogan asks.

"No. I have no interest in politics whatsoever."

"Thank God for that," Vi responds just as quickly as I did when she hears mine.

I chuckle as I go on to explain. "I am more than satisfied with being the CEO of Reyes Capital. Plus, it's not as if I was ever really exposed to any of that growing up. Not like Antonio and Esteban were, at least. The plan was for me to always be involved in our family business, what my father felt would be the best fit. He forced me to work my summers in those offices, ensuring that I understand it better when my time came."

"I didn't know that," Violet perks up a little. "So, as a teenager, you were forced to spend your summers in some stuffy office?"

"Most upper-class teenagers spend their summer vacations in much the same way." Lady Penelope informs my wife. "I worked in my father's firm as soon as I turned sixteen. Spent my summers, weekends, and holidays learning all about finance from the bottom up. How did you spend yours?"

A noticeable shift takes place at the table after that remark. My wife stiffens a little, and I catch one of the other women seated with us snicker.

"Something funny, Lady Zelda?" I ask, pointing her out.

"Be nice," Violet warns. "I'm sure it was an innocent question?"

"Was it? An innocent one, Lady Penelope. Or were you seeking to make some point about my wife's social class? The one she grew up in."

Lady Penelope glances around the table as if searching for someone to help her. When no one does, she shrugs nonchalantly.

"You don't know or you're afraid to answer my question?" I'm not backing down.

Lord Morgan answers for her. He after all is married to her, so I'm sure he hates that I'm attacking his wife. "It is no secret that Princess Violet got an immediate upgrade when she married you. I believe I read somewhere that she dropped out of school when she was sixteen. Got involved with some shady people. Even you have to admit that her past draws a person's attention, making them a little skeptical at first."

The table gets quiet again.

I take a few minutes to calm down. I need at least that to gather my thoughts so I can make a point without blowing up and causing a scene. "Well, it is a really good thing no one has dug into all of your past then, isn't it? Put them under a microscope and studied each one thoroughly." I give each of them a stern look, letting them appreciate just how true what I am suggesting is.

"Lenny, please don't." Violet tries to stop me.

But the thing is, she has no idea how important it is to stop all this before it becomes an acceptable topic amongst this group and their peers.

"Wow," this time it's Lady Nina who opens her mouth. "I'd never disrespect a man like the prince in such a way."

I'm about to give these arrogant individuals a piece of my mind, except Violet beats me to the punch.

"Honey, don't go there. I can assure you my use of that name is anything but disrespectful. It just goes to show how you don't know a damn thing about the prince. When I want to tick him off, that is when I call him Your Highness or Prince Lorenzo. When I wish to display affection or grab his undivided attention, I use the name he prefers those who know him use. And no one knows him better than I do, never has or ever will."

"And you made sure of that, didn't you, by trapping him?" Lady Zelda goes where she should not have.

"Maybe I am the one who trapped her. Did you ever think of that?" I beat my wife to it this time. "Decided that the only way to make her see reason, was to implant my seed inside of her so she had no other choice. Drastic times call for drastic measures."

That seems to give them something to ponder on. Well, until my wife slaps me and then voices her thought about what I've just done. "Are you fucking kidding me right now? You couldn't have left well enough alone, or even told the truth about it all. For a man who is not ashamed about..."

I don't let her finish. I grab her and kiss those mouthy lips hard. It is hard for me to resist her when she gives me shit. Even more so when she does it in front of a group who would never expect that response from a Princess. I kiss her until she is melting in my arms and I can feel her relax some.

"I am not ashamed. I have no regrets. Not about taking you to bed so I could show you what it felt like to be loved. Doing so before I asked you to officially be my wife. All because I believed that is what you needed, how you needed it even. I don't care that the math won't add up, once everyone tries to calculate when you conceived our child. Don't give a shit that others will not understand us or our family. All I care about, will ever care about, is that you do. That you understand why I fell in love with you. Know I married you because I love you. That this child you carry is a product of our love and nothing else. To hell with those who don't get us. It makes no difference to me what people think. No fucking difference."

"Well said Your Highness," Lord Cogan is smiling when he says it. "It's about time someone set the record straight. How ironic it is that we all seem to forget ourselves. We, for some unbeknown reason, expect you and yours to act better than the rest of us, but why is that exactly? Why do we feel the need to point out all your flaws, when we refuse to admit we have the same ones? I challenge my table mates to only pass judgment if they can declare to have lived up to those standards they have bestowed upon you. And since I very well know none of them can, because well... it seems an apology is in order."

Lady Zelda blushes but does just that, "I suppose my husband has a point. He often does. I shouldn't hold you to higher standards than I held to myself. Please forgive me."

The other ladies don't bother, only nod in agreement as if that is enough. It is what I had expected. They will never admit they aren't perfect.

Lord Cogan has always hated the way so many of them act, pointed it out as well. He rarely tolerates it. We've spoken often during events like this, laughed about it even. But he is well respected, and that means those around him listen, taking notes when he speaks up. A loyal supporter is what the man is, one we need moving forward.

We get through the rest of dinner with small talk. Not touching on any more sensitive subjects, thankfully. I am able to escort my wife around the party with ease. Introduce her to a few others that are known to keep the conversations light hearted and friendly.

And when I notice she's had about all she can take for one night. Smiled so much her cheeks probably hurt. I create an excuse that will allow us to make our exit. Send Violet to the lavatory while I call for our car.

I just hung up, when a man I'd not noticed until now, steps in front of me. I'm not surprised he is here. He has so many of these society types attending in his back pocket. Very involved in all things political, in hopes to keep his businesses under the radar, or at least appear as legitimate as possible.

"Viktor," his name alone puts a sour taste in my mouth.

"I believe it's Uncle Viktor."

"Not as far as I am concerned. Just because you married my father's sister, does not earn you a title that has meaning." Technically, he is right. Although we stopped referring to him as our Uncle when my father disowned them.

"Family is not something you choose; it is chosen for you. Your father should have taught you that." He scowls, and it is meant to intimidate me, although all it does is piss me off. "Blood is thicker than water. Blood doesn't lie."

"And we share no blood, do we," I retort. "Making you an outsider."

Something crosses his face I don't appreciate. An emotion that makes my blood run cold and has me wondering what is taking Violet so long.

"That wife of yours, I warned my son to leave her alone. But he refused to listen, always thought he knew better than I did."

"For once we seem to agree."

Viktor smiles about that and I hate it. "You see, what my son didn't seem to understand, was how crafty that little whore of his was. How she held the same fire inside of her as another female I once knew did?"

I see red. Not just because he referenced my wife as a whore, but for what he seems to be suggesting.

"I mean your Aunt not...", he laughs, "Now that would be an interesting twist. See, the problem he seemed to overlook was which one of his two women he should have put in charge. He should have made Lady Amber his mistress if he was so interested in keeping her. While her status helped make him appear a legitimate businessman, or it should have, that is all she was good for. He would have been better off grooming his whore instead of ticking her off. Because a woman like Violet is dangerous when not dealt with correctly. Given privilege to information, only someone you trust should have been granted. He was careless and has only himself to blame. I'd have taken care of her long before she ever had the chance to threaten me. However, now I have a problem that needs handling as well. One only your wife can assist me with. I hope you understand. As soon as she has done as I've requested, she will be rewarded with a promise that Ruben will never bother her again. Again, I hope you understand."

Right as he turns to walk away, there is a loud shriek from the corridor leading to the bathroom. The kind that has my feet running faster than they ever have before. I recognize that voice. Recognize who it is, and I wasn't wrong.

Violet is standing toe to toe with Lady Amber. Neither has noticed they've drawn a crowd. They are too focused on each other at the moment.

And when Lady Amber lifts her hand, displaying a needle filled with God knows what. My wife reacts instinctively, sending the other woman to the floor with one quick and swift jab right to the throat.

"Are you okay?" I ask, spinning her around, checking her out the best I can. "Did she stick you with that needle?"

"Fuck no. That fucking bitch could never get the drop on me." Violet is pissed, ready to go after the fallen woman still lying on the ground. "I swear to God she's lucky I'm dressed like this, or a throat punch wouldn't have been the only thing she'd have gotten. I'd have let her have a few more, maybe even performed one of those round kicks Cast showed me."

"Hold up, Rocky," I wrap her up in my arms and start walking her backward. "Let's let the professionals deal with her now. You've done enough damage for one night."

"God, that felt good," she grins at me with a fire in her eyes, one I recognize. "Did you see me? I did it exactly how Cast taught me."

I nod, still chuckling as I instruct the guards standing around. "Arrest her once she recovers. Bag that syringe so we can test it. And get all these nosey buggers out of here. It was self-defense. Lady Amber was threatening Princess Violet, and she got what she deserved."

Laney, who is bent over the body, glances up a little concerned. "I think she crushed her airway."

"Then perhaps she shouldn't have attacked my wife."

Laney shrugs. "I just thought you should know. I could have told her that. I've had a front-row seat during her training sessions. Your wife is a badass, and she doesn't mess around. She'll live, might have to be intubated while it heals. Bet she will think twice before doing something like that again."

On that note, I spin us around and lead us out the doors where our car is waiting. I need to get her out of here so we can get to the bottom of all of this once and for all.

Was Lady Amber doing Viktor's dirty work, or did she have her own agenda? Until I can speak with Violet, I won't know.

CHAPTER 31
Lorenzo

The Royals

The ride home is interesting, but not in a bad way, so not in a bad way. My lovely wife is high on adrenaline. No sooner do I get the partition up before I am jumped. She is straddling me while frantically working my pants. Practically destroying the zipper as she rips it open rather than taking the time to unzip it.

"In a hurry," I chuckle between the harsh fervent kisses she is providing me. "Hey, slow down. We have all night."

Gripping my dick in her hand, she squeezes just hard enough to make me nearly explode. "Still want to go slow?"

"Hell no," I groan as I shove her dress up around her waist. "So are you a big fan of these or..."

"Rip them off, you can buy me another pair."

I wrap my fingers around the string until it snaps and then let the material fall to the floor. They then dig into her hips as my thumb checks her folds to discover her more than ready, wet and throbbing even.

A whimper escapes when I press firmly against her clit, the kind that has me pressing harder until I notice she is close. Right before she does, I stop and get the look. The one she always gives me when I toy with her like this. I work it again and stop, again and stop, until I realize if I don't let her finish, she'll make me pay for it later. But before I do, I yank her forward, settling her on me, letting her walls work me without having to move.

"You're killing me," she moans as she tries to force me to help her get what she needs. "Please, Lenny."

I kiss her lips softly, barely letting them brush. Making it that much more intense. And then I press hard against her clit right as I slam into her. That move wakes her orgasm immediately. It sends us into a frantic need to drive the other person higher and higher until we tumble and fall together.

That's when I catch the car has stopped. Our guards have learned to never open a door. They've seen way more than they should. "We are home."

"Hmmm..." Violet mumbles. "So we are."

I lift her off of me and help get her back to being presentable again. Tuck myself in, although I don't bother trying to zip my pants. I know for sure they are going to need to go to the tailors for a new zipper. Instead, I fix them the best I can and get out where four cheeky faces are waiting on us.

"Hope we didn't keep you waiting long," Violet brushes her dress down before reaching inside to collect her destroyed knickers. "Here, you owe me a pair."

I shove them in my pocket as I jostle my head. "You all are free to go. We can discuss what happened earlier in the morning. I believe it should be able to wait until then."

Laney is the one to speak, "The initial report states that Lady Amber has a bruised esophagus, she'll definitely feel it for a while, but heal. Tapes have been confiscated and will be evaluated. But from what we've been told so far, Violet was approached by her and only did what she had to do."

"Good to know. Thanks. We'll touch base in the morning." I take off for the house and lock up behind us. Setting the alarm like I've done so many times.

I hear the shower running in our en suite when I enter the bedroom.

See Violet's dress draped over one chair. So, I pick it up and carry it off to the large closet so I can hang it for her. I toss my jacket, bow tie, and shirt onto a chair. Slip my shoes and socks off next. Yank my undershirt over my head and toss it into the laundry bin on my way back into the bedroom.

When I exit the closet, I head straight for the minibar we have in here. A nightcap would be a great way to settle some of my nerves. Help me decide how to approach Violet about earlier. I realize I told my staff we'd deal with it tomorrow, but I need to hear some of it tonight. Need to hear if she spoke with Viktor. And if she did, then I need to learn what was said. If not, then I have to establish if she knows what he believes she can help him out with.

Something about the entire situation rubs me the wrong way. Why in the world would Viktor think I'd ever allow her to help him, let her anywhere near him? He seemed way too sure of himself, way too confident that his promise to ensure Ruben would be out of her life for good, will make her bend. It all strikes me as odd.

I pour myself a scotch over a few ice cubes and swirl it around a few times. Bring it to my nose for a healthy sniff. A habit I often saw my father perform, one I picked up on. Then I sit it back down and stare at it a bit longer. Study the color while I let my mind recall the words spoken between Viktor and myself. I am almost positive there was some hidden message in his comment, one I am determined to figure out sooner rather than later.

Agitating my head, I pick up my tumbler and begin to tip it back when I catch something on the monitor. It was a shadow, one that moved quickly, but it was there. In a location where one should not have been. So instead of enjoying my drink, I spin around and type in the code to unlock the small safe. Reach inside and retrieve one of two pistols I keep in there. Then I think again and grab the other, heading straight for the bathroom.

The room is full of steam. She is standing under the waterfall pouring from the ceiling. "You okay?"

"Yep," she peaks around the wall and smiles. "You going to join me?"

"Soon. I just need to go check on something first." I tell her but don't mention the gun tucked in the back of my pants or the one I've placed under the towel by the sink. "If you finish before I get back, go ahead and crawl in bed. I know you've had a night and need to catch some shuteye."

She studies me closely and asks, "You okay?"

"Yep. Just want to check in with the guards. Update them before we call it a night." I step to her and kiss her lips just because I can. "Hurry up, it's getting late."

She smiles against my lips. "I love you."

Never gets old hearing those words. "I love you too. Now finish up before you pass out in here."

I stare at her for a few more seconds before I leave to go and check out what I believe I saw earlier. While I do, I send my guards a message to do a perimeter check and evaluate the surveillance tapes since we left. Then I send them another, advising them to do a system check. See if we have had any issues over the last week that looked odd. Something that at first, they wrote off as nothing, a glitch that seemed to check out. I know they will be able to read between the lines. Within a few minutes, they will have everyone on it, realize I've got a hunch that I won't let go until I've figured out why.

JAVIER: On it.

RICO: So far, so good. But you already knew that. What is it you are really saying?

ME: Don't really know. Just keep on it until we figure out what has my nerves on high alert.

LANEY: There was an issue with one of the alarm gates. It randomly seems to go off. Last went off a few hours ago. When it was checked, nothing appeared out of the ordinary. Tapes show nothing either. But now I'm thinking there is more to it than first suspected.

ME: Check the east garden. And have
someone bring Valentina back up here for
the night. I want her eyes and ears in the
house now that we are home.

GAYLE: We are on our way. Now that you
mention it, she seems a little anxious, more
than ready to head that way.

I tuck my phone into my pocket as I enter the kitchen. The house is
dark but not too dark, I can see well enough to make my way around
without needing light. Know each and every corner, shadow, and sound
inside this place. I've spent many hours in here alone listening,
watching, thinking. And while I don't see or hear anything out of the
ordinary. I feel it all around me, notice something is off.

I've never been happier that I talked Violet into letting Char stay
with Isabel tonight. We don't get a lot of nights without her, and I love
having her around. However, my little girl does love spending time with
her Aunt Isabel and Helena, my brother's head au pair. And since her
time in Aragon is limited to when they make a trip up here now that
school has started again, it was a win for us and them. I not only knew
that she was safer at the castle where security is airtight, I am glad she
isn't here so I can focus on only keeping one of my girls safe and not
torn between them both.

There is a bark before the front door opens. Valentina is let loose to
do what she often does. Run through the house checking for anything
out of place. She seems satisfied for now that all is well, so she darts for
me, demanding attention.

"Thanks for bringing her up," I tell Gayle as I rub the dog's ears.

She nods, "No problem. We've called in a few extras tonight. Will
up our perimeter checks, keeping them almost continuous to ensure
nothing slips past us. I called Darius to have one of his guys do a system
analysis, and you can bet he is putting his best guys on it. We will keep
you posted. Two of us will also be stationed inside tonight. Don't argue
that out, it is non-negotiable. We can discuss more tomorrow if you'd
like, but tonight Javier and I will stay in the maid's quarters."

"Rico okay with that?"

She barely blinks when she answers. "Do you want an answer to that question, really?"

I laugh and shake my head. "No."

"Didn't think so," she steps outside. "I'll let you know when we are ready. Until then, everything should be nice and tight."

Meaning that no one should be entering the home before. And if for some reason someone does, then that means that someone isn't one of them.

Valentina and I make our way back to our bedroom, taking a few extra moments to inspect doors, windows, and rooms. Closing the unused ones for the night just for precautions. Spending a little extra time in Char's room, letting Valentina have a solid sniff around before either of us are satisfied all is clear.

When we enter the bedroom, I'm not surprised to find Violet sitting there with the pistol on her lap. It was after all under a towel in the bathroom, put there for her in case she needed it.

"What's going on?" are the first words out of her mouth.

"Did you speak with Viktor tonight?"

"Viktor? No, I didn't even realize he was there. And when exactly was it you thought I might have spoken to him?"

I pull the gun out of my waistband and place it on the bar, grab my forgotten nightcap and swish it around again. "He approached me while you were using the restroom. I'm not sure I expected you to have talked with him, but..."

The lights flicker and then go off.

"Lenny." I don't like the frightened tone of her voice.

Before I can get to her, they are back on again, and it all seems too suspicious. Too strategic, planned even. Which is why I close and lock the door to our room. Snap my fingers and point to the closet, getting Violet and Valentina moving, not hesitating, or arguing about it.

Not yet, at least. But as soon as they are both inside, I place my hand on the sensor that disengages the door to the safe room and all but shove her in. Order Valentina to stay as well. The moment Violet realizes I'm not about to step in there with her, that is when I hear all those protests loud and clear. Right before the door sealing silences her.

Perhaps I am being a stupid arsehole. Taking an unnecessary risk that my guards are more than capable of handling. Trying to be the hero she doesn't need or want.

If this turns out to be bad, worse than bad, she'll never forgive me. But at least she is safe. And her safety, my children's safety, is all that matters to me right now. I'm done messing around. It is time to end this once and for all.

CHAPTER 32
Violet

The Royals

I am going to kill him myself when I get out of this goddamn room. I cannot believe he shoved me inside this box of hell without being by my side. What in the ever-living fuck was he thinking? Clearly, he wasn't and if I ever get out of here, I'm going to kill him with my bare hands.

Valentina seems just as perturbed about it as me. I reach down and pat her head, thankful that we are both likely assuming the same thing. She plops down and stares at the solid metal door, displeased with her master's dumbass decision.

"You should bite him in the arse when we get out of here," I tell her as I pace. "Take a solid chunk of flesh and not feel one ounce of guilt when you do. That is, if there will be a chunk of it left for you. I make no promises."

She offers me an approving growl, ready to pounce as soon as the door opens.

Making a fist, I pound on the door. Not that it does me a bit of good. He isn't likely there to hear my pounding, probably couldn't hear it anyway since this room is soundproof. Meaning the frustrated high-pitched scream I let out, only hurts Valentina's and my ears.

Once I've allowed myself a mini-meltdown, I take the time to survey the room we are stuck in for God knows how long. There is a wall of surveillance screens in front of me, exhibiting every freaking room in this large home. All the outside cameras as well, every one of them for me to study while I sit here in this room and can only watch.

For the longest time, I don't see anything. All is quiet, too quiet if you ask me.

Then I notice Laney and Gayle making their way inside. Taking a route anyone unfamiliar with the property would never use. Noticeably doing so to not alert an intruder, and my gut is telling me we most definitely have one.

I watch and let my mind reflect to earlier when Lady Amber approached me in the bathroom.

I'd not noticed her at first. Did my thing, then began washing my hands, checking my reflection in the mirror, noting how defeated I appeared.

It was then I caught her standing a respectable distance behind me, watching me all too closely. If it hadn't been for the other two women, also currently using the facilities, I imagine it might have ended differently. Their presence had granted me the opportunity to take her in fully, notice the way she seemed edgy, nervous about something, out of sorts even. It was her eyes that gave her away, the glossy unfocused eyes that suggested she was as high as a kite. Then I noticed her reddened nose. One that reminded me of all those I knew, whose choice of drug had been cocaine. And if her supplier was the same one who had once supplied me, I had no doubt that it was laced with something else. A substance that makes the high quicker, last longer, hook you faster.

As soon as the other women moved toward the door, I decided I had better follow them. A feeling deep inside warned me to act, not wait to find out what Lady Amber's scheme was. I'd just made it to the door, stepped into the hallway when I felt my head get yank back. Knew she'd grabbed my hair to stop me and I'd let out a yelp as I whipped around to break her hold on it. The echo made it sound louder than it actually was, catching the attention of those nearby.

"Get your fucking hands off me," I'd ordered as I struck her arm just right to sever her grip on my hair.

"Such a dirty mouth for a princess. Is that why he keeps you? He likes

the trashiness a whore like you can offer him. It is why Ruben kept you around, why I allowed it. He needed his little whore to give him what a lady could not afford. A good whore is what makes a marriage and keeps a man happy."

I hadn't bothered to respond. She wasn't worth my time or energy. Her words were only words, they held no meaning or played a part in what I had with Lorenzo. And since I was no longer concerned about why she or her husband had kept me around, I chose not to let it upset me.

"Trash needs to be disposed of properly. So far, you've not been, and that means it's time to rectify that. Ruben was right; until we get rid of you, our lives will remain unsettled. Time to take the trash out and let him decide just how to dispose of it."

We'd stood there for what seemed like forever, staring at each other with so much hatred. While I had wanted to walk away and leave, I wasn't about to turn my back on her again. She was going to have to make the first move and thankfully, she had.

The moment my eyes took in the syringe she'd pulled out of her handbag, I didn't think, I just reacted. It was quick and fast and done before she even realized it.

"I showed that bitch," I reach down and pat Valentina. "So, what do you think? What game do you suppose is being played here tonight?"

I continue to stare at the screens before me. Watched Lorenzo exchange a few heated words with his guards and chuckle about that. Serves him right to get chewed out like a disobedient child. Wait until he hears my thoughts on his little stunt. When I get out of here...

My eyes take in my surroundings again. Valentina and I are in a safe room, a room designed to keep others out until the danger has passed. Once the room has been engaged, the only way to open the door is from the inside. No code or key can open it from the outside, there is no override switch. It is why the switch to engage is also on the inside. The reason Lorenzo had to step out of the way quickly after he pushed the mechanism located high enough for only an adult to activate.

I remember when he first showed it to me, explained how it worked and what I should do if I ever found myself inside. This safe room was a system of rooms actually, connected by passageways. Once one was activated, they all were. Making it impossible for someone to get inside any of the rooms. Only allowing those in the structure to move around the house to the others. There was one in each bedroom. The unique feature was that it also activated locks to all those doors. A safeguard to allow an extra layer of protection. Giving an allotted amount of time to get everyone inside while keeping them safe. And since there being monitors in each main area, it made it possible to check each room before entering it.

Which means I can get out of here, and not only through the door I was shoved in. I have options that might be safer. Or possibly even let me sneak in on some unsuspected soul.

"What do you think, girl? Where do you suppose this intruder is hiding?" I ask, studying each frame carefully, looking for something to speak to me.

It's as if we both come to the same conclusion at the exact same time. Both realizing that the person inside was after one thing and one thing only.

Evidence. Evidence I had taken when I ran. Evidence that if it ever got into the wrong hand—or the right ones—could expose the truth about so very much.

Lorenzo and I had agreed it best he didn't know all the details. That we keep it as a safeguard and only ever use it if the time was right. All he knew was that should it ever get out, it likely meant the end of Ruben. And while I wasn't against letting him get what was coming to him, because he was more than due, I wasn't so sure I wanted to deal with the consequences of having this person he'd betrayed perceive me as some kind of threat. Nor was I willing to put my family in danger should this individual decide I knew too much and needed to be dealt with.

His head lifts as he stares directly into the camera. Without having to say a word, I know exactly what he is thinking. I realize what I need to do, where we need to go.

"Ready for an adventure, girl?" I ask as I stand and uncover what I am looking for.

The steel wall opens just to the left of me. I glance down at Valentina, who knows these passages better than I do. "Office girl. That is where we are going. Lead the way."

She tilts her head then briskly leads me, glimpsing back often to make sure I am close behind her. As soon as we reach our destination, I take a moment to search the room.

What this person is looking for isn't out there, it's in here. Hidden in plain sight. A discarded USB drive that has been tossed in a corner as if forgotten. I grab it before turning to watch the monitor, proving we were right.

Inside the office is Ruben. He's doing his best to not make any noise that would give away his position. Sitting at the desk staring at the computer, which happens to be hooked up to some external drive. He is clearly up to no good.

When the office door flies open, he picks up his weapon and aims. Ready to shoot the first person who steps through. Except no one does, not right away at least. And definitely not the person he'd been expecting. Not the person I'd even expected, not by a long shot.

"What were you thinking breaking into the home of your enemy? Have I taught you nothing?" Viktor shakes his head in disgust. "What is it you think you can accomplish by such an act?"

"Are you working with them now, father?" Ruben doesn't lower his weapon. He keeps it aimed right at his father.

"No. But do you really believe I am so stupid that I didn't know what it was you had been up to all along? That you could steal from me without me knowing. Make deals behind my back without me ever finding out. If your whore could figure it out so easily, what makes you think I would not?"

When Ruben starts to say something, his father holds his hand up to stop him. I have to admit it is rather fascinating to watch. Witnessing the power Viktor has over his son, how the man seems fearless even though he has a gun aimed at him. I wouldn't put it past Ruben to shoot him. Eventually, I do believe that was part of his plot. Kill his father so he could take over and run the family legacy the way he wanted. But it isn't easy to kill a man in Viktor's position, not even for his son.

While they are having this stare down, I decide to make a brave move and reveal myself. Let the door to the hidden room open behind Rueben, distracting him just long enough for Viktor to show his true intentions. As soon as Ruben turns the gun off of his father to focus on what is happening behind him, it becomes his fatal mistake.

I am smart enough to not be in the line of fire, keep Valentina out of it as well. We move into the corridor behind the steel door. As I'd predicted, Ruben didn't hesitate to let his weapon disengage. He fires rapid automatic gunfire directly into the room. Only hitting a few monitors and nothing else.

It is followed by a single gunshot and a thud.

"You may come out now, Princess. He will no longer be a threat to you or your family." Viktor calls out.

I hear the shuffling of feet, but don't move. I don't move until Lorenzo appears in the doorway.

And then I run. I run and leap into his arms, letting him secure me there like a small child. He carries me through the room and outside. I didn't need or want to see the body of the man who once ruled so much of my life. All I wanted to do was to get as far away from all of that as possible. Let someone else deal with the aftermath that is him.

Lorenzo walks me to the garden, with Valentina close by. He sits down when we reach a bench and just holds me.

Eventually, I speak and let him have it. "I'm so angry with you. Locking me inside there while you…"

"I didn't lock you inside," he interrupts and grabs my face with both his hands.

"At that moment it felt like you did." I glare at him, or at least I try.

He only sighs and pulls my head forward until our foreheads are touching.

"Don't ever do that again," I whisper with a shaky voice. "I… I can't do this without you. You… you are the air I breathe, Lenny. You… you are what keeps me from completely losing my shit. And if you pull something like that again, I will not be responsible for my actions. It's very possible I'll take your balls and wear them as a trophy."

"No reason to be so violent love, my balls are yours already. They also need to stay where they are so I can love you right, give you as many children as you will allow me to."

Not ready to think that far ahead, I bring us back to the present and ask the one question lingering in the front of my mind. "Why was Viktor here?"

"Apparently, he had been tracking his son, keeping a very close eye on him. When word got back to him that his son was here, he showed up and offered his assistance. There was only one catch, he wanted to speak to you when it was all said and done."

"And you agreed to that?" I have a hard time believing he would.

"No. Before we could discuss it, one of the silent alarms went off in the office."

"Letting you know where he was and what he was up to." I'd forgotten about all those silent alarms he has set up; they are everywhere.

"Sir," Gayle's voice breaks through the darkness. "Viktor would like a moment before..."

"It's fine," I answer for him, then slide off his lap and settle in next to him. "Might as well get this over with."

She steps back and allows Viktor to step forward. "I'll make it quick. After tonight, what was once between us is no more. No one will bother you or your family. You will forget what you know, and I will forget that you know it."

I reach inside my pocket and toss the USB drive at him. "I didn't really know anything. Only learned as little as I had to, and never really looked much farther than what initially caught my eye. Everything, however, is on that, and I have made no other copies. Meaning once you walk out of here with that, you also take everything I ever had on you and your family.

"But I cannot promise that the king won't continue his endeavor to rid you and yours from the kingdom. That he will look the other way or not make things difficult on you. That would be asking him to push aside everything he and his brothers stand for."

A cynical grin grows on Viktor's face before he answers. "That business has nothing to do with this. And those who were involved with the business my son was associated with will be dealt with properly. The way we deal with disobedient men in our organization."

Lorenzo waves a hand to stop him. "We don't need to know any of that. You can do as you please. One slip though, then we will do what we have to."

Viktor nods once before turning to leave, visibly done with us and all of this.

I lean into Lorenzo, really feeling the events of the evening pressing down on me. Making me even more than ready to put it behind me. As if knowing my thoughts, he scoops me in his arms and heads for the house. Letting his guards know that we are off to bed and not to be disturbed until we wake in the morning.

CHAPTER 33
Lorenzo

The Royals

I've noticed a change in my wife since the death of Ruben. She seems more relaxed, while at the same time there is this cloud hovering over her. It's not the same dreadful one that was once floating above, thankfully. It is however there, and I believe I understand why.

We've not slept in the house I once loved since that night. Instead, we've been staying in the guest cottage where she once briefly resided. At first, it was because of the investigation; we didn't want to be around while that was going on.

I've been inside the home more than once. Violet has not. She always comes up with an excuse for why she can't do it, legitimate sounding excuses. But now that a month has passed, I have come to the conclusion that she will never feel safe there again. The reason I've made a decision I hope she'll agree too.

I'm not so sure Aragon is the right place for us. It holds so many memories that haunt her daily. And if the king can move away and do his job remotely, I don't see why I cannot do the same.

Our time on the run, when we were hiding out in a rural location, that is where my lovely wife seemed the most relaxed. Therefore, I have decided to take her to the one place I have loved for so many years. A secluded location where I was allowed to be myself. My safe-haven away, where I didn't suffer under the scornful eye of those watching.

When my mother moved us away from Aragon, she did so because she wanted a more private and segregated life for us. It wasn't easy to find that life, but after a few years, it seemed the people respected her choice. Letting us grow up without always hovering.

De la Pena Citadel was no longer being used as a home. My mother has moved into Castile Vicente now that she plans on staying in Aragon. Antonio has suggested she become his advisor, took over the role abandoned by Esteban when he became Governor of the South. While she hasn't agreed to do it long-term, she has conceded to give it a trial run. Assist her eldest son, for now.

I'm guessing that once she begins to do the job, it won't take her long to realize just how perfect she is for such a role. A buffer between generations, a highly respected figure in this country.

I spoke with her last week to make certain she had no issues with my plan. She did not. Thought it was exactly what my growing family needed and fully supported it. The citadel is only a few hours northeast of Aragon, less if one uses one of the helicopters we have access to. Meaning that we will never be far from those we hold dear.

Today we are making the drive there. I'm driving us to Prieto so we will not be bothered with those things having our detail with us can cause. Our team is following, mind you; they are never far behind us these days.

I still consider Viktor a threat. He hasn't been seen since shooting Ruben. Later, disappearing into the night like men in his position often do. Lady Amber has gone missing as well, for that matter. It seems she disappeared shortly after being released.

I'm not worried about any of it, though. We received a message, not a direct message I guess, but a message we understood. It informed us Viktor had relocated and took it upon himself to make certain Lady Amber left with him. No one knew for certain if that meant she was paying a debt for her role in the plot Ruben had planned to execute. It was enough to let us identify she wouldn't be an issue for us. He was moving on like he said he would do. Taking care of matters the way he saw fit. There wasn't much we could do since he moved it all far away from Hermosa Islas. If he ever returned, that would be another story, but his return was very unlikely.

"Where are we going?" Violet finally asks as she watches the city disappear behind us.

I reach for her hand and squeeze it. "Someplace I believe you will like very much."

Her skeptical gaze tells me she knows I'm up to something. Instead of probing me for answers, she lets it go. Begins to stare out the window while taking it all in. Dozing off eventually.

The gravel crunching under the tires, stirs her a few hours later. "Where are we?"

"I see horsey!" Char shouts from the backseat. "I ride."

"That is Ulysses. He is a strong Thoroughbred. Gram has several horses. I'll introduce you to each one. I think you will like Aurora better, though. She is a very calm Morgan. Just what a little one like you needs when learning about horses. Gram raised Aurora from birth and rides her as often as she can."

Violet leans forward in her seat as she watches the large residence I was raised in come into view. "Why did you bring us here? It's so... peaceful. This is where you grew up?"

I put the vehicle in park and encourage Violet to get out. Once I have unbuckled Char, she is eager to join us. My mother has been here waiting, ready to help with her so I can show Violet around. As soon as our daughter spots Gram, she runs the best she can straight for her.

Sliding my arm around Violet, I lead her around the grounds. Words do not need to be spoken while we walk. The atmosphere here is so much less heavy. There is a peacefulness about this place that can be felt when strolling the land. A person does not feel like there are eyes on them, judging every move. Here you get the sense of being alone, something I myself love. Why I loved my home in Aragon so much. The open area gave me a small reminder of here.

Violet stops walking and takes a seat on one of the large boulders that can be found everywhere. She lets her eyes survey the estate and I wait. The heaviness she carries with her visibly lifts as she relaxes completely for the first time. I do not believe I've seen her like this before.

Dropping to a squatting position in front of her, I take her hands and stare into her eyes. "I have this idea."

"Do share," she says with a deep cleansing breath.

"I've discussed this with the family already. Cleared it with Antonio. There is no reason I cannot do my job as CEO of Reyes Capital remotely. Make a few trips to the city each month when needed. Plan my business trips abroad like I've been doing. It would take some adjusting, but it can be done." I see her nod.

"So, this trip is more about what exactly? We are not here to visit your mother." She is a smart woman.

"I'd like it to be our home. A fresh start. We can make new memories here. I can share all the happy ones I had as a child. What do you think?"

Violet tilts her head forward until it touches mine. "Are you sure this is what you want?"

"What I want is to see you look this beautiful every day. Watch our girls explore the land. Give them the freedom they will not have in Aragon."

I found out only yesterday that they expected the child growing inside Violet to be another girl. My heart melted while I stared at the image in front of me. The wiggly little blurb was my daughter, who's already causing all kinds of mischief.

I don't care what everyone is saying. They have no idea how much we needed this little one to help heal her mother's heart and soul. They don't get that, all because they live lives that nowhere compare to the one my Violet once lived. And I will in no way allow this child to ever be told that she was a mistake or an accident. She will learn she was given to us when we needed her the most. That she was the sunshine that burned away all the darkness that tried to sneak in and steal her mother's joy. I will always be thankful for her timing because it was perfect, ensuring she is the child God wanted us to have.

"You are not disappointed it's not a boy?" She asks me again like she did in Dr. Wilson's office shortly after we found out.

"Not at all. This baby being a girl helps guarantee that you will allow me the pleasure of giving you at least one more. Granting me that chance to prove I have a son inside me who wants to be born, he will get his chance when the time is right. Sunniva's time is now." I've been calling this little one that since the name came to me, determined to get Violet to agree.

A roll of her eyes tells me she is still debating if she likes it or not. "You know I could never deny you."

Just as I am about to let her prove that to me, the sound of gravel crunching stops me. I have one more surprise for her. This one I realize will take time to work out the way I hope, but one can pray for a positive outcome.

We head back for the house when the echo of children's voices catches Violet's ears. She turns to me when she recognizes one of them as a girl's. "Isabel has also come for a visit?"

"No," I shake my head. "I believe that is Juliet you hear."

"Juliet?" At first, she seems confused, but then it comes to her. "My Juliet?"

Again, I nod. "It seemed like it was time we met."

Tears flood her eyes as we clear the trees and see the children all gathered around my mother. She is a gracious host and determined to not let her status intimidate them in the least.

Char is chattering with them. Making them appear slightly more comfortable as she does her best to explain who her Gram is. "It is just Gram. Her the best Gram ever. You have a Gram? If not, I share her."

Brigham laughs. "We have a Nan. Mum's mother. We see her a few times a year when she comes for a visit."

"She brings us treats," Juliet adds.

"She sounds lovely." My mother smiles at them. "I bet she loves you both very much."

Char sees us before the others. "Papa looks. Brig and Jul came to see me. It was surprise. Why is mummy crying?"

The children all come running toward us. Violet bends down to greet them with open arms.

"Look how big you two have grown. I barely recognized you." She tugs them back and studies them very closely.

"I'm almost eleven. I'm not a kid anymore." Brigham announces in a voice that is just now showing signs of changing.

I extend my hand to him. "Hello. I'm Lenny. And you must be Brigham. It is very nice to meet you."

"He means Prince Lorenzo," the woman approaching informs them. "Don't be rude, Brigham. Remember your manners and show the good prince you have some."

Brigham gives me a slight bow and then does exactly as he is told to do. "Your Highness, it is a pleasure to meet you as well. Thank you for inviting us."

I reach out and rough the boy's hair as I kneel to greet his sister. "And you must be the adorable Juliet. The pleasure my lady is mine." I then take her hand and kiss it.

The little girl blushes and does a proper curtsey. "Thank you, Your Highness."

Violet tries not to laugh but isn't doing a particularly good job at it. "Oh, no. No, you all are not to address him like that. Family is not required to do formal introductions."

The woman, who I assume is their mother, speaks again. "We are not exactly family so..."

"But you are." I interrupt. "Hello. I'm Lenny. You will offend me if you call me something other than that. You must be Lady Marisol."

Marisol blushes, much like her daughter did when I take her hand in mine. "It's just Marisol. I'm not a lady."

Juliet seems a little eager to ask something while she stares at us curiously. It doesn't take her long to just do it. "Are you really a princess now, Violet?"

"I am." She stands with Char in her arms. "Charlotte is now a duchess."

"An honorary duchess," Marisol corrects, and I don't like it.

"There is nothing honorary about it. Char is my daughter. She carries my name."

Char proudly announces. "I Charlotte Lorenza Reyes. Him name is in mine twice." She holds up two fingers.

"But I thought," Brigham starts, then stops.

Violet must decide to switch to something less confusing. "So, what brings you to Prieto? This is a surprise, a good one."

"He didn't tell you?" Marisol raises her eyebrows.

"Tell me what, exactly?"

"That father agreed to allow us to move to Prieto so Brigham could attend the same school the prince attended when he was his age." Juliet sounds almost as excited about it as Brigham looks.

"Is that so?" Violet's eyes find mine, and I'm not sure if I'm in trouble or not. "He is full of surprises today."

"It was an offer we couldn't refuse," Marisol informs her. "A truly generous one."

"How generous, exactly?"

"Let us not get into all that now." I don't want to embarrass Marisol, make her feel like she is taking advantage of a situation.

It was I who approached Dolan and Marisol once I decided to move my family here. I knew that Brigham was close to the age the school I attended started accepting students. There were options it offered that others did not. Boarding being one, although I wasn't sure letting an eleven-year-old experience that was the best idea. While I had friends who had done that, I also witnessed how hard it had been on them. My own brothers had gone away and came back different, not as innocent or naïve as a child should be. I was prepared to offer alternatives if I needed to.

It seemed Marisol was ready for a change as well. She appreciated the opportunity to give her children the chance to get out of the hard life Dolan and she were living. Eager to do what she could and more than willing to find work near Prieto.

For an hour we walked around the land and talked with the children and Marisol. Violet letting her younger siblings lead most of the conversation. It was more than obvious how much she had missed them, how much she loved them. That she was looking forward to spending more time with them regularly.

After we sat down for a pleasant lunch, it was time for them to go. There were a few tears, most of them from her as she waved goodbye.

With my hands on her shoulders, I try to comfort her the best I can. Kiss the top of her head.

"Why?"

I almost laugh at her question. "Why what?"

"Why would you do that?" Violet leans into me, still following the dust their departure left behind.

"I know how important those two are to you. I realize that you feel as if you have missed out on so much with them. It seemed like it was time to do something to change that. Char needs to get to know them, all of them. It would be nice to get to know Dolan and Marisol as well. He is your father after all." I let my arm slide around her so I can draw her closer.

Char is running around with Valentina, chasing butterflies. We watch them for a while.

"I like it here," Violet whispers as she turns into me. "It feels like a really great place to raise a family."

I cannot help but smile about that. "I thought you might. We can do just that if it is what you want."

"How soon can we do that?" She asks, sinking in deeper.

"Today if you would like," I tell her. "I only need to make a phone call and we can pack our belongings and have them shipped in a few days."

"And what will you do with Hacienda Refugio Seguro?"

"Sell it. I have no need for a home in Aragon if we are to live here."

"Will you be happy living here?" Her head tilts back so she can see my eyes.

"I have always loved it here, Violet. The renovations are still underway, but I've been assured occupancy is not a problem. We can even bunker down in the carriage house, it has not been occupied for a few years now. When mother moved out, those who once lived here followed her to Aragon.

"My home where I will be happiest is wherever you are. Char, you, and little Sunniva are my home. You three are all I need to be happy."

And I mean that with all my heart. I could live in a shack and not care as long as I had them to keep me company. I need my girls, all of them, to be a happy man. Violet is the air that fills my lungs, and our girls are the blood the runs through my veins. Without them, I do not believe I'd survive.

Epilogue

VIOLET

The Royals

I still have a very hard time believing my life has turned out the way it has. That I've been blessed with so much after having to fight for so long just to get my life back.

We've been together for almost ten years. It seems like it has been so much longer, though.

My beautiful Charlotte is now twelve and still the apple of Lorenzo's eye. Along with the thorn in his side and the spice that makes his day. She has recently discovered boys, and her father refuses to accept that. He will not allow her to mention the young lads she favors. It is a game she loves to play with him just so she can watch her father react.

We are out on the trail when she starts in. "Papa, I need a new dress."

"Why?" He takes the bait way too easily this time.

"I've been invited to a party. I require a dress that will make me stand out." Charlotte kicks her horse, so it moves right next to his. "Can we go visit Gram's this weekend so she can take me to her friend's shop?"

"I want to go too," Amy whines from her horse.

"Hello, there is no way you are going to Gram's without me." That would be Sunny, letting everyone know she will not be left out.

"I want a new pretty dress. Can I have one too, Papa?" Jackie looks over at him from her spot on my saddle.

"Yuck. No. No. No. Char, no boys. No dress. No. No." Our beautiful boy announces from his spot in front of his father. "Girls. Oh boy. Too much."

Lorenzo laughs as he nods his head in agreement with his only son. "Why do I let myself get sucked in like this? Why can't you wear one of your other dresses, Char? You have a closet full of pretty gowns."

The expression on my oldest daughter's face has me laughing. She can hardly believe her own father would ask her such a silly question. "One does not wear an old dress to this kind of party, Papa. Especially the eldest daughter of a prince. Are you determined to ruin my social life?"

Lorenzo finally looks to me for the answer he isn't getting.

"Char, it will not ruin your social life just because you had to wear an almost new dress. And if the young baron turns his nose up, all because of a dress, then he is not worth your time." I inform her as I watch Lenny get that expression he gets when a boy is mentioned.

"Oh, no. No." He protests.

"No. No." Sal, his parrot starts in. "Oh, no."

"That's so not fair." Char isn't about to let this slide. "This will be the party of all parties. You are going to ruin my life if you don't let me go just because it's a boy/girl party. Everyone who is anybody will be there."

"Except for you," her father discloses.

I lift my hand to stop her from arguing and then send our three oldest back to the stables.

We have a total of four girls: Charlotte, Sunniva, Amarilla, and Jaqueline. I gave my dear prince one last chance to prove he had a son in him, and we were then blessed with Salvador.

I allowed my gorgeous husband to love me as much as he could. Five children later, we both came to the conclusion we had our hands full, so he took one for the team. If I told you I'd not thought twice about that decision, then I would be lying.

Having children with Lorenzo was an experience all in itself. I thought watching him love on Charlotte was a sight and particularly swoon-worthy. But parenting all these children with him has been ten times better. He was never afraid to change a dirty diaper, deal with a colicky infant, calm down a toddler's temper, or tolerate a preteen's crazy hormones. And with four girls, we are in for one hell of a ride. He always jumps in where he is needed. Never really complains about how difficult raising all these loud mouthy girls can be. And let me tell you, all four of our daughters are loud and mouthy. Payback for all the shit I caused, and my poor husband is paying dearly for it.

"She's not going," he mumbles.

"Lenny," I let my horse trot next to his.

"Don't," he grumbles.

I do my best not to laugh at him, but when he gets like this, it is so hard. "Please, will you just listen for one second?"

I almost lose it when both my guys turn to glare at me. The youngest barely two, giving me his best impression of his glaring father.

"You could allow her to throw her own party. Invite all those you are so worried about and see for yourself how harmless it really is."

"I've been to many parties like that Vi. I appreciate exactly what goes on."

"Then that is an even better reason to allow her to have her own party. You will know exactly what to look for, and can stop all shenanigans before they begin." I'm not sure why I am even suggesting this, I hate parties.

"But you abhor parties," he calls me out. "Avoid going to as many as you can."

"Yes, I do," I tell him as we stop just outside the corral. "So that should tell you just how important I believe this is for Char."

Once he has dismounted, he helps Jackie down so I can get off next. The children are all quickly gathered by our au pair. With five, we needed a little extra help.

And as soon as my feet hit the ground, I'm dragged off to the tack room for some privacy. "Lenny, we should..."

I don't get to finish because my husband is on me as soon as we are away from all eyes. This is the other reason we felt the need to take care of the baby situation. At the rate we were going, we'd have a dozen before long.

"Have I told you lately how these pants you wear when riding make your arse look spectacular?" he growls.

"You might have mentioned it a time or two. I do believe Sal commented on that today." I remind him of what his son said right before we headed out on the trail.

It was rather cute coming from him. My son was seated with his Papa when I climbed on to my horse, flashing my arse at them. Lorenzo whistled and Sal said, "Nice. Ride later. Right, Papa?"

He grabs my arse with his hands and lifts me easily. Settles me on one of the workbenches before moving between my legs. His hands cupping me, driving me insane.

"You honestly think throwing a party is the answer? You do realize if we throw one for Char, then Sunny will want one too. And once she gets one, Amy will demand one as well. It will be one damn party after another and so many fucking dresses." He closes his eyes as if picturing it clearly in his head.

And yes, my filthy mouth has trickled its way into my sweet prince's vocabulary. I have gotten better because I'll be damned if I am going to let my children sound less than sophisticated. I was not about to give the little pricks that surround them daily, a reason to bring up my past and make my kids think less of themselves. So, while we may slip up, we usually only do so when we are alone without precious ears to hear and then repeat.

"We'll have to have a family meeting and make it clear to the others when they will get their turn to have a party." He gives me that look and I chuckle. "What?"

"Have you met our children?"

My face hurts from smiling so big. "I have. They can be stubborn and hardheaded. Demanding even."

"They remind me of someone," he is now smirking and about to cop one.

After I pinch the spot under his arm, I continue. "But it's like everything else. We have to set the boundaries and not budge. Do you think you can do that?"

He shrugs and I know it will be up to me to make it clear to the other girls when they can throw their party. My soft prince has a difficult time telling any of his girls no, me included.

I'm not so sure he realized what he was signing up for when he first jumped into my life. I do realize that without him though, all the best things about my life would not exist. I might have survived and eventually found a suitable life for Charlotte and me, but a huge part of us would be missing. He is the father my daughter always deserved; one all my children are so very lucky to have.

Not to mention I have no idea how I'd have made it without knowing his kind of love. The man is in a league all his own. No one I imagine could have loved me the way he does. I'm glad I will never know if that is true or not. That the only man I will ever love is him.

My prince entered my life with a force I was not totally prepared to deal with. He didn't rush in to save the day or make demands he recognized I'd fight him about. This man, loving me so very completely now, recognized the best way to my heart was to be noble and valiant. Show his support by standing by my side and only stepping in when I myself needed a little extra support. I will forever be grateful and give him all my love for helping me fight for this new and wonderful life.

If you enjoyed the story of Prince Lorenzo and Violet, please consider leaving me a review on Amazon, Goodreads, or BookBub. Reviews are how an indie author gets recommended to other readers.

Here is the link to Her Royal Highness, book 4 in The Royals, the story of Angela and Edward.

I have several books available listed in the back of this book. Please check them out.

Thank you and Happy Reading!!!!

The Duke

FALCON GLOBAL NOVELLA

One kiss was all it took...

All I want is my freedom. All my father wants is to chain me to the highest bidder. I have one last opportunity to live on my terms before my choice is taken from me.

Darius Falcon, also known as The Duke, enters my world. He's an arrogant prick who won't take no for an answer. Refusing to change course once he sets his sights on me. Too bad he won't get to keep me for more than a week.

Then one day he materializes from the shadows to save me from a monster. It's then I wonder if now is my chance to take control of over my future. Maybe when you wish upon a hunk, dreams really do come true.

Only Available to Newsletter Subscribers.
https://dl.bookfunnel.com/xn53pw0g4o

Acknowledgments

I'd like to first of all thank my readers. You are who I write for, the people that keep me writing. Thank you, thank you, thank you.

To my all my beta readers. This time there are several and you all are equally awesome. Thank you to Marie, Becky, and Jacqui for taking on my book when it was still a little rough. The suggestion you ladies offered were awesome and helped me clear up a few minor issues. Thanks to Sally, Abby, Ashley, and Kimberley. You ladies had some great suggestions as well, making this book so much better. Each one of you found the little things others missed, assisting me in ways you will never know. I am very grateful for all of you and hope we can work together again in the future.

To my friend Alissa. Not only were you there to listen to me go on and on about this book, you were there for me. You forced me to have fun along the way, made me step away from it all and enjoy life. Then when it came time to get this book ready for all those dreaded line edits, rewording, and punctuation checks, you took it upon yourself to be my eyes when I could no longer see it clearly. You probably don't realize what will now be expected of you but I know one thing, you are stuck with me. Not just as my editor, but for life, as a friend who will keep me laughing and cheer me on when I need it most. We'll escape by doing a little research together when all else fails.

Last, I'd like to thank my family. I couldn't do this without their support. I love you all beyond words. None of it would be worth it without the three of you.

*updated 4/20/24

Also by C. R. Riley

Crystal Lake Series

Facing the Storm

Uncharted Waters

Light in the Shadows

When the Fog Lifts

Life Series

The Good Life

A Transformed Life

Love of the Game

Sneaky Quarterback

Tight End Comeback

Scoring the Birdie

Fielder's Choice

Catcher's Interference

Kohl Family Series

Untouchable

Unbreakable

Unforgettable

Unavoidable

Undeniable

The Royals

Suddenly Enthroned

Unexpected Princess

My Noble Fight

Her Royal Highness

Fearless Warrior

About the Author

Contemporary romance author C. R. Riley is celebrated for creating worlds and characters that don't always follow the rules, including those she futilely tries to set herself. But the best characters always find a way around them, often surprising her with their willingness to make each and every journey unique, if not emotionally satisfying.

Her Kohl Family series has been called the perfect epitome of contemporary romance with a twist of the unexpected. The characters tackle tough topics while making you fall in love with them, and despising those baddies who deserve it. Each story is a unique standalone. That cares over in her Modern-Day Royals series, which features characters who are unlike any royal put to the page before. And of course, combining her love of football and baseball she adds a steamy sports romance, Love of the Game which follows a family of athletes on their separate journeys to find true love.

You can find all her romantic and out-of-the-ordinary series on Amazon and free in Kindle Unlimited. Never miss a new project update or book release by signing up for her newsletter or follow her on social media, accounts listed below.

I'd love to hear from you and do my best to personally answer emails.
crriley@crrileyauthor.com